A Bouquet
of Love

Center Poin
Large Print

Also by Janice Thompson and available from
Center Point Large Print:

Weddings by Bella
It Had to Be You

Weddings by Design
Picture Perfect
The Icing on the Cake
The Dream Dress

**This Large Print Book carries the
Seal of Approval of N.A.V.H.**

Weddings by Design, #4

A Bouquet of Love

Janice Thompson

Center Point Large Print
Thorndike, Maine

This Center Point Large Print edition is published
in the year 2014 by arrangement with Revell,
a division of Baker Publishing Group.

The text of this Large Print edition is unabridged.
In other aspects, this book may vary from the original edition.
Printed in the United States of America on permanent paper.
Set in 16-point Times New Roman type.

ISBN: 978-1-62899-243-4

Library of Congress Cataloging-in-Publication Data

Thompson, Janice A.
 A bouquet of love / Janice Thompson. — Center Point Large Print
edition.
 pages ; cm
Summary: "Florist Cassia Pappas hopes to develop a strong professional
relationship with wedding coordinator Bella Neally, but when her Greek
family relocates to Galveston, she'll discover that a big family
complicates the best-laid plans, and two big families are a recipe for
disaster"—Provided by publisher.
 ISBN 978-1-62899-243-4 (library binding : alk. paper)
 1. Florists—Fiction. 2. Weddings—Fiction. 3. Large type books.
  I. Title.
PS3620.H6824B68 2014b
813'.6—dc23

                                                          2014025782

To the real Patti-Lou.
This is all your fault.

* * * * *

In memory of the awe-inspiring Judy Garland. She helped shape my life and my desire for the stage as a child, and she continues to inspire me as an adult. What fun to use her films and songs as chapter titles!

1

Strike Up the Band

You know you're Greek when you can't understand why McDonald's rejected your idea for the McFeta sandwich.

You know that old saying about how you should stop and smell the roses? Well, in my world, you would have to sniff your way past the garlic, cumin, and roasted lamb before you could pick up the scent of flowers. At Super-Gyros—my family's sandwich shop—we're known for drawing the customers in with both their noses and their eyes. So smelling the flowers is out. Sniffing the shish kebabs and freshly baked pitas is in.

What do flowers have to do with Greek food? To the average Joe, nothing. To a girl like me, everything. I can't think of one without the other. In my heart, I see myself owning a florist shop, arranging lovely bouquets, and bringing smiles to the faces of my customers. In reality, I see myself slapping together sandwiches, whipping up tzatziki sauce, washing dishes, and doing whatever else it takes to please my father.

Babbas. The best Greek papa on the planet. If

you don't believe it, just ask him. He'll tell you, using a wide assortment of descriptions from the Old Country. Not that he's ever actually been to Greece, mind you. Nor is he likely to go anytime soon. The man never stops working long enough to ponder a vacation. He's far too busy trying to open our new shop on Galveston Island.

I'm still not sure how the Pappas family ended up in Texas, to be honest. Just five weeks ago we were doing our normal thing in Santa Cruz, California, where we enjoyed a relatively boring existence, one that focused on our family-run sandwich shop on the boardwalk. Then suddenly, in a day, everything changed. Out with the old, in with the new. Goodbye, Santa Cruz. Hello, Texas. Crazy.

When Babbas makes an impulsive decision— say, moving the family a couple thousand miles to the humid south to open a second shop— he does so without consulting anyone. Except the Lord, of course. Babbas never moves without the Almighty's approval, so this trek to Galveston Island must've received a high five from heaven.

I don't usually argue with heavenly plans, but this move . . . well, it put me in a not-so-heavenly frame of mind. For one thing, the murky brown waters of the Gulf of Mexico don't come close to the Pacific. Did I mention that we lived in Santa Cruz, home of the world-famous board- walk, nestled against the white-sand beaches of the mighty blue Pacific? What could Galveston, Texas, possibly have to compare? The only thing I'd fallen in love with so far were the flowers. Galveston was loaded with them, and they took my breath away.

Imagine my joy as I glanced out our window that first Tuesday in May, my gaze landing on a colorful trolley clang-clanging its way up the Strand. On the side of the brightly painted car was an advertisement for a local flower shop, Patti-Lou's Petals, along with the words "Help Wanted" and a phone number: 1-800-PETALS4U.

Hello, possibilities!

I started humming the melody to one of my favorite Judy Garland songs—the one about the trolley—and pondered my dilemma. Working with flowers was my dream job. Definitely the ribbon on my proverbial bouquet. But Babbas would never allow it. Like every Greek daughter, I would remain tied to his apron strings until the day I married. Not that I had any prospects, especially now. What kind of a Southern gentleman would brave a relationship with a girl whose father ran around in a superhero cape and matching tights to promote his business? No, I'd be single forever. Might as well get used to the idea.

My gaze shifted from the sign on the side of the trolley to a handsome fellow seated inside. For a moment our eyes met. *Fate! Kismet!* Then, just as quickly, his attention shifted to a pizza joint across the street from our place. Just my luck. Still, this gave me a lovely glimpse of his gorgeous, wavy dark hair from the back. Be still, my heart! But his hair didn't hold a candle to those smoldering eyes I'd caught a glimpse of. Yummy.

The familiar Judy Garland melody soon made its way from my heart to my lips as the trolley clang-clanged on by. How could I help myself? My dreams would soon come true! I whispered the phone number "1-800-PETALS4U" and did my best to commit it to memory. Maybe I would work up the courage to apply for the job. Wouldn't that be something? The very idea put me in a remarkable frame of mind. I pondered the possibilities of my new life as I unloaded boxes, my heart now singing.

"You're humming again, Cassia."

I turned and looked beyond the stack of half-emptied boxes, bins, and cooking utensils until I located Mama. She stood off in the distance, her upswept hair falling loose in damp ringlets around her neck.

"I am?" Oops. Caught again.

She swept beads of perspiration from her brow and smiled, lighting up her overly painted face. The ruby-red lipstick might've looked better if she'd colored inside the lines, but Mama was never one for confines. In some ways, I appreciated that about her. The eye shadow—a theatrical shade of teal—came into full view as her eyes narrowed. "Yes. I love it that you're so musical." Mama retied her frayed Super-Gyros apron, which had come loose around her plump midsection. "I think you came out of the womb singing." She pulled up the ragged bottom of the apron and dabbed her upper lip, which caused the apron to come loose all over again.

"You think?" A little sigh worked its way out, much as I fought to keep it inside. "I just love those old show tunes. Did you ever see that Judy Garland movie, the one with the trolley—"

"Helena, I need you!" Babbas's voice sounded from the kitchen and Mama scurried out of the room to do his bidding, as always, still fussing with the temperamental apron. So much for finishing my sentence. Or my song.

I turned to the open boxes at my feet and spent the next few minutes pulling things out and trying to find a home for them. With the room in such a chaotic state, who could guess where anything went? How we would be ready to open by Saturday, I couldn't imagine.

When boredom set in, my gaze shifted out of the plate-glass window once again. This time my sights fell on the ever-growing lunch crowd at the pizza restaurant across the street. Must be a popular place. I shifted my angle to read the sign above the store. Parma John's. Cool name.

Something about the place drew me like the Pied Piper playing his merry little tune. I stepped outside onto the sidewalk and caught a whiff of pepperoni. Yum. I could almost taste the spicy goodness now, could picture it oozing with reams of melted mozzarella. What I wouldn't give to have a thick, gooey slice of pizza. But I couldn't. My father would kill me.

Still, it might be worth the risk.

Or not.

I sensed the presence of someone standing behind me and turned to discover my father had joined me. Oops. So much for daydreaming about pizza.

His thick salt-and-pepper brows furrowed into a perfect unibrow as he watched the crowd coming and going from Parma John's. "Looks like they have some sort of lunch special going on." My father's eyes filled with concern. The tone of his voice grew more serious. "But just you wait. Those customers will be mine. Soon."

"We don't open for a few days, Babbas." My little sister's voice sounded from the open doorway. I turned to give little Gina a smile. The precocious six-year-old skipped our way wearing mismatched clothes, as always, her loose ponytail waving in the breeze. She turned a couple of cartwheels on the sidewalk before squealing in glee. "But I love it here already."

"Stop that, Gina," Babbas scolded. "You're not

a monkey, you're a—" He stopped midsentence as a carload of teenagers pulled up to Parma John's and got out. "Hmm."

"I'm a superhero just like you, Babbas!" Gina struck a funny pose, one meant to show off the muscles in her upper arms, and I laughed. That wacky kid always made things better, even with her thick black hair in a never-ending state of messiness.

Babbas crossed his arms at his chest, his gaze never leaving Parma John's. "Then put your superhero powers to work, kiddo, and help me come up with a plan."

"A plan?" Gina did another cartwheel. "What sort of plan?"

"A savvy businessman is always thinking ahead." Babbas leaned against the streetlamp, his gaze never leaving the customers going in the pizza shop. "By the time Super-Gyros opens this weekend, everyone in Galveston will recognize our logo. We'll be the talk of the island. You know your Babbas, always making his presence known."

I knew, all right. No telling what he had up his sleeve this time. I had a suspicion it would embarrass us all, one way or another.

His eyes lit up with a familiar gleam. "I've hired a photographer to do a big photo shoot. She's just a couple of doors down." He gestured to a shop with the words "Picture Perfect" on the marquee. "We're going to use the photos to do a big splash in the local paper this week. And I'm making ten thousand flyers with the logo, offering free gyros to our first twenty-five customers."

Sounded like an expensive plan. I hoped it would pay off, for the whole family's sake. As far as the promotional stuff went, I didn't mind the shop's logo being seen by others, as long as Babbas didn't put a picture of himself in that ridiculous superhero costume again. Really? What grown man, especially one as hairy as my dad, wore spandex for fun? I still hadn't lived down the shame of the first time he'd shown up at my junior high in Santa Cruz dressed in that goofy getup.

Then again, my father seemed to thrive on humiliating his children. I mean, what other dad named his children according to the letters of the alphabet? Andreas, Basil, Cassia (yours truly), Darian, Eva, Filip, and our little mismatched monkey, Gina. Mama called her an afterthought.

I gave Parma John's another wistful look. So, Babbas had his eye on that place already, and not in a good way. He planned to give them a run for their money. When my father set his mind to something, well, he usually succeeded, or he plowed over a couple dozen people while trying. I couldn't help but wonder why. Couldn't we all just get along? Play nice? Eat together? Share a little Italian and Greek food across a common table?

Not while Babbas lived and breathed, judging from the scowl on his face.

"Helena!" he called out. "Come and see this! See what we're up against."

My mother appeared moments later, her makeup melting in the heat of the day. Miniature teal rivers trickled down from each eye, covering up the cotton candy–pink rouge, which had been applied with a heavy hand. Oy. If only she could see herself in a mirror.

"What is it, Niko? Yia Yia and I are busy setting up the kitchen. I can't leave her by herself for long. You know how your mother is. She'll put everything in the wrong place." With a swipe of the back of her hand to her moist forehead, Mama completely obliterated her painted-on brows. Well, mostly. Half of the right one remained, but not exactly in its original position.

"Never mind that." His nose wrinkled as he stared across the busy street. "We need to get busy out here before these Italians beat us at our own game. Help me come up with a plan."

"A plan?" My mother's eyes widened, drawing even more attention to the eyebrow situation. She sniffed the air. "For dinner, you mean? Smells good. What is that? Pizza?" Mama took a step toward the street but stopped when Babbas cleared his throat.

"No cavorting with the enemy, Helena."

Mama snorted and waved her hand in the air.

"I've never cavorted a day in my life, Niko. You know that." She used her apron to dab the perspiration from her face, and most of what was left of her right eyebrow came off in the process, thank goodness.

Babbas's face turned nearly as pink as Mama's cheeks. Nearly. "No one in the Pappas family will ever eat pizza from that place while I'm alive!" he spouted, his right hand raised high as if making a proclamation.

"We have to wait until you die to eat pizza, Babbas?" Gina's lip quivered. "That's going to take too long. I'm hungry for it now."

Filip and Eva joined us, both commenting on the yummy smells coming from across the street. Babbas turned red in the face as he waggled his finger in the air. "As far as we are concerned, pizza is the devil's food!" He went off on a tangent about the demonic origins of pepperoni, but I tuned him out, distracted by the flavorful aroma coming from Parma John's. If pizza was the devil's food, someone had better hand me a pitchfork and tail.

"Calm down, Niko, before you have a stroke." Mama shook a dishrag at him. "Working so hard has made you a grumpy old man."

"I am *not* grumpy!" Off he went on another tangent, ranting about his calm demeanor. Mama just patted him on his hairy arm and rolled her eyes.

Okay then.

She planted a tender kiss on his cheek, then snapped his bottom with the dishrag. "If you don't get in here and help me set up this kitchen, I'll show you what grumpy really looks like. I can't handle Yia Yia on my own, you know. Not when I'm setting up house, anyway."

Mama made her way back inside, muttering something about how my grandmother was going to be the death of her, if Babbas didn't kill her first. Not that my father appeared to notice or care. He stood in silence, eyes narrowed as he watched the crowd going into Parma John's.

My younger brother Darian joined us on the sidewalk, an open laptop in hand. He glanced up long enough to get my father's attention. "I did the research you wanted, Babbas. Parma John's is owned by the Rossi family, just as you suspected."

"Rossi." My father grunted. "I knew it. This is not good news."

"Who are the Rossis, Babbas?" Gina asked. "Are they bad people?"

"They are *busy* people," he responded. "They own half the businesses on the island."

"Oh, wow." That certainly piqued my interest.

"It's the same family that owns the big wedding facility on Broadway." My brother shifted the laptop from one arm to the other. "Club Wedding, or something like that. And they've got their fingers in a couple of other pies too." His brow furrowed, and for a moment he looked just like our father. Minus the unibrow. "We'll have to look out for them, Babbas," Darian said. "They're trouble."

"Wait . . . Club Wed?" We'd only been on the island a couple of weeks, but I'd already seen the traffic outside of that place on the weekends. I'd read about it in bridal magazines too.

"So they're in the wedding biz *and* the pizza biz." My brother closed his laptop and shrugged. "Sounds like an odd combination."

"Maybe." My father leaned down, his words now a strained whisper. "Or maybe that so-called pizza parlor is a front for something else entirely."

"Something else?" Darian and I spoke in unison.

"Did you ever think of that? Maybe *that's* why they're so busy. It's all a ruse." Babbas waggled his thick brows. "I saw *The Godfather*. I know how this goes. One minute you're nibbling on a slice of pizza, the next minute they're fishing your body out of the Gulf of Mexico."

"Babbas!" I slapped myself on the head. "That's ridiculous. The pizza parlor is just that— a pizza parlor. So don't worry about . . ."

I found myself distracted as a stretch limo pulled up to Parma John's. An older gentleman in a dark suit got out. He carried a large case of some sort in his hands. Odd.

"See?" My father pointed at the fellow. "Just as I suspected."

18

"Babbas, are you saying he's a bad man?" Gina hid behind the lamppost.

"Well, what do you suppose he's got in that case there?" Babbas lowered his voice, his words now laced with concern.

Gina's eyes grew wide. "What, Babbas? What?"

"A machine gun, that's what." My father gave an abrupt nod, as if that settled the issue once and for all.

"M-m-machine gun?" Gina ran back inside Super-Gyros, her shrill voice ringing out, "Mama!"

"You really think they're mobsters? I'm outta here." Darian shoved his laptop under his arm and scooted back inside the door, muttering something about how he wanted to go back to California, where people were normal.

Didn't we all.

Babbas followed him, but I lingered on the sidewalk, convinced we weren't dealing with mobsters. No, most of the people in the crowd looked just like us—perfectly normal. Not that anyone in the Pappas family could be called normal, but whatever.

The strains of a Dean Martin song drifted through the air as the door to Parma John's opened once again. I watched as a young woman not much older than me, judging from the looks of things, stepped outside. She carried a toddler on one hip, and a little boy ran ahead of her on the sidewalk.

She called out a name, D.J., and then waved at a man—*Wow! Real Texas cowboy material!*—who ambled her direction, his pointed cowboy boots clicking along the cobblestone road. The handsome stranger pulled off his Stetson and swept the young woman into his arms, brushed her dark curls out of her face, and then planted kisses on her lips. Okay then. Must be a couple. And judging from the way he tousled the boy's hair and then slipped the toddler onto his shoulders, he was the father of the kiddos. I was looking at a picture postcard of a true Texas family. Wow.

Maybe the great state of Texas wouldn't be so bad after all, not if all the fellas looked like this guy. Maybe he had a brother. Or a cousin. One could hope, anyway.

The young woman glanced my way before walking back into Parma John's with the cowboy and children. She squinted as the clouds above shifted and a bright, sunny sky caused a glare. Then she offered a welcoming smile and a little wave, which I returned.

See, Babbas? No mobsters here. Just friendly Texans.

"Cassia?" My father's stern voice sounded from the open doorway. "Your mama and Yia Yia need help setting up the kitchen. Besides, it's not safe out there. You don't know what those people are up to."

The smell of pizza drifted across the road once

20

again, and I fought the temptation one last time. I knew what they were up to, all right. Delicious pizza. Smelled good. Really, really good. But I knew better than to risk losing my inheritance— not that I really had one—over a deluxe pepperoni with extra cheese. Babbas would disown me in a hurry should I step foot over the invisible line he'd painted down the cobblestone street. No, I'd stay on the Super-Gyros side, where good Greek girls belonged.

Just when I thought I couldn't stand the temptation one moment longer, my grandmother joined me on the sidewalk. The midday sun gave her thinning white hair an angelic glow and made the soft, tissue-paper wrinkles on her cheeks even more pronounced. Standing against the oversize door of the shop, she looked disproportionately petite. Yet she always commanded respect, tiny or not.

"Babbas wants you inside, Cassia," Yia Yia's words were more instruction than suggestion. "Come, child."

I cringed at the word *child* and fought the temptation to respond with, "He always wants me *somewhere*." No point in hurting my grandmother's feelings. She'd given birth to the man, after all.

I stepped inside the shop and closed the door behind me. There would be plenty of time later to ponder the realities of pizza parlors and mobsters, flower shops and handsome guys on trolleys. Right now I had work to do. And when a good Greek daughter had work to do, well, she didn't waste any time smelling the flowers. She got right to it.

2

The Boy Next Door

You know you're Greek when your father spends so much time with his forehead creased that he looks like he has a unibrow.

There's something about the phrase "Everything's coming up roses" that always makes me smile. When I think of roses, my heart wants to sing. They're closed one day—barely a bud—and opened wide the next, ready to drink in the sun. Ready to show off their beauty. And the scent! Nothing could compare. That's why, when faced with the opportunity to work with flowers every day of my life, I longed to jump on it like a june bug on a daisy.

1-800-PETALS4U. I'd memorized the number that could change my life forever and hoped to put it to good use. But how? Babbas had other plans for me. To show him disrespect would be wrong on many levels, not to mention dangerous to my survival. I knew in my gut he would nix the flower shop job idea without giving thought to my wishes or dreams. The man had no time to stop and sniff the roses. Still, how could I pass up the possibility of working with roses . . . and orchids . . . and lilies . . . and a thousand other flowers I loved? And at a florist shop that turned out to be just down the street, no less? Seemed like the ideal position for a girl like me.

If only I could manage to convince my father.

Mental note: Cassia, you're twenty-three years old. At some point you really have to untie those apron strings.

I couldn't stop thinking about the words on the sampler in Yia Yia's bedroom: "God makes all things beautiful in his time." Was this the right time? Only one way to know for sure.

With courage mounting, I decided to take my chances. I would apply for the job at the flower shop—maybe pick up just a few hours a week—and continue to help my parents at the family business as well. And I wouldn't tell my father until I knew for sure the job was mine. Somehow it would all work out. I knew it.

First things first, though. I needed to figure out a way to sneak away for an hour or so without drawing attention. Once alone, I would head to the flower shop to hand over my résumé. And I would do it all undercover. Like a spy.

Very rarely had I done anything without running it by my father first. Strange, I know, being in my twenties and all. But when you've got different dreams than the rest of the family—say, you want to venture outside the family business to do your own thing—you don't dare ask for a parent's opinion on the matter for fear they'll give it. No doubt Babbas would consider me a traitor to the family for wanting to follow my own dreams.

And so I set out on my own Wednesday afternoon, claiming I wanted to take a stroll down the Strand to check out the tourist shops. Babbas was so busy installing the new stove that he barely noticed, anyway. I walked down the lovely old street, captivated by its Old World charm. The turn-of-the-century buildings had survived the Great Storm of 1900. Surely the area could survive a wacky Greek sandwich maker in a superhero cape.

Several blocks down from our store I located Patti-Lou's Petals. The bell jangled as I walked inside the quaint little shop. I paused, overwhelmed as I took it all in. The colors captivated me at once. Vibrant red roses, the color of Mama's lipstick. Shimmering yellow tulips, bright as the afternoon sun. Fuchsia gerberas. Orange gladiolas. Golden Asiatic lilies. I found them all in this gorgeous shop, and so much more.

My gaze traveled from the refrigerated bouquets in the large showroom case to the shelves, which housed all sorts of pretties, including flower girl baskets, greeting cards, ready-to-go bouquets, packets of seeds, yard art, and much more. Talk about variety.

The bell jangled behind me, and I moved out of the way as a handsome guy—tall with dark hair and broad shoulders—carried in buckets of roses. Wowza. A girl could get used to working with a guy like that. He wasn't the blonde, blue-eyed, boy-next-door type I'd known in Santa Cruz, but he definitely held some appeal.

Okay, more than a little appeal. His broad shoulders filled the white T-shirt he wore. My gaze traveled up to his handsome face, bronzed by wind and sun. The firm set of his chin suggested a stubborn streak, and the half smile, a definite joy of life. My kind of guy. And it didn't hurt the picture at all when his muscles rippled underneath the T-shirt.

Look away, Cassia! It's rude to stare!

But how could I help myself? Something about him seemed . . . familiar.

Might be better to focus on the flowers.

I walked over to the refrigerated case and peered through the glass doors at the beautiful bouquets and arrangements inside.

Well stocked. Check.

Behind the counter, a harried-looking woman waited on a customer whose smile was as bright as the golden daffodils the woman wrapped in delicate green paper. She thanked the elderly gentleman for his order as she took his credit card.

Great customer service. Check.

The man who'd made the purchase turned my way to show off the bundle of springtime flowers.

"The secret to a long, happy marriage. I buy a bundle of these every week." He gave me a nod and bounded from the shop.

Happy customers. Check.

The woman behind the counter still looked a little frazzled. She hollered something at a teenage boy and then gave some instructions to the muscular guy delivering the flowers, whose name, I learned, was Alex Rigas. I stepped out of his way as he came back through with another bucketful of roses and found myself swept away by those heavenly brown eyes.

Familiar eyes.

Oh, wow. The guy from the trolley. No way.

Those gorgeous eyes met mine for a quick glance, and I felt the edges of my lips curl up. Not that any sane twenty-three-year-old single girl would blame me. This guy oozed Southern charm and good looks. And did I mention the muscular physique?

Hello, handsome.

I cleared my throat and prayed I hadn't just said that out loud.

Focus, Cassia, focus.

The woman behind the counter finished waiting on another customer and then turned to me. "Can I help you?"

"Oh yes." If I could just get my hands to stop trembling. I felt like a kid standing in front of the school principal.

The woman glanced at her watch, then her gaze traveled to the clock on the wall before looking at me again. With my courage now rising, I dove right in. "I saw your ad on the side of the trolley," I explained. "And I love working with flowers. I've only been on the island a couple of weeks, but I really want to—"

"You're here about the job?" Before I could respond, she clasped her hands together and ushered up something in another language— maybe Italian?—and her eyes misted over. "Oh, thank God! I thought I'd never get anyone. The timing couldn't be any better. Praise the Lord and pass the pruning shears!"

"Oh? Well, that's good. Would you like to see my résumé? I stayed up half the night putting it together." I didn't mention that I'd worked through the night so that Babbas wouldn't find out about my secret plan. I reached inside my purse and came out with the paper. I couldn't help but notice it smelled like a gyro.

"Yum." She picked it up and sniffed it. "What is this?"

"Oh, sorry. Think I got a little tzatziki sauce on it." I used my index finger to wipe it off. "Sorry about that."

Great, Cassia. Wonderful first impression.

"Tzatziki sauce?" The guy from the trolley, Alex, set down a bucket of yellow roses and reached for my résumé. "Do you mind? I

28

haven't had a good tzatziki sauce in ages."

Did he plan to eat my résumé?

No, thank God. He only sniffed it, then offered up a sigh and laid it back down. "Smells great. Makes me miss my Yia Yia. She's been gone for years." With a nod, he added, "I'm half Greek."

Judging from the thick Texas twang, he was also half cowboy.

Still, I'd better get back to the reason for my visit. I returned my gaze to the woman behind the counter. "If you look at my résumé, you'll see that I have several years' experience working in a store. Well, not really a store. More of a shop. But I'm accustomed to working with customers and I can run a register."

"Perfect!" She glanced at my résumé long enough to seek out my name. "Cassia, is it? Bethesda?" I didn't even have a chance to say, "Bethesda's my middle name," before she said, "You're hired." She pushed the résumé aside and extended her hand.

I shook it. Sort of. She hadn't even let me tell her about my training in flowers. I'd better get right to it. "I went to a community college a couple of years ago," I explained. "On the West Coast. From there I got my accreditation with the American Institute of Floral Designers."

"Impressive." She nodded. "I don't even have that myself."

"I had to send in all sorts of pictures of my

arrangements and then do a live showing in front of judges." A shiver ran over me as I remembered that day. Talk about terrified. "I haven't really had a chance to use my expertise with flowers yet, but I've been dying to, so I was hoping I could work with you as your apprentice."

"Hmm? What? Apprentice?" The woman behind the counter didn't seem to be paying much attention. She spent much of the time scolding the teenage boy in the back room—who turned out to be her son Deany-boy.

I finally stopped talking when I realized I'd lost her completely. At least I thought I had. She turned away from her son and reached for my hand. "You're an absolute godsend," she said and then gave my hand a squeeze. "I'm Marcella, by the way."

"Great to meet you. I—"

"Can you ride a bike?" She gave me a pensive look.

"Ride a bike?" I tried not to let the panic show on my face. I hadn't ridden a bike since I was sixteen. "Um, sure. Can't everyone?" A forced smile masked my fear. I hoped.

"Awesome. There's a delivery bike out back with a large basket. If the customer wants something delivered and it's close by, I usually send one of the boys on a bike."

"Boys?"

"My kids. The older ones, I mean. They think

they're too old to help Mama now." She gestured to the back room, where the teenage boy continued to rant about the time. Sounded like they were late to some sort of ball practice.

"Between school and sports and youth group activities, they're really too busy to help me anymore." Marcella sighed. "Anyway, I could use someone else to make deliveries on occasion. Just wanted to make sure you're comfortable with that part."

Yikes. After all these years, riding a bike would be tricky enough. Riding with a bouquet of flowers in the basket? Impossible.

Okay, maybe not impossible, but the idea made me very nervous.

I made up my mind then and there to purchase a bike of my own so that I could practice riding with flowers on board. Whatever it took to keep this new job, I would do it.

"We're all about going green around here," she said. "That's one reason we buy all of our flowers local."

"If you want to call Splendora local." The handsome flower delivery guy chuckled. "Not exactly around the corner."

"True." She nodded and then looked back at me. "It's actually a couple of hours away. But you get the idea. Local is good."

"Right."

"Mom, c'mon! We've got to go!" The teenager

came out of the back room with a baseball bat tucked under his arm.

Marcella glanced at him then back at me. "I hate to put you on the spot, this being your first day and all . . ."

"What?"

"Would you mind watching the shop for a few minutes? I've got to run to my daughter's preschool to pick her up and then swing by and drop Deany-boy here off at baseball practice. Shouldn't take long. Maybe forty-five minutes?"

"Well, I . . . Does this really mean I'm hired?"

"Yes." She nodded and reached for her purse. "I'm sorry. I thought I already said that. You know how to run a cash register?"

"Well, yes, but—"

"Alex, would you stick around and help out?" Marcella gave him a pleading look.

He nodded. "Sure. Don't mind a bit."

Okay then. Maybe this wouldn't be so rough after all.

Marcella flew into action, grabbing her purse and slinging the strap on her shoulder. She glanced my way, her words now staccato. "A customer named Gabi is supposed to come by to look at the arrangement in the case." She pointed at a lovely bridal bouquet. "If she likes it, tell her we'll set a plan in motion for her wedding."

"Wedding?"

"Yes. She's got some pretty elaborate plans but

32

is on a budget, so we'll work with her. She's a brilliant dress designer and brings us lots of business, so anything we can do to help her out would be okay in my book. One hand feeds the other, you know?"

"I see." Sort of.

Mental note: keep an eye out for a bride with a penchant for dress design.

Marcella opened her purse and reached inside for a tube of pale lipstick, which she smeared on her lips without even looking. "Oh, and my mother-in-law is going to stop by to order some centerpieces for the Grand Opera Society's annual gala. Don't let her bamboozle you into a lower price just because she's family. You would be shocked at how family members try to take advantage of me."

Shocked? Um, no.

She sighed. "I still have to make a living."

"I understand, but . . ." I put my purse down and took a tentative step behind the counter. "Problem is, I don't know what to charge for anything."

She pointed at a paper taped down near the register. "Price list there."

"Ah. Okay." I ran my finger over the list and tried to take it all in.

"So, you're all right to handle things for a few minutes?" She sounded more than a little anxious. "With Alex's help?"

Before I could say, "Don't think so," she'd disappeared with her son on her heels, griping about how he was going to be late to practice.

And just that quick I found myself alone in the shop.

3

I Wish I Were in Love Again

Add "-aki" to the end of any American word and it becomes Greek.

Okay, so I wasn't exactly alone in the flower shop. The handsome Greek cowboy lugged in another bucket of gorgeous pink roses and placed it on the bottom level of the refrigerator case. I hated to stare at him as he worked, but with no one else in the place, what else could I do?

After a couple of awkward moments, he looked my way and offered a cockeyed grin. "I guess yer hired then." His thick Texas drawl pretty much gave voice to my thoughts.

"Guess so." Still, I felt completely lost.

"Better put on an apron so you look official and all."

"Look official?"

"Yep." He reached for a floral apron with the words "Patti-Lou's Petals" on it and tossed it to me. I caught it in midair, then stared at the pink, green, and white flowers on it.

At least it wasn't a superhero costume, right? I

slipped the apron over my head and glanced at my reflection in the glass on the flower case. Not bad.

"It suits you." The edges of Alex's lips curled up. "Like you were born for this."

"I think I was." My heart swelled at the very idea. Just as quickly, I pictured the look on my father's face should he see me in this apron. WWBD—what would Babbas do? Kill me, likely.

"I can't believe we haven't run into each other before if you're into flowers." Alex straightened the roses in the bucket, then closed the glass door on the refrigerator case. "My family supplies most of the florists in this neck of the woods. We run a nursery in Splendora."

"Splendora? I heard Marcella mention it. Is that a town?"

"If you want to call it that." He chuckled. "It's a really small town up Highway 59." This comment somehow morphed into a conversation about how Highway 59 was being converted into an inter-state, but he lost me after that.

Is it wrong to stare at someone's eyes while they're talking?

"You're not from around these parts, are you?" His teasing expression shared his thoughts on the matter.

"Well, I wasn't raised in Texas," I managed.

"Ah. Could've guessed that. Uncle Donny always says he wasn't born in Texas but got here as quick as he could. Guess you're the same, huh?"

"Um, right." I offered what I hoped would look like a convincing smile, followed by a thumbs-up, though I didn't have a clue who Uncle Donny was.

Alex didn't ask where I was from, and I didn't offer the information. Instead, I waited on an incoming customer who entered with a request for a prom corsage. Afterward I ran my finger back over the price list and did my best to memorize it.

After finishing up his work, Alex stacked several now-empty buckets. He walked into the back room and came out with two bottles of water. One he handed to me, the other he opened and drank from. I took a little sip and worked up the courage to speak.

"You're the guy from the trolley." Okay, that wasn't exactly what I'd planned to say, but there it was.

"The guy from the trolley?" He shrugged and then his eyes lit up. "Oh, I did ride the trolley yesterday. Is that what you mean?"

"Yeah." I felt my cheeks grow warm. Good grief. Now he knew I'd taken notice of him.

"Want to know why?" He leaned so close I could smell his cologne. Yummy.

Okay, I'll bite. "Why?"

"The trolley system just started up again," he said. "Hurricane Ike took out the whole line in

37

'08 and it's been down ever since. Until a week ago. So everyone and their brother's catching a ride as a show of support. We're hoping the tourists will take the hint and use it too."

"Oh, wow. So I got here just in time?"

"Yep." He took another swig from his bottle. "Where did you say you're from again?"

"I didn't."

"Not a Southern state, judging from your accent."

My accent? Was he kidding?

"I'm from California. Santa Cruz."

"Well, now . . ." He squared his shoulders and his eyes narrowed. "You're on a learning curve then."

"Learning curve?"

"Yer in the South now." He laid on the drawl extra-thick. "And that means yer fixin' to learn a few things."

"Fixin' to?"

"Yep. That's the first lesson. In Texas, we're always fixin' to do sumpthin'." He gave me a knowing look.

"Like what?" I asked.

"You name it, we're fixin' to do it." He chuckled. "Like, right now I'm fixin' to learn you a few things that should come in handy, now that you're livin' here."

"Okay." I looked around for a piece of paper and a pen, finally locating both in a drawer under the register. "Should I be taking notes?"

"Maybe." He nodded. "I'm gonna start by tellin' ya that *y'all* is a bona fide word in the South, and it's used every day, hundreds of times over."

"It is?" I asked.

"Yep. And the plural of *y'all* is *all y'all*."

"O-okay." I jotted this down. "What else?"

He continued to fill my ears with funny Southern sayings, and then the conversation shifted to stories about fishing and hunting. From there he dove into a funny story about his Greek father. Finally, something I could relate to.

"So, you really are part Greek?" I asked.

"I am." Alex's eyes twinkled. "But I'm also from Splendora, so you have to factor that into my heritage. Kind of changes up the whole thing, if you think about it."

I had no idea what that meant but didn't question him, and the thick Texas twang continued to tickle my ear. I'd never met anyone who looked like Adonis but sounded like Blake Shelton.

"I'm half Greek, half good ol' boy," he said with a wink. "Mama says it's the perfect combination. Just enough Greek in me to make me stubborn, just enough Southern to make me a gentleman."

He had the gentleman part down, no doubt about that. And if he had a stubborn side, I sure hadn't witnessed it. No, he'd captivated me, drawn me in like the heady scent of those roses

39

he'd delivered. Talk about easy on the eyes and comfortable to talk to. Wow.

At this point the shop filled up with customers, and I chatted at ease, offered suggestions, and took orders one after another. What bliss! I took the order from Marcella's mother-in-law, still puzzled by the last name. Rossi. Sounded so familiar. Not that I had time to ponder it for long, what with the shop so full and all.

"Are you a singer?" Alex asked me after the crowd thinned.

"Singer? No. Why would you ask that?"

"Oh, because you hummed the whole time you were putting together the arrangements for that last gal. I thought maybe you were with the Grand Opera Society or something. That's pretty big around here."

"Not at all. But thanks." A little giggle rose up. "I think there's just something about flowers that makes my heart come alive."

"It's always great to meet people who love flowers as much as I do." He shrugged. "Doesn't happen that often, but then again, I was raised around them. Same with you?"

"Not at all. My parents don't know a lily from an orchid." I bit the inside of my upper lip to keep from telling him that my father thought that flowers were a waste of time and money.

"Crazy." Alex laughed. "So what's your favorite flower?"

"Man, what a tough question. I've always adored lilies. Doesn't matter what color. Ooh, maybe it does." I pinched my eyes shut and could almost envision bright yellow Asiatics coupled with yellow button poms and Peruvians. A silly little sigh escaped.

"I've lost you, haven't I?" He laughed and I opened my eyes.

"Yep." But it felt really good to connect with someone who understood and appreciated my love for all things petaled. It didn't hurt that he happened to be as handsome as a Hollywood star posing for a close-up.

"I always like to compare people with species of flowers," he said. "Like, my mom is definitely a sunflower. It's not just that she's tall—my dad always says she's so tall she could hunt geese with a rake—but she's got the sunniest disposition of anyone I know."

He'd almost lost me at the rake comment. Still, I didn't dare laugh, at least not out loud, so I responded with, "I see what you mean. My mom's more of a poppy—overly colorful." When all of the color wasn't sweating off, anyway.

Alex carried on about his various family members but stopped when he got to one in particular. "Now, my aunt Twila, she's been a little harder to peg. You never met anyone so vibrant and outgoing. Seriously. Lots of pizzazz. Hope you get to meet her someday."

"Let me guess . . ." I put my hand up and thought it through. "She's a carnation?"

"Close." He shrugged. "We've pegged her a chrysanthemum." A crooked grin followed. "She's a little on the round side. Probably forgot to mention that part."

"Ah. Makes sense." I was swept away by the fact that he seemed to be taking such an interest in something that brought me joy. "So, this whole matching-the-flower-to-the-personality thing is something everyone in your family does?"

"Yep. We've learned a lot about people, believe it or not. Marcella's a hydrangea."

"She is?"

"Yep. She's a hydrangea. A little more on the subtle, elegant side. See what I mean? And you"—he leaned against the counter and gazed at me so intently that I could smell his cologne again—"are multilayered. Your flower unfolds a little at a time, revealing all sorts of mysteries beneath."

"O-oh?" He found me mysterious?

"I'm guessing, based on having known you . . . how long? Less than an hour?" He gave me a wink. "Anyway, if I'm right, that would make you . . ." The beginnings of a smile tipped up the corners of his lips, and I found myself fixated on that belongs-on-the-big-screen face. Man. The guy could've landed on the cover of a magazine. "A rose."

I could hardly believe it, but he'd hit the nail on the head. Maybe he really did know me, even after such a short time. I nodded and then gave him a full speech about a paper I'd written in high school about tea roses. An easy smile played at the corners of Alex's mouth.

"Our family's nursery specializes in roses," he said. "You wouldn't believe all the different species we have. And the colors. We're doing so much with color these days."

I was dying to hear all about it, but Marcella rushed in the door, totally interrupting our conversation. Bummer. She looked even more harried than before. "Had to stop to pick up snacks and some nasal spray for Deany-boy. Allergy season, you know. Sorry I took so long. What did I miss?"

Alex squared his shoulders and a thoughtful smile curved his lips. "Well, you missed this gal making some great sales. She managed to talk folks into all sorts of things."

"Wow." Marcella gave me an admiring look. "Well then, you're officially hired."

I didn't have time to respond. Alex dove into a story about how I'd saved the flower shop from certain ruin by selling a bouquet of flowers to a tourist. "Cassia's perfect for the shop, Marcella," he said. "You've got a winner here."

All right then. The boy thought I was a winner. Should I tell him what I thought about him? Nah, better not.

"I desperately need the help," Marcella said. "If you fall in love with the place, maybe I'll make you a really good deal on it. Someday, I mean."

"A really good deal?" Wait a minute. Was she offering to sell me the flower shop? We barely knew each other.

"I'd do the happy dance all the way to the bank." She laughed. "Don't get me wrong, I love working. But I'm worn out trying to balance the kids, the house, my husband, and the shop. It's just so hard. I can see myself handing over the reins someday. Soon. Maybe very soon."

The woman must be kidding. Buy the flower shop? I couldn't afford to buy a new bathing suit for the summer season right now, let alone a flower shop. Besides, Babbas would have me murdered in my sleep if I made such a drastic move without involving him.

"Well, I really don't think I'll be able to do something like that for a long time," I said. "One decision at a time."

"Right, right." She nodded. "No rush. It's just that my husband has been after me for a year to be a stay-at-home mom. I have a houseful of kiddos, and it's getting harder every day to juggle everything. I feel like I'm dropping balls all over the place. One of these days I'll need someone to take over the shop so I can retire."

"I definitely can't take over the shop just

yet," I said. "I have a family situation that demands several hours a week. So I'll have to balance my time between family and work too."

"If anyone understands that, I do." She reached to pat my hand. "Well, don't worry. It's clear the Lord has brought you here. We'll work out the scheduling. You take care of your family, I'll take care of mine, and between us we'll both take care of the flower shop. How does that sound?"

It sounded even better after she told me the hourly salary. Wow. I really could have my gyro and eat it too. If only I could figure out a way to let Babbas know.

Babbas.

A quick glance at the clock sent a shiver down my spine. By now he would be looking for me. I'd better get back to the real world . . . and quick!

4

Any Place I Hang My Hat Is Home

You might be Greek if you insist on standing right next to someone while you talk.

I rushed back to Super-Gyros to find my father perched atop a ladder inside the front of the shop. Judging from the expression on his face—what I could make out from down below, anyway—my absence had stirred up some negative emotions on his end.

"Where have you been, Cassia?" His tone indicated his frustration. "You can't just disappear on us like that. Leaving for nearly two hours when we've got so much going on? Where is your sense of family?"

"Sense of family?" Good grief. I hadn't abandoned the Pappas family, I'd just . . . Hmm. "I went for a walk down to the end of the Strand," I explained after thinking it through. "See, there's a great florist shop down there and I wanted to—"

"Life isn't all roses, Cassia." He wobbled a bit on the ladder, and I reached to steady him. "There are some thorns too."

Tell me about it.

"Time to get your head out of the clouds and stop sniffing the flowers."

Okay, that made no sense at all. Flowers in the clouds?

Babbas reached down to grab a lightbulb, then straightened back up to put it in. "I need you. Don't go wandering off." At this point he dove into a story about a time he'd lost me at the circus when I was a preschooler. How I'd turned up in the arms of a scary-looking clown. Great. Just the memory I needed to relive today.

I bit back the groan that threatened to escape. When would he stop talking to me like a toddler?

He managed to get the lightbulb screwed in, though he nearly tumbled from the ladder in the process. I did my best to steady it. Maybe the man really did need help.

"With your older brothers running our shop in Santa Cruz, I really need you, Cassia." His tone steadied in sync with the ladder, which finally stopped wobbling.

I could barely hear about my older brothers without envying them. Andreas and Basil were lucky ducks, getting to stay in California, even if it meant managing the old shop. Me? Not so lucky. Losing my older siblings to the Golden State put me in the running as oldest available child and most likely to take the heat from

Babbas for all things restaurant related. Yippee. Just what I needed.

Babbas climbed down from the ladder. He looked around the shop, still only about half put together, and clasped his hands at his chest. "My brother will be green with envy when my shop brings in more revenue than his."

"But Uncle Alex's shop in L.A. has been around for years." Darian approached, his arms loaded with imported food items to put on the shelves. "His sales last year were triple what we brought in, remember?"

Oy. Had my brother really just said that out loud?

I couldn't argue the point, of course, and neither could Babbas. Our uncle's shop in Van Nuys—the original Super-Gyros—had performed light-years better than our shop in Santa Cruz, though we'd fought valiantly to compete. Surely location had a lot to do with it. That, and my uncle's star clientele. My cousin Athena worked as head writer for a major network sitcom, after all, and she brought in tons of famous friends and co-workers to their sandwich shop. If we had their star power, our business might thrive too.

Darian continued to share statistics about our uncle's successes, at which point Babbas spewed a handful of adjectives, none of them acceptable in front of the younger kids, who happened to be entering from the kitchen with Yia Yia.

My grandmother must've picked up on my father's angst. She placed her hand on his arm, her expression reflecting concern. "What is it, Niko? What's eating my baby boy today?"

He scowled as he dragged the ladder several feet to his right, then began to climb again. "It's that Rossi family," he muttered.

Rossi. Why did that sound so familiar?

Rossi.

Oh. Help.

My heart rate skipped to double time as I made the connection. If Marcella's mother-in-law was a Rossi, then Marcella was a Rossi too. I'd just accepted a job working for the enemy.

"What have they done this time?" Yia Yia asked, the concern evident in her voice. "Tell Mama. I will take care of it."

Okay, from the evil look in her eyes, I had a feeling she could. And would.

"They own most of the businesses on the island," Babbas said. "The pizza joint, the wedding facility, even some sort of shop at the end of the Strand. Can't remember what Darian said that one was."

The florist shop. My heart skipped a beat just as my mother entered the room.

"Would you believe, they actually have a show on the Food Network." My father unscrewed a burned-out lightbulb from the ceiling, then passed it to Mama, who reached over to the counter for the box of new ones. "Some sort of Italian cooking show, hosted by the oldest members of the family. How am I ever going to compete with that?"

"Wait . . . a show on the Food Network?" Mama looked troubled by this news as she handed him a fresh lightbulb. "What show?" She tossed the old lightbulb into a nearby trash can and crossed her arms.

"*The Italian Kitchen*." Babbas began to spout— in Greek, of course—about what a ridiculous show it was, but I knew better. So did half of America, but I would never tell him that.

"I love that show." The words just slipped out. I didn't mean to say them, but who could deny the obvious? *The Italian Kitchen* offered not only great Mediterranean cooking but lively entertainment with the elderly husband and wife duo as hosts.

"I love it too," my sister Eva chimed in. "It cracks me up, the way that older couple, Laz and Rosa, bicker in the kitchen. They're hysterical." She started telling a funny story from a recent episode. From the top of the ladder Babbas sputtered and spewed more adjectives. This time in Greek, thank goodness.

"So that's the family we're up against?" Mama looked as if she might faint. Who could blame her in this heat? "You might as well hang up your hat now, Niko."

"Never! I will not give up and neither will any

of you. We are the Pappas family. We have superhero powers behind us." He tried to take a step down from the ladder and nearly fell. Eva and I grabbed it just in time and kept him from toppling. So much for superhero powers.

"Niko, we need to stop for a while. Take a break. Rest." Mama shook her head. "You're going to kill us all if we keep up this pace. We haven't had time to catch our breath for weeks."

"There will be plenty of time to breathe later." My father dragged the ladder a few feet more to the right and climbed back up again to deal with another burned-out light. "We open on Saturday, remember?"

How could we forget, with all of the work we'd done? Mama had worn herself to a thread, and even my younger siblings looked exhausted.

"We've been so preoccupied with opening the business that we've barely unpacked our boxes in the apartment upstairs." Mama huffed and puffed her way to the counter, where she grabbed the box of lightbulbs. "I swear, Niko, sometimes you wear me out. Five weeks ago I was settled in my home in Santa Cruz, dreaming of retirement. Now I'm in this humid place without even the benefit of lovely blue waters or white sand. Have you seen the Gulf of Mexico?"

He grunted.

"It's not the Pacific." Mama sighed and almost dropped the package of bulbs. "Not that I get to

51

go outside. I'm stuck in here, doing the work of three people half my age, and I have no idea why."

"You're here because this is where the Lord led me." He cleared his throat and reached down to transfer the lightbulbs. "Led *us,* I mean." His tone softened, and I could see the pleading look in his eye. "Trust me, Helena."

Mama pulled a dish towel out of her waistband and used it to wipe the back of her neck. "If I had a nickel for every time you asked me to trust you, I'd be rich enough to retire right now. We both would. Instead, we're here, in a place I've never even visited, opening a shop across the street from the most popular restaurant on the island and wondering if there's enough antiperspirant in the world to keep me from melting into the pavement. It makes no sense."

"Some of the greatest decisions in all of history made no sense at the time," Babbas said as he climbed one rung higher.

"Like boarding the *Titanic*, you mean?" Mama asked. "Buying stock in Enron? That sort of thing?"

"Like moving a family all the way from California to Texas. We are here now, and we will open on Saturday. In the meantime, we will all stick together. No strolling up the Strand to look at shops." He glared at me. "And no comments about how well our relatives are doing elsewhere. From this point on, it's all for one and one for all in the Pappas family. Understood?"

We all grunted in response.

My father climbed down from the ladder and moved it to a new location. "And as for those Rossis, I have an idea that will stop all of the pizza lovers on the island from ever going back to Parma John's. It's brilliant!"

"Oh?" This certainly got my attention.

"Yes." His eyes narrowed. "We'll place an anonymous call to the health department. Create a scare."

I could only hope he was kidding. "Babbas, that's a low blow. And what makes you think the health department would act on a complaint without finding out who had filed it? They'll come looking for you."

"Hmm. Something to think about." He shrugged. "Then for now, I will focus on making a television commercial. The villain will be a pizza shop owner." Babbas laughed. "Won't that be perfect?"

Hardly. But none of us would tell him that, at least not yet.

"If you're going to make a commercial, I hope you will shave first." Mama pointed to his stubbly chin.

"I do shave." Babbas put his hands on his hips. "Every day."

"Yes, but I've never seen anyone who can grow a full beard in a day. Your five o'clock shadow shows up at noon."

This got a snicker from my younger brother Filip, who then clamped a hand over his mouth and took a step back.

"Making a first impression is important," Mama said. "And you're always a stubbly mess."

Babbas stroked his chin. "Is it my fault if I'm a hairy man?" He started to climb the ladder once again. "What's next? You want me to shave my legs too?" He wiggled one in the air, kind of like a cancan dancer, and Gina laughed.

"Of course not." Mama pursed her lips. "Well, unless the hair gets in the way when you put on your tights."

"They're not tights!" Babbas's voice elevated to a higher pitch. "We've been over this a hundred times, Helena! They're *pants*."

"Whatever." Mama waved her dish towel in the air. "Point is, I saw a sign advertising a hair salon a few doors down. They do waxing."

"Waxing?" My father leaned down from the ladder, his presence even more ominous than usual. "I don't own a surfboard."

"I'm not talking about a surfboard, Niko. I'm talking about those bushy things you call eyebrows. They need to be thinned out in the middle."

"What's wrong with my eyebrows?" He reached up to rub the spot she'd referred to, almost falling from the ladder in the process. Filip reached out to steady him.

"When you're mad, they run together." Mama rolled her eyes.

"Are you saying I have a unibrow?" He looked down, revealing the bushy thing in all of its glory.

"Sometimes," Mama said. "But the reason I brought up waxing is because of that back of yours."

"My b-back?" Babbas twisted around on the ladder as if trying to see his back. A panicked look followed. "No one is going to touch my back with hot wax!" He raised one hand in the air, his voice so loud the neighbors could probably hear. "Not now, not ever!"

And this pretty much ended the conversation on waxing.

We dove back into our work, spending the rest of the afternoon organizing the restaurant in preparation for opening day. I never mentioned my hour in the flower shop. Wouldn't dare. And I certainly didn't say a word about meeting someone from the Rossi family. Babbas's blood pressure would skyrocket, and we couldn't risk that, what with him spending so much time on the ladder today.

Still, as I thought about the day's events, I wondered how I would balance the new job against my hours here. Babbas would eventually have to know. No way around that. How would this play out, though?

I pondered the various scenarios as I worked,

and all the more as I climbed the stairs to our apartment above the store. After a quick shower—really, what other kind could it be when you shared a one-bathroom apartment with seven other people?—I slipped into the tiny room I shared with my sisters and sat on the edge of the twin bed, my gaze landing on the curtainless window with its broken blinds.

Strange. We'd spent days organizing the shop downstairs, but barely ten minutes on our apartment. Maybe someday. In the meantime, I'd better snag this alone time to think through my job dilemma. Surely I could come up with a solution.

Minutes later Eva entered the room, her hair still wet from the shower. She took one look at me and her eyes filled with concern. "Cassia?"

"Yeah?"

"What's going on with you today? You're not yourself."

Eva might be two years younger than me, but she seemed to know me better than I knew myself at times. I wanted to tell her about the new job. Tell her that I'd rather work in a flower shop any day than open the new business with Babbas. But I couldn't. Not yet. After all, I hadn't even committed to take the job. Okay, I'd agreed to come back on Friday and work for four hours, but other than that, I'd given the woman—what was her name again?—no formal commitment.

"You look sad." Eva's nose wrinkled as she stared at me.

"Not really sad," I responded. "Just . . . confused." An awkward silence rose up between us. My sister continued to towel her long, dark hair. I finally finished my thought aloud. "Have you ever just wished you had a different life?"

"Like, wished you could trade places with someone else, you mean?" Eva slung the towel over the bed's footboard, then walked to the vanity mirror and gave her reflection a pensive look.

"Not really that." I rose and stood alongside her, staring at our dual reflections. "Just wished that things were different. Like maybe wished you had the courage to stand up to someone who micromanaged your every move."

"Oh, *that*." My sister groaned and turned to face me. "Why didn't you just say this was a conversation about Babbas?"

I sat in front of the vanity, frustration gripping me. "Because I'm twenty-three. I'm a skilled floral designer, but no one would ever know it, thanks to him. He doesn't think I can cross the street by myself without getting hit by a car."

"Well, there was that one time in Santa Cruz where you—"

"Why does everyone have a story about the way I was as a kid?" I slapped myself on the forehead. "The point is, I'm so tired of being treated like a child. I'm not. I'm responsible. Have I ever given him any reason to think otherwise?" My sister opened her mouth to respond, but I added, "Recently?"

"Not *recently*." She grinned and gave her reflection another look.

I rose and walked to the window. Peering outside, I surveyed the Strand under the glow of the setting sun.

"I'm twenty-three. Other girls my age are married. Have babies. They're not stuck at home under their father's thumb. They're chasing their dreams."

Across the street, something caught my eye. The door to Parma John's opened and that woman—the one with the gorgeous curly hair and svelte physique—stepped outside onto the sidewalk. The handsome cowboy followed with the adorable little girl in his arms. Behind him came the feisty little boy. I watched as they all made their way toward a truck parked nearby.

I envied her—the girl with the picture-perfect figure and flawless hair. No doubt she had a perfectly sane life, one not riddled with overbearing parents and wacky family members who were always in her business. Clearly she got to eat all the pizza she liked on top of that. Oh, and that dreamboat of a cowboy who always kissed her at every turn? I envied her for that too. Where did a girl have to go to find a guy like that?

My thoughts shifted to Alex, the guy in the flower shop. Apparently a girl didn't have to go far. Just up the street. At Patti-Lou's Petals, I could sneak away from my everyday life and spend a little time with a handsome Greek guy from . . . what was that small town called again? Oh well, it didn't matter where he came from. The conversation we'd shared almost gave me hope that I could one day settle into a happy relationship like the girl across the street had done.

I couldn't help the sudden burst of happiness that took hold of me as I thought about him. What a dreamy life that would be!

My sister tapped me on the shoulder. When I turned to face her, she grinned and said, " 'The Boy Next Door.' "

"Huh?"

"You're humming 'The Boy Next Door.' It's one of my favorites. Could've guessed it would be a Judy Garland tune. You've been on a kick lately with her music, haven't you?"

"Oh, sorry. Didn't realize I was humming."

"I know. You never do. But don't let that stop you. I love that you've got a song in your heart." Eva dove into the lyrics of "Zing! Went the Strings of My Heart" and sang it in multiple keys. Not that I minded. A Judy Garland song sounded great, no matter the key. Or keys.

I eventually worked up the courage to tell Eva my secret about taking a new job. Just when I'd fully unloaded on her, I heard a sound coming from the doorway and looked over, horrified to discover Yia Yia standing there with little Gina at her side, listening in.

Oh no.

My grandmother hobbled into the room, her stooped frame causing her to appear even tinier than usual. She gestured for me to sit on the bed and I did. Then she took the spot next to me and reached for my hand.

"Your father, he is a good man." Yia Yia patted my arm. "I raised him right."

"He's a *tough* man." I sighed as I thought it through. *Too* tough.

Yia Yia's wrinkles softened like a bar of chocolate left sitting in the sun. "He wants what's best for you, Cassia. Always. Like every parent."

"What's best for me is doing what I was created to do, working at the flower shop."

"Yes. Flowers. You always make them beautiful. And God . . ." She leaned over to whisper in my ear, "He makes all things beautiful, child, in his time." A pat of her wrinkled hand on my shoulder nearly brought me to tears.

All right then. God would make all things beautiful—like a fragrant bouquet—in his time. If I could just hang on for the ride.

5

A Star Is Born

You might be Greek if you were as tall as your grandmother (Yia Yia) by the age of seven.

The day after I landed the new job, chaos broke out between the Greeks and the Italians. It all started when the photographer—a very pregnant woman named Hannah—showed up to shoot some images of my father wearing his superhero costume. The shoot was supposed to take place outside our shop. Hannah suggested long shots of my "superhero" father in front of our newly installed Super-Gyros sign so that the Santorini-blue coloring in his tights would—as she put it —force the eye to gaze upward at the blue store sign above.

Unfortunately, complications arose at every turn.

For one thing, the lunch crowd across the street made things difficult. Hannah couldn't really figure out a good place to stand to get a long shot from the opposite side of the Strand. With the mob of people coming and going from Parma John's, she simply couldn't find a safe spot to stand for more than a second or two at a time.

"Sorry, Mr. Pappas," she called out from in front of the crowded pizzeria's door. "I'm doing the best I can. Could you scoot a little bit to the left so I can get your shop in the picture?"

Babbas tried to move, but a passing tourist nearly knocked him down. Or maybe it was the other way around. Either way, he sputtered and spewed like an '87 Chevy with bad gas.

A Parma John's customer got into his car and pulled away from the curb, and Hannah snagged the spot right away. She set up three orange cones to mark the area so that no one else could pull in, then gave Babbas a thumbs-up.

Apparently this decision didn't sit well with the elderly gentleman who ran the pizzeria. He came storming out into the middle of the street, waving his walking cane in the air.

It took a minute, but I finally recognized him as Laz from the TV show *The Italian Kitchen*. Oh, wow. Talk about starstruck. I wanted to rush his way and tell him just how much I loved his show. After he finished yelling at my father, anyway. Then I remembered . . . Rossi. Marcella. Flower shop. I hid behind a lamppost and peeked out to watch the rest of the goings-on.

In spite of the need for the cane, Laz carried himself with a commanding air of self-confidence. "What is this?" he hollered. His jaw tensed visibly as he gestured to the coned-off area.

"This is necessary for my photo shoot," Babbas responded.

"And what is *this?*" Laz pointed to my father's costume.

"This"—Babbas pointed to himself in his ridiculous costume—"is how you market a business."

"By looking like a schmuck in the middle of the street?" Laz spouted.

"I'm not the one standing in the middle of the street," Babbas countered.

I had to give it to him there. He was standing on the sidewalk, after all.

Okay, maybe he wasn't. My father had taken several angry steps toward Laz. Wow. I hadn't seen him move that fast since the Texas-size cockroach scurried across the kitchen floor a few days back. I pinched my eyes shut, unwilling to watch.

Only, who could look away at a moment like this? I opened one eye just a bit as Hannah hurried to the middle of the two men and did her best to calm things down, to no avail.

"Someone help that poor pregnant girl." My mother twisted a dishcloth in her hands. "Oh, I can't watch this!"

At this point Yia Yia began to pray in Greek. I couldn't make out much, but I got the part about delivering us from demonic spirits. Alrighty then.

I peeked out from behind the pole just in time to see Gina run into the street. My mother let out a scream as my little sister came within feet of a passing horse and buggy loaded with tourists.

"You nearly killed my daughter!" Babbas shouted at Laz as he pulled Gina to safety.

"I did no such thing!" Laz shouted, his face growing redder by the moment. "I just came out here to tell you that you people cannot cone off the area in front of my store. You are using my designated parking spots." He pointed at two spots marked "Designated Parking for Parma John's." Yep. Hannah's cones were clearly blocking the man's designated parking spots. Still, why the fuss? Couldn't we all just get along?

"Cool your jets." Babbas swept Gina into his arms and gave her a hug, then gestured for her to join us on the Greek side of the street. "We'll be done soon. Just go back inside and try to come up with a plan to save your business once all of your customers fall in love with my gyro."

"Your gyro." Laz spat on the ground. "That's what I think of your gyro."

Yikes. Babbas might be okay with someone criticizing his children, but not his sandwiches. Slam-dunking the man's gyro was nothing short of culinary blasphemy.

Babbas hollered something in Greek. Laz

reacted in fluent Italian, cane waving in the air. This went back and forth for a couple of minutes until they both stood face-to-face in the center of the road in a foreign-language duel.

Laz finally stopped and shook his head. "If you don't pick up those cones, I will call the police. This is a zoning violation. You are affecting my lunch crowd."

Babbas puffed his chest and squared his shoulders. "I'll show you a lunch crowd!"

Laz pointed at our shop devoid of customers. "Starting when? I don't see a lunch crowd. All I see is a pathetic excuse for a sandwich shop and a grown man wearing tights." He doubled over in laughter and the cane slipped out of his hand.

"These aren't tights!" Babbas pointed down at his Santorini-blue tights. "They are . . . are . . ."

"Skinny jeans?" my sister Eva offered from our side of the street.

This got another laugh out of Laz. He reached down to get his cane, then with a wave of his hand, he muttered something in Italian and walked back to his side of the street. "I'll give you five minutes and then I call the police," he called out in final warning. "They will set you straight."

Babbas walked our way and snagged the dishrag from Mama's hands. He wiped his sweaty face, straightened his twisted tights, and then signaled for Hannah to start snapping photos of him. Minutes later, just as an officer arrived, they wrapped things up.

Turned out the officer, a jovial fellow named O'Reilly, loved Greek food. Babbas invited him inside our unopened restaurant for a tour and a free gyro sandwich. "As a thank-you for protecting our community from crazy people!" Babbas proclaimed.

O'Reilly didn't argue. He followed my father into the kitchen and minutes later emerged with the largest gyro I'd ever seen. Go figure. Judging from the loopy grin on the fellow's face, we'd be seeing more of him. He gave my father a wave, thanked him, and headed off on his way.

Mama paused in the open doorway of our shop to give Parma John's a final look. Then she offered me a weak smile and said, "I think that went well."

Mama might cover her feelings with a fake grin, but I knew better. Situations like this broke her heart. She wanted friends. Needed friends. Especially in a new home. But Babbas's erratic behavior always seemed to isolate her from those most likely to connect with us—our neighbors. Sure, we'd eventually earn the respect of some customers, but customers and friends were two different things. Wouldn't it be lovely to sit and visit with the folks next door or across the street? Now we'd never get that chance, thanks to the man in tights. Er, skinny jeans.

Mama did what she always did when she needed to pacify herself. She went into the kitchen and baked. A couple of hours later we had several large trays of baklava and a few other yummy-looking desserts ready to sell on opening day. My mother's mood appeared to have lifted with the process.

She offered me a tantalizing piece of baklava from the plate in her hand. I gobbled it down in no time with a dreamy "Yum!"

"Thank you, sweet girl." She looked around the empty shop, then back at me. "Where is your father? Still bribing the police force?"

"No." I couldn't help but chuckle. "He's upstairs. Said he needed to work on the computer."

"The computer?" Her painted-on brows arched in perfect unison. "Interesting."

"I know, right?" Babbas never used it, at least to my knowledge. Might be fascinating to see him try.

Mama climbed the steps up to our apartment, still carrying the plate of baklava, and I followed behind her. She stopped as we reached the living room, and I nearly ran into her from behind.

"What are you doing, Mama?" I asked.

"As I live and breathe," my mother whispered as she gestured to the living room on our right. "Never thought I'd see the day."

I followed her pointed finger and saw Babbas

seated on the sofa, laptop in hand. Open. I didn't even realize he knew how to turn it on, let alone use it.

Turned out he didn't.

He glanced our way and grunted. "Cassia, come and help me." He gestured to the spot on the sofa next to him. "We need a plan."

I took a seat and took the laptop in hand. "A plan? For what?"

"I need to get on the internet and research advertising tips. Maybe come up with a slogan, a new way to promote the business. Something we can use in the commercial I'm writing."

Mama took a seat in the recliner on the opposite side of the living room, and against my better judgment, I focused on the laptop, scrolling from one site to another. We examined other restaurants' marketing strategies, but most seemed impractical for Super-Gyros. Too elaborate. Too costly.

One thing did seem doable, though, so I pointed it out. "It seems like they all have celebrity endorsements." I pointed at one site that featured a pro football player. "Customers show up because they trust the word of the endorser."

"Exactly. That's what we need." Babbas leaned back against the sofa, his eyes narrowing. "Someone big. A name that everyone recognizes."

"We don't know any famous football players," I

said. "Or basketball, for that matter. So we'll have to come at this from a different angle."

"Right. The sports thing doesn't really work, anyway." My father released a slow breath. "Maybe what we need—or who we need—is someone from Hollywood."

"Hollywood?" Mama and I spoke in unison.

"Yes. Hollywood has produced all sorts of superheroes over the years. Superman. Spider-man. A million more. Why not use Hollywood to promote Super-Gyros? It's the perfect idea!" Babbas rubbed his hands together and his voice took on a joyous tone. "I've got it! The answer was right under our noses the whole time. We have connections."

"We do?" I asked.

"Yes." He looked at me, his eyes now gleaming. "Your cousin Athena knows people."

"Athena?" My cousin might be an award-winning sitcom writer, but I doubted she would hand over the contact information for her Hollywood co-workers. No way.

"She knows famous people because of her job," Babbas said. "Maybe she could get what's-her-name from the sitcom to help us out. What's that one lady's name again? The blonde? Or maybe that fellow who plays the part of her husband. He might be good. I could see him as a superhero, couldn't you?"

Babbas began to list others from the sitcom,

but he'd lost me completely. I still couldn't get past the idea that he thought my cousin might be willing to connect us with these people.

"Brock Benson!" From across the room, Mama's voice roused me from my ponderings. "If you want to get people's attention, that's who you need. Brock Benson."

"B-Brock Benson?" I quivered like gelatin as I spoke the name of my favorite TV and movie star. "How would we get him here?"

"We will call Athena and invite her to come to Texas for a visit." Babbas stood and paced the room. "Once she comes we will mention—in a subtle way, of course—that we would like to meet with Brock to discuss a plan."

Like my father had a subtle bone in his body.

"When he arrives we will show him the commercial idea and ask him to star in it."

"Sounds dreamy, but we can't pay him," Mama said. "That's a problem. A big star like Brock Benson will expect to be paid a lot of money."

"Of course we can pay him," Babbas argued. "We'll offer him a lifetime supply of sandwiches. No one in his right mind would turn that down."

"But if he's friends with Athena, then he probably gets all of the gyros he wants from your brother's shop," Mama countered.

This garnered a couple of grunts from Babbas, as well as some mumbled words in Greek. "We will figure it out, Helena. The point is, we need to get Athena here. She and her husband can come for a visit to see our new place. Cassia will like that." He gave me a "please go along with me" look. "Won't you, Cassia?"

I would love to see Athena again. Very much. And meeting Brock Benson in person sounded pretty appealing. Still, I hated the idea of bringing my cousin here just to use her. She would never forgive me, and I'd never forgive myself.

"I've always loved spending time with Athena," I said. "But maybe we should wait until we have a real plan, Babbas. You know? We don't want to appear desperate."

"Waiting is good," Mama said. "We're not ready for visitors yet. Besides, where would they stay? Our little apartment isn't company ready. It's filled to the brim with people and boxes."

"Athena and her husband are famous Hollywood writers. They have money. They can stay at a hotel."

"Niko!" My mother looked horrified by this suggestion. "We can't put family up at a hotel. It's just not done. Imagine what your brother would think!" She began to argue the point, insisting that she'd never heard of such a thing.

I had a feeling Athena and Stephen wouldn't mind staying at a hotel. In fact, I felt pretty sure they would prefer that idea to staying in our tiny little apartment that was already crammed full. If we could talk them into coming. I still couldn't see why they would want to leave California and come to Texas just because Babbas asked them to.

"We can worry about where they will stay once they accept the invitation," Babbas said. "In the meantime, I need to create a commercial with a superhero theme. And we will need a jingle. Something catchy."

"A jingle?" Mama asked.

"Sure, you know. You hear them all the time on TV and radio." He started singing one from an insurance company commercial and Mama nodded.

Then my father decided to sing every well-known jingle that came to mind. He covered everything from McDonald's to Burger King to Oscar Mayer Weiner. Soon Mama was singing along. So were my brothers and sisters, who'd drifted in upon hearing the McDonald's jingle, likely hoping we were going out to eat for a change. Like that would happen.

When they finally stopped singing, Babbas rose and paced the room. "We need a jingle with a superhero theme. Something catchy. You can help with this, Cassia. You're musical."

I started to argue, but a couple of catchy ideas came to mind. Ten minutes later I'd written a tolerably good jingle for Super-Gyros. Where it had come from, I could not say. Still, Babbas fell in love with it, and even Mama offered a "Wow!"

My siblings joined me and before long we were all singing—with harmony, even.

"It's perfect, Cassia! And just right with your singing voice on the lead." Babbas snapped his fingers. "That's it! Our family will sing the jingle in the commercial!"

"Oh no." No, no, no, no, no. I would not, could not, sing in a commercial for the family business, especially not if my father—

"I'll wear the Super-Gyros costume and you can sing. It will be perfect."

The next thing I knew, we were talking about adding a stage in Super-Gyros where we could perform the song on a regular basis. No thank you. But how could I go about defying him when he looked so excited and so proud of my song?

"This will save the day, Cassia. Brock Benson will do a cameo in the commercial and your song will play in the background."

I had to admit, the idea of my song playing behind Brock Benson did hold some appeal. But from the devilish grin on my father's face, I knew he was up to something more.

"We will put those Rossis in their place." Babbas rubbed his hands together. "Wait and see."

Ack. The Rossis. I still needed to let Babbas know about my new job at the flower shop. Marcella would be waiting on me tomorrow morning, after all. Maybe I could tell him without mentioning the Rossi connection. Sure. He didn't have to know that part.

After releasing a cleansing breath, I dove right in. "Babbas, working with family has been so much fun. But you know how much I love to design flower bouquets—"

"Flowers." He snapped his fingers. "Excellent idea. You should wear a flower wreath in your hair when the commercial is filmed. All of the girls should. Oh, and your dresses—they must be traditional. Yia Yia can make them." He clasped his hands together and his eyes appeared to glaze over. "We will all look so . . . Greek!"

I didn't mean to groan aloud but must've done it involuntarily. Not that it stopped him. Oh no. On and on he went, ideas flowing as freely as the honey my mother had poured over the sumptuous baklava.

By the time the conversation ended, Babbas had pretty much planned out my future. Apparently it included several thrilling commercial appearances with me dressed as a young Greek virgin. Terrific. Now I just needed to figure out a way to balance my career as a jingle writer with my job at Super-Gyros. Oh, and my new position at Patti-Lou's Petals. I couldn't forget about that.

Or maybe, just maybe, I'd *better* forget about that last one. And while I was at it, I'd forget about the ache that consumed my heart every time

I thought about giving up on my childhood dream of working with flowers. Surely it would never come to pass now.

One thing remained clear—I couldn't do anything to stress out my father right now, not with Super-Gyros opening in two days. Our family's survival depended on keeping him in good spirits.

And so, with a smile plastered on my face, I rose and sang that goofy little jingle all the way into my room, where I climbed into bed fully dressed and pulled the covers over my head.

6

By Myself

You might be Greek if you're 5'4", can bench-press 325 pounds, and shave twice a day, but you still cry when your mother yells at you.

By Friday morning we nearly had the new shop ready for the following day's grand opening. Never mind the fact that my father flaunted our write-up in the local paper every chance he got and littered the island with flyers. Most of the passersby seemed genuinely interested. Many even promised to come by when the shop opened for business, especially those with the coupons for free gyros.

Midmorning on Friday Babbas prepped the fire to roast the lamb. Perfect opportunity for a getaway. He didn't even seem to notice I'd left. Then again, he rarely noticed anything once he got busy doing what he loved to do. When a Greek father babied his lamb, the rest of the family could do as they pleased. My sisters headed off to the beauty shop, and I bought myself a few precious hours working at the florist shop while Babbas tended to the meat.

I jogged the length of the Strand, past the luscious smell coming from Parma John's, to Patti-Lou's Petals a few blocks down. The bell on the door jangled as I walked inside, and Marcella looked my way and clasped her hands together. "Oh, good! You're back."

"I'm back." A whiff of the fragrant flowers made me forget all about the lamb I'd been craving.

"I'm just so thrilled you're here." Marcella rushed from one side of the shop to the other. "After you left the other day, I got on my knees and thanked God."

"Thanked God that I left, you mean?"

She giggled and tossed me an apron. "No, silly. Thanked God you'd come in the first place. Thanked him that you'd seen the advertisement on the trolley."

"So you've really needed help?" I tied on the apron, suddenly energized by its bright colors. My thoughts went back to Alex's comment about how it suited me. Yep. It suited me, all right.

Marcella continued to talk, oblivious to my thoughts. "Girl, you have no idea. I've been balancing motherhood with my work." She stopped to brush a loose hair out of her face. "I love both. I really do. But with a little girl in the mix now, as well as the two older boys . . . well, let's just say I've got my hands full."

She dove into a story about her husband and

his work at Parma John's, and I swallowed hard. Great. Just what I needed to hear. My boss's husband co-managed the pizza parlor with his uncle Lazarro. Perfect. Couldn't wait to share this news with the rest of my family.

Not.

Thank goodness the conversation shifted as customers flooded the store. We stayed busy until around noontime, when a familiar woman entered with a sleeping toddler in her arms. I recognized her as the young woman I'd seen across the street, the one the hunky cowboy had swept into his arms. The one with the picture-perfect life.

She headed Marcella's way, and seconds later the two were enmeshed in a quirky conversation about an upcoming wedding for Gabi, their mutual friend. Marcella made introductions, and the woman—Bella Neeley—drew me into the conversation. The three of us ended up chatting like old friends. Turned out the girl with the picture-perfect life had a picture-perfect personality too. And a great sense of humor to boot. And speaking of boots, she confirmed that the handsome cowboy with the Stetson was indeed her husband.

Bella had me laughing at least a dozen times as she shared stories from past weddings she'd coordinated.

"So you're a wedding coordinator?" I asked

after a particularly funny story. "Where do you work?"

"At Club Wed," she said. "On Broadway."

"Wait, Club Wed?" I clamped my mouth shut, unwilling to voice the obvious question that came to mind. *The one owned by the Rossi family?*

"Yes." The little girl in her arms began to stir, and Bella comforted her. "My parents owned it for years, but they passed it to me. I'm the manager and coordinator there."

Parents? But her last name's not Rossi.

"Bella's famous," Marcella said. "You wouldn't believe all the people she's worked with. Even Hollywood stars. Her themed weddings have made the news, and she's even been featured in *Texas Bride* magazine."

"Wow, that's amazing."

"I think so." Marcella sighed. "I hate to admit this, but I use Bella to promote my business. I mean, it's not every florist who has a sister-in-law who's been written up in a well-known magazine. You know?"

"Sister-in-law?"

"Yes." Bella nodded. "Marcella is married to my brother Nick."

Wait a minute. This girl—the really nice one with the great personality—was really a Rossi? If so, Neeley must be her married name.

I'd not only stumbled into my dream job at a

florist shop, I'd also stumbled headlong into a couple of new friendships from the enemy's camp. And much to my horror, these Rossis seemed really, really great. At least the female contingent. But would they still accept my friendship once they found out who I was? The subject of my last name had never come up again after Marcella shoved my résumé into the drawer, but she was bound to find out sooner or later. All she had to do was look at the tax forms I'd filled out. The woman was so busy she didn't care about my last name. Yet. But she would. They all would.

Bella rested against the counter and gave me a closer look. "You seem really familiar to me. Have we met before?"

She'd probably noticed me watching her from the upstairs window, but I would never say that. "No. Nope. Never met before."

"Strange. Feels like I've seen you before some-place."

For a moment it felt as if my tongue got stuck to the roof of my mouth. I couldn't force any words at all. Not that I wanted to. Who could come up with something logical to talk about when everyone else in the room was from the Italian side of the street and I was from the Greek side? Once they figured out my dad was working overtime to take out their pizza business, they would hate me.

Bye-bye, florist job. Bye-bye, new friends.

"You okay over there?" Fine lines appeared around Bella's eyes as she stared at me.

I finally managed to nod, then stammered, "Y-you're Bella Rossi."

She shrugged. "I'm Bella Neeley now."

"But you *were* a Rossi?" I asked.

"Sure." She shrugged again. "Once upon a time. And trust me, once a Rossi, always a Rossi. It's like a disease. You can't shake it." She and Marcella erupted in laughter.

I felt sick. "Well, that pretty much changes everything."

"Why does that change everything?" Bella comforted the little girl in her arms, who had started to fuss.

"Because you seem really nice."

Now she looked perplexed. "Well, thank you. But I'm not sure I understand what this is—"

"You're Bella Rossi. And you're related to Marcella."

"Who's also a Rossi." Bella put the little girl down in a chair and faced me. "My sister-in-law."

"Right. I think I've got it all figured out now." I smacked myself in the head and slid down into a chair, mumbling my epitaph in Greek. "You're all Rossis," I finally managed, this time in English.

"We are," they said in unison.

"I work for the Rossis and now I'm friends with the Rossis too."

Marcella nodded. "Well, of course we're friends. Is that a problem?"

"A problem?" I echoed, then swallowed hard. "Oh no."

Not unless you happen to consider a half-crazed Greek father a problem. Unless you're sure—really, really sure—the family you're working for is probably going to end up hating you in the end.

"Is there something you need to tell us, Cassia?" Bella asked.

"Just promise me one thing," I said at last. "Promise you'll never judge me based on my family."

This got Bella so tickled that she actually doubled over in laughter. "Me? Judge you because of your family? Oh, girl . . . you have no idea." She told a humorous story about her aunt Rosa and uncle Laz, and I felt myself relaxing as the truth surfaced—they were just as nutty as my dad. Maybe more so. Thank God.

"If you want to get together to talk family stuff, I'm your girl," Bella said. "But I'm pretty sure I can one-up you on any story you might tell. Just saying." She and Marcella shared a wacky story about the time Rosa chased a neighbor boy across the lawn with a broom, and my nerves lifted. By the time they covered their fourth—or was it fifth?—story, they'd long since forgotten about me.

Or not.

"Look, Cassia." Bella gazed at me so intently I thought she could read my mind. "Let's take a vow."

"A vow?"

"Yes. We'll never be offended by the other person's family members. I won't if you won't."

"Promise?" I asked. "Even if it turns out my family—well, at least one person in my family—is a little on the wacky side?"

"No offense." She stuck out her hand. "I promise."

I shook her hand and did my best to relax. Sooner or later they would have to know my deep, dark secret. For now, though, I would keep it to myself. Why ruin a new friendship on the very first day?

"Speaking of being offended, I might as well give it to you straight. Being in Texas is quite a wake-up call," Bella said. "I know this from my own experience. You'll have a thousand opportunities to get offended. You can't take anything personally, especially if it's spoken by someone with a Texas drawl."

"What do you mean?"

"Well, for instance, you absolutely can't be offended if someone calls you 'honey' or 'sweetie.' "

"It took me a while to get used to that too," Marcella said.

"Aunt Rosa hated it at first, but now she calls everyone 'honey' or 'sweetie.' " Bella laughed.

"Except Uncle Laz." A familiar male voice sounded from the door, and I looked over and saw that Alex had entered the shop with a bucketful of roses. "She's got a few other choice names for him. He tends to run on the hot-tempered side at times."

I'd seen that firsthand in the middle of the street during the photo shoot.

Alex's comment clued me in to the fact that he was a Rossi too. Maybe not by blood, but he knew the Rossi family well enough to say something like that about Rosa and Laz.

Man. Was everyone on the island connected . . . except me?

"So you're all friends?" I gestured from Alex to Bella to Marcella, then back to Alex again.

"Sure." He nodded. "I was supplying flowers to Bella and her family before they switched the name of the business to Club Wed. We've known 'em forever. Our families go way back."

"Of course, we've got the Splendora connection too," Bella said. "Gotta factor that in."

I didn't have a clue what all of this stuff about Splendora had to do with anything but just offered a shrug.

"Cassia's on a learning curve," Marcella explained. "She's from California."

"Santa Cruz," I said.

"Well, things are probably a little different here." Alex gave me a wink.

"No joke." I could lay out some of the differences, but I didn't want to run the risk of offending anyone by glowing about the home I missed so much.

"Maybe you should look at what the two have in common," Alex said.

"Like . . . ?"

"Like, both are coastal towns, right?" Alex said. "Can't be all that different."

"Oh, but it is," I countered. "Have you ever *seen* the blue waters of the Pacific? The Gulf of Mexico doesn't begin to compare. What color do you call that water, anyway?"

I fought the temptation to go off on a tangent, and all the more as Alex and Marcella began to brag about Galveston's newest attraction, Pleasure Pier. Clearly they had never been to the board-walk in Santa Cruz or they wouldn't waste their breath. And they'd obviously never seen a true coastal area, one complete with mountains and redwood trees, carved into a beautifully scenic landscape edged up to vibrant blue waters.

When they finished their lengthy, glowing report about Texas, I just shrugged.

Bella laughed. "Give her a break, y'all. She's only been on the island a few weeks. It takes time to win people over."

"But if you're not that keen on Texas, why

come?" Alex's question seemed genuine enough.

"I, um . . . well, I moved here after someone in the family made an impulsive decision. Let's just leave it at that." Biting back a sigh, I offered a little smile.

"Well, God bless whoever made the impulsive decision then." He gave me another wink, which sent tingles all the way down to my toes. If all Texans were as welcoming as this guy, I might be swept away after all.

"Besides, if anyone understands impulsive family members, I do." Alex dove into a crazy story about his controlling, over-the-top sisters, and I chuckled at how animated they sounded.

When his story ended, I gave all of my new friends a nod and released a slow breath. "I want you all to know that you're terrific people, and it's been great getting to know you."

"Well, it's been great getting to know you too, Cassia." Bella threw her arms around me and gave me a big hug. "Welcome to the island."

"I hope we can be friends," I added. "I really do."

"We're already friends." Little creases formed between her eyes. "At least, I thought we were."

"We are, but . . ." I paused and thought about my next words very carefully. I needed to prep her for the truth, even if I didn't share it all today. "You ever read *Romeo and Juliet*?"

"Sure. Didn't everyone?"

"You know about the ongoing feud between the

Capulets and the Montagues? It spoiled everything, and all because of family pride."

"Are you telling me you're Juliet and you've
got a Romeo hiding in the wings somewhere?"
Bella asked. "Some guy your family hates?"

For whatever reason, my gaze drifted to Alex,
who'd reached for the bucket of red roses.

"No. Not exactly that. But my father is . . . is . . .
different."

"I thought we already covered the family thing,"
Bella said with a wave of her hand.

Alex glanced our way as if to ask, "What did I
miss?"

"We promised not to judge each other based on
wacky family members," Bella explained. "And I
never go back on a promise."

"She's telling you the truth," Alex said as he
opened the refrigerator case. "And besides, have
you met the Rossi family? No offense to Bella,
but they're some of the craziest people I've ever
known, and I grew up in Splendora."

Again with the Splendora reference? Where was
this place? And were the people there really
nuttier than the Rossis? If so, they might just rival
my dad, the wackiest of all. Surely one day all of
these awesome people would see the truth for
themselves, and when they did my Romeo and
Juliet reference would make perfect sense. Until
then, I would relax and enjoy their company . . .
while they were still speaking to me.

7
Till the Clouds Roll By

You might be Greek if you were surprised to discover the FDA recommends you eat three meals a day, not seven.

On the morning of Super-Gyros' grand opening, the tantalizing smells of lamb, cumin, and garlic filled the air. Mmm. I'd always loved a gyro in the making. Apparently so did our new customers, who pressed through the front door in rapid succession. I watched as they made their way through our various selections of fresh hummus and pita bread to imported cheeses and kalamata olives. Yum. Who could even think of pizza on a day like today?

Apparently, no one on the island, judging from the slew of customers that streamed into our shop. Of course, many had come to redeem their free gyro coupon, but others were just here to sample the breakfast goodies and Greek coffees.

Mama smiled at a customer, an elderly woman with soft blue eyes. "Try the loukoumades," my mother said. "You'll never taste anything sweeter."

The woman reached for one of the tasty nibbles.

"Mmm." She grabbed another, then another, finally buying two dozen to take home with her.

Mama turned my way and held out the platter of loukoumades. Oh, yum. I loved them more than anything else. Well, anything except baklava. Making my way behind the counter, I reached for the plate of golf ball–sized fritters and popped one in my mouth, savoring the gooey honey and cinnamon topping. Yum. A second bite revealed another tasty treat.

"I love the extra walnuts," I said after licking my fingers clean. "They're my favorite." I reached for another, gobbling it down.

Off in the distance my father took the opportunity to extend the welcome mat to Officer O'Reilly, who'd shown up with three of Galveston's finest. Babbas offered them each a free gyro and a cup of Greek coffee. Black, of course. Within a minute, the officers were seated at one of the tables in the corner, laughing and talking.

Customers came and went for the entire morning, keeping us busy and excited. We couldn't provide the breakfast sweets fast enough, and by eleven o'clock the sandwiches were being snapped up right and left. Apparently my father's advertising campaign was working. And from what I could judge as I glanced out the window, the crowd on the Greek side of the street far outweighed the crowd on the Italian side. Not that Parma John's appeared to serve breakfast, but whatever.

The midmorning crowd finally thinned, and I worked up the courage to approach Babbas about my new job at the flower shop. I explained my reasoning and shared the plan I'd come up with to balance my hours between Super-Gyros and Patti-Lou's Petals. All of this I did at warp speed, hoping to spit it out before he could comment. And I left out the part where my boss and all of my new friends happened to be Rossis.

"I don't understand it, Cassia." Drops of moisture clung to his damp forehead. "You've always worked for the family. This is important. We're just starting out and we need you at Super-Gyros."

"I understand, Babbas, but with so many other children in the family, you have all the workers you need. To cover most of the shifts, anyway. I can still come and go. Marcella will give me a flexible schedule."

"Marcella?"

"The shop owner. She's great. And like I said, I can still help out. I'm not going anywhere. Not really. But I want to do something . . . different. Something unexpected." I paused and did my best to press back the lump in my throat. "Why do you think I took those classes in floral design?"

He gestured to the shop's decor. "So that you could help decorate the shop, of course. It never entered my mind that you might jump ship."

"Babbas, that's not what I plan to do. Not at all. You know I'll always be linked to Super-Gyros." Like I could ever get away.

A muscle clenched along his jaw. "We will discuss this later, Cassia. The lunch crowd should be here shortly. You ready to get back to work? I need you today more than ever."

Clearly the man hadn't heard a word I'd said. Or if he had, it had gone in one ear and out the other.

A voice rang out from behind me. "I'd like the Super-Gyro with peppers and extra onions. Scratch the sauce. I've never been a fan of tzatzi . . . tzatzi . . ."

I turned to see a local mailman standing there, licking his lips. Babbas stood, gave the fella a friendly pat on the back, and proclaimed that his sandwich would be half price. After teaching him the correct pronunciation of our homemade sauce. Minutes later, he had the fellow convinced that tzatziki—at least our version of it—was the perfect complement for the gyro.

In the middle of the lunch crowd chaos, the mayor appeared. She opted for the souvlaki sandwich—our top sirloin shish kebab on a pita with tomato, bell pepper, onion, and tzatziki sauce. Babbas offered it to her for free, but she wouldn't hear of it. Still, I could tell he'd won her over.

A cute guy wearing a surfboard shop T-shirt asked for a Super-Gyro. The woman behind him wanted a Greek salad. On and on the orders went. Just about the time we'd made enough sandwiches to feed everyone in the place, I was worn out.

I glanced around the shop, my gaze landing on a lady with three small children. She bit into a gyro, and a look of sheer bliss transformed her face from cranky mom to contented customer. In that moment, I understood why Babbas worked so hard to make Super-Gyros the best it could be—the same reason I worked so hard to create bouquets of flowers. To bring joy to people. To lift spirits. To make a difference in their lives.

Food has the power to transform. How many times had I heard him speak those words? Not that I had time to ponder them right now, with the crowd pressing in around me.

A woman who introduced herself as chairman of the island beautification committee stopped in to pick up food for a group meeting. "I'll have five spinach chicken pitas and three Super-Gyros." She watched as Mama—makeup easing its way down her face—whipped together the lamb and beef supersize sandwiches loaded with tzatziki.

I offered to put together the pitas. "What would you like on top?" I asked the woman.

"Everything else in the restaurant." Her gentle

laugh rippled through the air. "Seriously, load 'em up. Whatever you think we'll like."

I was up to my eyeballs in pitas when three nuns entered Super-Gyros chatting like school-girls. I braced myself, knowing what was about to happen. Sure enough, Babbas closed in on them and shared one of his "three nuns walked into a bar" jokes, and before long the sisters were laughing like hyenas. Then, when Father Harrigan joined them minutes later, they shared my dad's joke all over again. Go figure.

Over the next few hours I worked like a slave, just as I'd done hundreds—no, thousands—of times back in Santa Cruz. But as much as I hated to admit it, I had a blast all the while. These Galvestonians were a hoot. I couldn't get over the Texas twang from many of them. Maybe Southerners really were sweeter than folks from the West Coast. At any rate, I needed to give them a chance.

Speaking of sweet, more than once a customer asked for sweet tea. I just shrugged and pointed them to the soda machine or the coffee servers.

After waiting on an elderly couple, both wearing motorcycle jackets, I finally found a moment to catch my breath. As I packaged ready-to-go gyros, I listened in on the roomful of strangers. What blissful chaos.

Multiple conversations carried on at once around the room—in different languages, no less.

The laugh-a-minute car salesman talking to a co-worker. The local shop owners snagging a few minutes between customers. The young mothers with their little ones. The whole thing stirred together to create a sound so delicious you could almost taste it.

Off in the distance, the sound of my father's voice rang out above the noise of the crowd as he bellowed an order to my brother. Mama's response—in Greek—added just the right flavor to the conversation, drawing my ear. Darian called back in English and reached for a platter, which he dropped with a raucous clatter. This caught the attention of the customers, who stirred in their seats. They chuckled as my brother lifted the broken pieces of plastic and began to juggle them for their entertainment while singing a crazy song in Greek. Yia Yia took to dancing, and soon the customers started clapping out the beat.

Just about the time I found myself completely drawn in, the door opened and Alex, the handsome flower guy, walked in. Oh. No. I ducked behind the counter and pretended to count the pots and pans.

"You all right, Cassia?" Eva gave me a concerned look just as my brother's song came to an end.

"Yes. Just have a weird cramp in my leg." I did, actually.

"Probably from bending over like that." She

gasped and then squatted down to whisper, "You need to stand up and check something—er, someone—out. Adonis just walked in."

"I-I can't." The pain in my leg intensified. Ouch. And I certainly didn't want Alex to see me. He might blow my cover.

Eva must've lost herself in Alex's gorgeous eyes, because she didn't seem to notice that I crawled along the edge of the counter until I reached the kitchen. Once inside, I finally managed to shake the cramp out of my leg. I peeked through the open door at Alex, who ordered a gyro and a couple pieces of baklava, then left in a hurry.

Eva rushed my way, her eyes bright. "Wow, wow, wow. You missed it, Cassia. The most gorgeous guy . . . and I swear, he must be Greek. But you should hear the way he talks. Texas drawl, fer shure." She did her best impression and then giggled. "He's such a . . ."

"Southern gentleman." I couldn't help the words. They just slipped out.

"How did you know?"

"Oh, he just looked like it, I guess."

"Right." Her eyes narrowed and I could read the confusion in them. "But how did you know that if you didn't see him?"

"I saw him as he came in the door, but then I got a cramp." I rubbed the back of my leg. "It's better now."

"Well, that's good, because I need your help clearing the tables. Looks like we've got more people coming in the door." Eva headed back to the front of the shop, still chattering on and on about the guy she now called Cowboy Adonis. Great. Looked like my sister had her eye on the only guy I'd met so far on Galveston Island. Wasn't that just perfect.

I spent the rest of the afternoon waiting on customers right and left. Several times I glanced out the front window to check the crowd at Parma John's. They had their usual steady stream of customers, but nothing like what we were experiencing.

Babbas must've noticed too. At least once I heard him mutter under his breath, "I'll show you how to run a business, Mr. Food Network star!" Lovely.

As we wrapped up for the day, I managed to catch a few minutes on the sidewalk, clearing the outdoor tables. I couldn't help but smile as the trolley zipped by loaded with tourists, cameras in hand. Right away I started humming.

"Great," I grumbled. "Now that song is stuck in my head again."

My mother joined me, wiping her hands on her apron as she glanced my way. "Which song?"

"That Judy Garland one, about the trolley." I started humming it in spite of myself. "Did I ever tell you what happened the time it got stuck in my head and I couldn't shake it? I was clang-clang-clanging all day long."

"Funny." Mama chuckled. "But if you have to get a song stuck in your head, that's a fine one. Very cheerful."

"Yes, but not a hundred times in a row. I honestly couldn't get it to stop. Every time I tried to start humming another one, I'd end up back on that one."

"Well then . . ." Mama stopped working and looked at me. "Maybe the Lord was trying to tell you something. Did you ever think about that?"

"Trying to tell me that I'm supposed to ride the trolley?"

"No." Mama reached to touch my arm, her eyes spilling over with tenderness and passion. "Maybe you're going to meet your future husband on the trolley." She kissed her finger-tips and lifted her hands to heaven. "From my mouth to God's ears."

"Or maybe . . ." This time it was my father's voice sounding behind us. "Maybe we're sup-posed to take out an advertisement on the side of the trolley." He extended his hands as if creating a sign. " 'Eat at Super-Gyros and get a free token to ride the Galveston trolley.' " Babbas snapped his fingers. "Perfect!"

"I don't know, Niko." Mama went back to work clearing the tables. "The Super-Gyros logo is a superhero in flight, cape blowing in the wind. He's not riding a trolley. That doesn't make much sense."

"Just trying to tie the marketing into something islanders are familiar with," my father countered. "Work with me here, Helena."

"Of course, of course." Soon the two of them were coming up with the wording for the promo. I couldn't help but hum that goofy trolley song as I listened in. I wouldn't mind spending a jolly hour on a trolley if it meant meeting Mr. Right.

Mr. Right?

For whatever reason, my thoughts flitted back to the day when I first saw Alex riding the trolley. The moment I saw his face, I'd felt butterflies take flight in my stomach. They'd stirred again that first day at the florist shop. And today, when he'd walked in the door, I'd pretty much felt my heart burst into song. But the cramp in my leg had squelched the melody in a hurry.

My parents droned on about marketing strategies for the sandwich shop. I tried to act interested, but my heart just wasn't in it.

"I think the day went well." Babbas slung a dishcloth over his shoulder, then gazed across the street at Parma John's. The business on their side of the street appeared to be growing by the minute. People flooded inside, and strains of a Frank Sinatra tune drifted out. My father's brow wrinkled in concern. "But we can do better."

"Better?" I bit back a groan.

"Always looking ahead, Cassia," he said. "That's what a businessman does."

I was looking ahead too—to Monday, when I would go back to the florist shop for a few precious hours. Babbas hadn't approved the idea, but at least I'd worked up the courage to tell him my plan. Sort of.

Not that he cared about anything related to flowers. Or me. Oh no.

Darian joined us with a notepad in his hand. He rattled off clever ideas for marketing the sandwich shop, and Babbas listened in, eyes glazed over.

"We can sell coupon books at the register," my brother suggested. "Or maybe offer a discount card for repeat customers? Buy so many gyros and get one for free?"

"I always lose those cards," Mama said. "So I don't think that's a good idea."

"What we really need are interviews from local customers," Babbas said. "Maybe at the same time we film the commercial with the new jingle. We will ask some of our new friends to give an honest opinion about Super-Gyros."

"Unbiased, of course," Mama said.

"Yes." Babbas nodded. "Officer O'Reilly might be a good choice. He has the respect of the community. Although I might need to coach him just a bit, to make sure we don't have to use too many takes."

"You can't put words in the customer's mouth, Niko." Mama rolled her eyes.

"I wouldn't be so sure, Helena." He glanced across the street one last time, crossing his arms as he took note of Uncle Laz going into Parma John's. "Soon everyone on the island will be singing the Super-Gyros jingle that Cassia wrote. Just you wait and see. Our family—we will be television stars too. All of us, in our beautiful Greek costumes. And some people"—these last words he called out in a loud voice—"will learn to eat their own words!"

"Ugh." My cue to exit. I walked back inside the shop to help Eva clear the tables. She took one look at me and stopped her work, dropping the pan of dirty dishes in the process. I caught it before it hit the floor.

"Good catch." Eva smiled. "So what happened? Babbas again?"

"Yeah. Now he's determined to get us on TV, singing that stupid song I came up with. I could kick myself." I watched through the plate-glass window as he carried on in animated fashion, speaking so loudly I could hear him from inside the shop.

"It's your fault for being so brilliant," Eva said.

"Guess so." I sighed. "But the idea of doing what he tells me instead of what I want to is eating me alive." I made my way to the window and peered through the glass as Bella and her husband came out of Parma John's. Something about the duo always made me feel . . . Hmm. I couldn't find the right word to describe it.

"Something's bothering you." Eva joined me at the window, her gaze drifting to the Parma John's sign across the street and then down to Bella.

"Wouldn't mind trading lives with someone normal, that's all." I sighed as I watched Bella's husband slip his arm over her shoulder. She must've said something funny because he laughed.

"Well, I would offer to trade lives with you." Eva rolled her eyes. "But mine isn't normal either. I wonder if anyone has a normal life. You know?"

"Yeah." I still couldn't take my eyes off the two across the street. Bella glanced toward our shop, and I turned quickly so as not to be seen.

"You okay?" Eva asked.

"Yeah." I went to work clearing a table, my back to the window. After a moment I paused and leaned against the counter. "This is going to sound weird, but I feel really lonely sometimes. Do you?"

"Lonely?" Eva snorted as she scrubbed a nearby table. "Seriously? We're surrounded by people on every side, especially on days like today. Who could be lonely?"

"I know, but it's possible to be really lonely when you're in a crowd, trust me. Sometimes a girl just wishes she had someone . . . I don't know . . . someone to whisper sweet nothings in her ear." I craned my neck to catch a final glimpse of Bella and her husband as they made their way on down the street, hand in hand. "To tell her she's pretty. To tell her that she means the world to him."

"Yeah, I get it." My sister released a giggly sigh. "You're looking for Prince Charming."

"I guess. But I seriously doubt he's going to appear in Texas. You know? I always pictured him to be tall, tanned, and very Santa Cruz–ish."

"Oh, trust me, there are plenty of hunky guys here in Galveston." Her eyes lit up as she began to gush over Cowboy Adonis, aka Alex. I couldn't chime in, of course. To do so might give away my little secret. I'd seen those eyes first, and they'd captivated me too.

I found myself deep in thought until Eva looked my way and grinned. "You're doing it again," she said.

"What?"

"Humming 'The Boy Next Door.' "

"At least it's not that goofy trolley song," my mother said as she entered the shop, broom in hand. "I was getting a little tired of that one." She whopped me on the backside with the broom and I started laughing.

"Enough singing, already!" Babbas said as he made his way back inside. "Unless it's our new jingle. We have costumes to design, a commercial script to write, and dishes to wash!" He headed to the kitchen, carrying on about his plans to grow the shop into a coast-to-coast chain. "Before long there will be a Super-Gyros on every corner!" he proclaimed.

Alrighty then.

Crazy or not, my family always brought me back around to reality. Their version of it, anyway. And with a family like mine, who had time to dream of Prince Charming?

8

Zing! Went the Strings of My Heart

You know you're Greek when you teach all your friends curse words and tell them they mean "hello."

On Sunday morning we visited a new-to-us church. Not one of those megachurches. Babbas had sworn off those years ago, claiming it was too hard to make connections.

Interpretation: It's easier to sell people your wares in a smaller setting.

This new church seemed pretty great. I really liked the pastor and his daughter, who, it turned out, ran the bakery next door to Parma John's. I'd seen the Let Them Eat Cake sign, but I'd never dreamed I'd end up in church with the owner, Scarlet. We met, of all places, in the ladies' room.

Maybe it was wrong of me not to come clean about my last name or to introduce her to the rest of the family. Still, I needed time to figure out the best plan when it came to social situations like this. Not that gabbing with a new friend in the ladies' room is exactly something you could add to your social calendar, but we seemed to hit it off regardless. Might as well enjoy it before she met my father and realized he wanted to join her family-friendly church to garner new customers.

Somehow the conversation turned to my job at the flower shop. From there we shifted to a terrific conversation about wedding bouquets. Before long Scarlet filled my ears with stories of wedding cakes she'd made. My heart celebrated as she shared her vision for working with local brides. A soul sister! A fellow businesswoman, one who loved talking about weddings.

I hummed all the way back to the shop, then spent the afternoon looking over the brochure Scarlet had given me for Club Wed's vendor area. Maybe someday my bouquets would be put on display at the island's most famous wedding facility. Better yet, maybe I'd get a write-up in *Texas Bride* magazine. It could happen.

By Monday morning I could hardly wait to get to work. I said my goodbyes to the family— *Really, Babbas? Are the tears necessary?*—then walked down the Strand to Patti-Lou's Petals. I found Marcella inside, already looking frazzled.

"Oh, Cassia, I'm so glad you're here." She pointed at the little girl behind the counter. "This is my daughter, Anna. She's home sick from school today. I hope you don't mind. I'm praying she's not contagious."

The little girl let out a series of sneezes and

then started coughing. Looked like I'd have to use a lot of hand sanitizer today. Marcella took Anna into the back room to rest on the love seat, and I waited on a customer. After that, we turned our attention to a meeting with local bride-to-be, Gabi, a dress designer by trade. She brought several sketches for us to look at and once I saw the design of her gorgeous wedding gown, I couldn't help but gasp.

"It's exquisite!"

"Thank you." She blushed. "I've designed gowns for other brides, but coming up with something for myself wasn't easy."

I would think, with Gabi being a size 2 and all, that coming up with a design would be a piece of cake. Then again, what did I know about dress design? I did know flowers, though, so I gave her my ideas, all of which I tailored to go with the lovely gown.

"If you're going with an all-white theme, then I would suggest orchids and tea roses. Alex brought in the prettiest white tea roses the other day. Let me see if I can find one to show you." I snagged one and brought it back. "For the boutonnieres I would scale back on the orchids and use more of a rose theme. But if you decide to do corsages for the mothers and grandmothers, maybe just a hint of orchid mixed with a couple of the tea roses. What do you think?"

She stared at the flowers I'd pieced together

and then looked back up at me. "I think the flow of the orchids is perfect with the lace pattern in the dress. They're very much alike, actually."

"Yes, that's what made me think of orchids. When I saw the fabric I knew the flowers would be the perfect complement."

"You're so great at this." She gave me an admiring look. "What if I just left it up to you, Cassia? Be creative. I'll give you full rein. Seriously." She quickly glanced at the time on her cell phone and then rose. "I'm so sorry, but I have to make a stop by the fabric store before meeting Bella for lunch. There's so much to do when you're in wedding-planning mode." She thanked us both, gave Marcella a hug, and then swept me into her arms, gushing over me.

When she left, Marcella gave me an admiring look. "Well now."

"Hmm?"

"Girl, you really do love flowers," she said. "And you're great with them. Very inspiring. The customers are going to eat that up."

"Thank you. If you look at my résumé you'll see that I—" Yikes. I stopped right there.

"I can sense it all over you. This is more than a job for you."

"Oh, you have no idea. There's something about the scent of flowers that . . ." My eyes stung as a hint of tears threatened to spill over. "It's so goofy. I can't believe I get emotional over flowers."

"No, I think it's great," she said. "I wish I felt that way. I'm just so busy these days, I don't think much about the flowers anymore. They're more tools of the trade now. Not a passion. I can remember a time when I could look at the design of a dress or even the type of fabric in the gown and know instinctively what flowers to choose. These days I make suggestions and choices out of rote. I've done this so many times now. You know?"

"Oh, I'm sure you work with so many customers."

"You have no idea. Sometimes I forget how much the flowers I'm putting together mean to the people I'm selling them to. They're going to be given to graduates and prom queens, brides and spouses."

"That's what I love." My excitement grew as I shared my heart. "As I'm putting together the flowers, I'm thinking about the people . . . and praying for them."

"I need to do that," she said and sighed. "Just the other day I filled an order for a family that had just lost their mom. So sad. I hate working funerals most of all."

"I'm sure it's hard, but think of the comfort and joy those flowers bring." I gave her an encouraging smile.

"Weddings are still my favorite."

"Mine too."

Our conversation turned to fabrics and then to

Gabi's dress design. Before I knew it, Marcella had told me the whole story of how Gabi had fallen in love with her husband-to-be, a reporter for *Texas Bride*. Then her words grew more serious as she talked about her own marriage.

"I won't say it's all a bed of roses. Marriage is a lot of work, especially when you bring kids into the picture. But love—if you can find it—will change your heart forever. It will make you rethink the things you thought you wanted and give you a sense of purpose."

"Not sure I've ever really been in love," I said. "I thought I was once. I was seventeen." I giggled as I reflected on the boy I'd been so enamored with. He'd gone on to college in another state, and my heart had broken into a thousand pieces.

"Hard to know what love looks like until it slaps you upside the head," she said.

"I like to think about it." I rose and put the orchids and tea roses back into the case. "It gets me excited just dreaming about it. I figure it's kind of like waiting for a rose to open up. You know? I've been waiting a long time, but I know it's gonna be worth the wait."

I heard someone clear his throat behind me and turned to find Alex standing there. His cockeyed grin clued me in to the fact that he'd overheard our conversation. Oops. Well, what could I do about it now?

"Did I hear someone say something about

roses?" His eyes sparkled as he lifted the bucket filled with the most gorgeous reds I'd ever laid eyes on. "We have a new line with bolder colors than we've ever produced."

"Oh, Alex . . ." Marcella and I spoke in unison as we leaned in close to get a better look.

"They're beautiful," I added.

"Glad you agree." The warmth of his smile echoed in his voice. "My dad is sure this one's going to be our biggest seller. And based on what you just said, I'm going to tell my dad we should call them . . . brace yourselves . . ." He looked at me. "The Cassia."

"No way." Was he teasing me? Judging from the serious look in his eyes, no.

"I think it's a great idea." He put the bucket down and flexed his upper arms. "Impulsive decision based on our last conversation. Hope you don't mind. That whole story about waiting for them to open up was great. Seems like we've been waiting for this new line to bloom for ages." He pulled one from the bucket and passed it my way. "What do you think?"

"I love it."

"Great. Just wanted your stamp of approval before making the name official. There are over one hundred species of roses." His fingers swept over mine as he touched the rose in my hand. "I thought you might get a kick out of knowing you're now one of them."

"I'm so flattered." Really, *flattered* hardly described the feelings going on inside my heart right now. Zing-zing-zing! I breathed in the luscious scent of the gorgeous red bloom and sighed. "I just can't believe you would do this. You hardly know me."

"Oh, I know you, all right." He gave me a little wink. "You're a rose, remember? I can tell you anything you want to know about yourself, just based on that."

"Right, right." I hardly knew what else to say. In our family, things—and people—got named with ABCs for convenience's sake. No one took the time to focus on one person's name like this. To give it special meaning. I didn't know how to take such a grandiose gesture.

And how timely that Marcella and Alex had both made a point to tell me how much my love of flowers meant to them. It felt really good to have someone—in this case, a couple of someones—notice and even care about my interests. I certainly didn't get that sort of admiration at home. Not over flowers, anyway. Jingles, sure. Roses, not so much.

Alex continued to share his father's vision for the new Cassia line as he came and went from the shop, lugging in bucket after bucket. The reds had blown me away, of course, but those pinks! And the yellows. I could hardly believe the vibrant colors.

"These yellows are my mom's favorites," he said. "But then again they would be. She's a Texas girl through and through."

"Texas girl?"

"Sure." He nodded. "You're a Texas girl now too. All Texas gals love yellow roses, right, Marcella?"

"Yep." Marcella nodded.

None of this was making sense to me.

"Mama's from Splendora," Alex said, "so she's always been partial to the Yellow Rose of Texas." His eyes narrowed. "You know that story, right?"

"Not really." I shrugged, still distracted by the beautiful roses.

"Started right here in Galveston and involved a beautiful young woman named Emily who was kidnapped by Mexican forces while they ravaged the island."

Marcella shivered. "Such an awful story."

Alex leaned forward and spoke in hushed tones. Not sure why, since our only customer was on the opposite side of the shop. "According to folklore, Emily, um, distracted General Santa Anna and he let his guard down. This led to the Texans winning the fight."

He'd no sooner said the word *Texans* than an incoming customer started talking about the Texans—not the ones in the Battle of San Jacinto, but the football team. Turned out their victories were a bit more interesting to the guys.

Seconds later I'd lost Alex altogether, but I could hardly take my eyes off the red rose he'd given me. I still couldn't figure out what his story about Emily had to do with yellow roses, but I did like that fact that he'd called me a Texas girl. No one had ever called me that before. And strangely, it didn't bother me. In fact, it felt pretty good—nearly as good as this rose felt as I lifted it and ran the soft petals across my cheek.

Yep. I was a Texas girl, all right, one who couldn't stop humming. Over the next half hour I went through every song in the Judy Garland catalog, humming with abandon. I hadn't really noticed until a customer pointed it out.

After waiting on a woman ordering flowers for a memorial service, Marcella decided to take her daughter home for a nap. "Why don't you put the Out to Lunch sign on the door, Cassia?" she said.

"Oh, I don't mind staying here." My stomach grumbled and Alex laughed.

"I'll make her go to lunch, Marcella," he said with a twinkle in his eyes.

"I'll bet you will." Marcella gave him a knowing look, and I felt little butterflies flit through my stomach.

She left with Anna, and Alex turned my way, a pleading look in his eyes. "Okay, so what's it gonna be?"

"What do you mean?"

"What kind of food do you like?" Before I could

tell him that I'd brought my lunch—a Greek salad and loukoumades—he snapped his fingers. "If we had more time I would take you to Moody Gardens. There's a great restaurant there and we could look at the flowers. Ever been?"

"Not yet, but I've been dying to go. Sometime when I have a few hours to kill." Like that would ever happen.

"Agreed. You really need to take your time at Moody Gardens to get the full effect, especially if you're a flower lover." He looked my way, those gorgeous eyes now sparkling. "Oh, I know. There's a new place a few blocks down that's really great. A Greek sandwich shop."

"Super-Gyros." I bit my lip and forced myself not to say anything else.

"Yes." He nodded. "Great place. I ate there Saturday. The gyro was out of this world, and the baklava . . . Man. Never had anything like it. I could eat a whole tray."

Mama would love that news, but I couldn't comment. At least not yet.

"Have you tried the place?" he asked. "It's probably going to be really crowded, but it'll be worth the wait, I promise."

"Oh, um . . . yeah, I've tried it." I shrugged, unsure of what else to say. If I showed up at the Pappas homestead with a fella on my arm, Babbas was sure to grill him—and not on the kitchen stove. This guy didn't stand a chance, Greek or not. Besides, I wasn't ready to let any of my new Rossi-loving friends know about my family. Not yet.

Alex went off on a tangent about the moist lamb on the sandwich he'd eaten Saturday, and I could see I'd lost him. After a moment I cleared my throat, and he startled back to attention. His gaze met mine and he grinned. "Sorry. I love gyros."

"I've always been a fan too," I said. "But . . ."

"But?" His lips curled down in a frown. "There's a 'but'?"

"I, um . . . I ate there yesterday." Brilliant! And I didn't even have to fib.

"Aw, man. Okay." He shrugged. "Weird, though. I didn't think they were open on Sunday. But anyway, you already know how good the food is, and you're probably not wanting the same thing two days in a row."

"It's the best on the island." I didn't mean to do it, but the little jingle slipped out. Did I really just sing that out loud?

"Wow, that's cool." He looked duly impressed by my impromptu concert. "Haven't heard that one yet."

You will. Just stay tuned.

He hesitated and I could feel his gaze on me. "So, let's go someplace else. You like Italian food?"

Yikes! "Well, yes, I like it, but . . ."

A shimmer in his eyes clued me in to the fact that the boy loved his Italian food. "There's a great

115

place just down the street. Parma John's. It's a—"

"Pizza place," I finished for him.

"Right." He nodded. "I eat there all the time. In fact, the owners, the Rossis, own this place too."

"Yeah, I kind of figured that out already. I've pretty much decided the whole island is run by the Rossis."

Alex grinned. "Well, when you put it like that, it makes them sound devious. They're just normal people." He laughed. "Okay, I take that back. They're about as far from normal as any family I've ever met, but you've gotta love 'em."

Try telling that to my father.

"So, what do you say?" he asked. "You okay with pizza?"

"I really don't know if I should leave, especially with Marcella being gone."

"You heard what she said." His eyes melted into mine. "Besides, I've got to eat, you've got to eat . . ." A lingering silence filled the space between us. "Might as well eat together."

I looked into his gorgeous dark eyes, and my gaze traveled to his lustrous, wavy black hair and that engaging smile. My sister would flip if she found out that Cowboy Adonis was asking me to lunch. And I would be a fool to turn him down. So what if Babbas caught me going into Parma John's? I had to die somehow. Might as well be with this good-looking guy on my arm and pepperoni on my breath.

9

Yours and Mine

You might be Greek if you know someone who always feels the need to point out how much something they bought costs.

Pushing all reservations aside, I offered Alex a lame nod. "Sure. It's hard to resist pizza. I'm starving."

He gave me a funny look, one that almost said, "Is that all that's hard to resist?" but I turned away, my gaze shifting to the door. I walked over to it and hung the Out to Lunch sign, then ushered up a silent prayer, asking the Lord to send guardian angels to watch out for me should my father see me going into the restaurant owned by his archrival.

"Should we walk or drive?" Alex asked. "I've got the delivery van. You could ride in style."

I shrugged. "Seems pointless to drive, especially on such a pretty day. It's only seven blocks to Parma John's, anyway."

"Wow, you've got the number of blocks memorized?" He gave me an admiring look. "You must love that place."

"Oh, I've never actually been inside," I said. "I'm new to the island, remember?"

"Okay." He gave me a curious look. "But you know how far it is?"

"Yeah. I'm weird like that. I tend to memorize things." *Like how many blocks I have to walk to and from work.*

"Interesting. I memorize things too, but usually names and species of flowers, that sort of thing."

"I do that too," I acknowledged.

We both stopped and stared into each other's eyes. For a moment it felt as if the whole world stood still, like time had stopped. Then my phone beeped. Great. A text message. I glanced at it, surprised to see a note from Babbas.

How late are you working for these flower people? Mama needs you to make a run to the grocery store for sugar.

I quickly typed the response—*5:00*—then shoved the phone in my purse. "All done."

"Okay. Let's get this show on the road." He held the door open in gentlemanly fashion and I stepped through it, then locked it behind us.

A luscious breeze swept over us, coming off of nearby Galveston Bay. With the sun shining brightly overhead, the temperatures felt perfect. Great for a walk.

Still, walking side by side down the Strand with this fellow was too risky. Someone from the Pappas family would see me going into Parma John's, and my life would end right then and there. I needed a different plan.

"Oh, I know." I snapped my fingers. "I've been wanting to ride the trolley ever since I got here. What about that?"

"Sounds good. Should be along shortly. You mind waiting a couple of minutes?"

"Not at all."

He led the way to the trolley stop at the corner, and we waited for it to come by. Well, he waited. I stood behind him in case anyone in my family happened by.

Alex looked my way, brow wrinkled. "You okay back there?"

"Yeah. Just, um, checking to see what time the next trolley comes by. Shouldn't be long now."

He joined me and we stood reading the sign. Actually, he looked at the sign. I snuck another peek at his face, homing in on the clear-cut lines of his profile.

He gave me a warm smile. "Glad the trolley's up and running again."

"Me too."

"It took years to repair after the big storm. Everyone down here has been waiting on pins and needles to see it open."

"I would've been the first in line if I'd known. Growing up so close to San Francisco, I have a long running history with streetcars. I think that's one reason I fell in love with Judy Garland music in the first place, because of that trolley song."

"Trolley song?" Alex looked perplexed. "Don't

119

know it." The clanging of the trolley sounded and it squealed to a stop in front of us.

"You never saw *Meet Me in St. Louis*? Best Judy Garland musical ever. After *The Wizard of Oz*, I mean. I used to watch that movie when I was a kid."

"Which one? *The Wizard of Oz* or *Meet Me in St. Louis*?" Alex gestured for me to climb aboard and I did so in a hurry, still concerned that one of my family members might happen along and see me.

"*Meet Me in St. Louis*," I said.

"Ah." Alex followed behind me, and we took a seat near the back. "I think my mom made me watch that movie once. Is that the one with Margaret Mitchell?"

"Margaret O'Brien." I hated to correct the boy, but someone had to set him straight.

The trolley took off, and I held on tight as we zipped down the lane. Alex slipped his arm around my shoulders. "Right, right. I remember Margaret O'Brien." As the trolley moved along, Alex lit into a story about Margaret Thatcher. I didn't correct him this time.

My thoughts shifted back in time to my first trolley ride in San Francisco as a little girl. Babbas had taken me on a shopping spree. I'd forgotten until now. What a special day that had been. He'd treated me like his little princess, even bought me a ruffled dress.

"You're humming again." Alex gave me a funny look. "You do that a lot, you know. Noticed it at the shop. But I don't recognize half of the melodies."

"Oh, I'm sure they're Judy Garland songs. I've been on a kick lately."

"Well, since you're so musical and all, maybe you can help me come up with something poetic to help promote Rigas Roses. I'm supposed to be coming up with the perfect advertisement for our local Splendora paper, but I stink at rhymes."

"What have you tried?" I asked.

"Well, let's see. I came up with 'Roses are red, daffodils are yellow . . .' " He groaned. "See my problem? I can't find anything to rhyme with *yellow*."

"Nor should you want to." I laughed. "Trust me, that 'Roses are red' rhyme is too cliché, anyway."

"Still, it's familiar, and familiar brings in customers. How about this: 'Roses are red, lilies are white, buy from the Rigas family and you'll be . . . all right'?"

"But you want your customers to be more than all right, don't you?" The trolley stopped and several people got on.

"Yeah." He paused as the trolley started up again. "Okay, this one: 'Roses are red, carnations are pink, buy your flowers from us 'cause . . .' " He pursed his lips and appeared to be thinking. " 'Our service don't stink'?"

121

Crossing my arms at my chest, I offered him what I hoped would be a comforting smile. "An advertisement like that isn't the best way to connect with your customers. Just sayin'."

"Help me work on it?" He gave me a pleading look. "Our family business depends on it." I detected laughter in his eyes. "No pressure or anything."

Of course not. But who in the world kept spreading the word that I was good at rhymes and jingles? Crazy.

"I guess I could think about it. If anything comes to me, I'll let you know." I offered a hopeful smile.

The trolley drew near Parma John's, and I glanced across the street at Super-Gyros. Babbas stood outside, chatting with his new friend, Officer O'Reilly. Just what I needed. I ducked down in my seat and tried to figure out how to go about getting off this thing without being seen. Another peek from the bottom of the window revealed my father and the officer laughing.

"You okay over there?" Alex asked.

"Yeah, I, um . . ." I scooted farther down in the seat. "Oh, I . . . I need to make sure I've got my phone. Maybe I dropped it?" I reached into my purse and came out with it. "Nope. Here it is."

"Oh." He gave me a curious look. "I was worried about you for a minute there. Thought maybe you were on the run from the law."

"On the run from the law?"

He pointed out the window at O'Reilly. "I thought maybe you saw the badge and decided to slip out of view."

"No." Out of the corner of my eye I watched as Darian walked out of Super-Gyros and approached the officer with a sandwich in hand. O'Reilly extended his hand to receive the sandwich and dove right in, a delirious look on his face. At that moment, the three nuns we'd met the other day walked up and greeted the officer. Great. More people to hide from.

"Are you sure you don't want to go to the new Greek place?" Alex gave me a pleading look, and I almost fell into the trap. "You seem to be infatuated. Can't take your eyes off it."

I scooted farther down in the seat. "No. No, I don't. I . . . I might be allergic to tzatziki sauce."

"No way." He cringed. "That would be awful."

"Well, it hasn't been confirmed medically, but I get . . . hives." Okay, so maybe not hives, but I did have a little rash the last time I ate cucumbers. Then again, I'd been out in the sun too long that day, so it might've been a heat rash.

"Man, that would stink."

"Yeah. It's a problem."

And speaking of problems, I watched as my mother joined Babbas, Darian, and O'Reilly on the sidewalk. Great. Why not invite the whole family to watch my funeral?

"I just thought a good Greek girl like you would like Greek food." He gave me a little wink and my heart fluttered. "You did say you're Greek, right? Or am I just guessing based on your name?"

"My name?"

"Sure. Cassia—Greek. Bethesda—Greek."

"Bethesda? That's my middle name."

"Oh, sorry. I was so busy sniffing your résumé that I guess I read it wrong. Or maybe Marcella called you that?" He shrugged. "Anyway, sorry about the name mix-up. Not a very good way for a guy to impress a girl, getting her last name wrong. So what is your—"

"To answer your question, I am Greek. But I like lots of different kinds of foods." Another glance out of the window put me on guard once again. Babbas was pointing at the trolley, probably telling O'Reilly and the nuns about the sign he planned to put on the side of it.

"Great. You ready for some pizza then?" Alex asked.

I nodded and twisted in my seat to avoid being seen by my family members. "Sure. Sounds awesome."

Alex rose and extended his hand to help me stand. My hunched posture seemed to confuse him. "Sure you're okay over there?"

"Yep. I, um, have a little crick in my back." After all the twisting and turning, I didn't have to lie about that. Not one bit.

"Man. I'm glad we didn't try to walk those seven blocks. Hope you're okay." He helped me up. I followed along on his heels as he led the way off the trolley. Most of my attention, however, was focused on my father and O'Reilly, who followed my mother and brother into Super-Gyros. I breathed a sigh of relief and stood up straight just as we stepped down onto the street.

Alex extended his hand. "Mm-hmm. Thought so. Your pizza awaits, oh wanted one."

"W-what?"

He leaned close to whisper the rest, his breath warm against my cheek. "I have to believe you're on the run from the law. You were hiding from that cop, but now he's gone."

"Oh, I—"

"No point in denying it. You're as white as a ghost. But I won't hold that against you."

"Won't hold what against me?" I tried to sound lighthearted. "The fact that I'm on the run from the law or that I'm as white as a ghost?"

"So you are on the run from the law then." The wrinkles around his gorgeous brown eyes deepened. "This changes everything. I've never gone to lunch with a girl who's running from her troubles before."

I took his extended hand. "I'm not on the run from the law, I promise. But you might be right about the other part."

"Thought so."

"I'm just . . ." I shook my head and sighed. "Running." I hesitated. "Look, there's a perfectly logical explanation for my behavior, I promise. I'll tell you when we get—" I'd just started to say "inside" when my littlest sister came out of Super-Gyros. She waved and called my name. I immediately ducked behind a parked car.

Alex joined me, his posture hunched. "Why are we hiding?" His hoarse whisper conveyed his concern. "Are you really on the lam?"

"Lamb?" On a shish kebab, maybe.

"Is that kid an undercover officer or some-thing?" he asked, his voice more strained. "Or is she on our side?"

"Something like that." I groaned and slapped myself on the head. "I'll tell you everything when we get inside. If we get inside."

"Why wouldn't we get inside?" His dark eyes pierced the distance between us. "Wait. This isn't a mob thing, is it? There's not some crazed hit man waiting inside, ready to take us out, is there?"

"No." Just a crazed Greek father across the street, ready to murder his daughter for betraying him and the family business. But that was a story for a later time. Right now I had to get inside

Parma John's without Gina seeing me. I peered around the vehicle, holding my purse in front of my face. Gina stared at me, clearly perplexed, and I put my finger to my lips, hoping she would take a hint. After a moment of staring at me, she turned back toward Super-Gyros.

Alex cleared his throat. "Sorry, but if this keeps up, I'm going to starve to death."

Well, that would never do. I needed to keep this guy in fine shape, so I'd better get my act together. Another quick glance across the street revealed that Gina had gone back into the sandwich shop, so I stood, grabbed a very surprised Alex by the hand, and dragged him inside Parma John's lickety-split.

10
Me and My Shadow

You might be Greek if you tell your mama you're not hungry and she thinks you have an eating disorder.

We somehow made it inside Parma John's and were greeted by Bella, who seemed more than delighted to see us.

"Cassia, I'm so glad you're here! Your timing is perfect!" She grabbed my hand and gave it a squeeze. "Gabi just called and told me all about her meeting with you this morning. She loves your ideas for her wedding. Says you're a genius."

I melted like butter in the sun at this flattering remark. "Really? I enjoyed getting to know her. By the way, her wedding dress is a-*may*-zing. Gorgeous. And those bridesmaid dresses are going to be great too."

"She's a genius too, and that's good news for us. I have a feeling she's going to bring in even more business to the flower shop and Club Wed, now that she's got her own line of dresses. She has a knack for knowing how to merge fabrics and flowers."

"Awesome." I peeked at Alex out of the corner

of my eye to make sure he hadn't fallen asleep at the wheel while we talked shop. Nope. The boy looked interested, even.

"She's on her way here now to talk about the ceremony," Bella said. "Want to join us? I'd love to hear all about the flower choices. That will help me make some decisions about the decor in the chapel and reception hall. What do you think?" She looked back and forth between Alex and me. "Unless you two are . . . I mean, I don't want to interrupt your lunch plans."

For a moment I thought Alex might be bothered by her suggestion to turn our lunch-for-two into a lunch-for-four, but he seemed to take it in stride. Just one more reason to tumble head over heels for this guy. He looked like a real Greek hero but definitely had the manners of a Southern gentle-man.

Before Gabi arrived, however, Bella decided to introduce me to the entire Rossi clan. Well, all of those who happened to be at Parma John's that day. After following her into the kitchen, I met her brother Nick, who was Marcella's husband. Then Armando, another brother. Then Jenna, Bella's best friend. Then Sophia, Bella's sister and co-owner of Sassy Shears.

We headed back out to the front of the shop, and I offered a little wave to Bella's mother, who sat at a table with several other women. Then I followed behind Bella to the cash register to meet her uncle Laz. Not that he had time to talk, what with so many customers to tend to. I waited in silence, hoping he wouldn't recognize me from the other day when he'd stormed out into the street to confront my father.

Laz finished up with his final customer and glanced our way. As I got a close-up look at his aging face, I knew he wasn't a mobster. The twinkle in his eyes spoke of mischief, and the cane that he leaned on convinced me that age had taken its toll. He hobbled our way.

"Who have we here?" Bella's uncle narrowed his gaze and shifted his cane to the other hand. "Don't believe we've met before."

Thank goodness he didn't recognize me. I breathed a sigh of relief.

"Oh, that's because she's new to the island," Alex said.

"My name is Cassia." I deliberately skipped mentioning my last name.

"Cassia?" Laz's brow furrowed, and for a moment I thought I saw him glance toward Super-Gyros across the street. Just as quickly, he looked back at me. "Lovely name. Mediterranean?"

"Um, yes, sir."

"Well, any friend of Bella's is a friend of the whole Rossi family." He extended a wrinkled hand and I took it, offering a lame shake. "You can call me Uncle Laz. Everyone around here does."

"Guess that makes you family now." Bella

chuckled. "Welcome, sis." She then introduced me to the rest of the clan, but I could barely keep up. Rosa, who I recognized at once from *The Italian Kitchen*. Bella's brother Joey—a fellow shorter than me by an inch or two—and his wife. Someone named Bubba, who turned out to be Jenna's husband.

Really? Bubba? In an Italian family?

On and on the list went. She lost me when she started introducing some of the local patrons who were having lunch at the various tables, but my interest was piqued when I saw the photographer—what was her name again? Hannah something?—my dad had hired to photograph him in the Super-Gyros costume. I prayed she wouldn't remember me from the other day.

She didn't. Apparently she'd been too busy dealing with my crazed father to pay much attention to the rest of the family. The woman gave me a friendly nod, then went back to looking over the spread of photos on her table.

Something outside the window caught my eye. I looked across the street and caught a glimpse of my father sweeping the sidewalk in front of Super-Gyros, but I didn't mention it for obvious reasons. If Babbas could see me now, he would kill me. Slice me up with the meat cutter. Give my body parts to the nuns to dispose of in their convent's garden.

I hid behind a menu, imagining my funeral.

Wouldn't be much of a crowd. All of my friends lived in California.

Well, most of them.

"See something you like?" Alex asked.

"Yeah." I peeked out from behind my menu. "Lots of options, but I need to make a decision soon. I don't want to be away from the flower shop for long. Don't want to risk losing any customers."

"Would you like to try our special of the day—a large Mambo Italiano pizza with two cappuccinos for only $17.95?" Jenna asked. "That's my personal favorite."

Bella shook her head. "Lunch is on me today, so order whatever looks good." She offered us a table up front, but I claimed the sun would give me hives. *Really, Cassia? That's all you can come up with—another hives story?* She moved us to the back of the room, far from the sunlight streaming in from the windows.

"This okay?" she asked.

"Yes. Thanks."

"Really stinks, you being from California and having this weird sun sensitivity," Bella said.

"She's allergic to tzatziki sauce too," Alex said.

"Tzatziki sauce?" Bella's brow wrinkled. "What's that?"

"Oh, it's a great dressing for salads and sandwiches," I said. "And for dipping. You take yogurt and cucumbers and dill and mix them together, then you add lemon and olive oil and some spices. Then you spread it on anything and everything." I went into a lengthy discussion of the sauce, pretty much giving away Mama's secret recipe to all who were within earshot.

"Man, it sounds good. Might have to try that myself." Bella laughed. "But if I do, don't tell Uncle Laz. He made us take an oath that we wouldn't eat anything Greek now that the competition has moved in across the street." She gestured with her head to Super-Gyros, and I swallowed hard and tried to keep a straight face.

Peeking around my menu, I looked at the Super-Gyros sign. It looked pretty good from this angle. Really good, actually.

Bella kept on talking, oblivious to my thoughts. "But seriously, Cassia, if you have a problem with the sun, you might need to live in Colorado or someplace like that."

Right now I'd like to live in Colorado. Or Kansas. Any landlocked state would do. Anyplace where a nutty father wouldn't come looking for me.

Thank goodness I didn't have much time to fret over Babbas. Seconds later Parma John's door swung open and Bella greeted Gabi, the gorgeous bride-to-be. The two women chatted with ease, and I leaned over to make sure Alex wasn't put off by the interruption.

"You okay with this?" I whispered.

133

"Sure, why not." His expression reflected his ease. "We can always do lunch next time at that new place across the street. We'll just skip the tzatziki sauce. Oh, and we'll sit in the back of the shop, away from the sun. Maybe over there we'll have some peace and quiet . . . time to ourselves."

Sure we will.

But from the look in his eye, I could tell he wanted time alone with me. Flattering. Not that I had time to think it through. Bella pulled over a chair and gestured for Gabi to join us.

She took a seat and grabbed my hand. "Oh, Cassia! I'm still on cloud nine from our meeting earlier. I told Bella that she'd better snag you up quick."

"Snag me up quick?" What did that mean? I already had a job. Make that two jobs.

"Sure." Gabi's long lashes fluttered as she grew more excited. "For Club Wed. The Vendors Square area. Your work is amazing. She needs to add you to her list of preferred vendors."

"Oh, I see."

"Do you mind if we talk flowers while we eat?" Gabi asked. "I'm starving."

"Oh, of course not." I could talk flowers over food, as long as Alex didn't mind.

He began to talk about the new species of roses he had named after me, and before long we were all engaged in a conversation about wedding flowers once again.

"Looks like I've lost all of you." Bella chuckled. "That's okay. Gabi and I can talk about the ceremony later. I'll put in your pizza order. Do you guys know what you want?"

"Cassia's never been here before," Alex said. "So she gets to choose."

I perused the menu and tried to make a choice. Pepperoni sounded good. So did the Mambo Italiano, the special of the day. That would explain the Dean Martin song playing repeatedly overhead. I'd noticed the themed music the moment I walked in. Still, they didn't have my favorite pizza—the Greek Zorba. Weird. What sort of pizza place didn't carry the Zorba?

"What strikes your fancy?" Bella asked. "You like pepperoni?"

"Yes." I must've wrinkled my nose or something because she gave me a curious look.

"What is it? Don't see what you like?"

I'd never had a very good poker face. "Well, I have a favorite, but I don't see it listed. It's a Greek pizza we used to get back home in— anyway, it's no biggie. I love pepperoni."

"What is this Greek pizza?" Uncle Laz appeared beside me, looking more than a little interested.

"Oh, well, it's really just a combination of things I love—lamb, kalamatas, feta, spinach, a little lemon on the crust. Loaded with flavor and good for you too. Heart healthy."

"You've said the magic words!" Laz clasped

135

his hands together, his cane falling to the wayside. "I need to add more heart-healthy choices, especially now that I . . ."

Rosa joined us and finished his sentence. "My Laz had an episode with his heart a while back, and we've been looking for ways to get him to mind the doctor."

"She has the perfect solution, Rosa." Laz tried to reach down to grab his cane, and Bella snagged it before he toppled over. "And this will work on multiple levels."

"What do you mean?" Rosa asked.

"This is the perfect plan to beat that new restaurant owner at his own game." Laz's eyes gleamed as he rattled off something in Italian. Then he made a proclamation in English. "This young woman has just given me all the ammunition I need to draw people who love Greek food over to our side of the street!"

Oh. No.

Lord, please don't let them bury me in that pink dress Yia Yia loves so much. I look awful in pink! And if there's any justice at all, please don't let Mama do my makeup.

Bella looked back and forth between me and her uncle, a bewildered look on her face. "I don't know, Uncle Laz. We don't really know that much about Greek food. Besides, people come here for great Italian cuisine, you know? Seems kind of silly."

"But we've got to fight fire with fire, and that man across the street is hot under the collar already." Laz's deep chuckle had a bit of an edge to it. "Just wait till he sees our new Greek pizza advertised on the board outside. That should do the trick!"

That should do the trick, all right. Babbas would flip.

"Won't be healthy for his heart, now will it!" Laz gave me a hearty whack on the back just as I took a sip of my soda, which came shooting out of my nose. Perfect. Talk about making a great impression on Alex. He seemed mesmerized by this whole conversation.

"Thank you, young lady," Laz said. "I owe you."

I couldn't manage anything but a weak nod, but Laz didn't appear to be paying attention to me anyway. Instead, he hollered across the room at an incoming patron, telling him all about my brilliant-beyond-brilliant idea. Great. Before long everyone on the island would know I had inspired the new Greek pizza. Maybe he'd even name it after me. That would just be the icing on the cake.

Cake. Mmm.

My gaze shifted to the opening between Parma John's and the bakery next door, Let Them Eat Cake. The smell of baked goods drew me in, almost distracting me from the problem at hand.

In that moment an idea occurred to me. I knew just how I would get out of here without raising suspicion from the other side of the street. After we finished our pizza, I would come up with some reason to go into the bakery—maybe buy a cake or something—and then go out the bakery door. Perfect. That way, if I was spotted from the opposite side of the street, no one would question my loyalty.

Just as I settled this issue in my mind, I caught a glimpse of a familiar man out of the corner of my eye. A shiver ran down my spine as I took in the fellow in the expensive suit, the one who'd gotten out of the limousine the other day. His confident stride spoke of authority as he headed right toward us. In his right hand he carried the dark case, the same one Babbas had insisted held a machine gun. As the well-dressed fellow lifted the case onto the counter by the cash register, I fought the temptation to duck under the table. I couldn't die at Parma John's. I just couldn't. My father would never forgive me.

"You okay over there?" Bella asked.

I nodded but didn't mean it. "Just, um, wondering about that man over there." I spoke in a strained whisper. "The one with the case."

"Man with the case?" She turned and saw him, then grinned. "Oh, perfect timing! I've been waiting on him." Bella rose and waved. "Gordy!"

The man grabbed his case and rushed our

way. "Bella!" He kissed her on each cheek, then reached to open the case.

I pinched my eyes shut and braced myself for shots to ring out. This wasn't exactly how I'd planned to meet my Maker.

Turned out the dark case held a musical instrument—a saxophone. Gordy, I learned, directed a swing band, a band that Gabi had hired to perform at her wedding.

Go figure. The limo didn't belong to a mobster. It transported band members to and from gigs.

I felt like a fool.

On the other hand, at least I wouldn't die one. Not today, anyway. And not at Parma John's, under the watchful eye of my father's mortal enemies.

11

Fly Me to the Moon

You might be Greek if there were more than twenty-eight people in your bridal party.

Turned out Gordy was quite the character. He kept us in stitches, and not the kind you get at a hospital. I found myself caught up in conversation just as our pizza arrived. Gooey blobs of melted cheese graced the thick red sauce and tantalizing crust, but what really drew me in was the scent—no, the sight . . . no, the scent—of the pepperoni. Oozing little rivers of greasy goodness all over the cheese and red sauce, the yummy-looking circles practically begged me to reach out and grab one of them for a taste. So I did. In fact, I downed the first piece so quickly that Alex gave me an admiring nod.

"Guess you were hungry." He took a bite and a contented look settled over him.

"Guess I was." It might not be the Zorba, but I hadn't had anything this tasty in ages. After I finished my second piece, a quick glance at the clock sent me into a tailspin. Had I really been gone from the flower shop for nearly an hour?

Ack. I had to make a clean getaway from this place and get back to work.

I worked out a plan in my mind, a way to protect me should anyone across the street be watching. "Do you mind if we stop off at the bakery on the way out?" I asked Alex. "I need to look at something."

"Don't mind a bit. That's my usual exit route too." He waggled a brow and then laughed. "Wait till you taste Scarlet's cheesecake."

Sounded tempting. So did making it out of Parma John's alive.

Bella insisted on covering our lunch tab. We thanked her and rose to say our goodbyes to the Rossi crew. Uncle Laz caught us just as I headed into the bakery. "Before you go, you must tell me your name once again. My memory . . . it's not so good. I want to name the new Greek pizza after you."

Oh. Help. I'd never wanted to lie so badly in my life.

"Well," I finally managed, "my name is so boring. Why don't you call it something that people will recognize—maybe something like the Venus de Milo?"

I knew that Babbas would laugh his head off at that name. He would think it amateurish. And he would never, ever suspect that I had played a role in naming the pizza.

"Venus de Milo." Laz shrugged. "Might work.

I'll run it by the family." He offered me a gracious smile. "And speaking of family, you're a member of the Rossi clan now, whether you realize it or not. There's no turning back now."

Oh please, God, don't let Babbas show up for my funeral wearing those spandex tights.

I swallowed hard and fought the temptation to say, "Well, I might need a new family after this." Instead, I managed a pleasant and calm, "Well, thank you, Mr. Rossi."

"None of that Mr. Rossi stuff. It's Uncle Laz to you." He threw his arms around me in a bear hug, his cane swinging through the air and nearly clipping Alex in the head.

Through the plate-glass window I saw my father in front of our shop, wearing his superhero costume. Yikes. He appeared to be looking for something. Or someone. Maybe me. He glanced directly at us, and I ducked through the opening into the bakery, then turned back toward the men.

Laz gave me a strange look, but not half as strange as the look from Alex, who followed along behind me. "Did you decide what you want from the bakery?"

"Oh. Um, yes." I paused, my thoughts tumbling. "My mother's birthday is coming up." *Next January.* "I'm going to buy her a cake."

"That's nice. Well, you've come to the right place. Scarlet makes the best cakes in town. She even won a decorating competition on TV. I think you two will get along great."

"I met her at church yesterday, actually," I said. "She seems really nice."

"Oh, you went to her church? What did you think?"

"I liked it a lot." *Hope my dad doesn't get us excommunicated.*

"I've been there quite a few times myself. Scarlet is sweet, and the hardest worker I know," Alex said. "She's also tough as nails, but I guess you'd have to be, to be married to Armando."

Married to Armando? Which one was Armando again? I couldn't remember.

I made my way across the crowded bakery to the glass counter, where I gazed down at the panorama of sugary delicacies. Oy vey. This might be the death of me.

Scarlet greeted me with a smile. "Well, hello, stranger. Didn't take you long to stop by. I'm tickled you're here."

She went on and on about how great it was to see me, but I couldn't get past the fact that Alex had called her Armando's wife. In that moment, as she stood across from me chattering on without a care in the world, it hit me.

Armando. Bella's brother.

I swallowed hard and faced Scarlet head-on. "Scarlet, your last name is Rossi?"

"Well, sure." She reached into the glass case

and straightened a tray of M&M cookies. "Still consider myself a honeymooner, though, so I forget my own last name at times. You know how it is when you first get married. You have to remind yourself of the new name." She beamed. "But I'm so happy to be a Rossi now."

Of course she was. They were all happy to be Rossis.

I slapped myself on the forehead. "You're a Rossi. Bella's a Rossi. Marcella's a Rossi. You're all Rossis." A little sigh followed. "And you're all great."

"Well, thank you." Scarlet giggled. "Technically I'm only a Rossi by marriage, but if that makes me great in your eyes, I'll take it."

Yeah, you're pretty great, and you're a Rossi. Which definitely means my chances of keeping you as a friend are going down by the minute. So long, new friend. After Babbas finds out your last name, we won't be visiting your father's church anymore.

She rambled on about the goings-on at the church's youth group—something about how she needed to bake more M&M cookies for some big event—but seemed to have lost Alex to the sweets. He pressed his index finger to the glass case in front of the turtle cheesecake and released a contented sigh.

"Which one are you going to get?" Alex turned back to me.

"Which what?"

"Which cake? For your mother?" Tiny creases formed between Alex's brows.

"My mother. Right. Her birthday." *Next January.*

"This one's nice." He pointed at an expensive number, all frilled out in cream cheese frosting. "That's the one I would get for my mother."

"That's the one you bought for yourself last week, goober." Scarlet laughed. She looked at me, an amused expression on her face. "I've never known a guy who has a sweet tooth like Alex. He's worse than any woman I've ever known."

"Keep on humiliating me like that and I'll just start buying my sweets across the street." He pointed at Super-Gyros and my breath caught in my throat.

"Oh yeah?" Scarlet's brow wrinkled in concern. "They sell baked goods over there?"

"Only the best baklava I've ever had in my life," Alex said. "But I wouldn't worry if I were you. They only had a million customers buying it right and left when I was there on Saturday."

Scarlet's brows elevated. "Be serious. Do you think I should add baklava to my lineup?"

"You make the best sweets on the island," Alex said, "but I don't think you want to give these people a run for their money when it comes to baklava. They're Greek."

"Ah." She sighed. "Well, I guess I'll stick to what I know."

The bakery filled with customers, and I took another look at the time. No way. I'd been gone an hour and ten minutes? Marcella would have my head. If the man in the superhero cape didn't kill me on the way out of here.

"I need to go. Now." Taking hold of Alex's muscular arm distracted me from making a quick getaway.

"You gonna get the cake for your mom later then?" he asked.

"Yeah. I've got plenty of time." *Several months, in fact.*

He led the way out of the bakery door onto the street, and I hid behind him as my sister came out of Super-Gyros to clear the tables on the sidewalk.

"Just keep walking," I said to Alex. "I'll explain in a minute."

He headed away from Parma John's in the direction of the florist shop. When we reached the first street corner, I breathed what must've been a visible sigh of relief.

"I knew it." Alex snapped his fingers. "You're on the run from the law, aren't you?"

"No." I laughed nervously. "But I am on the run. You've got that part right."

"From . . . ?" He took a seat at the trolley stop and gestured for me to join him.

"My father."

"Your father?" Alex's expression tightened. "Is he abusive?"

"No, nothing like that." With a wave of my hand I dismissed that idea right away. Babbas was tough, no doubt about it. But never abusive. Oh, he occasionally ranted about giving the little ones a swift kick in the rear every now and again, but he didn't mean it.

"So why are you on the run from him?"

"It's kind of funny, really." I gave what I hoped would be a convincing smile. "My father would kill me if he knew I was at Parma John's, having pizza."

"Because you're allergic to pizza too?"

"No. Because he really doesn't like to see me cavorting with the enemy."

"Cavorting with the enemy?" Alex asked. "Now I'm really intrigued."

"Here's the problem," I whispered. "The whole island is filled with Rossis."

"That's a problem?"

"Well, not from my vantage point, but my father . . . he, well—"

"Doesn't like the Rossis? Is that it?"

"Yeah, but there's a little more to it than that."

He thinks they're evil and wants to see them destroyed.

I'd just opened my mouth to explain when the trolley came to a stop in front of us. Alex reached for my hand and helped me on board. We found ourselves smack-dab in the middle of a tourist group from Japan—approximately thirty people, all snapping photographs of the buildings along the Strand, and all speaking Japanese. Loudly.

With so many people on board, we couldn't even locate seats, so we had to stand on the platform in the back along with three other chattering tourists. Before I had the opportunity to explain about my father, we were back at the florist shop, which was flooded with customers. Marcella gave me a "thank God you're here" look, and I sprinted to the counter to help her. Hopefully she would forgive me later.

And Alex . . . hopefully he would forgive me too. No doubt he thought I was a nutcase.

He grabbed a large stack of flower buckets from the back room and gave me a little good-bye wave, which I returned with a smile. I didn't even have the chance to thank him for the lunch invitation before he was out the door. Hopefully I could make it up to him, and soon. If anyone deserved an explanation for my wacky behavior, he did.

12

More Than You Know

You know you're Greek when you say "Opa!" every time someone drops or breaks some-thing.

The next couple of days were spent going back and forth between the flower shop and the family restaurant. Thank goodness Babbas hadn't seen me going into Parma John's. For now I was off the hook.

Well, sort of. He kept me hopping during the hours I worked at Super-Gyros. Marcella kept me hopping too. Seemed more and more she needed time off, which left me manning the flower shop. I didn't really mind. In fact, I rather enjoyed helping customers make decisions.

On Thursday morning I worked harder than ever putting together six bridesmaid bouquets. The little poppies in the bouquets reminded me of *The Wizard of Oz*, so I hummed "Somewhere over the Rainbow" as I worked. While I was in the middle of putting them together, Bella came in to place an order for one of her brides. She and Marcella worked on the order while I pieced together the bouquets, which looked lovelier by the moment.

When I finished, I placed them in the walk-in refrigerator in the back, then came back out to the front of the shop, still in a happy-go-lucky mood.

Both ladies turned to face me as I entered the room.

"So what's this fascination with Judy Garland?" Bella asked.

I shrugged. "I've always been a fan. Love the music. Love the movies. Love the flower connection."

"Flower connection?" Marcella's eyes narrowed.

"I get it," Bella said. "That whole poppies scene in *The Wizard of Oz*, right?"

"Well, that, and the fact that she had her own flower shop," I explained.

"What?" Marcella still looked perplexed.

"It's true." I started tidying up the worktable, clearing it of broken flower petals. "Judy Garland opened her own florist shop on Wilshire Boulevard when she was just fifteen years old. The money she made was put into a trust that she wasn't able to touch until she got older."

"No way. Judy Garland, the movie star, was a florist?" Bella shook her head. "What, did she sing 'Somewhere over the Rainbow' as she put together wedding bouquets?"

"Probably. I know that she balanced her work at the shop with her work at MGM studios. She waited on customers, filled orders, all sorts of things. There's a really cool picture of her online, one where she's pinning a boutonniere on Jimmy Stewart's lapel." I wrinkled my nose. "No, it wasn't Jimmy Stewart. It was that other guy, the one with a similar name." I paused a moment and then snapped my fingers. "Jimmy Durante. That's his name."

"Are you making this up, Cassia?" Marcella asked.

"No, it's totally true. At the same time she was filming *The Wizard of Oz*, she would work at the studio during the day and hit the flower shop for a couple of hours in the evening. The whole thing was her mom's idea—sort of an investment—but she couldn't touch the money till she turned eighteen. Still, it gave her an interest outside of showbiz."

"So what you're saying is Judy Garland worked in a family business." Bella chuckled. "Then I have more in common with her than I knew." This led to a discussion about how crazy her life was, working with family members. I wanted to chime in and say "Me too!" but couldn't, for obvious reasons.

A call from Aunt Rosa sent Bella scurrying back to Club Wed. After she left, Marcella gave me a few hours off as a thank-you for my hard work. "Go," she said. "Be with your family."

Of course, she still hadn't met my parents and siblings—or even asked about them—but that didn't seem to matter to her. I wouldn't call the woman self-absorbed, but she seemed too engrossed in her own family to wonder much about mine.

I walked back down the Strand, smiling as the trolley went by. Memories of being with Alex flooded over me. What I wouldn't give to have a second chance with him. He'd been noticeably absent from the island over the past few days, though. Weird.

When I reached Super-Gyros, I noticed the whole family standing out on the sidewalk, staring across the street.

"What's happening?" I whispered to Eva.

She pointed at Nick Rossi, Marcella's husband, who was hanging a new sign outside Parma John's advertising the new pizza, the Venus de Milo. I eased myself behind Eva just as Uncle Laz walked out of Parma John's and glanced our way. Yikes.

"What's this?" My mother's voice was tinged with concern.

Babbas went off on a tangent—in Greek—about how the enemy had come to our doorstep to roost, whatever that meant. If he knew the real enemy here—me—he would send me packing in a hurry. I had to find some way around this without making things worse. But what could I do, hiding behind my sister?

As soon as Nick got the sign hung, my father

pointed at it and snorted. "Look at that. No imagination at all. So what if they have a Greek pizza? They're calling it the Venus de Milo." He snorted again. "The Venus de Milo. That's price-less. Do they realize how ridiculous that sounds?"

"Venus de Milo was beautiful," Gina chimed in. "Wasn't she?"

"Beautiful, yes," Babbas responded. "Tasty, no. It's a stupid name for a pizza."

"But we don't say *stupid,* Babbas." Gina's little nose wrinkled.

"You're right, baby girl." Mama gave Babbas a warning look. He didn't seem to notice, because the next several phrases—all muttered under his breath—included the word *stupid* and a few more that Gina shouldn't hear.

We all stood in silence after that, watching as passersby responded to the sign.

"See?" Babbas chuckled. "No one's even paying any atten—" He stopped as a group of tourists in Hawaiian shirts pointed at the sign and then walked inside Parma John's. "Hmm."

"Don't worry, Niko," Mama said. She slipped her arm around my father's waist. "They wouldn't know a Greek pizza if it jumped up and bit them. And besides, we've got the best tzatziki sauce on the island. Everyone knows that."

"Everyone?" Eva looked around our near-empty sandwich shop. I nudged her with my elbow to shut her up. I must've nudged a bit too hard because she stumbled to the right, which left me completely visible to the other side of the street. I crouched down behind a nearby table and pretended to pick up some crumbs, but I was just a second too late, because Uncle Laz caught a glimpse of me and waved. Well, waved for a second, then furrowed his brow, his hand falling to his side.

Please, God, don't let Eva sing "Somewhere over the Rainbow" at my funeral. Her pitch is awful.

"See, Niko?" Mama nudged my father. "Those Rossis aren't so bad. That nice man is waving at us." She waved back, but my father pulled her hand down.

"How many times do I have to ask you not to cavort with the enemy, Helena?" He pursed his lips and gave Laz a solid stare.

"Cavort?" Gina tugged on Babbas's waistband. "What's *cavort?*"

"It means your mother is dancing with the devil right now," my father said. He turned and headed back into Super-Gyros.

Little Gina's eyes grew wide as she stared at our mother.

I did my best to inch my way inside without Uncle Laz seeing me, but I felt sure he'd taken notice of me once again. Great. Now I couldn't go into Parma John's for fear of my father seeing

154

me, and I couldn't go into Super-Gyros for fear of Uncle Laz seeing me. Just one more reason to come clean with my dad and tell him the whole sordid tale. Surely he would understand. Maybe he would laugh and realize the only solution was to make peace with our new neighbors.

Just as soon as the lunch crowd cleared I approached him. "Babbas, I want to talk to you. It's important."

"Important enough to interrupt me when I'm roasting the lamb?"

"Yes." I sucked in a deep breath and plowed ahead. "I think we need to come up with a new solution for the issue with the pizza place."

"Issue?" He turned from the lamb and waved the tongs. "It's more than an issue. It's a matter of pride. Culture. Heritage!"

Next thing I knew, Yia Yia had joined us and was telling a story about the Old Country. About how good Greeks always supported their own. Never betrayed the family. Great. Just what I needed to hear.

Now fully convinced my father would not be swayed to fall in love with the Rossis, I turned to Mama. I found her finishing up a phone call. She set her cell phone on the counter and looked at me. "Well, that's interesting news."

"What?"

"Your cousin Athena and her husband are coming to the island for a visit in a couple of weeks. She seemed perfectly happy with the idea of coming. I'm so relieved."

"That's wonderful." I hadn't seen my cousin for two years. We'd grown up spending a lot of time together, but the years had drawn us apart. I envied her life, to be honest. Her job as head writer for *Stars Collide*, one of Hollywood's hottest sitcoms, seemed like a dream gig to me.

My mother leaned in to whisper when a customer walked by. "Something's stirring with Athena. She's up to something."

"Do you think she's pregnant?" I asked.

"I don't know. I got the feeling it had something to do with the sitcom. Or the network. Or something like that. There's a reason she's coming to Galveston, and I don't think it's just to visit with us or talk to your father about filming a commercial."

"Really?" That certainly piqued my interest.

"Wouldn't that be awesome? Maybe she'll bring you-know-who with her someday!" Mama let out a girlish squeal, which scared the customer, causing her to drop a block of packaged cheese.

Babbas gave us a warning look. Better get back to work. Not that we had a lot to do, with so few customers in the place. Maybe the dinner crowd would pick up. I reached for a rag and some window cleaner and started cleaning the large plate-glass windows in the front of our store. This gave me the perfect opportunity to keep an eye on things across the street.

I noticed that Bella's brother and uncle had gone back inside, but the Venus de Milo banner hung proudly over the restaurant, along with all of the details of the Greek pizza Parma John's now offered. Talk about feeling torn—I was half proud that Laz liked my pizza idea and half mortified that I'd given away a family secret. Hopefully Yia Yia would never find out. She would definitely think I'd betrayed the family, and a good Greek girl never did that.

I eased out to the sidewalk and started cleaning the glass on the outside. With my back to Parma John's, I should be safe.

The familiar sound of the trolley passing by caught my attention and I turned. It stopped at the corner, just yards away. My breath caught in my throat as I saw Alex seated inside . . . staring right at me. His brow wrinkled, but seconds later he waved at me and called my name.

Ack! Now what?

Mama must've heard him. She came outside and watched for a moment, her face lighting in a smile. "That young man is calling for you, Cassia. Do you know him?"

"Oh, I, well . . . Yes. I met him at the flower shop."

"He seems to be waving." Mama waved back and shouted, "Hello there!"

Alex got off the trolley and came bounding our way. I could read the curiosity in his eyes as he looked at me. "Hey, Cassia. I thought it was you. You . . . work here?"

What could I say, really? The boy had caught me red-handed with a bottle of Windex in one hand and a rag in the other.

"Work here?" Mama chortled. "That's funny. She lives here. The whole family does. Welcome to Super-Gyros! I'm Helena Pappas."

This, of course, garnered a wide-eyed stare from Alex. All I could do at this point was shrug and fix my gaze on the sidewalk. Anything to avoid the obvious. Only, someone needed to make introductions. A good Greek girl didn't stand like a statue staring at the ground, even in rough circumstances like this.

Mama beamed when I told her Alex's last name, then she grabbed his hand. "You're Greek?"

"My father is. My mother is from Splendora."

I still had no idea what that meant but didn't ask for details.

"Well then, you've come to the right place." Mama gave him a pat on the back. "How would you like a nice gyro?"

"Oh, I had one on Saturday. It was great. Best ever." He rubbed his belly and a satisfied look came over him.

"I must tell Niko you said that! Oh, what

glorious news. Cassia has a new *friend!*" Mama took off in Babbas's direction.

Alex and I lingered behind for a moment. He gave me a pointed look, and I could read the confusion in those gorgeous eyes. "This is your family's restaurant? But you never said anything about it when we went to——"

"Come inside." I took his arm and pulled him toward the open door, then whispered, "Please. Don't. Say. Anything. About. Parma. John's."

He nodded and stepped inside the store, then stopped cold. His eyes drifted shut and he stood there, breathing in and out. "Oh. Wow." Alex continued this deep-breathing routine, a delirious look on his face.

Babbas walked toward us, his unibrow securely in place as he stared at Alex. "Everything all right over here?"

Alex's eyes popped open. "Oh yes, sir," he drawled. "I'm just loving the way it smells in here. I'd forgotten how great it was."

"Niko, this is Alex . . . Cassia's *friend.*" Mama giggled and then added, "He's Greek."

"Nice to meet you, sir." Alex extended his hand, but my father just grunted.

"Cassia's friend, eh?" Babbas crossed his arms at his chest and squared his shoulders, then muttered, "We'll see about that" under his breath. "Name's Alex, you say?" My father stressed the

159

name, but not in an admiring way. "I have a brother named Alex."

"Oh, that's great," Alex said. "I've always liked my name. I'm actually named after my grandfather. He—"

"My brother is a showboat," Babbas said. "Always trying to outdo me. He's a puffed-up so-and-so. And you"—he jabbed his finger into Alex's chest—"have his name."

"Babbas!" That was hardly fair, judging a person because of his name. Even my hot-tempered father didn't usually stoop that low.

The happy-go-lucky expression on Alex's face faded immediately, and he fell silent. I didn't blame him. Finally he said, "I can't help my name, sir."

"Besides, Alex ate here on Saturday and loved our gyro." Mama was trying hard to smooth things over, judging from her forced smile. "Isn't that wonderful?"

"Ah." Babbas's face widened in a grin, and he gave Alex a boisterous pat on the back. "Well, why didn't you say so? I always love to hear from a happy customer. Maybe you would give us an endorsement? I'm putting together an advertisement for the local paper."

"I'd be glad to." Alex nodded.

Babbas wrapped him in a fatherly embrace. "In that case, come on in, son."

Something about the way he said *son* brought

joy to my heart. It seemed to put Alex at ease too. Before long the two fellas were fast friends. Babbas showed him around the shop, going through every detail of the business. My siblings trailed along behind them, especially Eva, who seemed a little too interested in every word coming out of Alex's mouth.

I half expected the handsome Greek cowboy to fold under the pressure, but he held up well and never mentioned our trip to Parma John's once, even when my father made an ugly comment about Lazarro Rossi. Instead, Alex gave me a "now I get it" look. There would be plenty of time to fill him in on the particulars later.

By the time they got to my father's detailed description of our new meat slicer, I could tell Alex was getting hungry. Babbas shaved off slices of lamb and passed them his way. We almost lost the boy after that, judging from the "I'm over the moon for this stuff" look in his eyes. Babbas rambled on about the restaurant, feeding Alex all the while. Not a bad way for the guys to get to know each other. Food always had a way of pacifying the masses.

"We've got the best tzatziki sauce on the island." Babbas reached into the refrigerator and grabbed the batch I'd just made.

Alex swallowed his piece of lamb and nodded. "Can't wait to try it with the lamb. I'm sure it's great."

"Oh, it is. Cassia makes it fresh," Mama bragged. "Try it." She opened the container and stuck in a spoon.

"You like it," Yia Yia chimed in.

Babbas gave him another piece of lamb and he slathered it with the stuff. The whole family gathered around to watch him take his first bite.

He ate and ate, those gorgeous eyes fluttering closed in what appeared to be complete delirium. "Oh, man. It's great, Cassia." He opened his eyes and looked right at me. "Must stink, though."

"What do you mean?" Yia Yia looked perplexed.

Alex licked the spoon and shrugged. "Must stink that she has to make the tzatziki sauce when she's allergic."

"Allergic?" Mama gasped. "Say it isn't so!"

"Heaven be with us!" Yia Yia dabbed her eyes with her apron and went into a lengthy prayer in Greek.

"Cassia?" Babbas gave me a strange look. "Is there something we should know?"

"I, um, get hives." This wasn't completely untrue, anyway. I did get hives the last time I ate tzatziki sauce. Of course, I'd lathered it on top of zucchini. Might've been the zucchini.

You would've thought someone in the family had died. Yia Yia gave me a hug and whispered, "We will find a doctor. He will know what to do."

Babbas shook his head as if in mourning, then

looked at Alex. "Still, it's a good sauce, no? Worth risking your life for?"

"The best, sir. And if I die, I want it to be with Cassia's tzatziki on my lips."

Okay, I read a little more into that, and the wink that followed from Alex made my heart do a crazy flip-flop thing.

My father slapped him on the back once more, this time a little harder—*Welcome to the family! You're getting smacked around now!*—and then offered to show him our new state-of-the-art oven. Alex trailed along behind him, and I breathed a sigh of relief that no one brought up my allergy again. Babbas was too busy gabbing, and it was clear he hadn't clued in to the fact that Alex and I were more than passing acquaintances.

Until Alex gave it away.

"I haven't known your daughter long, sir," he said. "But I've already discovered we have a lot in common, not just our love of Greek food."

My father took several steps in our direction, giving Alex a stern look. Yikes.

"You two are *friends?*" The way my father emphasized the word told me he suspected more. "I see."

"Sure, we're friends." Alex nodded. "But I was saying we have a lot in common. We met at the flower shop."

"You were buying flowers?" No doubt Babbas found this idea ludicrous.

"Oh no, sir. I'm in the flower business."

"Oh." Babbas chuckled and slapped his thigh. "I *see*." He slapped Alex on the arm. "For a minute there, I thought you were going to tell me you had a thing for my daughter. I worried for nothing. So you're into *flowers,* are you?"

Alex's brows arched. "Sir, just because I'm in the flower business doesn't mean I'm . . . I'm . . ."

"Babbas!" I interrupted the conversation. "Alex's family has a nursery in a small town north of Houston."

"Nursery?" Now my father really looked confused. "You do babysitting on the side?"

"No, sir. The only things I babysit are roses. Well, and a host of other flowers. But no kids. Definitely no kids."

My father's gaze narrowed. "You lost me back at the nursery part."

"Alex's family has a profitable flower distribution company in a town called . . ." Hmm. I couldn't remember the name.

"Splendora, sir," Alex said.

"They provide a variety of species to florists all over the state," I added. "Including the shop where I work."

"Actually, we're number one in the state, sir," Alex said. "My grandfather passed the business to my father, and he has poured his life into it."

"Sounds like your father and I have a lot in common." Babbas began to talk about his passion for our family business, carrying on for quite some time.

When he paused, Alex said, "I think that's admirable, Mr. Pappas. Oh, and to answer your original question . . . I might just be a little bit interested in your daughter."

For a moment everything went silent. Babbas looked as if he'd been turned to stone. I kind of felt like it myself. Well, all but my heart, which did a weird thump-thump thing. I looked around for something to hide behind but decided the meat slicer wasn't big enough.

Had this handsome Greek cowboy just publicly declared an interest in me?

Judging from the shimmer in his eyes, yes.

And judging from the rock-hard look in my father's eyes . . . Alex would definitely have his work cut out for him.

13

You Go to My Head

You might be Greek if you were spanked by your friend's parents because your parents gave them permission to.

Whenever someone in the Pappas family took up a new habit—say, bowling or golf—it usually ended up involving everyone. Take the time my oldest brother decided he couldn't live without a skateboard. Yia Yia nearly ended up in the hospital with a heart attack the first time he took a tumble. And that time Eva decided she wanted to be a figure skater? Yeah, Babbas still joked about how she fell flat on her face in her first lesson. My family members didn't usually grace you through the learning curve. No, they made sport of you at every possible turn.

That was why, when I took a couple hundred dollars out of my savings account to buy a brand-new bike on the Thursday after Alex's visit to our shop, it didn't surprise me that my family members all took a vested interest. I would prove to them that I was still capable after all these years. Hopefully.

Mama in particular seemed intrigued by the

idea of riding. With all the bickering going on between her and Babbas lately, I had the strangest feeling that she might just climb on my bike and take off . . . permanently. I'd have to remember to buy a lock and chain.

On the morning of my first ride, my family clustered around my new bicycle—a Mongoose cruiser in a really sweet shade of forest green.

"What's this, Cassia?" Babbas asked.

One thing I never understood about parents—they always seemed to state the obvious. Like, when I didn't finish my food, Mama would say, "What? You didn't finish your food, Cassia?" And when I showed up late, Babbas would say, "You're late, Cassia." Clearly they could see a bicycle standing in front of them. Why ask, "What's this, Cassia?"

Oh well. I'd better answer before Babbas decided to forbid me from bicycle riding on the grounds that it would be bad for the business.

"It's my new bike," I said. "I bought it from a store on the seawall. Got a really good deal on it."

"A bike." He stared at it as if he'd never seen one before.

"Can I ride it?" Filip reached for the handlebars, but I grabbed them first.

"Maybe. Someday. But I want to break it in."

"Get on it, Cassia," Mama said. "I want to take your picture to send to the relatives in California!" She ran inside the shop, came out with her camera, and started snapping photos. Great. I'd probably land front and center on her Facebook page. I always loved it when that happened.

"Ooh, I have a brilliant idea!" Babbas went into the shop and came out with a sign advertising Super-Gyros. "Now let's see . . . where can I hang this from your bike?" A pause followed as he surveyed the bike. "Guess you'll have to wear it, Cassia, like a sandwich." He slapped his knee and laughed. "Get it? Sandwich?"

Seriously? Apparently there were worse things than landing on your mom's Facebook page—like landing on the front page of the *Galveston Daily News* with a promo for your dad's business strapped to your back.

"Oh no!" I put my hand up in the air. "I didn't buy this bike to promote the business."

"Why did you buy it then?" Crinkles formed around Babbas's eyes. "I've never known you to ride before."

"I'm going to be making deliveries for the flower shop," I explained. "It's part of my job."

"Flowers." Babbas spat on the ground. "I should have known it." This led to a lengthy sermon about how a good Greek daughter would support her father, not a perfect stranger in a flower shop, but he lost me about the time he starting criticizing roses. The man could say whatever he liked, but he'd better not go messing with my roses, now that I had an entire species named after me.

Babbas headed back into the shop to wait on our first customer of the day, an elderly lady who happened to be visiting us for the first time. He gave a "come with me" grunt to Mama—*Wow, what amazing communication skills, Babbas!*—and she followed along behind him.

"Are you going to ride it or not?" Darian asked.

"I-I guess so." I hadn't exactly counted on trying it out for the first time in front of an audience. What if I fell?

I reached down and unsnapped the helmet, which I'd hung from the handlebars. "Guess I'd better get suited up."

"You look like a pro," Eva said. "Very cool."

"Thanks. Marcella made me promise I would always wear a helmet when I rode. Don't want to risk getting hurt." I swung my leg over the bar and almost tumbled over in the process.

"Do they have helmets that cover the whole body?" Filip teased.

Thanks for the show of support, folks.

"I'll be fine," I said. "Don't worry about me."

"I'm not worried, Cassia," Gina said. "Not at all! You're so good at pedals." She pointed at the bike pedals and giggled. "You're always talking about them."

"Huh? I am?" It took me a minute, but I finally got it. *Petals*—I was always talking about them. Ha.

"Now you have two of your own," Gina added.

I giggled and gave her a little kiss on the brow. "Looks like I do, at that." I eased my bottom onto the seat and placed my right foot on the pedal, preparing to kick off with the other foot.

"You gonna ride with the stand down?" Darian pointed at the kickstand.

Right, right. I attempted to nudge it upward without getting off the bike and almost toppled once again. This got a good laugh from Darian, but the "drop it!" look I gave him shut him up pretty quickly.

"Laugh now," I said. "But just wait and see if I ever let you ride." This seemed to do the trick.

With my siblings looking on, I managed to take off. Figuring out the various gears was a little tricky. So were the handlebar brakes. When I reached the first corner I grabbed them with such force that the bike skidded to a rough stop. This caused a flip-flop–wearing tourist to walk right into me. I made my apologies and kept going. At a snail's pace.

After just a few blocks my thighs felt like they were on fire. Still, what kind of wimp stopped after such a short ride? To return home now would be to admit my defeat in front of the whole family. Instead, I pointed my bike toward the south end of the Strand, determined to get as close to the seawall as possible.

Okay, so I didn't make it that far. But riding as far as the end of the Strand was admirable for my first attempt. I paused at the flower shop and noticed Alex's delivery van, wondering if I should go inside. The idea of seeing him held some appeal, but the idea of working did not. Marcella would probably expect me to dive right in, in spite of already giving me the day off. No, I'd keep riding.

With the breeze in my face, I headed farther south, where I rode for blocks and blocks. Eventually I turned back toward Mechanic Street. Maybe I could ride as far as the Tremont Hotel before going home again. Might be nice to imagine myself a society girl circa 1900, making her way along the boulevard.

Or not.

I felt the wind go out of my proverbial sails at the corner of Mechanic and 19th. How long had I been gone, anyway? Should've brought my phone to keep track of the time. Maybe install one of those bike-riding apps so I wouldn't get lost. Either way, I should probably head back to the shop now. Babbas would be looking for me, no doubt.

Before I had a chance to think it through further, Alex pulled up next to me in his delivery truck and called out my name, followed by, "Hey, little lady."

I laughed and nearly tumbled off the bike. "Did Marcella put you up to this?"

"Up to what?" he asked.

"Tailing me. Does she need me to work?"

He shrugged. "Nope. Just happened to be passing by on my way home from the shop."

"Ooh, what were you delivering?"

"Only the best orchids I've seen in years. But don't go back to look at them. They'll still be there tomorrow. Maybe." He gave me a little wink and my heart skipped a beat.

"Can't wait."

For a moment neither of us said anything. Then another driver happened by and honked at Alex, who was taking up too much of the intersection.

I didn't really mind the break, what with the exhaustion from my ride.

Alex must've noticed. He pulled the van off to the side and got out. Extending his hands toward me, he said, "Here. I'll put your bike in the back and drive you home."

He took care of the bike and then offered me a hand to get into the passenger seat. The luscious aroma of flowers seemed overpowering in here, in a good way. Their heady scent almost made me forget myself. Until I caught a glimpse of Alex's muscular arms as he pulled himself into the driver's seat. Then suddenly I remembered who I was. Who he was. Who we could be . . . together.

I felt like a giddy schoolgirl riding in the front seat with him. In fact, I could hardly string two sensible words together. Not that he seemed to notice.

I settled back in my seat and gave the interior of the van a quick glance. "I've never been inside of one of these before," I said. "Very . . ."

"Boxlike?" The edges of Alex's lips tipped up in a gorgeous smile. "I know. It's not much, but it gets me where I'm going and the flowers arrive in good shape. And just enough room to fit your bike inside."

"Lucky break." Of course, anytime I could snag a few minutes of alone time with this handsome flower guy, I considered myself lucky.

"Yep." Alex pulled out onto the road and eased his way along. "Hey, speaking of which, I'm glad to see you got a bike. I like to ride myself. Sometimes I drive down to the island and rent a bike to ride along the seawall."

"No way." I couldn't help the little chuckle that slipped out. "Wow."

The edges of his lips curled up in an embarrassed smile. "Yeah. Does that surprise you? Make me sound like a kid or something?"

"No, I just . . ." Should I tell him how much I'd loved the feel of the wind against my face, the smell of the salt water in the breeze as I made my way toward the coast? "Today was my first time in years, but I loved it."

"Really?" This seemed to pique his interest. "Maybe we should go together sometime."

"Sure. I'd love that." Oh boy, would I ever. My imagination went off on a little tangent as I thought about the possibilities of strolling the seashore hand in hand with this awesome guy. Strange how he'd snagged such a large piece of my heart in such a short period of time. I reflected back to that first moment when I'd seen him on the trolley. The words *Fate! Kismet!* had crossed my mind. Now, seated beside him, I had to admit our blossoming relationship did feel like fate. Divinely ordained.

He dove into a story about a ride he'd taken on some trails in the Sam Houston National Forest, but my mind shifted. "You should buy a bike and leave it at our place. That way you wouldn't have to rent one."

"I own a great one," he said. "But it's a long drive down from Splendora. Maybe I should buy another and keep it here . . . if you don't think your parents would mind, I mean."

"My parents?" With a wave of my hand I dismissed the idea. "Nah. You know how easy-going they are." Ha.

When we arrived at the shop I asked him to pull around to the back so I could unload the bike. After getting it situated I gave it one last look. I couldn't help the smile that rose up. Riding with soft wisps of hair in my face had been freeing. Totally freeing.

"You hungry?" I asked.

His "I thought you'd never ask" look left little to the imagination. I took him into Super-Gyros the back way, chatting all the time. Imagine my shock when I saw Yia Yia inside weeping.

She took one look at me and began to offer up a heartfelt prayer in Greek. "Oh, Cassia, thank God!" Yia Yia threw her arms around me and began to wail. I couldn't figure out why, though. Had someone died?

"Yia Yia, what's happened?" I asked. "What is it?"

She began to ramble in unintelligible Greek sentences, completely losing me. Alex seemed to be trying to work on the translation and eventually leaned toward me to whisper, "They thought you were dead."

"W-what?" I looked at my grandmother. "Why would you think that?"

"You leave on that—that—bicycle! And you never come home again."

"What else could we think, Cassia?" Mama clutched her cell phone in her hand. "I've been on the telephone with the police."

"The police?" My heart skipped a beat. "Are you serious?"

"You should tell us your plans," Mama scolded. "So we won't worry."

"You knew I was going out to ride my bike," I countered.

"Yes, but that was an hour and a half ago," Mama said. "We expected you to be gone ten minutes. Maybe twenty. But an hour and a half?"

You thought I would only last ten minutes? Thanks for the show of support, people!

"Do you know how many people die in an hour and a half?" She shared a gruesome story she'd recently seen on the evening news, and I bit back a sharp retort. Seriously? I couldn't go out for a bike ride without getting the whole family worked up?

At this point Mama seemed to notice I wasn't alone. She welcomed Alex by handing him a sandwich. He opened it and took a bite. Go figure.

My little sister wrapped herself around my leg. "Don't go away again, Cassia! Promise?"

"Well, I—"

"We were afraid those Italians had kidnapped you." Gina's eyes, filled with anxiety, met mine. "I thought maybe they locked you up in the kitchen at Parma John's and forced you to make the new Venus de Milo for them."

Where did the child come up with such nonsense? Then again, a Greek pizza did sound really good right about now.

Babbas joined the group, his face red. "So that Rossi family wasn't behind your disappearance?" He crossed his arms. "If they had anything to do with this, I'm going to—to—" He ranted in Greek, and I interpreted enough to pray the little ones couldn't understand the translation.

"I'm telling you, Babbas, I just went for a bike ride. By myself."

176

"Yes." He glared at Alex. "I can see you were by yourself."

"Oh, I just happened along, sir. I found her looking pretty winded on the corner of Mechanic and 19th and offered to drive her home."

"A good Samaritan!" Yia Yia took Alex's face in her hands—quite a task, with him being so much taller—and gave him a kiss on either cheek.

"I rode to the end of the Strand and then a few blocks farther south toward the seawall area," I explained. "Then I turned back. By the time I got to Mechanic and 19th I was a little . . . tired."

"The seawall?" My mother reached for a menu and began to fan herself. "You rode in all that traffic?"

"I didn't make it that far." I pinched my eyes shut and pictured myself riding along, the salty island breeze nipping at my heels, the crash of waves off in the distance.

Turned out the only thing crashing was the plastic bowl Eva had been holding. It had slipped out of her hands and hit the floor.

My father waggled his finger in my face. "I still say you need to beware those people across the street. They're out to get us."

I couldn't help but notice Alex's eyes widening as he listened in. Still, he didn't join the conversation, thank goodness.

"Babbas, they're not," I said. "I'm sure they're perfectly good people who—"

"Who are intent on forcing us out of town. Getting rid of us because we're the competition."

"Why do you say that?" I asked. "What have they ever done to make you think that?"

"They have not extended the hand of friendship to us."

"That's probably because we've only been open awhile. Besides, they're busier than ever now that Scarlet's bakery is part of the restaurant. You know what it's like when you add something new."

"They're pretty crowded over there," Alex said. "So I'm sure they don't get to take a break very often."

"Sure, sure, rub it in that they're doing good business." His eyes narrowed to slits as he turned to me in slow motion. "Wait. Who is Scarlet? You've been in this bakery?"

Oh. Help.

If I told him about my lunch at Parma John's, it would be the end of me.

"The only thing you need to know is that I wasn't kidnapped. And there's no reason to call the police, trust me."

Too late. Officer O'Reilly and a couple of his finest men rushed into the sandwich shop just as I finished my sentence, ready to send out a search party for the kidnapped Greek girl. Just what I needed, more press.

Less than thirty seconds after clearing up the

misunderstanding, Babbas offered the officers free coffee and gyros. Several minutes later, the poor fellas were a captive audience for my father, who filled their ears with tales from the Old Country.

Again with the Old Country stories, Babbas? You've never even been to Santorini. Or Athens. Or anywhere else in the Mediterranean.

Didn't seem to matter. My father described each gorgeous locale with the gusto and admiration of a true Greek patriot. And my, what a stance! Shoulders back. Chest puffed out. Chin jutting forward. Zeus on steroids. And apparently his superpowers included charming cranky police officers, from the looks of things.

"Are you going to give my daughter a ticket, Officer?" Babbas gave O'Reilly an imploring look.

"I, um, well, I don't know what I would cite her for." The officer took another bite of his gyro, a contented look on his face. "What did you call this sauce again?"

"Tzatziki." I shrugged. "And I don't really see how you could give me a ticket for anything. I did nothing wrong."

"She rode the wrong way down a one-way street," Yia Yia called out.

"On the sidewalk!" I said.

"And she nearly ran over a tourist at the first corner," Gina added. "But he lived."

This led to a strict discussion from Officer O'Reilly on sidewalk etiquette. Really?

By this point Alex was laughing out loud. I didn't blame him.

"I guess I'll just give you a warning this time." O'Reilly took a swig of his coffee. "But next time you might not be so lucky."

"I guess I'll take my chances," I said. "And if you're ever in the neighborhood again, I'll be sure to get kidnapped to make things more interesting."

"That would be just fine." He took a bite of his sandwich. "Anything to give me an excuse to come back here for lunch."

The officers walked out of the shop with baklava in one hand and to-go cups in the other. Across the street, Bella's uncle Laz looked on, likely wondering what all of the squad cars were doing here. I stayed inside so as not to raise further suspicions. Maybe he would think we'd been robbed or something exciting like that.

Completely humiliated, I sank into a chair at a nearby table. Alex joined me and finished up the last of his sandwich. "I hate to leave just when things are getting good," he said. "And trust me when I say we don't get this kind of excitement in Splendora. But I wanted to ask you something before I left."

Being a good Greek mama, my mother hovered around us like a spaceship coming in for a landing. No doubt she wondered what he might ask. I kind of wondered myself.

"I've talked a lot about our family's place up in Splendora," he said. "And you've seen the roses. Some of them, anyway. But how would you like to see the whole place?"

"Go to Splendora?" I asked. Wow. I couldn't help but wonder what I might find there, what with the big buildup and all. Not that it mattered. My Southern Adonis wanted me to take a trip to this place he called Splendora. So I'd take a trip to Splendora.

"Mom and Dad are getting tired of hearing about this girl I've named the rose after. And they're not the only ones."

"O-oh?"

"Yep. Don't mean to alarm you, but there's a passel of folks up that way wantin' to see if you're a figment of my overactive imagination or if you're real."

"Oh, I'm real all right."

He brushed the crumbs from those gorgeous lips and then leaned my way, the smell of lamb still fresh on his breath. He whispered, "Well, that's good. 'Cause I'm all done with pretending. What about you?"

I had a feeling he meant a little more by that, but I didn't say anything in response. Then again, with my tongue stuck to the roof of my mouth, I couldn't really speak, now could I?

14

Journey to a Star

You might be Greek if you thought everyone got pinched on the cheeks and money
stuffed in their pockets by their relatives.

The rest of the week seemed to drag by. I could
hardly wait for Saturday, when Alex and I would
head north to this until-recently-fictional place
called Splendora. He made his early morning
delivery to the shop around 8:00 and then picked
me up at Super-Gyros.

"What is this?" he asked, pointing up to the new
banner Babbas had hung the evening before.
"You're selling meatball subs now? Buy one, get
one free?"

I did my best not to groan out loud. "Yes. Don't
ask." Why my father had decided to counter Laz's
Greek pizza with an Italian sandwich, I could not
say. We'd never sold anything but Greek food at
Super-Gyros. Didn't make a bit of sense to branch
out to other cultures, even to draw in business.

Oh well. At least I didn't have to spend the day
fretting over anything related to the sandwich
shop. I had to make a trip to a very intriguing
place called Splendora.

My nosy family members gathered in front of

182

Super-Gyros to see me off. My father, of course, griped that he couldn't manage the Saturday lunch crowd without me, but Yia Yia and Mama offered to take up the slack. I had a feeling the ladies were just tickled to see me heading off on a date with the handsome flower guy.

The Rigas Roses delivery van wasn't exactly a luxury limousine, as I'd already learned, but it provided an interesting way to travel, and it was spacious, especially without my bike taking up so much room in the back.

"Didn't really give the van a close look last time," I said. "You've got a lot of room in here."

"If you think this is big, wait'll you see the double-wide my parents live in."

"Double-wide?"

"Trailer." He gave me a warning look. Well, a playful warning look. "Only, don't call it that, okay? Mama calls it a manufactured home."

"Manufactured home." I repeated the words to make sure I got them right.

"But just for the record, they started building a big two-story house a few months ago. It's not done yet. Too much going on with roses being in season right now."

I wasn't sure what roses had to do with a house being built but didn't ask. In fact, I found myself pretty tongue-tied for the next several minutes as my nerves kicked in.

Thank goodness Alex was proficient at small

talk. He chatted with ease until we got to the Galveston Causeway. The expansive bridge crossed over from the island to the mainland, but I'd only been across it a couple of times over the past few weeks, usually to pick up supplies for the restaurant.

"Hold your breath," he said as we approached the expansive bridge.

"W-what?"

He gestured to his mouth, pinched tight, and puffed his cheeks out. I drew in a deep breath and held it until I thought I might explode.

"Beat you!" he said when we got to the mainland side of the bridge. "That's a little game my sisters and I have played ever since we were kids, by the way. I always win."

"Gotcha. Guess I'm not as full of hot air as you." Where the comment came from, I had no idea, but he laughed.

"You got me there." We rode on a bit longer in silence. After a couple of minutes I noticed Alex watching me out of the corner of his eye.

"What is it?" I asked.

He shrugged. "Just thinking how nice it is to have someone to share this ride with. I come up and down this stretch of road all the time by myself. Glad you came with me today."

"Me too." He had no idea how glad.

"I-I really enjoy your company, Cassia. Maybe a little more than I've said."

"I like being with you too."

A delicious silence filled the van.

"I can't remember the last time I felt this at home with someone," he said after a few moments. "I really mean that. We were destined to meet. Destined to be right here, right now, headed to—"

"Splendida?" I offered.

"Splendora." He chuckled.

"Right, right." I shrugged, overcome with embarrassment. "Splen*dora*."

"I hope you like it," he said, then gestured to the acreage to our right and left. "It's not like this. There's not much to look at here. But as we get farther north I think you'll enjoy it."

I enjoyed the view already, but it had nothing to do with trees and such. That gorgeous face. Those eyes. That solid physique. Just thinking about what a lovely job God had done putting Alex together made my cheeks grow warm. *You're wrong, Alex Rigas! There's plenty to look at here.*

"It's not exactly California," he said, then laughed. "But we've got some nice scenery up north."

"Up north?"

"Well, Splendora is north of Humble, so we still have a ways to go."

This led to a discussion about the Humble Oil Company, which had been bought out by Exxon. This somehow led to a conversation about the price of oil, which in turn led to a lengthy speech about drilling in the Gulf of Mexico. To be honest, I didn't know a thing about drilling—unless you happened to be talking about drilling a hole in a phyllo roll-up to put in the custard—so I had nothing to offer. Still, I enjoyed listening to the cadence in his voice, the lilt as he talked about the things that mattered to him. And the way his eyes sparkled as he talked about his family . . . wow! I could stare at those gorgeous eyes all day.

"So, tell me who I'm going to meet when we get to Splendora," I said when he stopped for breath. "I don't know anything about your family, except that they're in the flower business."

"I grew up in a family of women," he said. "My dad and I were totally outnumbered."

"Oh?"

"Yeah. I have three older sisters. One is married, but the twins are both single and still live at home with my parents."

Sounded familiar.

"They should both be there today."

"Twins? What are their names?"

"Lily and Jasmine."

"Oh, wow. Should've guessed. Flower names. I like that."

"You think *those* are interesting, you should meet my married sister."

"Let me guess." I paused to think about it.

"Rose?" When he shook his head, I tried again. "Daisy? Iris?"

Alex laughed. "No. Her name is Blossom. Like the old TV character."

"That poor girl." I shook my head and tried to imagine her pain.

"I think she's gotten used to it now, but she took a lot of ribbing in school. You wouldn't believe what she went through."

"No doubt. Does she live in Splendora too?"

"Yep. Her husband Darrell washes trucks at Uncle Donny's truck stop."

I still didn't have a clue who Uncle Donny was but didn't ask.

As Alex switched gears to talk about his brother-in-law's time in the military, my thoughts shifted back to his earlier comments about living in a double-wide trailer. Er, manufactured home. Alex had grown up in a humble setting. Maybe he wouldn't be so put off by my family's apartment above the shop. Not everyone lived in a huge two-story house like the Rossis'.

"This is all so new to me." I gestured to the pine trees to my right. "I've never been in Texas before."

"Ever?"

"Nope. Lived in Santa Cruz my whole life. I enjoy looking at the difference in terrain." I pointed out to the highway with its surrounding greenery. "Everything here is so . . . flat. And green. Very, very green."

"I never get tired of the green, but the flat part is an issue. I'd love to visit the mountains. Still, we've got great flowers here, at least in my neck of the woods. Wait till you see our nursery. And Mama's gardens out front. I think even you will be impressed."

"*Even* me?"

"Oh, I'm just saying you know your flowers. You're a pro. So you're probably more discriminating than most."

Wow. No one had ever called me a pro before. Leave it to Alex to set my heart to fluttering. My face heated up as I thought about just how special he made me feel. And from his description, the family was pretty wonderful too. Suddenly I couldn't wait to get to Splendora.

About thirty minutes into our trip we turned off Interstate 45 onto a road marked Highway 59 and headed through the heart of downtown Houston. I had to admit, the Bayou City was pretty impressive. I looked to my left and took in the expansive skyscrapers. Then I shifted my attention back to the five-lane freeway, which serpentined ahead. Thank goodness Alex knew where he was going. I'd end up driving around in circles if you put me behind the wheel.

About twenty minutes later the area around us grew more wooded. Majestic pine trees now surrounded us on both sides of the road, their deep green bristles breathtaking.

"Is this Splendora?" I asked.

"Nope. We're almost to Humble. Then King-wood. Then Porter. Then New Caney. Then Splendora."

"I see." Only, I didn't. Not really. But I did see tall pine trees stretching to the expansive blue sky. I also saw reams and reams of bluebonnets and Indian paintbrushes. I must've said "wow" a thousand times.

When we arrived in Splendora, Alex pulled off at a truck stop with an odd name. "Hope you don't mind a pit stop," he said. "I need to get some gas, and it wouldn't hurt to stop in for a visit with Uncle Donny."

"Your uncle works here?" I asked.

Alex shrugged as he turned off the engine. "Well, he's not technically my uncle. He's D.J.'s uncle. But everyone in town calls him Uncle Donny. He runs the place." Alex gestured at the Donny's Digs 'n' Dogs sign above the truck stop.

Digs? Dogs? Huh?

"Hope you're hungry. He's got the best hot dogs in the state. I suggest the number three: extra cheese and heavy on the onions."

Um, no thanks. I'd never been a fan of hot dogs, especially loaded with onions.

But when we walked inside, the luscious aroma of the hot dogs cast some sort of spell on me. Before long I was nibbling on the number three and talking to an elderly fellow with a twang so

189

delightfully thick that it captivated me and carried me away to a different place.

The man smelled of gasoline, but I was so intrigued by his conversation that the scent took a backseat.

"Has she met the family yet, Alex?" Donny asked.

"Nope. We just got here. I called Mama last night to give her a heads-up that company's coming. She said she's gonna roll out the red carpet."

"Well then . . ." Donny smacked his lips. "What time should we be over for supper? If she's rollin' out the red carpet, that means she's deep-frying catfish and hush puppies, and I wouldn't want to miss that."

"No doubt. And I'm sure Mama would love to have you and Aunt Willy over for supper."

"Aunt Willy?" I couldn't help but repeat his words. Was this some sort of code? And how in the world could I possibly eat another bite after such a huge hot dog?

"Well, folks call her Willy," Alex said. "But she's really Wilhelmina. She's Scarlet's aunt."

"And my lovely bride," Donny said, his face lighting in the most delightful smile. "And what a bride she is."

"I see."

Turned out the petite woman served up baked goods at the truck stop and appeared to do quite the business. Donny raved about his wife's baked goods, proclaiming them to be the best in the state.

"Is your aunt Twila going to be there?" Willy asked. "I owe her a cheesecake. She won it at the church in a raffle. I could bring it tonight."

"Oh, I'm sure she'll be there," Alex said. "You know how it is when our family gets together. And Dad's frying up a mess 'a catfish outside in the fryer. Plenty for all, even with Aunt Twila there."

This got a laugh out of everyone, but I didn't know why.

Alex shared a funny story about his aunt's over-the-top eating habits and then turned to me. "I can't wait for you to meet Aunt Twila. She's quite a character."

"Aunt Twila?" I snapped my fingers. "Oh, I remember the story about her. She's a chrysan-themum."

"Yep, and she's also a singer. Started out at our local church, and now she sings all over the place with her two best friends—Jolene and Bonnie Sue."

"They all sound like characters from a sitcom."

Donny and Willy laughed.

"Wait'll you meet 'em," Donny said. "They pretty much are characters."

"But they're very real," Willy added. "Though sometimes I have to wonder."

Alex nodded. "Yeah, they're real, all right. You're about to get all the proof you need. All of these fine folks live right here in Splendora, just a hop, skip, 'n' a jump from the old homestead. Not that a trailer is a homestead exactly, but you get the idea."

"Don't you mean *manufactured home?*" I teased.

"Yep, 'n' thank you fer the reminder, little missy," he said. "Mama would have my hide if she heard me callin' it a trailer." Strange how his twang deepened the closer we got to his old homestead.

The mention of catfish now made me a little queasy. My stomach already ached from eating the massive hot dog, which made climbing back in the van quite the task. I found myself growing more nervous as Alex turned off the highway onto the back roads.

"Are we getting close to where you grew up?" I asked as the road ahead narrowed and a canopy of trees enveloped us overhead.

"Yep. Not far from D.J. Neeley's place. You met him, right? Bella's husband? He was ahead of me in school several years."

Before I could answer, Alex pointed to a beautiful patch of land to our right. "We're here."

"Wow." I'd never seen a property like this one. The trailer—er, manufactured home—was nestled up against the new house, which was still well from completion but on its way. Alex wasn't kidding when he said the family was building a two-story house. It was a sprawling wood-framed beauty with large porches both upstairs and down.

And the garden! It took my breath away. Colorful azaleas—really, a rainbow's worth—filled the largest bed to my right. A pathway ran through the bed on the left, and the lush foliage surrounding the gazebo literally made me gasp.

"A traditional English garden!" I felt the sting of tears in my eyes at the sheer beauty of it all.

"Yes, complete with a bridge over a little creek and some pretty magnificent trees that my grandfather planted when he was my age."

"Oh, Alex." I held my breath, unable to take it all in at once. "I've never seen anything like it."

"Glad it meets with your approval." He turned the van off and then reached for my hand and gave it a squeeze. "If you think this is great, wait till you see the nursery. After supper I'll take you for a walk. If we can ever get some time to ourselves."

"I would love that."

Before our feet had landed on the ground, a tall woman slightly on the rotund side rushed our way. She flung her arms around Alex's neck and gave him a kiss on the cheek. "How's my boy?"

Alex's face flushed an appealing shade of pink, which served to put me at ease. "I'm good, Mama. Good."

"And this"—she took my hands and gave me a

solid once-over—"must be our little rose." She threw her arms around me, my face landing squarely in her ample bosom. If I didn't suffocate, I'd greet the woman.

"Nice to meet you, Mrs. Rigas," I said when I came up for air.

"Not half as nice as it is to meet you, honey." She gave my hands a squeeze and then winked. "You don't mind if I call you *honey,* do you? We're not big on formality round here, and we sure love our pet names." She released her hold on my hands and gave Alex a nudge with her elbow. "Right, little buddy?"

He grimaced. "Mama, I'm not 'little buddy' anymore."

"Well, shoot. You'll always be my little buddy-boy."

This led to a conversation from her about the "bud" angle—apparently it had something to do with his green thumb with the roses when he was a little boy.

I followed behind Mrs. Rigas into the manufactured home, which was a lot bigger on the inside than it looked. Not at all what I'd pictured. Neither was the fellow in the recliner, who stood when we entered the room and greeted me with a smile.

"So this is our Cassia!" The man swept me into his arms. "I'd know you anywhere. You're our little rose."

I looked up, up, up into the eyes of this kind stranger, convinced everyone in Splendora was tall. Must be something in the water. "So I've been told, sir."

Mr. Rigas was an older version of Alex, only with a plusher midsection and graying hair around his temples. Though he reminded me of Babbas in appearance, this fellow's warm greeting convinced me that their personalities must be opposite.

"Hope you're ready fer a crowd," Mr. Rigas said with a grin. "I'm about to fire up the fryer for the best catfish you ever ate, which means folks'll show up soon as the wind blows the scent their way." He slipped his arm around his wife's ample waist. "Not that I'm the only one working, mind you. My sweetie here knows how to throw a great shindig."

It warmed my heart to hear him refer to his wife as his sweetie. For a moment I wondered how Mama would respond if Babbas ever gave her a love name like that.

I didn't have time to give it much thought because two of the prettiest young women I'd ever seen entered the room, arguing with one another. Man. They reminded me of the kind of girls you'd see in the Miss America pageant—gorgeous.

"I want you to meet my sisters Lily and Jasmine." Alex lowered his voice. "But whatever you do, don't mention the name Fred in their presence. Promise?"

"Fred?"

He put a finger to my lips. "Don't. Go. There."

"O-okay." I looked back and forth between the girls, intrigued by two things—their overwhelming beauty and the fact that they looked nothing alike. "I thought you said they were twins," I whispered.

"They are, but not identical. The one on the right is Lily. The one on the left is Jasmine." He pointed as he spoke.

Lily, much like the flower she'd been named after, was long and lean and had delicate ivory skin. Long auburn curls hung gracefully over her shoulders. Quite a contrast to Jasmine's dark locks. She took several steps toward us, almost ballet-like in movement. Jasmine was a bit shorter and moved a lot faster. Her eyes sparkled with energy. I had a feeling we would be fast friends.

Alex made the necessary introductions, and before long we were all engaged in a friendly conversation. After a few moments I tagged along on their heels as they walked outside to greet more incoming guests. Lily made polite conversation and then greeted the pastor and his wife, who arrived in a hearse.

Really? A hearse?

This didn't stop Jasmine from socializing with me. Within minutes the vivacious brunette had shown me around the new house—what there was of it, anyway—shared her weight, and told me all about her love life. Apparently she'd stolen a fella from her twin sister. A fella named Fred. I kept my mouth shut, of course.

"Guess we'd better get back to the party," she said after spilling the beans about her sweetie. "Mama's rolled out the red carpet."

Apparently rolling out the red carpet meant inviting the whole of Splendora over for an outdoor fry. Less than two hours after our arrival, the smell of frying grease filled the air. I watched, mesmerized, as Mrs. Rigas covered the catfish in cornmeal batter and passed it off to her husband, who started the frying process. I couldn't help but think Mama would've loved this.

Apparently everyone in Splendora loved it too. No sooner did the scent of fish hover over us than the cars started arriving one after another. They must've used the smoke as a signal, just as Mr. Rigas had suggested.

I'd never seen so many people in one place in my life. I'd already met Pastor Higley and his wife, who'd brought a casserole dish with some sort of gelatinous mixture and cottage cheese in it. Now Earline Neeley, Bella's mother-in-law, arrived with her husband. They rolled up on motorcycles wearing "Bikers for Jesus" vests. Interesting. More interesting still, they'd somehow managed to haul a tub of potato salad on one of the bikes. Crazy.

Donny arrived with Willy a few minutes after six. She carried the most luscious-looking cheesecake I'd ever seen in my life. Now, I'd tasted some yummy Greek goodies—baklava making the top of the list—but I had never seen anything that made my jaw drop like this turtle cheesecake. Yum. My hunger returned with a vengeance, and just in time for the first round of catfish to emerge from the fryer.

Unfortunately, I didn't have a chance to eat. Not yet, anyway. I found myself distracted as a large minivan pulled up and three of the most unusual-looking ladies climbed out. Nearly as round as they were tall, this trio exited the vehicle with so much fanfare you would've thought the paparazzi were waiting behind the bushes in the English garden.

"Let the party begin!" one of them hollered out as she clasped her hands together at her overly buxom chest. "The Splendora Sisters are here!"

"Splendora Sisters?" I glanced at Alex, more curious than ever as I took in the vivacious trio of women in their glittery blouses and spandex pants.

"It's my aunt Twila and her best friends," Alex said. "Remember? I told you about them."

"Right, right." I remembered the Aunt Twila part, anyway—she was a chrysanthemum. But I had no idea what to expect from the others. We hadn't covered their flowers yet.

He leaned down and whispered, "Consider yourself warned. And guard your cheeks, whatever you do."

"My cheeks?" I sure hoped he meant the ones on my face.

"Yep. These ladies are brutal. Think Texas tornadoes with pink lipstick and teased hair. They blow in like a gust of wind and leave a trail behind. They pinch a lot of cheeks and offer advice, especially when it's not warranted. But most of all, they'll hug you to death. Just . . . duck."

Duck?

"Take my word for it," he whispered. "Trust me."

"O-okay."

From the looks of things—the three ladies all now completely visible—he'd gotten the "pink lipstick and teased hair" part right. All three of them—Twila, Jolene, and Bonnie Sue—were as skilled as Mama with the makeup brush. Maybe more so.

Oh, wow. I've never seen eyeliner in that color before.

When the ladies gathered me into their arms for a group hug—*Really? Does everyone in Splendora hug total strangers?*—I understood the "duck" comment. Getting swallowed up in Mrs.

Rigas's bosom had been rough enough, but I nearly stopped breathing when Twila, Jolene, and Bonnie Sue swept me into the fold. Er, *folds*.

Twila proved to be the largest of the three women. Like the others, she carried most of her weight on the top half. And talk about glittery. I'd never seen sequins on a woman of that size. Not at a catfish supper, anyway. She took one look at me and her overly made-up face lit into the prettiest smile I'd ever seen.

"You were right, Alex. She's a rose, all right. No wonder you named the new line after her. I get it now."

Okay then. Looked like I was pretty famous round here. Just the idea got me tickled. A little giggle escaped as I thought about it. Alex must've given them quite the buildup about me. The very idea made me care about him even more.

"She's a Greek beauty, just like you said, sweet boy." Jolene leaned over and ran her index finger over my right cheek. "And doesn't she have the loveliest pores."

Lovely pores?

"Your skin is like porcelain, honey," Twila said, examining me so closely that I felt like I'd been shoved under a microscope. "You've discovered the benefits of great skin care, I see."

Actually, my only skin-care regimen was a bar of soap and a washcloth, but I wouldn't tell her that.

"She has youth on her side," Bonnie Sue added.

"True, true." Twila nodded and then wiped the back of her neck. "Well, I don't know about the rest of you, but it's so hot out here the trees are beggin' for a dog." She fanned herself, and I looked at Alex, unsure of how to respond.

"Not as hot as yesterday. I'm pretty sure I saw the chickens laying omelets." Bonnie Sue slapped herself on the knee. "Oh, that's priceless."

"The temperature's higher today, Bonnie Sue," Twila argued. "But it's nothing a big, tall glass of sweet tea won't cure."

"C'mon inside, everyone!" Mrs. Rigas called out from the front porch of the manufactured home. "I've brewed up enough sweet tea to keep everyone cool and comfortable for hours to come."

"Sweet tea?" I looked at Alex and whispered the next part. "Do I have to?"

"What? You don't like sweet tea?" He looked as if he didn't quite believe me. Still, how could I lie to the boy?

"It's not that," I said. "I've just never had sweet tea before."

The silence that followed was deafening. Apparently the entire town of Splendora now knew that I'd never had their national beverage. Great. Just one more reason for all of these folks to consider me an outsider.

15

We Must Have Music

You might be Greek if at least five of your
cousins live on your street and all five of
those cousins are named after your
grandfather.

Thank goodness I was accustomed to being
surrounded on every side by family members. But
my parents and siblings had nothing on the
town of Splendora. Mrs. Rigas poured a deep
glass of liquid from a large pitcher, and all of her
guests gathered around me while I attempted
my first-ever glass of sweet tea. I took a little sip
and almost choked. She hadn't done the "sweet"
part justice.

"Wow," I managed. Tasted like the time Mama
accidentally put too much syrup in the soda
machine.

"She likes it!" Twila patted me on the back so
hard I nearly spewed tea all over Alex's mother.
"You're one of us now, girlie! Once you go sweet,
it gets in your veins."

No doubt. I took another little sip, the flavor
growing on me. Hopefully it wouldn't throw me
into a diabetic coma or anything.

"Would you like a little tea to go with your sugar?" Twila giggled, then jabbed me with her elbow. "That's the way we drink it down here."

"We call it glucose tea," Mrs. Rigas explained. "I drink several glasses a day. That's why I'm so sweet."

That might also account for her girth, but I'd never say such a thing. I could only imagine the calories in a glass of tea this sweet.

"Cassia's parents own a Greek restaurant," Alex said. "And I'm pretty sure there's no sweet tea on the menu."

"Well, that's a shame," Twila said. "I just can't imagine drinking it without the sugar. The sweetness is the fun part." Her nose wrinkled as she took a sip of her own tea. "Guess it takes foreigners some time to get used to our ways."

"She's not exactly a foreigner, Twila," Mrs. Rigas said. "She's just from California, not another country."

"I went to California once." Twila rolled her eyes, which drew my attention to a smudge of mascara just below her left eye. "Seemed like a foreign country to me."

I couldn't really argue that point. I took another little sip, then looked at Alex's mother. "This is growing on me. I'm sure I'll end up falling in love with it. I've always been a fan of tea. In fact, I'll have to give you my mother's recipe for the Louisa. If you like lemon verbena, I mean."

Mrs. Rigas shook her head. "Sorry, but you lost me at Louisa. What's that?"

"I'm sorry. It's a Greek herbal tea. I . . . well, I thought you were Greek." Not that she looked it, but one could never judge by appearances.

"Heavens no," she said with a wave of her hand. "My hubby's got Greek blood, but not me. I grew up little Eula May Skinner." She gestured at the largest of the Splendora trio. "Twila's my big sister."

"*Big* being the key word." Twila gave a wink as she swallowed down a hefty bite of Willy's cheesecake. "Ain't sayin' I enjoy being plus-size all the time—say, when I'm havin' to weigh in at the doctor's office—but I'm a big girl and proud of it."

"Twila, I wasn't referring to your size." Mrs. Rigas rolled her eyes. "I just meant you were my *older* sister."

"Heck, I'd rather be called *big* than old." Twila shrugged. "But never mind all that. I still have to get to know this beauty queen." She leaned forward and ran an index finger over my cheek. "I see you've discovered the benefits of a good moisturizer."

"E-excuse me?" I pulled away.

"I just can't get over your pores. They're lovely. Must be the sea air."

"All those years of living on the coast in California," Mrs. Rigas added.

"Ah. Surprised your pores aren't filled with fruits and nuts then." Twila giggled.

I offered a polite chuckle and glanced over at Pastor Higley's plate of catfish. Yum. How could I get these ladies to stop talking long enough to fill a plate with some of that luscious goodness?

Twila didn't hear my stomach rumbling, apparently. She started telling a story about how her beauty secrets had garnered national acclaim after appearing in an article in the paper.

"National acclaim, my eye." Bonnie Sue rolled her eyes. "Just because you got a little write-up in the *Splendora Gazette* doesn't mean you've made the national news, Twila."

"I was referring to the *Houston Chronicle*, but since you brought up the *Gazette*, you might as well know that I don't read that rag anymore."

"Rag?" Jolene put her hands on her ample hips. "I'll have you know my cousin Rosalie works for the *Gazette*."

"All the more reason not to read it," Twila said. "That old gossip rag is just an exposé of who's bickerin' with who and what's on sale at the Piggly Wiggly."

"Speaking of the *Gazette*, y'all read about poor old Nancy Jane?" Bonnie Sue fanned herself. "She gave up the ghost on Tuesday. I read it in the obits."

Man. I always hated to hear of someone passing away, but this news really seemed to shake them.

"Always loved Nancy." Twila brushed a tear from her eye. "Visited her every time I went to the Cut 'n' Strut. 'Course, the woman couldn't cut hair in a straight line to save her life, but she always brought a smile to my face."

"Cain't believe she's gone," Jolene commented. "Who's going to trim my hair next time?" A little sniffle followed her words.

Somehow this conversation morphed into one about Nancy Jane's poor husband, which somehow reminded Twila of a funny story about the time he brought deer sausage to a church social, which then morphed into a conversation about deer hunting.

Really? Deer hunting? How did we get here?

"You look pale, honey." Jolene rested her hand on my arm. "Are you all right?"

"Oh, it's just that I . . . well, I never really went hunting before. The idea of shooting a sweet, innocent little deer just . . ." I couldn't finish the sentence.

"Oh, hon, you don't have to shoot 'em." Twila doubled over in laughter. "Leave that to the fellas. They live to use their huntin' rifles." She nudged me with her elbow again—*Really? What's with all the touching?*—then leaned my way. "And besides, you just ain't lived till you've spent quality time with your fella in a deer stand. Round here, the first day of deer huntin' season is like a national holiday."

"What do you mean *like* a national holiday?" Jolene asked, her brow wrinkled. "It *is* a national holiday."

That started a lengthy dispute between the two that was interrupted by Mrs. Rigas. "Twila, don't throw a hissy fit. It's not becoming of a woman your age."

"True, true." Twila's scowl faded. "I think I'll have another glass of sweet tea to brighten my disposition. Would you like some more, Cassia?"

"Oh, no thank you," I said. "I'm fine with what I've got." I somehow managed to take another swallow. The sugar didn't choke me this time, thank goodness. In fact, I found myself rather enjoying it.

"All right, sweet pea. Well, I'm so hungry I could eat a horse." She took a couple of steps toward the food table, then turned back and looked at me. "Jeet?"

"I'm sorry . . . what?"

"Jeet?" the three ladies repeated in unison. Okay, so they were posing some sort of question, but I couldn't make sense of it.

Alex whispered in my ear, "Did. You. Eat?"

"Oh!" I shook my head. "No, I haven't eaten yet. But it smells divine and I'm starving."

"You have to try my hubby's fried catfish." Mrs. Rigas reached for a paper plate. "He uses a special recipe. Top secret." She leaned toward me and whispered, "Between you and me, he double-fries them."

"Can't wait. I hardly ever get to eat anything fried," I said.

This drew a wide-eyed stare from all three sisters.

"Well, that's a new one to me too. And I thought the sweet tea comment was odd." Bonnie Sue fanned herself with the folded *Splendora Gazette*. "If you can't go chicken-fried, what're you gonna do with your okra?"

"*Kotopoulo me Bamies*," I responded. "Chicken with okra stew. Mama makes it all the time. But it's not fried."

"I just don't know if I could eat it like that." Twila continued to fan herself. "Guess I'll have to try it sometime, though I doubt I could ever pronounce it." She giggled.

"I heard about a gal who ate her catfish blackened." Jolene's nose wrinkled. "Seems like a waste of a good piece of fish to me." She patted me on the arm as if I somehow needed her empathy. "Skinny as you are, you should eat two or three pieces of that luscious *fried* catfish, hon. Can't be bad for you. It's the other white meat, after all."

This drew a confused look from Twila. "I thought pork was called the other white meat."

This led to an argument between the two. They ended their bickering when Jasmine and Lily approached.

"Well, blessing on blessing!" Twila embraced one twin and then the other. "Always happy to see my darling duo."

I could see Lily cringing at this proclamation, but Jasmine slipped her arm around her aunt's hefty waist—well, sort of—and gave her a kiss on the cheek. "Love you, Auntie T."

Twila looked my way, her shoulders now squared. "Cassia, did you know my girl here is an award winner? She was voted Queen Bee at our last Honey-Do Festival."

"No, Aunt Twila." Jasmine shook her head. "I was Empress at the annual Mosquito Festival, remember?"

"Oh, that's right." Twila clamped a hand over her mouth. "Silly me." She grabbed Lily's arm. "Our Lily here took the prize of Queen Bee."

"And she never lets me forget it," Jasmine whispered in my ear.

They'd lost me a couple of lines back in the conversation. "Mosquito Festival?" I asked, convinced I'd misunderstood.

"Well, sure." Jolene swatted the air. "You're in the South now, honey. Every event is named after a fruit, vegetable, or animal."

"Or grain," Alex said. "Remember the Sugar Cane Festival?"

"Oh, I miss that one," Jolene said. "Just hasn't been the same since the big drought a couple of years back."

"Jasmine won a cooking contest at that one," Alex said. "High honor."

"Oh, you like to cook?" I turned to face the young woman, who blushed with abandon.

"Actually, I make candies," she said. "Specialty candies, I mean. Uncle Donny's selling them up at the truck stop, and a few other local shops have them too. I hope to branch out."

"Oh yes," Twila cooed. "Her homemade candies are incredible. You have to taste them, Cassia. They're all the rage. Of course, they're bad for my girlish figure." She giggled as she placed her balled-up fists on her plump hips.

What to say? What to say?

Twila turned to face Jasmine. "Oh, and speaking of your candies, I ran into Fred the other day up at Donny's truck stop, and he told me that he's gained six pounds since the two of you started dating. Poor fella!"

Everything grew deathly silent. I could hear Alex next to me, sucking in his breath. Jasmine too. Seconds later Lily turned on her heels and marched away.

Twila put a hand over her mouth, then slowly pulled it down. "Oh dear. I've gone and done it now. Put my size 10½ shoe straight into my big fat mouth."

Jasmine looped her arm through her aunt's and grinned. "Oh well, Auntie T. She has to get used to it sooner or later."

"So, is Fred coming today?" Twila asked, looking around as if expecting him to materialize.

"No. He's fishing with Jimmy-Dee and Skeeter. I told him it'd be for the best."

Jimmy-Dee? Skeeter?

Alex looked at me and chuckled. "Now you've been properly introduced to the family. And the South. Better have another sip of that sweet tea. You're gonna need it to recover from the chaos."

No doubt about that. I took another drink, now savoring the sweetness. So this was how people got addicted to sugar. Before long I'd have to join a twelve-step group for recovering sweet tea–aholics. Of course, finding a mentor in the state of Texas might be difficult, if one could judge from the crowd I now found myself in. While pondering that fact, I took another little sip. Then another. Yum.

Alex slipped his arm through mine and we walked to the food table. I had to give it to them— one piece of Mr. Rigas's catfish wasn't enough. So I had two. Make that three. With coleslaw. And three glasses of sweet tea. By the time the meal ended, I was pretty sure I'd put on at least six pounds like Fred. When Alex asked me if I wanted to take a walk through the gardens and into the nursery, I wondered if I would make it.

"Do it, honey," Twila said and then winked. "Tiptoe through the tulips with that sweet boy for a while. You never know what might bloom!"

"Ah, young love!" Jolene added. "Makes me wish I was in my twenties again." She released a lingering sigh. "Those were the days."

Bonnie Sue put her hand on my arm. "Don't miss this opportunity. Take a walk down the primrose path with him, sweetie."

And so I did.

Alex took hold of my hand to lead me over a rocky place in the pathway. We approached a small bridge over a little ravine, and I realized he hadn't let go of my hand. Not that I was complaining. Not one bit. It felt perfectly natural.

I breathed in the fresh, pine-scented air and sighed with contentment. "It's beautiful here, Alex." Then again, every moment I spent with him felt beautiful. And the bellyful of sweet tea and fried fish offered an additional sense of contentment.

"Thank you. I've always loved it." He gestured to the bridge that ran over the little creek. "You wouldn't believe what my grandparents had to go through to clear the land for the rose garden. We're pretty thick in the piney woods."

"Clearly." I glanced off in the distance at the towering pines. But he'd said something that piqued my interest. "Wait . . . grandparents?"

"Yes. This nursery was my grandmother's baby."

"Did she . . . I mean, is she . . ."

"She passed away when I was fourteen." The sadness in his eyes let me know just how much he had loved her.

"I'm sorry, Alex."

"Me too. This place was Yia Yia Melina's dream. She always had a green thumb and loved roses, so my grandfather started clearing a spot for a small rose garden. By the time my dad was born, Yia Yia had grown it into half an acre. By the time he was five, it covered two full acres."

"And now?" I asked.

"Well, that depends. Are you talking about the rose garden or the tulips? Or the orchids? We grow so many different types of flowers now."

"But you kept the Rigas Roses name?"

He nodded. "We'll always keep the name. My grandmother loved it."

He grew silent and we continued to meander along, hand in hand, through the various gardens to the nursery area behind his parents' home. I couldn't help but gasp when I saw the roses—zillions and zillions of them in colors so vast they looked like a rainbow.

"I thought you might want to see the new strain of roses." He gave my hand a little squeeze. "The Cassia."

We started walking again, finally landing next to the most breathtaking red roses I'd ever seen. "Oh, Alex." I could hardly catch my breath. Their beauty held me spellbound. I closed my eyes and drew in the scent of the flowers, feeling a little delirious.

"The only problem with planting gardens in Splendora is the pine trees. We've had to cut down so many of them. They're as thick as thieves."

I chuckled at his funny expression.

"I'd bet I've hauled a hundred loads in the wheelbarrow in the last six months alone. We're always clearing trees to make room for more gardens."

"Doesn't look like you run the risk of having too few." I pointed to a thick woodsy area to our right. "I've never seen so many."

"Welcome to Texas." He laughed and led me down a cobblestone path through the reds and into the pinks. He stopped when we got to the yellow roses and pointed at a small mosaic stepping-stone in the middle of the pathway. "See that stone right there?"

"Yes, it's lovely."

"Notice the handprints in the middle?"

I leaned forward and took a closer look. Sure enough, someone had pressed their palms into the concrete before it dried, then encircled the stone with bits of stained glass in varying shades of blue and yellow.

"That's beautiful," I said.

"Those are my grandmother's handprints," he explained. "The week before she passed away, my mother took us to the hospital to see her. She was barely able to speak and didn't seem to have full control of her faculties. But when Mama pulled out the little kit to make the stone, you should have seen Yia Yia Melina's eyes light up. She never minded getting her hands messy, especially in the garden." His eyes misted over. "That was as close as we could get her to the garden that day, but it seemed to do the trick. And I've always enjoyed the fact that we've kept the stone right here, in the spot where my grandfather planted her first little rose garden."

"Alex, that's an amazing story. I hope you'll always keep the stone there."

"We will. One day I'll tell my kids, and then they will tell theirs. It's part of our legacy. Kind of like your family's sandwich shop."

Ugh. "Yeah, that superhero costume is some legacy, let me tell you." I had to laugh. What else could I do?

Alex slipped his arm over my shoulder. "Well, I didn't mean that, necessarily. I just mean that a family business is something to take pride in. It meant so much to my grandmother to leave this to us. And I know it means a lot to your father that you kids are growing his business."

Would it be wrong to sigh aloud?

We continued our stroll through the gardens as the sun set overhead. With the vivid rays of orange and pink settling down over the flowers, they seemed illuminated. My heart felt so full I could hardly contain all the emotions.

We paused at the bridge over the little creek once more, and I turned to face Alex. "I can't thank you enough for bringing me here."

With the tip of his index finger, he brushed a loose hair from my face. "You're welcome," he whispered, his breath tingly against my cheek. "I see it all the time, so it's very familiar to me."

"I've never been to a nursery that compares, so it's unfamiliar to me," I said. "But I love it. Impressive."

"Thank you. Yia Yia would be happy to hear you say that." He placed his palms against mine, comparing the size of our hands. "I'm glad to find someone who loves flowers. Not everyone appreciates them like I do." He laced our fingers together. "I'd have to say we're a perfect fit."

I would have to agree. But with my heart now beating out of control, I couldn't manage to find the words.

Alex slipped his arm around my waist and drew me closer. I trembled in his arms as his eyes met mine, the "come hither" look more than evident.

Under the canopy of vines, the evening breeze gently drifted in through the pine trees. My eyes fluttered shut. Then, with the luscious scent of flowers providing the perfect backdrop for our first kiss, I waited for the inevitable.

Just as Alex's lips brushed mine, just as the

moment I'd dreamed of all day came to pass . . .
my cell phone rang.

No. Way.

"Can you ignore it?" he whispered.

"Yes. Just let me . . ."

My words drifted off as I lifted my phone to see
who had called. Babbas. Seconds later, a text
message came through from my father: *Need
you. Work to do. Got to put those Rossis in their
place.*

A second message came through directly on the
heels of that one, this time from my mother: *Hate
to interrupt your plans, but Babbas has arranged
a meeting with a videographer tomorrow
afternoon to film the commercial and needs you
here ASAP to go over the harmonies to the jingles
with the other kids. He's in a mood this evening!
Ack!*

I shoved the phone back into my pocket,
aggravation fully rooted in my heart. I wasn't sure
which bothered me more—the fact that my special
moment with Alex had been interrupted, or the
idea that my mother had referred to me as a kid.

Okay, the interruption definitely took the cake.
Ruined the moment and ruined my mood. But
maybe Alex and I could get it all back, recapture
what had been lost on the evening breeze. If I
closed my eyes, I could almost picture myself in
his arms once again.

I looked over at him, but he'd turned his

attention to a ragged-looking flower—one of the Cassias—in a pale shade of yellow. He knelt and plucked the pathetic-looking thing off the bush, then tossed it aside.

Just as he stood and looked at me, the three Splendora Sisters came marching our way with large slices of Willy's turtle cheesecake in hand. "Yoo-hoo, you two!" Twila called out. "You're missing out on all the fun!"

"And the cheesecake too!" Jolene shoved a plate into Alex's hands and he dove right in.

Yeah, we were missing all the fun, all right. I took the piece of cheesecake that Bonnie Sue offered and swallowed down a huge bite. It did little to soothe the turmoil going on inside me. For in that moment my heart felt just like that poor, pathetic little rose Alex had tossed away . . . completely wilted.

16

Babes on Broadway

You might be Greek if every Sunday afternoon of your childhood was spent visiting
Papou and Yia Yia or extended family.

On Sunday morning we went back to Scarlet's
church. I loved every minute, especially the
worship service. Scarlet led the songs, her voice
as pure as angels singing from on high. Armando
sat on a stool to her left, playing the guitar. They
sounded great together. Maybe one of these days
I'd work up the courage to ask if I could sing
along with them. My years on the praise team
back in Santa Cruz had afforded me plenty of time
to grow my skills.

Still, I'd better not ask Scarlet about it just yet.
After all, I didn't know if we'd be staying at this
church. And if she met my family, she might just
mention that I'd been to her bakery after visiting
Parma John's. And heaven forbid she should
wish my mother a happy birthday. Wouldn't that
just be the icing on the cake?

I scooted out of the service quickly and
followed along behind my siblings as we made
our way to our aging minivan. I glanced wistfully

at another family as I overheard their lunch plans. How great would it be to go out to dinner on a Sunday afternoon? Hang out? Not work?

Wouldn't happen in the Pappas family, especially with the new business. After all, Babbas had made plans for us to spend the day filming the new commercial using some local teenage boy he'd hired as a videographer.

When the teen canceled at the last minute, Mama tried to convince my father that we should rest. "Even the Lord took one day off, Niko," she said as she took her seat in the van.

"He could afford to. He owns the cattle on a thousand hills." My father gestured for my younger siblings to get into the van. "My cattle— er, lambs—are mortgaged. We will rest when the new shop is stable. In the meantime you will call Athena to set up a plan for her visit. The kids and I will do inventory."

And so, after a quick lunch—food from the shop, of course—we dove right in. Mama called Athena for the third time in as many weeks, and we "kids" got to work alongside Babbas. Turned out the inventory didn't take as long as we'd expected. By midafternoon I found myself curled up in bed with my sisters snoozing in their beds nearby. Though I tried valiantly to read a book, I found my eyes drifting shut.

A knock at the door roused me.

"Come in."

The door eased open a few inches and Darian peeked inside.

"Hey." I smiled. "What's up?"

He took a couple of steps into the room and noticed the other girls were sleeping. "I need some advice," he whispered.

"That's priceless. You're the one who needs to be dishing it out, not me."

"Not this time."

I could tell from the concerned look on his face that something had him troubled, so I gestured for him to come in the room. "What's up?"

He took several steps toward me and then looked back at the open door. "I, um, have a problem." His words came out in a strained whisper.

Wow. Very out of character. "What is it, Darian? You can tell me."

He took a seat on the edge of my bed and remained silent for a moment as he gestured to our sisters.

"They could sleep through a hurricane," I said. "Don't worry."

"Okay." Another pause followed before he dove in. "See, I, um, I've been hanging out at the ball field, hoping the coach might need help."

"Great idea. I know how much you loved to play ball in high school."

"Right. Would still love to play if I could. Turns

out the coach is a great guy, but he's in over his head, so I ended up giving him a hand."

"Are you saying that you're coaching a baseball team?"

"Not officially. I'm just helping this guy Bubba out."

"Bubba?" Why did that sound so familiar? "Well, that's nice." I set my book aside and shifted the pillows behind me. "You could use a friend outside of the family."

"Yeah." Darian's gaze shifted to the ground. "Only . . ."

"What? He doesn't like your coaching tips?"

"No. Nothing like that. He's . . ." Darian uttered a groan and my little sister stirred in her bed. She fell back asleep right away, and my brother gave me a sheepish look. "He's really nice," he whispered. "And I didn't mean to be his friend. If I'd known his wife Jenna works for the Rossis, I never would've done it." He sighed. "But the next thing you know we were talking about what it's like to work for family and then he was asking if I wanted to have some pizza."

"Wait. Back up."

"I know, I know." Darian put his finger to his lips to quiet me, then shook his head. "I'm a traitor to the family."

"Are you trying to tell me you've been to Parma John's?" I whispered.

Darian looked horrified. "No! Not—not yet,

anyway." He gave me a pleading look. "Do you think I'm awful? It's not about the pizza, really." He released a sigh. "Okay, maybe it is . . . partly. Smelling it day after day is wearing me down. You have no idea what I'm going through."

"Um, yeah, I do."

"But it's more about the friend part. I guess the little ones wouldn't get it," he said. "But moving here has been tough. Being away from the family . . ."

"Away from the family?" I snorted and Eva snored in the bed next to me. "Funny."

"No, I mean the cousins."

He had a point there. In California we had reams of cousins and other extended family members to spend time with.

"I'm used to having a lot of guys my age to hang out with, but I don't have that here. School is the only chance I have to be . . . normal. Working with Dad is okay. I like the marketing stuff. But I really want to play ball. Hang out with the guys."

"Ah."

"Would it really be so terrible if I made some new friends? Hung out with Bubba and the guys and ate pizza? What's so wrong with that?"

Nothing. Absolutely nothing. Except the obvious.

One thing he'd said suddenly caught me off guard. "Wait a minute. Did you say your friend's name is Bubba?"

"Yeah."

"And he's married to Jenna, who works at Parma John's."

"Right. Why?"

I bit back a laugh and said, "Oh, never mind. Let's just say I totally understand your predicament and can sympathize on many levels." I released a yawn. "I'll tell you all about it soon, I promise. But don't feel like you're alone, okay?"

He gave me a curious look before responding with, "Okay."

Before he left, I gave my brother as many words of encouragement as I could. I pondered his situation as I settled down in the bed to rest. I couldn't shake his comments about needing friends.

I'd just dozed off when Eva's gentle voice woke me up. "You still awake, Cassia?"

Biting back the complaint that threatened to escape, I managed to mutter, "I am now."

"Good." She sat up in the bed and plumped her pillows. "Just FYI, I heard every word Darian said."

"Oh, man." I sat up in the bed and looked at her. "You're not gonna rat him out, are you?"

"Are you kidding? Just the opposite." She lowered her voice and checked the other bed to make sure Gina was still sleeping. "I need to talk to someone or I'm going to bust."

"Oh?"

"Yeah." She leaned toward me. "Houston, we have a problem."

"Join the club."

"Yeah, I'm a member of the club, all right." She released an exaggerated sigh and lay back against the pillows in dramatic fashion. "I went to have my hair cut at a new place a few doors down. Sassy Shears."

"Great cut, by the way."

"Thank you." She fussed with her hair. "I took Gina with me. She needed a trim."

"Okay." Couldn't figure out where this was going, but that was often the case with Eva's stories.

A delightful smile tipped up the edges of my sister's lips. "The girl who cut my hair was great. Well, actually, she wasn't a girl—she's in her late twenties, I guess. The age part didn't really matter. Her name's Sophia, and we totally got along. We just started talking, and before I knew it an hour had gone by."

"That's good, Eva. I'm glad you're making friends."

"Me too. The best part was we had so much in common. She loves great hair, I love great hair." Eva chuckled. "She's really into fashion, I'm into fashion. She has an older sister, I have an older sister."

"That's great. I'm glad you're finding people to connect with. It's good for you."

"Yes, but . . . you didn't hear the rest." Eva leaned close to me again and lowered her voice. "Her family runs a business, our family runs a business."

"Sounds like a divine appointment."

"Only one teensy-tiny problem." Eva bit her lip. "Her last name is Rossi. Well, at least it used to be. She's married now, so she has a different last name. But she's a Rossi, and there's nothing I can do about it."

"Oh no." I couldn't help but laugh. "Another one?"

"I think they're everywhere." Eva smiled. "You know that girl we keep seeing come out of Parma John's? The one with the perfect life? That's Sophia's older sister—"

"Bella." I said her name and sighed with relief. It would feel good, really good, to tell someone in the family about my friendship with Bella and Marcella.

"Wait, you know her sister?" Eva shook her head. "Are you serious?"

I nodded and then told her all about the Marcella/Bella/Rossi connection at the flower shop.

"You had no idea when you took the job, though?" She seemed mesmerized by this. "Crazy."

"I know. But I love it there. And Marcella and Bella are totally great."

"So's Sophia."

"And apparently Bubba's been a good friend to Darian."

Eva sat back and closed her eyes. "We're doomed."

"*Doomed* might be a little dramatic."

"Maybe. Maybe not." Her expression tightened. "Still, I hate this trapped feeling. There's got to be a way out. If someone doesn't do something"—she stared me down—"I'll never get out of here in one piece. I'll be tied to Babbas's apron strings forever. You know?"

Of course I knew. Those apron strings were choking the life out of me even as we spoke.

"Sometimes I just want to run away from home." Eva rolled over in her bed. "Go back to California, where people are normal."

I wasn't sure about that last part, but I did fight that running-away-from-home feeling . . . a lot. Only, now I couldn't run. Not with Alex in the picture. To leave him would be heartbreaking.

Eva's words about the apron strings bothered me all evening. When I awoke Monday morning, I still found myself troubled by our conundrum. What sort of family felt trapped by their father? Sure, we were instructed to respect our parents, but at what cost? Self-worth? Lack of friendships?

I must've been wearing my troubles on my face when I entered the flower shop because

Marcella and Bella both gave me concerned looks.

"Everything okay?" Bella said from behind the counter.

"Hmm?" I put my purse away in the back room, then came back out to join them. "Not really."

"Want to talk?" Marcella asked.

"No." I shook my head. "You two are busy. I'll be okay. I need to go through last week's deliveries and prune out the dead flowers."

Bella still looked concerned. "No, we're just talking about centerpieces for a wedding that's months off. I have a feeling you're dealing with something a little more pressing than that."

Pressing. Sounded like the right word. With Babbas demanding so much of our family, I felt like he was pressing, all right—pressing the air right out of my lungs.

"How can we help?" Bella asked. "I mean, I know I'm not involved in the situation—whatever it is—but I want to be there for you. That's what friends are for. You know?"

How could I resist the hand of friendship Bella was offering? To do so would be ridiculous.

"Sometimes it helps to have an outsider weigh in," Marcella said. "To give an unbiased opinion. That sort of thing."

"But that's just it." I turned to face them, the sting of fresh tears in my eyes. "You're not outsiders. And Bella, you're wrong to say you're not in the situation. You're involved. You just don't know it." Moisture spilled over my lashes and down my cheeks.

Bella rose and took several quick steps toward me. "I'm sorry, but I'm so confused. Have I done something to hurt you? To offend you?"

"No, not at all."

"Is it me?" Marcella looked worried. "I've been leaving you at the shop alone way too much. I knew it. You're feeling taken advantage of."

"No, it's nothing like that. It's just . . ." I brushed tears away with a swipe of my hand. "I'm not supposed to like you." A dramatic groan escaped, and I slapped myself on the forehead.

"Not supposed to like me?" Fine lines appeared on Bella's otherwise perfect brow.

"I think she was talking to me." Marcella drew in a deep breath and held it as if preparing for bad news.

Bella shook her head. "No, she was definitely talking to me."

"I . . . I'm referring to both of you. I'm not supposed to like anyone in the Rossi family. Not Marcella. Or Bella. Or Scarlet. Or Uncle Laz. Or Aunt Rosa. Or Bubba. Or Sophia. Or anyone else whose last name is now or has ever been Rossi." I slid down into the chair behind the counter and put my head down.

"Why?" Bella sat next to me.

"Because you sell pizza." I lifted my head and glanced her way.

"Technically, neither of us sells pizza," Marcella argued.

"True. But you're both Rossis and the Rossis sell pizza. Really, really yummy, gooey, amazing, can't-wait-to-have-it-again pizza. On the Strand."

"And this is a problem because . . ." Bella said.

"Because my family is Greek."

"Okay." She looked more perplexed than ever.

"Greek. As in . . . Greek food." *Just come out and say it, Cassia. She's going to find out anyway.* "My parents own the restaurant directly across the street from Parma John's."

"Super-Gyros?" Her gaze narrowed. "The new place?"

"Yep. The finest in Greek cuisine, run by a man—my father—who happens to have the most competitive spirit on the planet. He won't stop until . . ." Nope. Wouldn't finish the sentence.

Bella's brows creased. "So, the guy in the photo shoot—the one who has Uncle Laz so worked up. The one with the tights. He's . . ."

My gaze shifted to the window. Oh, how I'd hoped to avoid this conversation. "Yeah. That's him. My dad. Niko Pappas, superhero extraordinaire, star of stage and screen. Well, he will be, as soon as the new commercial airs. We were supposed to film it yesterday but the videographer had to cancel. And that reminds me, I wrote a

230

perfectly ridiculous jingle for Super-Gyros, so I'm about to be famous too. For all the wrong reasons, I mean."

"Oy." Marcella's hand covered her mouth and she grew silent.

Bella's eyes widened. "This changes everything."

"Yeah. Pretty much. But it doesn't mean that we can't be friends, right?"

"Right." Bella nodded, but I could read the concern in her expression.

I looked Marcella's way, and she nodded too but didn't say a word.

"Of course we'll still be friends." Bella smiled, but it looked a bit strained. "We can't let our silly families separate us."

I could tell she was trying to sound convincing, but I didn't buy it. Not for a minute. My heart felt as if it had taken a swan dive into the icky waters of the Gulf of Mexico.

"What are we going to do?" I asked.

"What can we do?"

"I dunno." I gave a little shrug. "Something to end the feuding? A peace treaty?"

"You obviously don't know my uncle Laz." She sighed.

"And you obviously don't know my dad. He's got this mentality that everything he does has to be bigger. Better."

"Kind of like *My Big Fat Greek Wedding*?" She quirked a brow.

"Yeah, only he's not interested in weddings unless he happens to be catering one, and even then it's all about the money he can make off the bride. Now that I'm in the flower business, he'll probably count on me to send brides to him for food. See what I mean? With my dad, it's all business all the time." I paused and thought about that last line. "Well, that's not true. Babbas loves the family."

"Babbas?" Marcella looked perplexed.

"That's what we call him."

"Ah. Interesting." She shrugged.

"And my grandmother is Yia Yia and my relatives are nuts and we really are a lot like that family in the movie you just mentioned. Only weirder."

"Impossible." Bella released a chuckle. "I saw that movie. They were nuts. The whole family."

"Oh, we are too. I have six brothers and sisters and we all have ABC names."

Bella shrugged. "No idea what that ABC part means, but congrats on all the brothers and sisters. I come from a huge family too. You met my siblings."

"Yeah, they're great too. But imagine living with all of them—or most of them—in an apartment above your store."

"Lots of families do." She snapped her fingers. "Wait . . . I've noticed someone sitting in the window, looking down. Couldn't really make out the face, though. Are you saying that was you all along?"

"Yeah. Me. And my sister Eva, who, by the way, has struck up a friendship with your sister Sophia."

"Priceless." Bella shook her head.

"We've been watching you and your husband, dreaming of what it would be like to have your life. Seems so . . . perfect."

"Perfect?" She erupted in laughter and then looked at Marcella, who sniggered. "That's so funny." The chuckles turned into full-fledged guffaws, and before long Bella and Marcella were doubled over in laughter.

While my friends laughed themselves silly, my sister's comment about the apron strings consumed my thoughts once again. I forced back the lump in my throat. This might seem funny to them, but I couldn't find the humor in the situation at all. No, all I saw were a thousand reasons my father could bring all of our new relationships crashing down around us in one swift move.

"Sometimes I just want to leave. Get out of here. You know?"

Both women stopped laughing at that proclamation.

Marcella looked at me, her eyes widening. "Oh, Cassia, it all makes sense now. I understand why you're so infatuated with Judy Garland." She gave me a knowing look. "It's that whole 'Somewhere over the Rainbow' theme. You're subliminally longing for a different life."

I couldn't help but sigh. She'd hit the nail on the head, after all. "Do I drive you crazy with the Judy Garland songs?" I asked.

"Drive me crazy? No." Marcella laughed. "But I think we'd be safe to say you've covered every song in her repertoire since you started working for me."

Embarrassment swept over me.

"Even *I've* noticed." Bella pointed a slender index finger at me. "And I have to agree with Marcella. I think she's on to something. Maybe you want to run from your situation—kind of like Dorothy did in *The Wizard of Oz*."

"Maybe." I shrugged.

"Well, remember, it didn't solve her problems. She ended up doing battle with the Munchkins."

"No," I countered, "she didn't battle the Munchkins. She battled the monkeys and the Wicked Witch."

Bella waved her hand in the air. "Still, it wasn't all roses."

"Poppies."

She rolled her eyes. "Whatever. Weren't the roses—er, poppies—bad or something?"

"Poisonous," I said. "The Wicked Witch cast a spell on them."

"Right, right." Bella shook her head and leaned against the counter. "Anyway, when you run away

234

from home, it never really ends well. You get chased down by an old lady riding on a broom, and then you have to walk a really long way down a yellow road."

"Yellow *brick* road."

"Right."

"Point is, you've got to face your challenges and march through them," Marcella said. "Not run away from them."

"Not that I'd get very far anyway. Babbas would hunt me down. He'd come all the way to Oz to fetch me back to Kansas again. Er, Galveston. I'm never going to get out from under his thumb. That might not make sense to the average person my age, but it's my reality."

"Then we have more in common than you know." Bella's expression grew more serious. "I remember a time in my life when I wanted nothing more than to break free from the confines of my very large, crazy family. They are crazy, you know."

I sighed. "Tell me about it." When she gave me a funny look, I added, "My family, I mean. They're crazy."

"Our two families are so much alike it's nuts. In fact, they're so much alike that maybe they could be related." She paused, then snapped her fingers. "Or friends, at the very least. That's it, Cassia."

"What's it?"

"That's the way we get Uncle Laz and your father to play nice. Point out all the things they have in common. Get them to see that they are more alike than they are different." She started giving me all sorts of facts about our two cultures being related, even stating that Greeks and Italians were technically kissing cousins. Her suggestions to merge the two, however, went in one ear and out the other.

Get Babbas and Uncle Laz to play along? Yeah, it sounded good in theory. In reality, I could already hear the Munchkins singing in my head. Or maybe those voices were the evil monkeys. Either way, I'd never find my way out of Oz with Babbas controlling every aspect of my life from behind the proverbial curtain.

17

Come Rain or Come Shine

You might be Greek if you hate going out in public with your family because people always think you're fighting when you're really just loud.

On the Saturday after my heart-to-heart conversation with Bella and Marcella, I went back to work at the flower shop. Marcella had somehow over-looked a large order for a wedding and needed my help pronto. Thank goodness we had plenty of flowers in stock. I still couldn't figure out how she'd managed to forget something this important, though. She seemed to be slipping up a lot.

We worked at a record pace. Marcella spent much of the time thanking me for helping her pick up the slack. "I truly don't know how I would manage without you, Cassia," she said. "More and more I find myself distracted." She gave me a winsome smile. "I guess my heart's just at home with my family. You understand."

"After our conversation the other day, you think I want to spend more time with my family?" I laughed, then shame washed over me. "I'm sorry. I guess it sounds like I don't love them. I do. Very much." Even Babbas, though he drove me nuts at times.

"I understand, Cassia." Her eyes misted over. "We've been through so many ups and downs in our marriage . . ." She grew quiet, then shook her head. "Anyway, I know what it's like to keep up appearances. It's better just to come clean and let your emotions out. Don't let things build up."

"Right."

She gave me a motherly look. "God has done so much in my relationship with my husband over the past few years. And with his family too. I truly believe he can mend whatever is going on between you and your father if you ask him to."

"I have asked."

"Well, don't give up. Keep asking and keep believing. We don't know God's time frame, but we do know that he wants us to be in good relationships with each other. One of these days you'll be proud to be a Pappas."

I was proud of it already, though it rarely showed.

"Hey, speaking of your name, I want to apologize." She laughed. "I actually thought your last name was Bethesda. I feel awful that I didn't even give your résumé a close look. Will you forgive me? I was so . . ."

"Distracted." We spoke the word together.

"It's probably for the best that you didn't realize I was a Pappas at the time," I said. "Maybe you wouldn't have hired me."

"Not sure if it would've influenced me or not. But to my credit, Bethesda sounds like a last name. Never heard it used as a middle name."

"Right? And you probably won't again." I quickly lit into a story about how and why I'd been given such an odd name. "My great-grandmother on my mother's side was a Bethesda before she married, so I was given her name."

Oh, wow. I realized in that moment that my parents hadn't just slapped together ABC names for their kids. Each of us had a middle name from a family member who'd gone before.

"*Bethesda* means 'flowing water,' " I explained. "Or 'house of mercy.' I've always been drawn to the water."

"Isn't there a Bible story with that name in it?" Marcella looked up from her work, curiosity in her eyes.

"Yes. A crippled man at the edge of the pool of Bethesda. The waters had curative powers."

"Well, think about it, Cassia." Marcella gave me another one of those motherly looks. "God has graced you with a name that has a special meaning. He wants to use you to bring healing to relationships. That should bring you some comfort as you think about the situation with your dad, right?"

I pondered her words as we continued to work. I'd never once given thought to the idea that God would use my name as a reminder that he longed to bring healing in my life. Now I couldn't shake the idea.

With the sting of fresh tears in my eyes, I nodded and whispered, "I think you're right. I'll pray about that."

For whatever reason, this conversation reminded me of Alex—of the feud between his twin sisters. Everyone else in the family seemed to get along fine, but those two sisters just couldn't see eye to eye, especially with a fella in the mix. Why did some family situations have to be so complicated?

Marcella went into the back room to put the bouquets in the walk-in cooler, and I sat in silence, my thoughts firmly rooted in what she'd said. If only Babbas wasn't so . . . difficult. Then perhaps I could see things through hopeful eyes like Marcella did.

A short while later the bride-to-be's mother picked up the bouquets. I stretched my back, which was aching from working all morning. I prepared to head home but then ended up taking care of an elderly customer named Frank instead. I'd heard all about him from Marcella. Apparently this dapper fellow showed up every Saturday to purchase two dozen carnations, which he handed out to the widows at his church on Sunday morning. "So they never forget they are loved," he always said.

In spite of his slow gait, Frank looked pretty chipper in his seersucker suit, bow tie, and circa 1980 shoes. I also noticed his trendy hairdo. Interesting.

"How are you today, Frank?" Marcella asked.

"Oh, the arthritis is giving me fits." He put his hand on his right hip as he moved slowly in our direction. "And getting a good night's sleep is getting harder with this bad shoulder of mine. But I'm still blessed by the best."

His response brought a smile to my face.

"You want your usual order?" Marcella asked.

"Well now, yes and no." He rested an elbow on the counter and I noticed the twinkle in his eyes. "I'll take my usual two dozen pink carnations, but throw in a pink rose too."

"A pink rose?" Marcella looked perplexed.

I walked over to the case and started pulling the flowers out.

"Yep. And wrap it separate."

"Something we should know, Frank?" she asked.

"Maybe." He arched a brow. "When I'm ready to talk. Right now just hand over the flowers and no one will get hurt."

This got a laugh out of us. Marcella got busy with another customer, so I wrapped the flowers —all of the carnations in one bundle and the rose by itself, per Frank's request—and then handed them to him. After giving me his usual cash payment, all in ones, he leaned toward me and whispered, "There's a certain lady I've got my eye on, just so you know." He gave a little wink.

"I thought so," I whispered in response, then gave him his change.

He looked at me kind of funny as he examined the money. "You didn't charge me for the rose."

"It's on me." I smiled. "You just go nab that lady friend of yours."

"Will do, will do." He turned and whistled his way out of the store.

I reached into my pocket for money to cover the rose, but Marcella stopped me. "Oh no you don't."

"But—"

"Nope. This one's on me." She chuckled and the wrinkles around her eyes spoke of mischief. "But just FYI, you have no idea how many times I've given away roses to that man. He's had his eye on at least five or six of the widows in his church over the past six months."

"Oh. Oops." I laughed as I tried to picture Frank courting the ladies. Couldn't envision it. Still, the ladies had to be flattered. Or creeped out.

I walked home from the flower shop that afternoon, my arms loaded down with leftover roses that Marcella insisted I take home with me. As I sniffed the roses, I thought about Frank. Some men aged gracefully, retained their charm.

Some men—like Babbas—seemed to get rougher with age. Maybe when I got to heaven I could take this up with the Almighty. He could surely let me know why I ended up with a grumpy man for a father. Of course, by the time I got to heaven, that probably wouldn't be a top priority on my list. I'd be too busy singing in the heavenly choir or planting flowers in my heavenly garden.

This last thought led to some great internal questions about what flowers would be like in heaven. My imagination went crazy as I tried to picture the vibrant colors and luscious scents.

Thinking of flowers, as always, reminded me of Alex. I couldn't help but smile as I thought about how great I always felt when we were together. I decided to shoot him a quick text just to let him know that, followed by "Wish I could see you." He responded moments later with "We need to remedy that. Soon." My heart burst into song, and I nearly forgot about the situation with Babbas. Nearly.

When I arrived at Super-Gyros, I put the roses in vases and used them as centerpieces on the tables. While I worked, Mama filled me in on the day's details. I learned that my cousin Athena had called to let us know that she and her husband planned to come to Galveston the following week. To celebrate that great news, I decided to go for a bike ride. I put on my new riding shorts and brightly colored T-shirt and reached for my helmet.

Eva's curiosity must've gotten the better of her. She followed me out to the storage room where I kept my bike, chatting all the way, first about Athena's visit and then about my desire to ride.

"What's up with all the bike riding, Cassia? Why do you go out so much?"

I slipped the helmet on my head and clicked the ends of the strap together. "It's the only time I can truly be alone, away from all the chaos of the shop and the hundreds of people who surround me on every side. When I'm on my bike, I'm . . . free." I didn't mention the fact that my family— God bless them—was the loudest I'd ever known. The screaming, even the friendly bantering, was so high-pitched I could hardly stand it at times.

"Could I go with you sometime?" she asked.

"Sure. But we'd need to get a second bike."

"I think I'd like that."

I gave her a smile and climbed aboard. After waving goodbye, I set the music on my phone to exactly the right song—"Somewhere over the Rainbow"—and stuck in my earbuds. Then I took off, ready to be free from all of life's struggles, including the obvious ongoing issues with my dad.

Well, until the trolley rolled my way. As it went on by, I noticed a new sign on the side: "Parma John's Pizzeria, the island's favorite eatery. Now featuring the Venus de Milo, a tasty Mediter-ranean pizza."

Oh. Help.

Babbas would have a fit.

I rounded the corner, the wind blowing against my face. My thighs felt the burn as the breeze offered a little more resistance than normal. With my earbuds in, the music provided the perfect backdrop to convince me to keep going.

Off in the distance I caught a glimpse of seagulls circling a trash can. If I pinched my eyes shut for a second—not a wise move on my bike, of course—those seagulls might just resemble my family members, hovering around me at every turn.

The song on my phone changed, and I found myself caught up in a familiar worship tune. The upbeat melody kept my feet firmly on the pedals, which moved in perfect timing. Talk about a great motivator.

After a couple of minutes, I turned onto a back street and slowed my pace as the music shifted to a new tune. The words to the worship song hit my heart, and I pondered the situation with my parents, how I'd come to resent the fact that Babbas expected so much from me. Seconds later I felt a tug on my heart as the Lord whispered words of peace over the situation. I thought about what Marcella had said, about how my name meant healing.

In that moment, I saw hope for my situation. Maybe my father would never change, but I could. My heart needed an adjustment, a shift.

As I rounded a bend in the road, the gulf came into view. With the sunlight reflecting off the water, it took my breath away. Sure, I'd bragged that the Gulf of Mexico couldn't hold a candle to the Pacific, but the glistening waters called out to me, drawing me in. I pedaled toward the seawall, slowing as I reached the crossing point. After waiting for the traffic to clear, I made my way across and went to the sidewalk on the other side. There I parked my bike and walked to the stairs, then headed down to the sand.

While I strolled along the water's edge, I was reminded of everything Bella had said, how she had suggested I play up the similarities between Babbas and Uncle Laz. Maybe we really could bring the two together. I would implement a plan as soon as I arrived back home, and I would do so with a new attitude and greater patience.

Turned out the ride home was tougher than I'd imagined. The breeze picked up and worked against me all the way. By the time I got back to Super-Gyros, I felt winded in every sense of the word. Still, I needed to talk to Babbas, and I needed to do it now . . . before my courage slipped away on the afternoon breeze.

18
What'll I Do?

You might be Greek if you think that activated charcoal, garlic, and vitamin C are the solution to all medical problems— including broken bones.

I passed off my bike to Eva, who looked terrified to get on it. Moments later, however, she took off down the Strand, all smiles, and I went inside the shop. I located my father in the kitchen, working alongside Darian. Perfect opportunity.

"Babbas, I really need to talk to you. It's important." I drew in a deep breath, whispered a prayer for God's help, and waited for my courage to rise.

Babbas continued to work, not even looking up. "What is it, Cassia? I'm busy."

"I know, but this is important. I want to talk to you about the situation with the Rossis."

I noticed Darian cringe, but he said nothing.

"Rossis?" Babbas mumbled something under his breath. "I know all about it, Cassia."

My heart went a little crazy at that proclamation. "Know about . . . what?"

"Their new sign on the trolley. Yia Yia saw it.

But don't you worry. Our sign will go up in a few days." He spread his hands as if showing me the sign. " 'Enjoy the finest Mediterranean food on the island at Super-Gyros. Now featuring a meatball sub. Buy one, get one free.' "

"Well, that's great, Babbas, but that's not really what I meant."

"What, then?"

"I've been thinking about what a great thing it would be for our customers if you and Mr. Rossi got along. Made peace."

"Made peace . . . with that man?" Babbas turned to face me, a large slab of lamb in his right hand. He shook it in my direction. "Over my dead body! And explain to me how conceding to the pizza lovers will help grow our customer base?"

"It will, Babbas," I said. "They will see you as gracious and hospitable, and that will make them want to come back."

He grunted and kept working.

"I think Cassia is right," Darian added. "I've been researching, and Italy and Greece are like Uncle Alex's children and your children. They're both Mediterranean cousins."

"Why did you have to bring my brother into this?" Babbas's face turned red, and he slapped the piece of meat on the counter. "Not all cousins were meant to get along!"

"But Athena is coming soon," I said. "Surely you want me to get along with her while she's here. Otherwise why would she want to help us?"

"That's different." The regret in his eyes was palpable. "I know that you and Athena are close."

I chose my next words carefully. "You and Uncle Alex could be too. For that matter, you and the Rossis could eventually be close. Did you ever think about that? We could all be friends, and honestly, Babbas, we need friends."

He looked out the window at Parma John's, which was teeming with customers. "Italy might be our cousin, but that doesn't mean we have to get along. There's no law that says we have to."

"Only that whole 'love your neighbor as you love yourself' one in the Bible," I countered.

Wow. Did I really just say that out loud?

Judging from the scowl on my father's face, yes.

"It makes sense from a spiritual standpoint," Darian said. "And from a cultural one. It's good to meet people who care as much about their heritage as we do."

Another grunt followed from my father. He took the meat tenderizer and started whacking with abandon at the piece of lamb on the cutting board. Apparently this whole approach wasn't working.

"Darian is just saying that the two countries have strong cultural ties," I explained.

"And historical ties," my brother added. "The friendship between the two goes all the way back to ancient times."

"You and your research." Babbas muttered under his breath as he pounded the meat.

"Point is, Greece and Italy are brother nations." Darian stood a little taller, his shoulders now squared. I liked that confident look on him—a lot. "You might be surprised to learn how many Italians live in Greece, and vice versa."

At this news my father spouted that he would rather live at the top of an active volcano than ever visit the country of Italy. "We may be cousins," he said. "We may be distantly related. But that doesn't mean I'm living on their land . . . or eating their pizza!"

"Even if they came over here and ate our food?" I asked. "Then what?"

"You're telling me the Rossi family will come here and eat our food?" Babbas stopped pounding and stared at me. "That, I would pay money to see."

"But if they ever did," I said, "then you would make peace?"

"It will never happen." With a wave of his hand he dismissed the idea as foolish. "So stop with all of this talk about Italy and Greece." He pounded piece after piece, the only sound in the room the whacking of the tenderizer against the raw lamb.

I needed a different approach. I put my hand on my father's shoulder and felt his muscles flex as he reacted. "It's for your own good." I lowered my voice. "We worry about you, Babbas. We all do."

"Worry about me? Why?" He held the tenderizer but stopped pounding, his back still to me.

I squeezed his shoulder, tenderness rising in my heart as I spoke. "You're so wound up all the time. It can't be good for your health. We want you to relax."

"Relax?"

He started pounding again and I pulled my hand away. "Yes. You work yourself to death. Never take a day off."

"I take Sundays off. Never miss a church service."

"Yes, but even then you're promoting the business. I hear you talking to the choir director, the Sunday school teacher . . . anyone and everyone."

"No harm in that. Even God approves of marketing."

That piqued my interest. "Oh?"

"Yes. The Bible says that every tree that doesn't produce good fruit will be cut down and thrown into the fire. I'm not willing to be tossed into the fire, so I must bear fruit."

"Agreed. But sometimes I think you over-produce, Babbas, and you're too serious."

He set the meat aside, wiped his hands on his apron, and started lifting cans of fava beans off the shelf. "If I want to feed my family, I must work. I will be found faithful in this."

"Yes, but don't you think it would be fun to take a vacation?"

"Vacation?" He snorted and nearly lost his grip on one of the cans. "Not anytime soon. There's too much to do."

"Then a mini vacation," I suggested. "You and Mama should go bike riding like I do. She would love that."

"Bike riding?" He turned my way, eyes widening. "You can picture your old Babbas on a bike, wind whipping through my—" He stopped cold and pointed to his thinning hairline. "Scalp?"

I pressed back the giggle that threatened to erupt. I still couldn't get past the fact that my father had the hairiest arms, legs, and back on the island but was showing signs of baldness on top. "Yes, I can picture it. And besides, you'll be wearing a helmet, so no one will notice your scalp."

"Over my dead body I'll wear a helmet."

Okay, there would be plenty of time to argue the importance of bike safety with him later. Right now I had to convince the man he could actually step away from his business for a few minutes to take a ride with Mama.

"Who would man the store if Mama and I both left at the same time?" he countered. "You're hardly ever here anymore, and Eva has her head in the clouds."

To my right, Darian cleared his throat.

"Babbas, you have to trust Darian to take a more active role sooner or later." I nudged my brother with my elbow. "He wants to help you more. He's loaded with ideas, in fact. Right, Darian?"

"Right."

I nudged my brother again, but he didn't chime in further. Instead, he shook his head.

"Did he tell you his ideas about articles in the paper?" I said. "And he always wants to help research new ways to get the word out."

"I know, I know." Babbas waved his hand in dismissive fashion. "I hear it all the time."

"And Eva is great with marketing. She wants to go to school to study it."

"Go to school? There's no time for that. I need her here."

"But she would be so good at it. She's outgoing and bubbly and gets along great with all kinds of people. She's a good writer too, Babbas. She could do an article about the shop for the local paper."

"That last ad I put in the paper didn't bring in much business," he said.

"No, I don't mean an ad. I'm talking about an article about the family, something more personal."

"Personal, schmersonal. This is about business, not family."

Ouch.

"Well, here's an idea for you," I said. "It's time to add sweet tea to the menu."

"Sweet tea?" My father narrowed his gaze. "And why is that?"

"Because people in the South expect it. It's part of the experience. If you want to grow your business, sweeten the pot by adding sugar to the tea."

Babbas shut us down at this point, claiming he had heard enough. I left the kitchen and headed upstairs with Darian at my side.

"How do you think that went?" I whispered.

He shrugged. "I think you planted a lot of seeds."

"Hope they take root."

When I got to our apartment, Darian headed off to his bedroom. I found Mama in the living room on the laptop. She saw me coming and closed the computer quickly, her face growing red.

"Mama?" I sat down next to her. "What's going on?"

"What do you mean?"

"Mama."

"You wouldn't understand, Cassia." Her eyes glistened with tears, and my heart lurched. Maybe she was shopping for plane tickets, a way out of here. Wouldn't surprise me, to be honest.

She put a finger over her lips and glanced at the stairs as if expecting Babbas to appear at any moment. "Okay, I'll tell you, but it's top secret. Just between us, okay?"

"Okay. Sure." I'd never known my mother to be secretive before, so this intrigued me.

"What I'm going to tell you is a terrible confession." She clutched the laptop in her hands so hard that her knuckles turned white. "I've never betrayed your father. Never."

"Betrayed him?" I almost lost my breath as I pictured what she might say.

"Yes. I've made a friend."

Ack. What kind of friend? I forced myself to remain calm, knowing my mother pretty well. She'd always been the friendly sort. Lots of people had gravitated toward her in Santa Cruz, and she'd certainly won over her fair share of people since arriving on Galveston Island.

"It happened so innocently," she said. "I was making a delivery to the opera house the other evening and met a lady. We had so much in common it was kind of funny. I think you'll appreciate the story, honey."

"Oh?"

"Yes. She has a large family, I have a large family. She's proud of her culture, I'm proud of my culture. She's got a daughter in the wedding business, I've got a daughter in the wedding business. Don't you find that ironic? I mean, as different as we are, we're still very much the same in the ways that count. So much so that I believe we could turn out to be wonderful friends."

I'd just opened my mouth to argue that I wasn't

exactly in the wedding business when it hit me. "Mama?" I stared at her, dumbfounded. "Are you by any chance talking about Bella's mother, Mrs. Rossi?"

Mama clamped a hand over my mouth and nodded, her eyes wide. "Don't. Let. Your. Father. Hear. You." She whispered the words and released her hand from my mouth. "He's already beside himself about the Rossis. He would kill me if he knew I'd been cavorting with the enemy."

I had no doubt he would flip—and not like a gymnast. And she had the cavorting part down. I'd heard him use those very words.

Mama went on to explain that she and Mrs. Rossi—whom she fondly called Imelda—spoke by email or instant messenger nearly every day. "This puts me in an awkward spot," she said. "Because it turns out you-know-who is really very nice. And she feels the same way about me, judging from our chummy conversation. She called me a kindred spirit."

"Kindred spirit?" My father's voice sounded from behind us. "Who called you a kindred spirit, Helena?"

"O-oh . . ." Mama's cheeks blazed red. She glanced at the clock and then said, "Look at the time, will you? I've got to get busy on that baklava for tomorrow's lunch crowd."

"Tomorrow is Sunday." Babbas crossed his arms at his chest and glared at her.

"Monday," she said. "I meant Monday. Better get to it." She scurried down the stairs and into the shop below, laptop still tucked under her arm.

Babbas kicked off his shoes and settled onto the recliner. "I can never make sense out of half of what she says, but I love her. Always have, always will."

"You're a lucky man, Babbas," I said. "Such a wonderful wife."

"Yes, I'm blessed, all right," he said. "No doubt about it."

Still, I couldn't help but wonder what he would do if—when—he found out that Mama had befriended Imelda Rossi. But maybe Mama's new friendship could work in my favor. I mean, if Babbas got distracted fretting over my mother's friendship with Imelda, he wouldn't have time or energy to worry about my relationships. Surely my friendship with Bella and Marcella would pale in comparison. Right?

Not that I planned to tell him anytime soon. One thing at a time. God would show me exactly the right time and right place. Until then, I would keep on working, keep on riding, keep on praying.

19

On the Sunny Side of the Street

You might be Greek if you serve your guests anything you happen to have that's available. And they'd better accept it.

Later that afternoon, Alex surprised me by showing up at Super-Gyros with a fistful of yellow roses. Cassias, of course. My heart pitter-pattered at the sight of him and those luscious roses. Oh, how this Greek cowboy had captured my heart!

My family members gathered around me, just like the seagulls over the trash can earlier in the day, gushing over the flowers. Well, the ladies gushed. The guys shrugged off the visit as if they weren't really interested. Babbas didn't fool me, though. He was keeping a watchful eye on this situation between Alex and me.

"Do you have time to go for a ride?" Alex asked me.

"A ride?" I reached for a large plastic cup and put the roses inside. Not bad for a makeshift vase. I'd have to add water later. Nothing would stop me from spending time with Alex, not even roses.

He nodded. "Yep. I took you up on that suggestion and bought another bike to keep down here on the island. If you're okay with storing it for me, I mean. It's in the delivery van."

"She's already been for a ride today," Gina said.

"But I love riding," I argued. "I don't mind going again. Not at all." Especially with Alex.

"But I need her help with the dinner crowd," Babbas added.

Mama slapped him on the arm. "Niko, let them go for a ride."

My father headed behind the counter as a couple of customers entered the shop, and I followed Alex out to his van. He opened the back door and I caught my first glimpse of his bike—a gray cruiser. Basic but nice. He pulled it down, and we talked as he wheeled it around the back of the shop to our storage area. I got my bike out, and minutes later we were on our way.

"Where do you want to go?" I asked.

"To the beach." He pulled up next to me, and we talked as we rode. The time passed quickly. We reached the seawall just as the afternoon crowd started to thin out. Perfect!

"Want to stop?" I asked.

He nodded and pointed to a spot just east of Pleasure Pier. "Here?"

I pulled my bike over and came to a stop, then climbed off. Alex followed suit, and minutes later we descended the steps from the seawall to the sand below.

"I love coming at this time of day," he said. "It's not as hot and you can actually find a patch of sand that's not taken up by tourists."

I pulled off my shoes and held them in my hand as we walked along the water's edge. After a few moments of quiet reflection, I opened up and told Alex about the conversation I'd had with my dad earlier in the day.

"How did he take it?" Alex asked.

I shrugged. "About like I expected. Just acted like he didn't hear me."

"Do you think he'll make amends with the Rossis after some time has passed?"

"I don't know. I hope so."

We stared out at the water. Alex reached for my hand and gave it a squeeze, which caused my heart to flutter. "You'll figure out a way to let your dad know that you're working for the Rossi family. And I'm sure your mom and your brother and sister will eventually face your dad and tell him about their new friendships too. He has to get over it. He doesn't have any choice."

"Oh, he has a choice. Problem is, he usually makes the wrong ones, at least when it comes to relationships."

"Just because he has a history of doing that doesn't mean it has to take down your whole family."

"Hope not."

Alex gazed into my eyes. "Do you mind if I ask a question? It's not really my business. I'm just curious."

"Sure. What is it?"

"Why does your father hate your uncle Alex?"

"Ah." I paused a moment to think about that. "He doesn't hate him. He envies him."

"Why, though?"

"Because Uncle Alex has had a lot of success with his business. Babbas has always struggled to keep up, and I know it has to frustrate him. I think it goes back to when they were kids. My father is the younger brother and always had to work harder to achieve anything. It's always bugged him."

"I guess I get that. You met my sisters. They're always competing. It's tough, feeling like you're not good enough."

"Tell me about it."

He gave me a winsome look. "But if I've learned anything in life, it's this: staying bitter doesn't help you on the road to success. You've got to let that go."

"Mama has tried to tell him that, but he has a hard time letting go. I've never seen anyone so tightfisted. He's . . . well, he's Greek."

"Aren't we all?" Alex grinned. "But our culture or heritage is no excuse for hanging on to things like that, especially when they drag us down."

"I know. And I worry about him. He's already had one episode with his heart. It was just a scare, thank God, but I know the man's blood pressure has to be through the roof. He gets worked up so easily, and he never rests. That's a deadly combination." A shiver ran down my spine as I thought about the possibilities.

Alex laced his fingers through mine. "Did you know that Bella's uncle Laz had a heart attack a while back?"

"No."

"Kind of a similar scenario. He worked himself into a breakdown trying to do the show, manage the shop, and do all the other things he had going on. The doctor made him take a break. Several months off."

I tried to picture Babbas taking a break. Nope. Couldn't do it. "I can't even imagine my father handing over the reins of our new store. You should've seen what it took to get him to trust my older brothers with our store back home."

"So he's jealous of your uncle and will work as long and hard as it takes to prove himself an equal. Sounds kind of like he and Laz are two peas in a pod."

"Yeah, I've said that all along. They have a lot in common."

I seemed to lose him after that as he stared at the waves rolling in and out. After a few moments he spoke, his words sounding weightier than before. "It's the same ocean, if you really stop to think about it."

"What do you mean?" I stared out at the murky, gray waters of the Gulf of Mexico and tried to figure out his words.

"I'm just saying all of the oceans were created by the same God, and they all run together. The Gulf of Mexico turns into the Caribbean, the Caribbean stretches into the Atlantic, the Atlantic wraps on around and connects with the Indian Ocean, which eventually hooks up with the Pacific, and so on. Eventually it all connects." He slipped his arms around my waist.

"Hmm." I leaned back into him, suddenly overwhelmed with the comfort of his nearness and the vastness of God. A girl could get used to this feeling. Very used to it.

"We humans always divide things up. Give them names. But when God looks down on this earth, he probably doesn't see it like that. To him, it's one beautiful ocean." Alex paused and a holy silence rose up between us. "I guess the same is true of people too. We divide ourselves into groups. Cultures. Races. But God looks down on us and says, 'Hey, you're one big happy family.' Kind of like the oceans. We all overlap."

I gave a definitive sigh. "Would you mind telling my father that? To him, everything is divided. And he's not keen on the idea of merging."

"We just need to pray that God opens his heart to the idea. We can't do that, but the Lord can."

In that moment, I totally believed him. God could do it, and I would continue to pray to that end.

Alex held me close, wrapping me in a tender embrace. I felt so comfortable, so peaceful, I could spend the rest of my life in his arms. And when he placed little kisses along my hairline, I leaned in a bit closer. His kisses spread to cover my cheeks, then his lips found mine. There, with the waves crashing nearby, the overwhelming sense of perfection grabbed hold of my heart.

We spent the next few minutes walking hand in hand along the water's edge. Then, just about the time I felt sure my family was calling the police to report me missing, Alex suggested we ride back to the shop. The bike ride home seemed shorter. I wanted to spend every minute I could with Alex, without others looking on.

When we got back to Super-Gyros we parked our bikes outside. The dinner crowd had shown up in force, and I felt sure Babbas would give me grief for being gone so long once I got inside.

If I got inside.

Man, did we have a lot of customers.

Thank goodness my father didn't seem to notice my return. I dove right in, and Alex, in true Alex fashion, worked alongside me, stuffing pitas, mixing sauce, and serving up yummy slices of baklava. Seemed totally natural and comfortable.

Things went smoothly until about an hour later, when a delivery van pulled up to the front of our shop and parked in one of our spots.

"Are we expecting a delivery, Niko?" Mama asked.

"No." He walked to the front door and gazed outside.

The delivery driver opened the back of the truck and started rolling out pallets of food products. Instead of coming our way, however, he headed across the street.

"Wait one minute!" Babbas called out. "Where are you going?"

The driver looked our way. "To Parma John's. Why?"

"Because you're in my designated spot."

"Sorry, mister," the guy said. "I don't have any choice. They're all full over there." He pointed to the parking spots outside of Parma John's, all of which were filled.

"You will move your truck immediately or I will report you." Babbas clenched and then unclenched his right hand, as if ready to take this guy down. Uh-oh.

Really? You have to do this in front of Alex?

Things got even scarier when Laz came out of Parma John's to see what all the hollering was about. I scooted back inside and watched through the window. Babbas hollered something in Greek. Laz hollered back in Italian. Seconds later my father came storming back in the shop, fuming over "those Italians across the street."

Just as he reached for his phone to call Officer O'Reilly, the front door of Super-Gyros opened and three familiar women breezed inside. I recognized them as the trio of women from Splendora.

"Aunt Twila!" Alex came out from behind the counter and embraced his aunt. "You ladies all done with your visit with Bella?"

"Yes. We had the yummiest new pizza." Twila rubbed her plump midsection. "Something called the Venus Flytrap."

"No, Twila." Bonnie Sue rolled her eyes. "It was the Venus de Milo."

"Right, right." Twila shrugged. "Anyway, we left your sisters over there to visit with Bella and Sophia. I'll tell you all about it later."

I hoped she wouldn't mention Parma John's in front of Babbas, who stepped out from behind the counter with Mama at his side. They gave the three glittery guests curious looks, and I made introductions right away.

"Mama, Babbas, this is Alex's aunt Twila." I gestured to her first. "And these are her best friends, Bonnie Sue and Jolene."

Mama gave the ladies a broad smile, but Babbas couldn't seem to close his mouth as he took in the women with their over-the-top blouses and teased hair.

"Oh, Mr. Pappas!" Twila grabbed his hand, her eyes filling with tears. "I can't begin to tell you how much we love your daughter."

"My daughter?"

"Oh yes." She glanced my way but never let go of my father's hand. "For one thing, we heartily approve of the match."

"Match?" My father's already furrowed brow seemed to contort further.

Jolene joined in. "She and Alex are perfect for each other."

I glanced at Alex, who almost dropped the pita he happened to be stuffing.

"I always say the apple doesn't fall far from the tree," Jolene added, her voice now carrying a singsong quality. So you and Cassia's mama must be darling people. I can tell just by looking, and I'm a good judge of character."

At this proclamation, Babbas squared his shoulders. "Well, thank you. But back to this comment about approving of the match—"

"They are a match made in heaven," Bonnie Sue chimed in. "And don't you think they'll make lovely babies together?"

I happened to be taking a sip of a diet soda as she delivered this line and almost choked on it. From across the room, Alex cleared his throat and then shot out of the room. Chicken.

"B-babies?" Mama's eyes widened.

Both of my parents turned to look at Alex, who

had disappeared into the kitchen, the swinging door clanging behind him.

"Well, yes." Jolene giggled. "Lovely little things they'll be, don't you think? Alex with that tall, handsome, boy-next-door look about him, and Cassia with her lovely dark hair and beautiful teeth?"

Beautiful teeth? I'd have to remember to check them in the mirror later tonight. If I lived that long. Judging from the look on Babbas's face, I might not.

"Cassia Bethesda Pappas, is there something you wish to tell me?" My father turned to me, crossing his arms at his chest. "Are you . . ." I almost thought he would say "expecting," but thank God, he did not. Instead, he said, "M-married?"

"Me? Married?" I shook my head. Violently. "No way. I would never do that, Babbas."

"You mean you wouldn't ever get married?" Twila pouted. "That's disappointing news. I felt sure you and Alex would be perfect for one another."

"No, I mean I wouldn't get married without my father's approval," I explained. I offered Babbas what I hoped was a convincing smile. "And I would never ever consider getting married without Babbas giving me away. Never. Ever."

From the look in his eye, he would be willing to give me away at this very second. Toss me out of the family ASAP. "So, you're not married," he said. "But these women are talking about babies. Perhaps there is something else we should be discussing"—he glared at the women and then back at me—"privately."

"No, no!" Twila waved her hand in dismissive fashion. "You've misunderstood, Mr. Pappas. We are simply commenting that Cassia and Alex would make a lovely couple. Someday. And maybe, with your approval and blessing, they might someday marry."

"And make lovely babies." Jolene jabbed my father in the side with her elbow.

I squeezed my eyes shut and tried to avoid the glare. Finally courageous enough to give Babbas a peek, I opened one eye.

Twila gazed at my mother. "I see where Cassia gets her beauty. This one is a Greek goddess." She stepped in Mama's direction and leaned in close. Maybe a little too close.

"Greek goddess?" My mother's cheeks, already rouged beyond what was acceptable, flamed in a rosier-than-usual shade. "Why, thank you. I think."

"Great bone structure," Jolene said. "And so tall and stately, all of you."

"Th-thank you." I hardly knew what else to say.

Twila gave my mother's overly made-up face a close look. "I hope you don't mind my saying so, but you're quite the artist."

"Artist?" My mother looked around the room and then shrugged. Apparently she didn't get it. Twila was clearly referring to Mama's makeup job.

If I had any lingering doubts, they were answered when Jolene pointed a plump index finger at Mama's teal eyelids. "Your use of color is . . . so creative!"

"Oh, you think so?" My mother reached inside her pocket and came out with a small travel-size makeup case. "If you like that one, I've got plenty more. Caribbean turquoise, sunset magenta, purple pizzazz."

The three Splendora Sisters gathered around her like chicks around a mama hen.

"I've always loved a good color palette," Twila said. "But it's what's underneath that counts."

"What's underneath?" Mama looked perplexed.

"Good skin, lovey," Twila explained. "Great pores. I always say a house is only as firm as its foundation."

"Ah." Mama glanced at her appearance in a small compact mirror. "And my foundation is . . . ?"

"Solid as Mount Ararat." Twila took the compact and stared at her own reflection, smacked her lips, then gave it back to Mama. "The perfect canvas for a spectacular masterpiece."

I wasn't quite sure how to take that last comment but decided not to chime in. Mama and the women became fast friends within minutes. This warmed my heart, in part because my mother really needed friends. I went to the kitchen to fetch Alex, who joined us again, relieved to be past the awkwardness from a few moments before. If our relationship survived today's chaos, we were truly destined to be together.

A short time after the ladies arrived, Jasmine and Lily showed up. Jasmine had something on her blouse—red sauce of some sort. When Twila pointed it out, she shrugged.

"What do you expect? We just had the yummiest pizza ever. You know I'm a mess when I eat pizza."

"Pizza?" Babbas came close. "Did someone say pizza?"

Before the girls could answer, I distracted them. "Babbas, Jasmine here is a candy maker. You should see some of the things she's done. Maybe we could sell them here at the shop."

"Do you think?" Jasmine's eyes lit up. "Oh, that would be wonderful. I could do some really fun molds. What do you think? The Parthenon? Greek statues? Ooh, it would be so much fun." She looked at my father. "I work in chocolates. Sometimes caramel and hard candy, but mostly chocolates. Do you like truffles?"

Minutes later we were gathered around Darian's laptop looking at pictures from Jasmine's Facebook page.

"Do you share the recipes?" Mama asked. "I'd love to learn."

"Never!" Jasmine laughed. "You're asking for top-secret information."

"She won't even tell me." Lily rolled her eyes. "Not that I'm really interested in candy making."

"Well, I am." Mama practically drooled as she looked over the photos on the screen. "Man, this is making me hungry."

As she flipped through the pictures, I found myself growing hungrier by the moment. Yum. This girl didn't just make candy, she created masterpieces. I watched in awe as photos of dozens of themed candies rolled by on the screen. Baby shower goodies, birthday sweets, Valentine's treats, but most of all, wedding-themed candies. Gifts for brides to give their bridesmaids, favors for wedding guests—on and on the goodies went.

My favorites were the bride and groom cameos, perfectly defined in white and dark chocolate. Then again, the chocolate roses really took my breath away. So did the sea salt caramels, the chocolate and pecan turtles, and the chocolate seashells with their various colors. In the end, though, a wedding cake composed entirely of chocolate candies won my heart. I'd love to have that at my own wedding. Someday.

By the time we finished looking at the photos, I was practically drooling too.

"Want a sample?" Jasmine whispered. "I take some with me wherever I go."

"Are you serious?"

She opened her large purse and came out with a bag of sweets. Babbas's eyes bugged out of his head as she laid out the goods on the counter. It all looked so tempting, but I hated to eat something she'd probably spent hours making.

That didn't stop me, however. I nibbled one of the chocolate cameos first, then a turtle. Oh, yum.

Babbas loved the peppermint-flavored chocolates and decided to repay Jasmine's kindness by offering her a tray of baklava to take home to her family.

When the chocolates were gone, the conversation really took off. Eva and I served up samples of our food to our new guests at no charge—Babbas insisted. They sat at the table nearest the counter and gabbed with Mama at length. The time passed quickly, the sound of laughter ringing out across the shop all the while. I couldn't remember when I'd ever had a better time.

Several times I looked at Alex, who gave me a wink. My heart fluttered whenever our eyes met. If life got any better, I might just have to throw a party. Then again, we were already having one, weren't we? Yes, with the ladies now fully engrossed in a song—one with three-part harmony—we even had entertainment at our little soiree.

Babbas, never one to be outdone, decided the Pappas family singers needed to show off the new jingle. As much as I hated to do it, I led my siblings and parents through the song for our guests, even clapping at the end.

Twila proclaimed it to be the best she'd ever heard.

That was when an idea hit me. I glanced at Alex. "There's your answer, Alex. You need a jingle for your family's company? These ladies are perfect to sing it."

Apparently that line opened up a whole new discussion. Twenty minutes later the three ladies had not only written the perfect little song for Rigas Roses, but they'd developed harmonies and a great tagline to go along with it.

"How do you do that?" Mama asked.

"Oh, it's just a gift, honey." Twila giggled, then she turned her attention to me. She reached for my hand and I gave it to her, not quite ready for the hearty squeeze that followed. "In all the excitement of the day, I keep forgetting to tell you how thrilled I was to hear the news."

"News? About Alex naming the new roses after me?"

"Oh, well, that too, but I'm talking about the pizza!"

At this, you could've heard a pin drop.

Twila continued to squeeze my hand, her face beaming. "Bella told me that Laz named his new Greek pizza after you! That Venus Flytrap one."

She'd no sooner spoken these words than my father stopped working behind the counter and stared at me. I heard the Munchkins—no, the evil monkeys—singing in my head, their piercing voices nearly drowning out Twila's next words.

"We had several pieces of that yummy deliciousness less than an hour ago, and it's perfect, just like you!" Twila let out a girlish sigh and released her hold on my hand. "Laz said your recipe was the best thing that's ever happened to Parma John's, and I'm inclined to agree."

"Easy on the figure too." Bonnie Sue placed her fists on her ample hips. "I like that."

"Just had a large slice," Jasmine said. "So yummy."

Babbas took a step from behind the counter and cleared his throat, his presence quietly menacing. The evil monkeys increased their song. *Oh-EE-oh. Oh-OH-oh.*

Twila looked back and forth between my parents and me. "I think it's just the sweetest thing, your two families getting along so well. Brotherly love does the heart good. God bless you all."

"Oh my, yes," Jolene agreed. "Other restaurants might compete, so it pleases the Lord's heart to see folks being neighborly." She turned and faced my mother. "And I just think it's the sweetest thing in the world that you and Imelda

275

are so friendly and all. She cherishes your little notes, says they always brighten her day."

Mama froze in her tracks. Behind me, I heard Eva make a mad dash out of the room. No doubt she figured she'd be next. Darian eased his way into the kitchen. Coward.

Babbas didn't say a word. Not a word. Neither did Mama, though her eyes now bugged out of her head. No doubt my father would wait to kill us until after the guests left. Keeping up appearances and all that. With our secrets now told, I could sense the man behind the curtain controlling levers that would send all of us to a place we didn't care to go.

If I could find a hot air balloon right about now, I'd climb aboard and sail away—far, far away.

20

For Me and My Gal

You might be Greek if you show up late for
most of your appointments but would
never consider being late for a day with
the guy (or girl) of your dreams.

From the moment the Splendora Sisters left
Super-Gyros on Saturday evening, I braced
myself for the inevitable. At any moment Babbas
would blow like a top. The rest of us tiptoed
around him all night, but he never said a word.
Not a word. Of course, his tight expression spoke
volumes, but at least those volumes were silent.

Poor Mama. She moved like a robot, scurrying
around the apartment, cleaning everything in
sight. When Babbas fell asleep in the recliner, she
left him there. Probably a wise move on her part.

Sunday we all went to church, as usual. No
longer concerned that my father would discover
my friendship with Scarlet, I visited with her
after the service while my parents chatted with
her father. Everything felt so . . . normal.
Miraculously normal.

The miracles continued into Monday morning,
but they didn't involve my father. No, this time

they involved my love life and my career.

Now, I'd seen a lot of romance movies over the years. I'd dreamed of the perfect guy a thousand times. Even thought I'd found him a time or two back in Santa Cruz. But never once did I picture my love life getting a jump start in the walk-in refrigerator at a florist shop just days after my father found out I'd betrayed him.

It happened Monday morning, a couple of hours after I arrived at the florist shop. Alex came by to make his delivery and asked me to hold the door of the walk-in refrigerator while he stepped inside with the buckets. When he lost his hold on one of them, I ran to his side to catch it. As I did so, the door closed behind me.

I didn't really give it much thought for a minute or two. After all, we were pretty busy picking up flowers from the floor and putting them back into the bucket.

Only when I tried to open the door and found it sealed shut did I start to wonder if we might have a problem. Seconds later a chill set in and I started shivering.

Alex took a couple of hesitant steps in my direction and opened his arms in invitation. "C'mon. Don't worry. I'll warm you up."

Before I could think of a way to say, "Good Greek girls don't cuddle," he'd swept me into his arms and held me close.

"Feeling better now, little missy?"

"Mm-hmm." I nodded and felt myself start to warm up.

He kissed the top of my head, and this time the shivers that ran down my back were for a completely different reason. By the time his lips reached mine, I didn't care about the temperature anymore.

Who says it's cold in here?

After several more kisses, Alex took a little step back. "Don't want to get too carried away," he said, then winked.

I would've winked back, but my eyelashes were starting to ice over. The shivering started again, and Alex pulled me close once more. "Don't worry," he said. "I get locked in here at least once a week. But it's never really locked. The seal around the door is just tight."

"I got stuck in our fridge in Santa Cruz once," I said. "But my brothers were just playing a trick on me. They were blocking the door from the outside."

"Boys." He laughed. "Can't live with 'em, can't live without 'em."

"Not so sure about that last part." I chuckled and then gave him a little kiss on the cheek. "If you ever met my older brothers you'd know what I mean." No sooner were the words spoken than I regretted them. "Shouldn't have said that. Both of my older brothers are still in Santa Cruz, running the restaurant there. I miss them."

"In spite of their pranks?" he asked.

I nodded and another shiver wriggled over me.

Fortunately—or unfortunately, depending on how you looked at it—Marcella opened the door just a few seconds later. Her mouth rounded into a perfect O as she took in the sight of the two of us wrapped in a tight embrace. "Want me to close the door?" she asked and then giggled.

"N-no." My teeth chattered as I shot out of Alex's arms and into the warmth of the shop. "I j-j-just need to w-w-warm up." I sprinted to the front door of the shop and swung it open, grateful for the heat streaming down on me as I stood in direct sunlight. Through the plate-glass window I caught a glimpse of Alex chatting with Marcella, who now stood behind the register. He must've said something to make her laugh, because she doubled over.

A few seconds later, he joined me outside. "You okay out here?"

"Yep. Just warming up." *And trying to get over the embarrassment of being caught in your arms.*

"Oh, I don't know. I thought things were warming up nicely in there." He gave me a little nudge with his elbow, and I nearly lost my balance.

"I should probably get back inside. Marcella's going to wonder why she's paying me."

When I arrived back inside, Marcella was on

the phone. Turned out the call was for me. Bella. I took it with some degree of hesitation, wondering if my father had done something to set off alarm bells on the Greek/Italian end of the Strand.

"Hey, Cassia." Bella's happy-go-lucky voice sounded as normal and chipper as ever. "Just wanted to run something by you."

"Oh?"

"Yep. Can you swing by Club Wed tomorrow afternoon for a meeting? I've already cleared it with Marcella. She's fine with giving you some time off."

"Sure, but . . . a meeting? What for?"

"I've got plans, and they involve you, Cassia."

"Me?" This certainly got my attention.

"Yes. I've set up a new vendors' area in the front of the wedding facility. You can ask Marcella about it. Some of Gabi's best dresses are hanging there. A couple of sample cakes from Scarlet—dummies, of course. And photographs that Hannah and her husband Drew have taken. They're all on my preferred vendors list. I recommend these people to my incoming clients."

"I heard about it. Sounds great."

"Thanks. I'm grateful to Gabi's fiancé for helping spread the word in *Texas Bride*."

"No way." The local vendors were all featured in a major magazine? Lucky ducks.

"I've been promoting Marcella and the flower

shop all along, but now it's time to add you to the list."

"Me?"

"Yep. Now that you're going to be taking Marcella's place at the shop, it only makes sense. But I'll need a good photo of you, one where you're surrounded by flowers. Do you have one like that?"

"No—wait. Taking her place at the shop?" Had Marcella told Bella that she'd offered to sell me the business? I hadn't agreed. Couldn't possibly.

Bella didn't answer my question. She seemed far too preoccupied planning my future. "Just c'mon by tomorrow afternoon if you can, okay? I'll get Hannah to stop by to grab some photos of you out by the gazebo. We've got some beautiful azaleas blooming out there."

She'd lost me back at the moment when she said I'd be taking Marcella's place. Surely she'd misunderstood something I'd said. Or maybe something Marcella had said. Yes, that was it. Just a big misunderstanding.

Still, how could I in good conscience show up for a photo shoot like the one she continued to describe? I needed to talk to Marcella, to get her perspective on all this. She could straighten things out with Bella. We needed to move quickly, though, what with Hannah agreeing to meet me at Club Wed tomorrow afternoon at three to take the photos. Man.

On the other hand, what would it hurt to have a few photos taken with some lovely flowers? Even if they didn't land in the vendors' area at Club Wed, they might come in handy at the shop someday. I reluctantly agreed to meet the ladies at Club Wed.

We ended the call a few minutes later, and I toyed with the idea of talking to Marcella about what Bella had said. Only one problem—with so many customers coming and going, I didn't find an opportunity to do so.

About half an hour later, Alex finished up his work and joined me behind the counter. "You hungry?" he asked.

I shrugged. "Hadn't thought about it."

"It's almost your lunch break."

"Lunch break? This early?"

"It's not early. It's ten till twelve. Besides, I know of this great little Greek place just a few blocks down. Great gyros. Family atmosphere. I really think you're gonna like it there."

"Ha. Well, as long as you don't take me back to Parma John's, I guess we're okay. Last time I nearly risked my inheritance sneaking into that place."

"Yeah, I keep forgetting to ask how your dad reacted after I left the other night. Did he blow like a top?"

"Weirdly, no. He acted perfectly normal . . . only quieter. Totally bizarre."

"Wow. Maybe God's working on him."

"Or maybe . . ." I shivered. "Maybe he's like a volcano, just waiting to blow."

This seemed to concern Alex. "Do you think it's worth the risk going back there for lunch then? I'm dying for a gyro, but not if it's going to be awkward for you."

I was dying for a hero too, but didn't say so out loud. Besides, it looked as if one had already come my way, one intent on riding the trolley from the florist shop to my family's restaurant. Go figure. This guy just couldn't seem to get enough of that trolley, could he?

Less than five minutes later we sat side by side on the trolley. Alex couldn't stop talking about the new Super-Gyros sign on the side of it. I still couldn't stop shivering in spite of the warm air outside. Alex slipped his arm over my shoulder and I nestled close. Very close.

"So, tell me more about that conversation I sort of overheard a while back," Alex said. "About roses."

"About roses?"

"Yeah, the one about waiting for the rose to open up." The edges of his lips curled up in a delicious smile.

"Oh, *that* conversation." I bit my lip and pondered what I would say. "A lot of work goes into getting a rose—fertilizing, growing, pruning, budding, blossoming." I stopped and shrugged. "I have no idea why I'm telling you all of this. Roses are your business. I've never even grown one myself."

"You should try it sometime. You're right, it's a process."

"Well, what you overheard me saying to Marcella is that I look at love the same way. It's a process. One minute God is doing a work in your heart, planting seeds of hope that there will one day be a blossom. The next day he's tilling the soil. Then relationships begin to grow, like the rosebud coming to life on the vine. And then one day—when the timing is just right—that bud blooms."

"And that's how love is?" His eyes sparkled with mischief.

"I'm guessing. I've never actually . . . well . . . been in love before." A lengthy pause followed and my heart skipped a beat as the reality of how I felt about him kicked in.

"I see." He gave me a pensive look. "Never . . . ever?"

"I, um, well . . ." My face heated up. "Anyway, I guess what I'm saying is that it will be worth waiting for. In the end, that rose is gorgeous. You never think about how long it took to get it to that point, you only see it for what it is in the moment." The trolley bell rang as it jolted to a stop. I did my best not to tumble out of the seat.

"I like the way you think." Alex leaned over

and gave me a little kiss on the cheek, then stood and led the way up the aisle as if nothing had happened.

Had that really just happened? Here? On the trolley? In the middle of the afternoon?

I followed behind him to the door. Alex got off the trolley and extended both his hands. I reached to take one of them, but he swept his hands around my waist and lifted me to the ground. A little squeal came out—I couldn't help it.

"Catch you off guard?" he asked.

"A little." My breath caught in my throat, but I finally managed to get hold of my senses. Not that Alex had released his hold on me. Nope.

I continued to gaze into his beautiful brown eyes. Crazy how the expression I found there made me want to throw my arms around his neck and give him a kiss square on the mouth.

I felt my face grow hot at the very idea. Seriously? Kiss him? Here on the Strand? In front of my father's place of business? With a banner advertising the new meatball sandwich waving in the breeze?

I had the strangest feeling Alex was thinking the same thing, if one could judge such things by the twinkle in his eyes. Well, not the part about the meatball sandwich, but the kissing in front of my family part.

My heart slowed its pace, but neither of us moved. Or spoke. We stood like department store mannequins in the middle of the road, both of us grinning.

Well, until Eva hollered at us from the Greek side of the street. "You two gonna stand there all day and get run over by the next trolley? I'm no good at CPR."

"No CPR necessary." Alex released his hold on my waist as he hollered back his response.

Easy for him to say. I could've used a little intervention right about now. Maybe some oxygen to help steady my breathing, at the very least.

I tagged along on his heels into my family's shop, willing my heart to stop the strange little dance it had begun seconds earlier.

The next half hour was spent in giddy delight as I took Alex behind the counter at Super-Gyros and put him to work making his own gyro. Turned out he was pretty good at it. So good, in fact, that Babbas—who hadn't spoken a word to me since the Splendora Sisters ratted me out—offered him a job. Without pay, of course.

"There you go," I whispered in his ear. "You're really one of the family now. Working for no pay is the highest form of flattery around here."

Alex laughed, then ate his sandwich and offered to help with the lunch crowd, which was larger than usual now that school had let out for the summer. Babbas asked him to make a gyro for an incoming customer. He did an admirable job.

"Not bad, not bad," Mama said and then gave

me a little wink. "I think this one's a keeper, Cassia."

Yes, he was a keeper, all right. I thought back to our conversation on the trolley. Strange sensations drizzled over me as I reflected on what we'd both said. Something was blooming, for sure. No denying the obvious anymore.

A quick glance at the clock reminded me that I needed to get back to the flower shop. Babbas didn't even seem to mind. He was so thrilled with Alex's help that he had nothing but flattering words to say. Go figure. Either the man had forgotten what the Splendora ladies had told him, or God had truly worked a miracle of biblical proportions. I'd take it, either way.

After saying goodbye to the family, Alex took my hand and we headed to the corner to wait on the trolley. Once on board he led the way, not to a seat, but to the platform in the back. We stood in silence waiting for the trolley to start moving. Alex slipped his arm around my waist and drew me close. I turned to face him, my heart once again doing that crazy *clang, clang, clang* thing.

Alex brushed his index finger along my cheek to push a loose hair out of my face, and I found myself leaning into his palm. He left his hand resting against my skin and drew me even closer. My eyes fluttered closed and I leaned into him.

What happened next would've made an excellent scene in a Judy Garland movie, though Alex made a hunkier hero than any Hollywood hottie. He tilted my face upward and I opened my eyes, heart nearly dancing.

Gazing up at him, I noticed the joy in those gorgeous eyes of his. They gave me the courage to do what I'd been dying to do for hours. With no one around to tell me otherwise, I flung both arms around the boy's neck and gave him a kiss that nearly sent both of us tumbling off the trolley platform and onto the street below.

Bliss! Joy!

The sound of Gina's voice rang out, and I realized she was watching us from the sidewalk. "They're kissing!" she hollered out with such enthusiasm that the patrons at both Parma John's and Super-Gyros looked our way.

I felt my face grow hot and wanted to hide. Judging from the way Alex tipped me backwards and planted a big one on me, he had a completely different plan for dealing with the onlookers.

By the time I stood upright, a crowd had gathered around the back of the trolley from both sides of the street. Babbas and Mama. Bella and Aunt Rosa. They all watched us as the clanging of the trolley bells rang out.

"Something you two want to tell us?" Mama asked after a moment.

Alex nodded. "Yes. Yes, actually, there is."

I looked at him, wondering what he would come up with. The trolley started moving and he held me close to keep me from falling. He made a broad, sweeping gesture and hollered, "Rigas Roses are in bloom, people!"

I knew what he was implying. Reflecting back on our earlier conversation, I had to conclude his little statement meant more than the obvious. Not that I had time to think about it. The trolley zipped along, my family and friends growing farther and farther away.

I giggled before I could control myself. Alex put his arms around my waist. Then, face-to-face, with half the population of Galveston looking on as we buzzed down the Strand, he gave me another kiss worthy of a moment on the big screen.

21

Get Happy!

You might be Greek if you think that everyone who is in the selling business is a
crook and everything is always overpriced.

Babbas's behavior over the next several hours
was strange, to say the least. We could hardly get
the man to say a word, good or bad. I had a feeling
something big was brewing in that mind of his,
and I half expected him to blow at any moment. I
got my answer on Tuesday morning, when he
placed a written manifesto on the door leading
from our apartment down to the shop. I paused to
read it and got a sick feeling in my stomach.

"What is it?" Eva whispered as she took a step
closer to try to read it.

"Apparently it's an ultimatum for all Pappas
family members. We're not allowed to talk to,
socialize with, or share a meal with anyone who is
connected to the Rossi family."

"Puh-leeze." Eva ran her finger along the words
of the manifesto and then slapped herself on the
head. "Well, that takes the cake." She began to
rant about how she would go back to California
before she would ever submit to anything that

ridiculous, but I found myself distracted, thinking about cake. If we couldn't get Babbas calmed down, I'd never get to taste Scarlet's Italian cream cake.

Darian looked wounded as he read our father's stern words, but the person who seemed to take this manifesto the hardest was Mama. She took one look at the piece of paper and erupted in tears, then headed downstairs to bake. I had a feeling some pretty awesome baklava would come out of her angst.

The timing of the manifesto was particularly awkward for me, what with the fact that I needed to be at Club Wed for my photo shoot in a few hours. If Babbas found out, there would be a huge price to pay. Still, someone in the family needed to stand up to him.

Listening to Judy croon "Forget your troubles, c'mon get happy" all the way from the Strand to Broadway soothed my troubled nerves. That, coupled with the breeze in my face, turned my attitude around. What was the worst that could happen if Babbas found out I'd gone to Club Wed to meet with Bella? He'd fire me? Cut back my pay? Ask me to move out of the apartment? Fine. I'd figure out a plan. I'd been socking away money from the florist shop, after all. What would be so bad about getting my own place? The more I thought about it, the more hopeful I felt.

By the time I pulled my bike into the driveway

at Club Wed, I'd almost forgotten about my woes. I slowed to a halt and stared at the Rossis' huge Victorian home next door to Club Wed. Beautiful. Who lived in a place like that?

After climbing off the bike, I parked it at the front steps and pulled off my helmet. No doubt my hair looked frightful. Who showed up for a meeting with the island's most important wedding planner looking like the bride of Frankenstein?

Bella didn't seem to notice or care. She greeted me with her little girl on one hip and a cell phone pressed to her ear. After she gestured for me to follow her into Club Wed, I tagged along on her heels, trying to focus on the decor, not her conversation with her mother.

As we walked through the foyer, the strangest sound greeted us. A loud "rat-a-tat-tat" rang out and I stopped in my tracks. The little girl started to cry as the noise continued. Bella pulled the phone away from her ear and shouted, "Enough, Guido!"

I realized the noise was coming from a colorful parrot perched on an indoor tree to my left. The rowdy creature let out a shriek and then hollered, "Go to the mattresses!" The child's wails became ear-piercing at this point.

Bella ended her call, turned my way, and said, "Welcome to my world."

Wow. And I'd looked down at her from my window, thinking she had such an easy, ideal life. Maybe we all had our problems.

"Before we go into my office, I want you to see our vendors' area—Vendors Square." Bella took me into a small room to the left of the foyer, where I saw some terrific displays for Hannah's photography studio, Scarlet's bakery, and Gabi's dress designs.

"Guess who's next!" Bella said. She shifted her daughter to the other hip and tried to soothe her. "You do so many interesting floral designs that I've never seen before. Do you have a portfolio?"

"I usually take pictures of the bouquets as I make them. They're on my phone."

"That's fine. Let's combine them into a portfolio book. People will love looking through it."

"Sounds great." I looked around Vendors Square, drawn in by everything I saw.

"Hannah will be here soon to take your pictures," Bella said, "but I'd like to meet with all of you for a few minutes first to share some news."

We didn't have time to carry the discussion any further because the other ladies arrived. Bella passed her daughter off to Aunt Rosa, who'd appeared from the house next door, and we went into Bella's office to meet. She gestured for us to sit, and I took the chair nearest her desk.

Bella sat behind the desk, looking more official now that she'd handed off her daughter. "Two things I want to let you know before we start the photo shoot. First, I'm opening a wedding facility in Splendora."

"No way." Hannah put her hands to her mouth, clearly stunned.

Scarlet clasped her hands together. "I knew it!"

"You've talked about it for ages," Hannah said. "You're really going to do it?"

"Yep." Bella nodded. "It makes perfect sense. I'm calling it Town and Country Chapel—the best of city luxury with the quaint feel of country living."

"Perfect!" Hannah clapped her hands. "I love the idea."

"The longer I'm in this business, the more the Lord seems to be linking me to Splendora. It's D.J.'s hometown. His parents still have a place up there. Twila, Jolene, and Bonnie Sue are there. D.J.'s uncle Donny. Even Scarlet's aunt Willy lives up there, and you guys know she's the best baker in the state. She'll be perfect to help out."

Scarlet cleared her throat.

"Best baker in the state next to you, Scarlet, of course." Bella chuckled.

"Nah, my aunt's light-years better than I am." Scarlet laughed. "I'm not offended."

"Well, you get my point." Bella nodded. "We've got some great connections up there, and they will give the place a professional feel."

Gabi looked a little concerned. "But they're not

wedding coordinators. You'll need someone to manage the place, right?"

"Wait a minute." Scarlet paled. "Is that what you're getting at, Bella? Please tell me you're not moving away. I don't think I could handle that."

"No." With a wave of her hand Bella seemed to dismiss that idea. "That's the fun part. I've been thinking of asking someone else—actually, a couple of someones—to work for me. They could run the new facility."

"Who?" Scarlet asked. "Oh, let me guess . . . Twila and one of the other ladies?"

"No." Bella laughed. "I can't even imagine what they would do with the place. They'll help me grow the business, I'm sure. They're so well known and loved by their community." Her eyes sparkled. "But that's not who I had in mind to run it. I was thinking of Alex's sisters, Lily and Jasmine."

"Oh, Bella." I could hardly catch my breath. "That's an awesome idea. Does Alex know you're thinking about this?"

"No. I haven't told him yet, but I think he'll like the idea," she said. "I like it too, but I want to pray about it before asking the twins. I'm not a hundred percent sure how they'll do working together since they're nothing alike. On the other hand, they're young and ambitious, and I know they could potentially bring in great clients."

"Would they ever!" I agreed.

"You might not know this, but Lily has a business degree," Bella said. "She's been dying to start her own company, so this will be perfect. She's so graceful and sweet."

Hmm. I'd only seen her in mad-at-my-sister mode, so I couldn't really comment on the sweet part. But she had come off as graceful for sure. And the business degree was definitely a plus.

"This will be great for Alex's family too," Bella added. "They'll have business around the clock at the new wedding facility. And we can have a great vendors' area up there too."

"Speaking of which, have you tasted Jasmine's candies?" I asked. "She's got a whole line of wedding-themed chocolates. They're so good."

"Oh yes." Bella rubbed her stomach. "The last time I went to Splendora she gave me a gift basket as a thank-you for recommending her to one of my clients. She will definitely keep on making her candies."

"Thank goodness." I could practically taste them all now.

"She's a big wedding fan, trust me." Bella jotted down a note, then looked back at us. "Speaking of which, I need to remember to set up a vendors' area for Jasmine's candies here at Club Wed. That's the beauty of this new arrangement. We'll all be working together." She gestured to each of us. "And I do mean all of us. I truly believe

God has brought us together. We'll just keep on growing, adding more wedding-themed businesses that brides have to choose from, no matter where they live in the great state of Texas."

Great state of Texas. For the first time I could say those words and mean them. I'd finally fallen for more than the flowers—I'd tripped head over heels into friendships and a relationship with the greatest Greek cowboy ever to yee-haw his way into my heart.

Bella rose and smoothed her blouse. "Now, one last thing before we head outside to take Cassia's pictures. I wanted to tell you that I've had an idea, one I think you're going to like. All of you, I mean. I talked to Brock Benson a few days back. You all know he's a good friend of ours."

"Wait—*Brock Benson?*" I shook my head. "You know him?"

Bella appeared stunned at my reaction. "Sure. He's been here several times over the past few years. I figured you knew about our connection to him. Didn't Athena tell you?"

"You know Athena too?" Was I hearing things? Bella knew Brock Benson? And my cousin? Crazy! Were these Rossis tied to everyone?

"Well, I know *of* her," she said with a nod. "Brock told me all about her the last time he came to town. He loves his gig on *Stars Collide.* I think it's calmed him down to do a weekly show instead of movie after movie. And that's where he met his wife, so his ties to the show are pretty strong."

"Yeah. I just didn't realize that you knew all of this . . . and him." I shook my head, still perplexed.

"The writing is stellar," Bella added. "Brock says Athena's the best writer he's ever worked with. Sharp as a tack. Guess he should know, right? He's done a ton of movies and TV shows now."

"Right."

At this point the other ladies in the room started sharing stories about their favorite Brock Benson movies, finally agreeing that his pirate movies were their all-time faves.

Bella finally got us to calm down by clearing her throat. "Anyway, Brock sings Athena's praises all the time. That's the point." She gazed at me. "And I'm going to assume that you know Brock too. Through Athena, I mean?"

"I don't really know him personally," I said. "I just feel like I do because of all of Athena's stories. He seems like a great guy. Babbas has been talking about getting him to come to the island to make a commercial for our shop."

"Funny you should say that. My idea was . . . similar." The edges of Bella's lips curled up in a smile. "I think if I approach this just right, I might have the perfect plan for all of us."

She went on to lay out the most amazing idea I'd heard in ages. It seemed almost too good to be true. By the time she reached the end of her plan, I felt my spirits lift. If we pulled this off— if Bella and Athena, working together, could really get Brock to come to Galveston and do us this one teensy-tiny favor—it would not only bring an end to the feud between the Pappas and Rossi families, it might just bring in tourists to all of the shops on Galveston Island.

I whispered up a prayer of thanks for a friend with such a creative imagination.

"Is it okay if I tell my father what you're thinking?" I asked. "I really think it would go a long way in helping mend his relationship with your uncle Laz."

Bella's nose wrinkled. "Hmm. Well, before you do that, let me make a call and ask Brock. I don't want to make promises until we know for sure he'll come."

And so she did. Just like that, she picked up her phone, punched in a number, and chatted with Brock Benson like they were old friends.

Okay, they were old friends, but she talked about everything from the weather to his role in *Stars Collide* to his life as a new dad. From there, the conversation shifted to her idea. I could tell from the smile on her face that he liked it. Obviously very much, judging from the pitch of her voice as the conversation continued.

By the time she ended the call, I knew we had a winner.

"He's on board," Bella said. "It's going to be great. And best of all, Athena is already on her way down to the island, so he said he'll fly down next week. He's going to bring his wife with him, so you'll get to meet her too."

Scarlet, Gabi, and Hannah all chimed in, talking over one another. Seemed all of them were tickled by this news. Then again, who wouldn't be? Brock's willingness to help us out was great news for everyone in attendance.

"So it's okay to tell my family?" I asked.

"Yep. Soon as Hannah snags a few shots of you in the gazebo, I'll head to Parma John's to let Uncle Laz know. He's going to be tickled pink." She looked at me intently. "This is going to solve the problem, Cassia. I know it will. And it won't just help the two restaurants, it's going to help all of us."

My heart wanted to burst into song. In fact, it did. As we headed back to the gazebo, as Hannah snapped photos right and left, I just couldn't stop smiling.

Later, as I rode my bike back to the restaurant, I sang with great gusto, "Forget your troubles, c'mon get happy!" This time I really meant those words. With Brock Benson on our side, we really could get happy. Oh, and what joyous news about the new facility in Splendora! Alex's sisters would be blissful if Bella asked them to co-manage it.

Alex.

I sighed with pure delight as I replayed our kissing scene from yesterday, the one on the back of the trolley. At that moment my phone changed songs and—wonder of wonders!—"The Trolley Song" came on. Coincidence or a sign from above? Didn't matter. It kept me singing all the way up the boulevard.

When I arrived at Super-Gyros, I didn't bother parking my bike out back. No time for that. I left it at the front door, ready to race inside and tell my father the good news about Brock.

It totally threw me when I found the Closed sign on the front door. I tried to push the door open, but someone had locked it from the inside. After I knocked, Darian unlocked it and gestured for me to come inside.

I found the shop strangely quiet. My father sat behind the counter looking glum. Beside him, all of my siblings sat in a row, somber looks across their faces. At once my heart went to my throat. Something terrible had happened.

I took several cautious steps toward Babbas, a lump growing in my throat. "Babbas? Did someone . . . die?" I looked around for Yia Yia but couldn't find her. My heart plummeted to my toes.

"No, Cassia." He rubbed his brow with his fingertips. "It's your mother."

"Mama?" I began to shake all over. Something had happened to Mama?

Babbas reached for a dish towel and mopped his sweaty brow. "She . . . she . . ." He looked at Eva. "You tell her, Eva."

My sister released a slow breath and then looked at me. "She ran away from home."

"W-what?" I could hardly believe my ears. "Is this a joke?"

"No joke." Eva shook her head. "She's gone. She's been gone for hours."

"She left a note." Babbas handed me a piece of paper filled top to bottom with Mama's beautiful handwriting.

I read it silently, taking in Mama's emotion. She had snapped, all right. And judging from this letter, she didn't plan to come back anytime soon.

"Oh, Babbas. She's just reacting to your manifesto this morning. She'll be back."

"That manifesto . . ." He shook his head. "I wrote it in anger. But I will win her back. If I can find her."

"No idea where she's gone?"

"I just pray she hasn't gone back to California." His eyes misted over. "If she's left me to go back home—"

The front bell jangled, interrupting him. "Did someone say California?" a familiar voice rang out.

I turned at once, my heart sailing to my throat

303

as I laid eyes on my cousin Athena and her husband Stephen.

Oh. Help.

Athena rushed my way, all smiles, and threw her arms around my neck. "It's so good to see all of you!" she squealed.

Yikes. Now what?

Athena and Stephen greeted the various family members one after another. Finally, when they'd made the rounds, Athena slid her Gucci purse off her shoulder, laid it on the table, and asked the question I'd secretly hoped to avoid.

"Where in the world is Aunt Helena? I've been dying to see her!"

22

After You've Gone

You might be Greek if your family
inheritance includes olive trees.

Athena looked around the shop, then glanced
my way. "I can't wait to hug Aunt Helena's neck!
And to have a piece of her baklava." She put her
finger to her lips and then giggled. "Don't ever
tell my mama I said this, but Aunt Helena's
baklava is so much better."

Babbas squared his shoulders at this exciting
news. Still, how could we broach the subject of
Mama's absence when we didn't even know
where she was?

My father cleared his throat and shifted his
position. "Your aunt Helena is out for a while," he
said after a moment or two. "But she'll be back."

We hope.

Athena smoothed the wrinkles on her trousers.
"That's a bummer. I wanted to see her." She gave
me a little wink. "But a piece of her baklava will
tide me over until I do."

"I've got to taste this to believe it," Stephen
said. "Athena's been singing her aunt's praises all
the way from L.A. to Texas." He looked around

our shop and nodded. "This is a nice location, Mr. Pappas. You've done a great job with it."

Babbas stood even taller at this proclamation.

"Let's start with the baklava," Athena said. "Then you can give us a tour."

Eva went into the kitchen and came back with a large tray of baklava. Athena and Stephen tore into it like they might never get to eat again. Before long their eyes were rolling in delight.

"See?" Athena licked her sticky fingers as she looked at her husband. "Didn't I tell you?"

"Yeah." He took another bite, then spoke around it. "I promise not to tell your parents, but you were right."

Babbas led the way, showing them around the new shop. Athena oohed and aahed at all of the right times, which brought a smile—first one I'd seen in ages—to my father's face. I led her up to our little apartment and cringed as I tried to envision what it looked like through her eyes. Stephen followed on our heels, chatting easily with Darian and Filip.

"Oh, it's charming!" Athena glanced around the living room and then walked over to the sofa to sit down. "Your mama has done a nice job making it look . . . homey."

That was one way to put it. I couldn't help but think that Mama would flip if she knew that Athena was here when the room hadn't been adequately tidied up.

We headed back down to the shop a few minutes later, and Babbas offered them food.

Athena shook her head and reached for her purse. "No Greek food for us this evening, Uncle Niko. Brock made us promise we would try something else instead."

"Oh?" Babbas looked confused.

"Yes." Her eyes sparkled with mischief. "Brock said we have to start our vacation on Galveston Island with a visit to Parma John's pizzeria. He made me promise to have the Mambo Italiano special."

Oh. No.

Babbas's smile faded, but to his credit, he didn't say a word. Not a word.

Athena looped her arm through mine. "We have so much catching up to do! You have to come with us."

"Oh, I, uh—"

"You and Bella are friends, right?" Athena said. "I heard you practically work together."

I swallowed hard and nodded. To my right, Babbas cleared his throat. Hopefully he wasn't gearing up for a tirade.

"I had a call from Brock just a few minutes ago." Athena's face beamed with obvious delight. "He told me all about the new commercial idea that Bella came up with. It sounds wonderful, and I'm sure it's going to bring in business!"

Babbas's face lit into a smile. "Brock is going

to do the commercial? You've arranged it?"

"Yes." I nodded. "That's what I was just about to tell you when Athena got here. But Babbas, *Bella* is the one who arranged it. Not me and not Athena."

"Bella . . . Rossi?" My father's eyes narrowed to slits. "She arranged for Brock to film a commercial for Super-Gyros?"

"Sort of." I couldn't give him all the particulars. It was clear from the look on Athena's face that she knew the real story, but she didn't spill the beans, thank goodness.

"Brock is coming next week to film a commercial, yes," Athena said. "But in the meantime, he insisted I go to Parma John's." She gave my father a knowing look. "It's part of the deal, Uncle Niko. We play nice with the neighbors."

My father grunted.

I was pretty sure that Mama—if we ever found her again—would burst into song at all of this.

"Now, who's coming with me?" Athena looked around the room.

Eva, Darian, Filip, and Gina all looked terrified . . . but intrigued.

"C-can we go?" Filip looked at Babbas and then at me.

"I'm going." Eva pulled off her apron. "You're going." She pointed at Darian. "We're all going."

"But pizza is the devil's food." A tear slipped down little Gina's cheek. "I can't eat the devil's food until Babbas is dead in the ground!"

"The devil's food?" Athena knelt down in front of her. "No, honey. Angels' food is more like it! Pizza is yummy, gooey goodness on a plate." She took my little sister's hand as she rose. "We don't need to wait until anyone dies to eat it. We're all going to have some right now!"

Babbas grunted again.

"And we're going to send a text to Brock from Parma John's to let him know we're there. With a picture attached!" Athena went off on a tangent about how she'd better make sure Bella was in the picture. And Uncle Laz. And Aunt Rosa, who—according to Athena—was Brock's all-time favorite Rossi.

My father, God bless him, didn't say a word. I could almost hear the internal wrangling going on in that head of his. If he argued, he would lose Brock Benson. Still, this must be killing him, watching his family march directly into the enemy's camp in his presence. He begged off to the kitchen, muttering all the way.

We stood on the sidewalk in front of Super-Gyros moments later, facing Parma John's. Athena would never know the significance of that first step. I'd tell her sooner or later. With my cousin and her husband leading the way, we marched across the street and into Parma John's, heads held high.

I entered Parma John's to the sound of "Pennies

from Heaven" playing through the sound system. From across the room, Jenna hollered out, "Welcome to Parma John's. Would you like to try our Tuesday special? One large pizza covered in sliced meatballs with four soft drinks for $24.98." She looked up from the register and our eyes met. Her mouth rounded into an O as she took in the whole family.

Apparently seeing the whole Pappas family caused quite a stir among the Rossis. Bella rushed our way, a terrified look in her eyes. "Cassia? Did someone die?"

"Nope."

"D-does your dad know you're all over here?"

"Yep."

"Should we call in extra security?" She released a nervous laugh.

"We brought security along." I pointed to Athena and Bella squealed.

"Oh, I know who you are!" She threw her arms around my cousin's neck and gave her a squeeze. "You're just like Brock described you." She looked back and forth between Athena and me. "Wow, you two could be twins. You look so much alike!"

No way. I'd always considered Athena to be my pretty cousin.

"Are Rosa and Laz here?" Athena looked around the restaurant. "Brock said I have to get to know them. I feel like I already do, like they're members of my own family. We watch *The Italian Kitchen* every week, don't we, Stephen?"

"Yeah." He shrugged. "She makes me watch it."

"I do not. You love that show!" This led to a playful argument between Athena and Stephen, who ended up admitting that he loved the show too.

"Well, I'm sorry, but Rosa is at home this evening. She, um, has a lot going on." Bella gave me the oddest look, one I couldn't quite decipher. "Anyway, c'mon in, y'all." She gestured to the restaurant's largest table. "You'll be our guests of honor. The pizza's on the house! And I'll send Uncle Laz over to get acquainted."

Laz arrived at our table moments later and chatted with Athena, asking all sorts of questions about Brock and his wife Erin. I still couldn't get over the fact that the Rossis knew so much about my cousin and her job. Crazy.

Bella spent the next several minutes fussing over us and gushing about Athena's beautiful hair. But I could tell something wasn't quite right where she was concerned. Several times she looked at me out of the corner of her eye, and once she mouthed the words, "We. Need. To. Talk." After placing our order, she leaned down to speak to me privately. "Cassia, can I steal you away for a minute?"

"Sure." With the others engrossed in friendly chatter, they would never miss me. I rose and followed her into the ladies' room. Odd place for a meeting.

She closed the door and leaned against the wall. "Oh. My. Gosh. I thought I was going to explode out there! I have something to tell you."

"W-what is it?"

She glanced toward the door again, as if expecting to be interrupted at any moment. "It's about your"—her voice lowered to a whisper—"your mother."

"Mama?" I swallowed hard and braced myself for whatever she had to say.

"Your mother is at my parents' house."

My heart skipped a beat. "No way."

"Yeah." Bella nodded and gazed at me with greater intensity than before. "They put her up in the spare bedroom, and she plans to stay until further notice. This according to my mom, who called just before our meeting today. I should have told you then, but Mama said your mother hadn't even arrived yet, and she wasn't completely sure she would carry through with it. But obviously she did."

"I just found out she was missing when I got home from your place," I said. "Babbas was devastated. But when he finds out she's at your parents' place . . ." I paced the small bathroom, unsure of what to say next.

"From what I can gather, our mothers are really good friends." Bella shrugged. "Who can blame them? They have a thousand things in common. And your mother seems to have connected with Aunt Rosa too. They're all very chummy."

"Still . . ." Staying at the Rossi home? This would be the ultimate insult to Babbas.

"I stopped by my parents' place after our meeting this afternoon, just to see if she'd shown up, and there she was," Bella said. "She seemed a little embarrassed to be found out."

No doubt.

"I think maybe she's trying to make a point with your father, but she doesn't seem to be in a hurry to leave. When I stopped by, Aunt Rosa had her in the kitchen cooking up a storm for the family. I ate some of her homemade tzatziki sauce. Man, that's good stuff."

"Oh no." Giving away family recipes? Babbas would have her head.

"She seems happy as a lark. And that really worries me."

"Me too." Mama? Happy, living with the enemy? Boy howdy, Babbas wouldn't be happy if he found out. I mean, he would be happy to find Mama, of course. Happy to know she hadn't fallen off the planet. But the whole part about cooking with the Rossis? Ouch!

"So what do we do?" I leaned against the counter, ready to admit defeat.

"It's more complicated than you know. They're hiding her from Uncle Laz. That's why he's here and Aunt Rosa's there. They're going to make sure your mama is in the guest room with the door closed before he gets home." She sighed. "As competitive as your father is, Uncle Laz is even more so. You know? This is such a dilemma."

"Especially with Athena here." I shook my head. "I'm guessing Mama forgot we had family coming today."

"Likely. Seems like she has a lot on her mind."

"You have no idea."

Bella checked her reflection in the mirror, then looked my way. "Well, let's go back out there and act like nothing's wrong. I don't want to ruin Athena's good time, and you need time to process all of this. We can talk after. I just . . . well, I just wanted you to know."

I gave Bella a hug and thanked her for telling me about my mother, though I still couldn't process it. After sucking in a deep breath and ushering up a prayer for God's miraculous intervention, I headed back out to the table. I somehow made it through our meal and then hugged Athena and Stephen before they left for their hotel. At this point I had two choices: I could go home with my siblings or take Bella up on her offer to go to the Rossi home to check in on Mama. I chose the latter.

Eva gave me a curious look when I told her I wasn't ready to go home yet. "Everything okay?" she asked.

"I'll let you know," I whispered. "You just make sure Babbas doesn't kill any of the little ones before I get home, okay?"

"Oh, sure. Leave me to deal with him while you run away from home like Mama!" Eva spit out a nervous laugh.

I wasn't running away. Well, not for long.

Bella drove me to her parents' home. When we arrived I got out of the car, my heart as heavy as lead. My stomach felt nearly as heavy, what with all the pizza I'd eaten.

We walked inside the grand old home, and I took in the stately foyer with its wooden floors and high ceilings. Wow. But I couldn't get distracted by the Rossi lifestyle. Not yet, anyway.

Off in the distance voices rang out, followed by laughter.

"Sounds like they're still in the kitchen." Bella put her purse down on a little table in the entryway. "Not unusual around here, by the way. Our family sometimes spends all day in the kitchen."

"Technically ours does too." I forced a smile.

I could hear peals of laughter emanating from the other room, but I wasn't prepared for the look of pure joy on my mother's face when I saw her standing in the Rossi kitchen, wearing an apron that read, "Kiss me, I'm Italian!"

She stopped talking midsentence when I walked in the room, and her eyes widened in surprise. "Cassia!"

For a moment I couldn't speak. This all felt so . . . surreal. Finally I managed to squeak out the only word that made sense at that moment.

"M-Mama?"

23

Puttin' On the Ritz

You might be Greek if you think the intercom in Walmart is a family walkie-talkie.

For a moment no one said a word. I spent that time gazing at my mother. I'd never seen her look so beautiful. Gone was the frumpy hair, gone was the usual over-the-top makeup job. Standing before me now, she looked like a completely different woman.

"I . . . I hardly recognize you, Mama. You've done something different."

"Do you like it?" She fussed with her hair, which had been curled and pinned up on the sides.

Like it? I loved it. But the hair didn't come close to the makeup job. Mama's usual look had been replaced with something far more stylish and elegant.

"Imelda is a skilled beautician." Mama waved a sauce-covered ladle toward Bella's mother.

"Oh, it's nothing." Imelda took the spoon out of Mama's hand and took a little taste. "I've always loved to dabble with a brush and paint. Nothing spectacular. And my years of working at the opera house have taught me a lot about color combinations." She pointed the ladle at my mother's face. "Your mama has the most gorgeous wide eyes, so I just accented them a bit with a more subtle color. Don't they look beautiful?"

"Wow. Yes." I could only imagine what Babbas would say.

Babbas.

"Mama, I need to talk to you about . . . well, you know."

"Talk all you like. I'm not going home."

I watched the play of emotions on her face and wondered at the pain in her eyes.

"But Mama . . . what are you doing here?"

She placed a hand on her hip and stared at me. "Living my life, Cassia. Something I rarely get to do."

At this point Rosa slipped out of the room with Bella behind her. Imelda gave Mama one of those "are you going to be okay if I leave?" looks and my mother nodded, so she left too.

"But Babbas . . ." I couldn't get the rest of my sentence out.

"Your father gets what's coming to him." Mama raised the ladle like a weapon. "He needs a wake-up call."

"Are you planning to stay away forever?"

"Depends on your definition of *forever*." She gave me a knowing look. "I will stay away long enough for him to come looking for me. Then I will make my decision. Until he comes looking, I stay here, sharing recipes with my friends."

"Oh, he's looking."

She looked around. "Where? I don't see him."

"Mama. He doesn't know where to look. The man never leaves the shop. He doesn't even know anything about the island. His whole world is inside Super-Gyros."

"Exactly. And it's about to move outside. If he wants me back, I mean. I will stay away long enough for him to acknowledge that he can't manage the business without me." Her eyes narrowed and she put the ladle down. "He can't, can he?"

"Things are falling apart at the seams without you, Mama. Surely you know that. *He's* falling apart at the seams."

"Well, good. Just what I wanted to hear. Don't you go out of your way to make things easier. I want him to see just how much I do. And don't expect a word out of Yia Yia either. She's not going to come to his rescue this time. You can trust me on that."

"Wait a minute. Are you telling me that Yia Yia knows you're here?"

"Knows I'm here?" Mama tipped her head back and laughed. "Yes, she knows I'm here. She's the one who suggested it."

"No way."

"Yes. She gave me the idea. Did the same thing

to your grandfather years ago. Maybe one day you'll run away from home too. It will be a family tradition."

"Trust me, I've already been tempted."

But if I marry Alex, I'll never run away. Won't need to.

Marry Alex? Where had that come from?

My face heated up at the very idea. "We don't need to run away for long, Mama. Things are about to change. Bella came up with a plan that will change everything."

I shared Bella's idea and Mama looked intrigued. In spite of this, she didn't seem to be in a hurry to come home.

"We shall see how it goes. In the meantime, just hold down the fort."

"So you don't want me to tell Babbas where you are?" I asked. "Because he's going to worry himself into a heart attack or something."

"Fine, fine, tell him where I am. I don't care. But also tell him that I won't be back until I'm ready."

"It's going to be harder to keep things under wrap now that Athena and Stephen are here." I didn't mean to sigh, but a little one escaped.

"Oh no." Mama looked mortified. "I totally forgot about your cousin. Does she . . . does she know?"

"Know you've run away from home? No. She was asking for you earlier, but we told her you were out. She didn't seem suspicious."

"Fine. You can bring her here to visit. She won't have to know I'm staying here."

"I don't know, Mama." I'd no sooner spoken those words than a text message came through on my phone. From Athena.

Any chance you could come by the hotel for a few minutes? I have a little confession to make.

I quickly typed, *What is it?*

Her response didn't give me much to go on: *I'll tell you when you get here.*

I ended the conversation with Mama a short time later. No point in belaboring things. If she wanted to stay, let her stay.

After giving her a hug and thanking Cosmo and Imelda Rossi for opening their home to her, I hitched a ride with Bella to the Tremont Hotel, just a few blocks from our family's shop. Athena met me in the lobby. I could tell from the gleam in her eye that something was up.

"I would invite you up to the room, but Stephen's sawing logs. Passed out the minute we got here. Must've been the pizza." She laughed.

"Well, I'm dying of curiosity." I took a seat on a beautiful antique chair, and she sat across from me in one equally nice.

She placed her hands on her knees and sat up straight as an arrow. "I won't keep you in suspense any longer. I have news."

"Wait." I put my hand up. "I think I can guess

what this is about. Are you having a baby?"

"No." She laughed. "Well, not at the moment, anyway. This is business related." A little pause followed her words. "I didn't come to Galveston just to hang out with you, though I would have. I've missed you."

"I've missed you too. It took a while to make new friends, but nothing's the same as hanging out with you." I flashed a smile, which she returned. "So why are you here, really?" I asked. "To help Babbas?"

"Your father . . ." She rolled her eyes.

"I know, I know. But no one can say he's not passionate about his business."

"True." She reached for her drink. "I do think we can help your dad. In fact, if you're okay with Bella's idea for the commercial, I think we can help all of the businesses on the island."

"I'm so glad you love the idea too. I'm all over it."

"I do!" she said. "A commercial that promotes Galveston's tourism will benefit all of the shop owners on the island. And Brock is the perfect one to do it. He's something of a legend around here, from what I can gather."

"It's true. And I'm so grateful he's willing to help out."

"He's not the only one. My good friends Tia and Jason are coming down to the island next week with Brock."

"Don't think I've met them."

"Tia's the director of *Stars Collide* and Jason is a camera operator. They're married. They've agreed to oversee the commercial while they're here, but that's not really why they're coming to Galveston." She gave a mischievous wink.

"Surely they're not vacationing here when they live so close to the Pacific."

"No, not at all. This all goes back to Brock, actually. And Bella." Athena shifted in her chair. "Brock is probably more tied to Galveston than you realize. You know that he's really good friends with the Rossis, right?"

"Yeah, just found out about all of that." I laughed. "Trust me when I say that everyone I run into is either married to a Rossi or friends with a Rossi, so I probably shouldn't be surprised."

"Okay, well, let me get to it then." Her eyes sparkled as she spoke, and her voice grew more animated. "The network has approached me about writing a pilot for a new sitcom . . . set here in Galveston."

"A new sitcom? Here?"

"Yes." She leaned forward in her chair. "So, cousin, get ready to see more of me. Lots more. I'm here to scope out the place for the next few weeks, to get a feel for the city, the people, the accents—all of it. Every nuance will be recorded in this brain of mine and used in upcoming episodes."

I could hardly believe it. What amazing news! I couldn't help but wonder about one thing, though. "This is awesome, Athena, but does it mean you're leaving *Stars Collide*?" My heart thump-thumped. "The show's not being canceled, is it?"

"No." Athena chuckled. "Nothing like that. This would be a spin-off idea."

"Well, I love it! What's the show about?"

"That's the best part." She moved a bit closer and lowered her voice. "It all started with Bella. She shared a story idea with Brock and he shared it with me. You know how I am. I can't hear a good idea—especially a funny one—without wanting to fictionalize it a little."

"That's what makes you such a good writer," I responded. "And that's why the *Stars Collide* viewers love the show, because of your great sense of humor. You're . . . hysterical. And people love that."

"Thank you. Please remember you said that, okay?"

"Sure. But why?"

"Because, Cassia, the idea that Bella shared with Brock involves your family."

"It does?" What did the Pappas family have in common with a Hollywood sitcom? Nothing that I could see.

"She told Brock in passing about the feud between her uncle Laz and your father. She must've exaggerated the story."

"Probably not."

"Well, Brock thought it was hysterical, so he told me. When he shared all of the wacky details of things your father had done, I couldn't resist. I mentioned it to our producer, and he said it sounded like a great idea for a sitcom." She slapped her knee. "I could just see Brock Benson playing the part of the Greek shop owner's son. Won't he be great?"

"Are you serious?" I could hardly breathe at this news.

"Yes! Our producer took the pilot script I came up with—I think it's hysterical, by the way; you're gonna love it—and he started talking with some guys at the network, and the next thing you know they're on board. This is going to be perfect as a spin-off to *Stars Collide* because Brock's character is already Greek. See? It's the ideal segue to tie the two shows together."

I wanted to form words but couldn't. My entire world was about to be fictionalized for all the world to see? And this was a good thing?

"Anyway, I decided to come to Galveston to soak myself in the culture. So far the only thing I've soaked is my blouse." She tugged at her collar. "It's hot here."

"So, let me understand this." I put my hand up to stop her from carrying on about the heat. "You're here to help us film a commercial, but the real reason you're here is to watch Babbas and Uncle Laz try to outdo each other with their restaurants? To fictionalize the feuding between the families to use in this new sitcom?"

"Bingo!" She crossed her arms at her chest and nodded. "Of course, we'll change the names to protect the innocent."

"You mean the guilty." I shook my head. "Man, I hope this doesn't backfire on you, Athena."

"Nah. We'll exaggerate the story enough that your father and Bella's uncle will think it's a hoot. That's what makes comedy work, after all —exaggeration."

"You won't have to exaggerate Babbas's character much, trust me. He's pretty over-the-top as it is."

"Yep. But he's also going to be famous in his own right once the show airs. And it should draw all sorts of new customers to the island and both of the restaurants. So you can see now why we were all so thrilled with the idea of Brock doing a tourism commercial for the island. It will benefit the new show, and vice versa. It's a win-win for all involved."

"Should we tell Babbas?" I asked. "He's going to have to know sooner or later. He'll probably have to agree to his story being fictionalized, right?"

"Yes, we will have to get his permission, and Laz's too. And probably the other family members as well, which means you might be signing some legal documents before all of this is over. But let me take care of that. I'll come up with a way to tell your father."

"Good luck with that."

"He just needs his ego stroked. I don't want this whole project to come to a grinding halt because he's offended."

"Hmm. Well then, you might want to wait a few days. Babbas is going through a bit of a . . ." How could I put it? "Transitional time with Mama."

"Transitional?" Athena looked confused. "He's going through a midlife crisis?"

"No." I drew in a deep breath. "I think *she* is. Mama ran away from home today."

"She what?" Athena started laughing, then clamped a hand over her mouth. Pulling it down, she whispered, "Do you know where she is?"

"At the Rossis' house, cooking Italian food with Aunt Rosa, when I saw her a little while ago. Babbas is going to flip when he finds out."

"Oh, this is perfect!" Athena rose and took a step in my direction. "We'll have to use this in the sitcom, of course."

"Good luck convincing my father of that."

"I'm pretty sure I can," she said. "We'll hire him as a consultant. He can help with story ideas. We want this to be as authentic as possible."

Good grief. I could almost see it now. Before long Babbas would be sitting in the director's chair, calling the shots. Or worse. Maybe he'd want to star in the show.

"You know he'll want to play the role of the Greek father, right?" I gave her a knowing look.

"I guess we'll cross that bridge when we come to it. But we'll be filming mostly in L.A., so I don't think he would really give it serious thought, do you? I mean, you guys just moved here. Surely he's not ready to trade it all in just yet."

Strange, I would've jumped on the idea of going back to California just a few weeks ago. Now the idea of leaving made me feel queasy. So much had changed, so very much.

"No. He would never leave the shop, trust me. Once Mama comes back and things get back to normal, I think we'll be planted here forever. Especially now, with the sitcom idea brewing."

I couldn't help but smile as I thought it through. Staying here forever sounded very appealing now that Alex and I were a couple.

Alex! I needed to call him and fill him in on the day's events. He would be shocked, no doubt. I was still reeling myself. In one day my whole world had changed. I'd been asked to link arms with Bella and the other Galveston wedding vendors, Brock Benson was coming to town to film a commercial that would benefit all of the island's businesses, Mama had run away from home, and my father was about to become a lead character in a sitcom that could very well change all of our lives forever.

Other than that, it had been a pretty normal day.

24

You Made Me Love You

You might be Greek if your guests get out of their car and the first thing they say is, "How did you find this place?"

The following morning I found Babbas pacing the shop, looking completely bewildered.

"What do I do, Cassia?" he asked. "Without your mother here to do the baking, I'm lost."

"I can stay home from the flower shop today," I said. "But I have a better idea. Why not close up the shop for a couple of hours?"

"Close up shop? Never!"

"Even if it meant going to see Mama to try to talk some sense into her?"

"What?" He took several steps toward me and reached for my hands. "You know where your mama is, Cassia? Why didn't you tell me?"

"I just found out last night, and you were already sleeping when I got home. I went to see her, Babbas. She's . . . well, she's not keen on coming home just yet. I think she has a lot to work out in her heart and mind."

"I will go to her. I will close the shop."

At that last proclamation, I felt pretty sure I heard a heavenly choir singing "The Hallelujah Chorus." My father never shut down the shop, no matter what. Stranger still, he insisted that the whole family come along. Maybe he felt safer with the little ones gathered around him, or maybe he thought Mama would take one look at Gina's little face and melt.

We made the drive to the Rossi home, all of us weirdly silent. I could read the fear in my father's eyes as we pulled up to the beautiful Victorian mansion.

"This is where your mama is staying?" he asked.

When I nodded, he fell silent for a moment. When he finally spoke, his words sounded strained. "She'll never want to come home after this." He dove into a discussion about how a woman as good as my mother deserved a lovely home like this one, how he should have given her all she wanted and needed.

A strange surge of affection coursed through me as I thought about what he must be feeling. "It's not about the house," I said. "It's about the people in it and how they treat you."

"Do you think I need to treat her better?"

I think you need to treat us all better.

But I would never say that aloud, at least not during such a vulnerable moment. "I think she needs to hear how much you love her and how much she's missed. Every woman wants to be missed, Babbas."

Eva chimed in, and so did Darian, who surprised me with his candor.

We got out of the car and crossed the beautifully landscaped front yard, then climbed the steps to the veranda. When I rang the bell, my father ran his fingers through his thinning gray hair as if trying to groom himself. "How do I look?" he whispered.

"Fine. Just fine."

He did too. Until Bella's uncle Laz opened the door. Oops!

No one said anything for a moment. Laz finally offered a nod and ushered us inside with a gruff, "They're in the kitchen."

Babbas didn't say a word as he made his way past Laz Rossi. Must've taken a lot of restraint to keep his thoughts inside. What would he say, anyway? "Thank you for taking care of my wife"?

When we arrived in the large modern kitchen, my father paused to take in his surroundings. I could tell from his expression that the room impressed him. Apparently so did the woman standing behind the trays of garlic rolls. Mama looked even prettier today than yesterday, and that was really saying something. The new hairdo and makeup job made her look a good ten years younger, and the dress she wore took several pounds off of her.

Babbas took a tentative step into the room and cleared his throat. Mama looked up from her work and her eyes grew wide. "So . . . you're here." For a moment I thought she might hide behind Rosa, who looked as if she could take my father down at a second's notice. But no, Mama held her own. Still, Rosa hovered nearby with a spatula in her hand, which no doubt she would use against my father's backside should he come any closer.

"Yes, I'm here, Helena," Babbas managed. "I've come for you."

"Well, thanks for stopping by, but I won't be leaving. Some big changes will have to take place before that can happen."

Rosa let out a grunt and smacked the spatula into a pan filled with ground beef.

"Helena, what are you trying to prove here? What is this?"

"I'm living my life, Niko. That is all."

"But . . ." He raked his fingers through his hair. "You already have a life." He pointed to us kids, but we were all too busy taking in the fabulous home. I heard Eva let out a little sigh.

Mama muttered something under her breath, then put both hands on the countertop and glared at him. "Remind me again why you've come?"

"I've come to . . ." He hesitated and looked around the Rossi kitchen. "Is that a double oven?"

"It is." She nodded. "I've used it several times

since they invited me to stay with them. I've always wanted a double oven."

"I know, Helena. And maybe someday we can—"

"There are a great many things I've always wanted, Niko. Things I've done without so that we could have a restaurant."

"Are you sorry I brought you to Galveston?"

"I'm sorry you never asked my opinion. You told me what we were doing, and I went along with you to keep from stirring the waters."

"You are unhappy here?"

Darian cleared his throat, obviously uncomfortable with the conversation. My other brother and sisters looked uncomfortable too. Still, what could we do but pray at a time like this? Well, pray, and drool over the garlic twists on the large tray in front of us. Yum.

"You brought us to this God-forsaken place. Hot. Humid. And you won't even let us befriend our neighbors. We have to hate them just because they have a restaurant."

"But Helena—"

"At home I had friends. People I could call on. Here I have customers. People who see me as an outsider." She pointed to Rosa, who blanched and took a step back. "Do you see this woman here?"

"Of course I see her," Babbas growled. "I'm not blind, woman."

"You are blind, Niko. That's the problem. You see her as an enemy. I see her as someone willing to open up and share her life, her home, her recipes with me. That sort of person, Niko, is called a friend. You wouldn't know because you don't believe in them." Mama slung her arm around Rosa's shoulder.

"Well, I . . ." Babbas seemed at a loss for words.

"And I'm not allowed such friendships, am I? At least in California I had a few acquaintances who met with your approval. Here my hands are tied. I have to hide my friendships from you." Her hand slid off Rosa's shoulder. "Or worse yet, give up on them altogether and pretend I'm okay when I'm not."

"Are you saying you want to go home to California?" Babbas flinched as he spoke the word *home*. Surely he'd said it by accident.

"I don't even know where home is anymore." Tears filled Mama's eyes. "I miss my old life. I miss being a normal family. I miss relationships with other women, talking about things that women talk about. And I miss spending time alone with you."

"You . . . you do?"

"The old you. The one who talked to me about life. Things that mattered. Not just questions about how many trays of baklava I'd baked and how many gallons of tzatziki sauce I'd made. Remember when we used to talk about retiring? Taking a trip to Greece?"

"But we must keep the business running,"

Babbas said. "How could we possibly leave when there's so much to do?"

"The business, the business, always the business!" Mama huffed across the room, then turned back to face us, eyes brimming. "That's the problem, Niko. The business is the main thing with you. When are the people in your life going to be the main thing?"

The silence that followed was deafening, but not nearly as deafening as the intense sobs from my father. I'd never heard a grown man weep like that, so it caught me off guard. Must've scared Rosa too, because she scooted out of the room. Gina rushed to Babbas and threw herself around his legs, then began to weep with him. Mama looked equally as shocked.

"Niko, what is it?"

For a moment he didn't answer. When his words finally came, I could barely make them out. "I . . . I . . . love . . . my . . . family!" This sentence was followed by a string of words in Greek. Or possibly pig Latin. I couldn't really tell through the emotion, but I got the gist of it. The man didn't like being accused of putting business before family. That much I got.

"I do not question your love, Niko. I question the way you show it. You are harsh to those you love and even more so to those you don't." Mama's voice softened. "This sets such a bad example for the children."

"Bad example?" He looked her way and dabbed at his eyes.

"You say one thing and do another. You go to church on Sunday and even spout the Scriptures from the sermon, but then you bark out orders to your family. This is not the best way to show us that we are loved or appreciated. Worse still, you teach the children to hate their neighbor. This is the opposite of what the Bible says we should do."

"It's not hate." He shrugged. "It's marketing."

"Marketing schmarketing." Mama walked over and placed her hand on Babbas's arm. "I'm sick to death of that word. What ever happened to winning people over with love? With real relationships? This is what being a Christian is all about, Niko. Not letting your anger and your jealousy get the best of you."

His eyes puddled again and he shifted his gaze to the floor. "So, I am a hypocrite?"

"I'm just saying you're a temperamental man, Niko, and it hurts your testimony."

"Hurts my testimony?" Tears trickled down his cheeks and his voice quivered. "Because I get emotional, you doubt my faith?"

"I'm not doubting your faith." Mama's voice lowered. "Just the example you are setting. You can call it emotional if you like. I call it anger. Temper." She raised her index finger to silence him before he could interrupt. "And before you go telling me it's because you're Greek, just know that I've heard that line before. If we're going with that theory, then we have to also say that our heritage controls our emotions, and I refuse to believe that."

"B-but—"

"You need to take a look at your temper and stop making excuses for it, because the way you act confuses people." She gave him a compassionate look. "I know your heart. You're not a mean man on the inside."

"I'm not." Tears dampened his red cheeks again, and he swiped them away with the back of his hand. "If people really knew me, they would know that. I guess I just . . ." His words drifted off, and he ran his fingers through his hair.

"You just get carried away in the moment and start bossing people around," Mama said. "It comes naturally."

Obviously.

"Someone has to be in charge," Babbas said. "Every ship needs a captain."

"A captain, yes," she countered. "Not a tyrant. Sometimes I feel like you've forced the rest of us onto the ship without consulting us first. Then you set out to sea and make us swab the decks while you bark orders. It's not a fun way to live."

Babbas sighed and slid down into a chair at the breakfast table. He looked at my siblings, then his gaze shifted to me. "Do you feel the same,

Cassia?" he asked. "Do you think I'm a tyrant?"

Wow. Talk about being put on the spot. Still, I couldn't help but speak the truth, hard as it might be in the moment. "I think sometimes you react out of emotion, Babbas. We all do."

"But you think I'm . . . mean?" This question was directed at all of us.

Gina answered it best by scooting behind me to avoid his gaze. The rest of us just stood in silence.

Is there an exit nearby? I need a clean getaway, Lord!

"I'll take that as a yes." Babbas brushed his hands on his slacks and drew in a deep breath. "And do you all agree that I've kidnapped you on my pirate ship and set out to sea without consulting you?"

More silence.

His shoulders rolled forward and he looked tired. "I've made a mistake coming here." His words came out in a hoarse whisper.

"Coming to the Rossi home, you mean?" Mama crossed her arms at her chest and gave him a pensive look.

"No." He stood and looked into her eyes. "Coming to Texas. It was a mistake. We were doing fine in Santa Cruz. I brought the whole family here on a whim, and look at the trouble it's caused."

Actually, I could name any number of good

338

things that had come from that decision, but this probably wasn't the time or place.

Babbas leaned forward and placed his head in his hands. For a few seconds he said nothing. I wondered if he might be praying. With his face now hidden from view, who could tell? He finally came up for air and faced us all, tears still trickling down his cheeks.

"I must change my ways. I must come up with a new plan. Will you pray for me? I need God's help in this . . . and yours too."

You could've heard a pin drop in the room. Surely the idea of our father changing his ways had sent a shock wave around the room. Possibly the planet.

Gina broke the silence by stepping out from behind me and flinging herself into our father's arms. "It doesn't have to be a big change, Babbas," she said, and then the tears flowed like flower petals down her precious pink cheeks. "J-just a little b-bitty one in your heart. Th-that's what my Sunday school teacher said last w-week."

My baby sister had a good point. A little bitty change would probably go a long way in a situation such as this. If Babbas really opened himself up to the possibilities, it could change the entire dynamic of our family. Maybe we could be more like Alex's family—calm, cool, collected. Or maybe we could meet in the middle and be more like the Rossis. Either way, I could sense changes coming, and not the kind that would make for wacky television.

Television.

With Mama and Babbas now on speaking terms, things were definitely looking up, but I needed to tell them about the upcoming sitcom idea. Athena's plan could change just about everything. They also needed the details about the commercial, which should help bring tourists to the island in droves. Maybe they wouldn't have to work so hard. Maybe they really could take that trip to Greece.

I looked back and forth between my parents—Mama with her firm stance and Babbas with his shoulders slumped forward in defeat—and decided the timing wasn't right to spill the beans. With Athena's help, I would tell them tomorrow. Or the next day. Right now we just had to get Mama home and figure out a way to get back to our normal lives.

Judging from the pained expression in my father's eyes, however, I had a feeling "normal" was a long way off.

25

Stormy Weather

You might be Greek if your mom reads every label in the grocery store.

For the next twenty-four hours we all moved like robots around Mama and Babbas and prayed neither would blow like a volcano. The uneasiness in the air was thicker than an overworked batch of tabouli. By the time we opened the shop on Thursday morning, I found myself praying harder than ever, convinced the worst was yet to come.

Alex must've picked up on it too. He showed up for lunch on Thursday but didn't seem as interested in his gyro. He sat in the front booth, gyro in hand, and watched the interaction—or lack thereof—between my parents. His nearness brought a comfort I hadn't felt in days. My heart always seemed to beat more steadily when Alex was nearby.

"So what's the deal with your mom and dad?" he asked between bites.

I gestured for him to wipe the dribble of sauce from his chin. "It's so strange," I whispered. "If you didn't know any different, you'd say everything was normal, but I get the creepiest feeling the top's about to blow off the well, if you know what I mean."

"Yikes." He took another bite.

"Mama really let him have it before she came back home. But this isn't over yet."

He looked at my mother, who worked in silence. Babbas gave her a tight nod and then turned back to a customer.

"Yeah. Something's about to blow. Hope I'm not here when it happens."

"Same here."

"What about your cousin?" He gestured to a nearby booth, where Athena sat with her laptop open in front of her while nibbling on a Greek salad. Across from her, Stephen sat with his open laptop, typing madly. "Has she picked up on any of this?"

I shrugged. "I told her most of it, so she's aware. She's a writer, and you know how those writers are. They're always paying attention to the little nuances. She's probably taking notes for the sitcom. You've got to admit, my parents would make great characters on network TV."

"No doubt." He watched as my father forced a smile while waiting on an irritated customer. "Might have to limit the show to cable if your dad decides to blow like a top. Could be scary."

"Yeah. I know it freaked my brothers and sisters out to see him cry. They've never seen him like that before."

"Have you?"

"Hmm." I paused to think about it. "Only once, when my grandfather died. Babbas cried like a baby." My heart twisted as I remembered the depth of pain I'd seen in my father's eyes that day. What was that old expression about still waters running deep? He covered his aces ordinarily, but when the going got tough, my dad melted down like a Godiva chocolate in the afternoon sun.

"Man." Alex took a swig of his soda.

"Well, I hope whatever he's got up his sleeve with the fake smiles and kind words to strangers ends up in a sitcom and not the evening news."

Alex let out a laugh and then reached for a napkin. After composing himself, he waggled his finger at me. "Don't ever do that again."

"Do what?"

"Say something funny when I'm taking a drink. You could've killed me."

"Are you two fighting?" Gina came close, looking troubled.

I turned to my little sister, perplexed by her question. "No way. Why would you think that?"

"Alex's face is red and he said you tried to kill him."

"Just an expression."

"Expression? What's an expression?"

"It's just a . . ." Alex shrugged, then took another sip of his drink. "Never mind, kiddo."

She walked away, but not in her usual monkey-like way. No skipping. No smile. Nothing.

"It worries me that she assumes men and women have to bicker in order to communicate." A little sigh wriggled its way out. "She's only ever known raised voices and arguments. Sad."

"Oh, I don't know." Alex reached for his soda again. "At least your parents talk to each other. Some of the families I know, the mom and dad don't communicate at all. Loud communication is still communication."

I glanced at Mama, who worked in eerie silence next to my father. Very, very unusual. Yep, this situation wasn't over yet. No doubt we had big troubles ahead.

As if sensing my concerns, Athena rose from her spot behind the computer and headed my way. "Hey."

"Hey."

"So what do you think, Cassia?" she said. "Is the timing right? Now that your mama's back, I think I should tell them about the sitcom."

"Maybe." I looked at my parents again, feeling conflicted.

"C'mon. I'll do most of the talking. Just follow my lead." She extended her hand and I took it, then stood.

"Okay, but if this goes south, we'll need a backup plan."

"Nah, no backup plan needed."

Alex stood and joined us. "Okay if I listen in?" he asked. "This is too good to pass up."

"Yes, please." I slipped my arm through his, feeling the security of his presence. "I need you." I needed him, all right, but not just in situations like this. More and more, my heart convinced me that I could not live without him. Even a day apart was too much. I gave him a little smile, and he leaned over and kissed the tip of my nose, further convincing me. Oh, how I adored this guy.

"This will end well, Cassia," he whispered. "Just have faith."

I nodded and we walked toward my parents.

"Uncle Niko, I need to talk to you," Athena said. "Do you have a few minutes?"

"I . . . I suppose. Should we sit?"

"No need, but we might be better off talking in the kitchen so we have some privacy." She led the way, my father following behind her like a whipped puppy. Mama trailed on his heels, and Alex and I took up the slack behind her.

Once inside the kitchen, Athena unfolded her idea. She handled it gracefully, kind of like the petals of a flower peeling back one at a time. First she talked about the commercial, which would promote all of the businesses on the island. Babbas took this news better than expected. In fact, he said nothing in response. Then she shared the news about the sitcom.

"W-wait." Babbas shook his head. "You are saying that my shop is going to be featured in a television show?"

"Well, not your shop exactly," she said. "We'll change the name of it. And we'll change Parma John's to something else too. But the idea of the competition between the two will remain the same." She placed her hand on his arm. "We'll make it funny, Uncle Niko, I promise. It will be so exaggerated you'll hardly recognize it. The viewers will eat it up." She laughed as she realized what she'd said. "Eat it up—ha! The point is, they'll love it."

Mama paced the kitchen, then turned back. "I don't know, Athena. This will make fools of us all. I've had enough of that."

"It won't, Aunt Helena." Athena gazed at her with tenderness. "I care too much about you to let that happen. It will be fun, and it will bring so much business to Super-Gyros."

"And to Parma John's." My father's words were spoken softly. I couldn't tell if that part of it bothered him or not.

"Yes, Parma John's too. And if we do our job well with the show and the tourism, all of the businesses in town will prosper. Don't you see? This will be so good for Galveston, and from all of my research, the island really needs an economic boost right now. Bella told us things haven't been the same since Hurricane Ike."

346

She went on to explain that very little of the show would actually be filmed in Galveston and then delivered her final bit of news. "We want to hire you, Uncle Niko. To be a consultant, I mean."

"Hire me?" I could almost read the next question in his eyes. "But how will I keep the shop running?"

"Don't worry, Babbas," I said. "We will make sure everything runs smoothly when you're gone."

"Gone . . . how long? Would I have to go to L.A.?"

"Only for a few days at a time. After a while we could communicate by Skype."

"What is this . . . Skype?" he asked.

"Darian will teach you," I said. "But think of it, Babbas. You'll get to help write the show. It will be authentic. Greek. See?"

"Yes, I see." His unibrow slid into place as he absorbed the idea. "But all of this would be easier if we lived in California, no?" Babbas looked back and forth between Mama and Athena. "If we still lived in Santa Cruz, I could drive to L.A. in less than a day. Spend more time with the family and still do as you say."

My heart pounded as I listened in, and my grip on Alex's arm tightened. "What are you saying, Babbas?"

"I'm saying it makes more sense to go back home. To California. That's what I'm saying.

Mama was happier there. You kids were happier there. And now Athena's telling me that I will need to be in Los Angeles to help with this show of hers."

Mama held her poker face really well. I had to give it to her. If this news excited her, you wouldn't know it.

"Wait." I shook my head, confused. "You mean we're going back to Santa Cruz?" When he nodded, my heart rate doubled—but not in a good way. "Are you serious?"

"Yes. I've been praying about it all night, and I asked the Lord for a sign." He reached to take Athena's hand. "This is my sign. I can never thank you enough." He looked up to heaven and whispered, "Sometimes the Lord moves in mysterious ways."

This was mysterious, all right.

"Oh, but Uncle Niko, I didn't mean that you should leave Galveston." Athena tried to explain that the show's Texas angle would be compromised if we didn't actually live here, but Babbas wasn't having it.

"No." He put his hand up. "We know enough about Texas to add the right flavor to the show. So don't worry about that. My head is filled with ideas." He sighed. "Besides, I'm sure the Rossis will be glad to see us go. They've probably had enough of us as it is."

I tried to argue that point. So did Alex. Even

Athena joined in, stating that the competition between the two restaurants was key to the story idea. But Babbas would not be swayed.

"I have prayed. God has answered. We will go home as soon as we can find someone else to lease the space. I will start working on that tomorrow." With tears in his eyes, he turned to Mama and squeezed her hand. "You will be happy again, Helena. I promise. The older boys are doing such a fine job with the Santa Cruz store without me, maybe I can retire. We can spend more time together."

Mama's eyes widened and she leaned into his outstretched arms. Still she said nothing. Was this the answer she'd been hoping for? I had no idea. Her face showed no emotion.

Me? I was teeming with emotion, none of it good. If you'd told me weeks ago that we'd be going back to Santa Cruz, I would've jumped for joy. Now the idea made me queasy. I could never leave Alex. Never. To do so would kill me. And what about my new job? My new friends? Surely God hadn't brought me here to give me all of that only to snatch it away again.

Babbas's face lit in the broadest smile I'd seen in years. He led the way back into the shop and called the family together. Eva, Darian, Filip, and Gina joined us in the kitchen while Babbas shared the news that we were going back home to California.

"But Babbas . . ." Eva began to cry. "I've made friends here. Sophia and I are supposed to go to the movies next weekend."

"I've got new friends too." Darian's gaze shifted to the floor. "And my coaching. I can't give that up. Next year they want to hire me full-time."

"They do?" I looked at him, surprised by this announcement.

"Yeah. I just found out."

Babbas slapped him on the back—a little too hard. "Don't worry, Son! There are baseball teams in Santa Cruz. You can coach all you like." The exaggerated smile from our father seemed out of place on his usually stern face.

I couldn't smile. No way. California was part of my past, not my present. But the idea of staying here while my family went back to Santa Cruz held no appeal either.

I suddenly felt sick inside. Darian did too, judging from the look on his face. Mama looked . . . perplexed. I couldn't really tell what my other siblings were feeling. The conversation took off like a horse out of the gate and the volume level rose with each new sentence. Who could figure out what anyone was thinking or feeling?

I kept a watchful eye on Mama while the others talked around her. She never came out and said, "Woo-hoo! We're going home!" Neither did she argue with the idea. Maybe she'd decided to hold her cards close for now. Likely we'd be hearing her true feelings later, when we parted ways with the crowd.

The clanging of the bell over the front door alerted us to the fact that a customer had entered, so we moved our conversation—now hushed— back out to the shop. Athena walked to the booth and sat across from Stephen, her face loaded with unspoken emotion. No doubt she felt awful about all of this.

Mama waited on the customer. Babbas shushed the little ones and sent them to the back, likely to keep the incoming customers from wondering what the crazy Greek family was up to now.

Alex seemed frozen in place behind the counter. "So, that's it?" He lifted his hands up in the air, clearly frustrated. "Just like that, you're all gone?"

"I don't know. I really don't." A mist of tears sprang to my eyes. "I need time to think, Alex. To process."

"You don't have to go with them." He reached for my hand and squeezed it. Hard. His eyes came up to study my face. "You're twenty-three."

"But my family means everything to me," I countered. "I can't even imagine leaving all of them for . . ."

For what, I couldn't say. Alex and I had shared so many special moments. So many sweet kisses. Our hearts were permanently linked, and I wouldn't want to unlink them, not ever.

"But I don't want you to go. Not now. Not when I . . ." His words drifted off, and I thought for a moment I saw pain in those gorgeous brown eyes. "Cassia, you have to know how I feel about you."

"I . . ." *I do.* But he'd never come out and said it, had he?

He pulled me into his arms, then pressed a kiss into my hair. "You mean so much to me. You have to know that. If you go away, it will kill me. I'll—"

He didn't get a chance to finish his sentence. The clanging of the bell at the front door alerted us to the fact that more customers had entered. I took a giant step backwards—a good Greek girl would never be caught in a compromising position, after all—and shifted my attention to an elderly woman who wanted to order sixteen sandwiches for her Bible study group.

Minutes later Alex received a work-related call and had to leave. Looked like I would have to wait to hear what he had to say. Not that I had time to really think about it. A larger-than-usual lunch crowd swarmed the place, nearly running us out of lamb and ready-to-go salads.

Babbas served up gyros with a broad smile, looking happier than I'd seen him in ages. Mama worked in silence but offered a convincing smile to our guests. My brothers and sisters bused tables, swept, and mopped, but kept their thoughts to themselves. And Athena and Stephen ate their lunch and made a few calls on their cell phones, then got back to work at the front table, where they'd pretty much taken up residence.

Around 1:30, a text came through on my phone. I half expected it to be from Marcella, wondering why I hadn't shown up for my afternoon shift at the florist shop. Instead, it was from Alex. Three words . . . but they caused my heart to twist inside me as I absorbed the depth of their meaning.

Please.

Don't.

Go.

26

Buds Won't Bud

You might be Greek if your only vacation
is back to the homeland.

The next couple of hours I managed to carry on a
hushed conversation with Athena, who sat in the
front booth with Stephen working on their sitcom
idea. Well, in between waiting on customers I
talked to Athena, anyway. Most of our conversation revolved around our family's situation, but
some of it ended up being about my job at the
flower shop.

I shifted gears after my heart grew heavy and
redirected the conversation back to Athena and
the sitcom. "Do you think you'll go on writing
forever?" I asked.

"I hope so." She ran her fingers across the
closed laptop. "Can't imagine giving up something I love."

Ugh. She would have to say that. If I went back
to Santa Cruz, I wouldn't just have to give up my
blossoming romance with the man of my dreams,
I'd also have to give up working at the flower
shop. The very idea broke my heart. Sure, there
were florists in California, but starting over held

no appeal, not when I loved my job here so much.

Stephen looked up from his open laptop and shook his head. "Athena will never quit writing, trust me. She'll draw her last breath seated at the laptop, typing out her final thoughts."

"What would you write?" I asked. "If you knew it was the last thing you would ever get to write—if you could really say whatever was on your heart—what would it be?"

She appeared to think about that. "I guess I'd say that life, as sweet as it is, is just a glimpse of what's coming next. That heaven is our real home. It's not a fictional story, like the sitcoms I write. It's real."

Wow. I hadn't expected something this serious from my over-the-top funny cousin.

"And then I'd say that we have to have a relationship with Jesus to get there," Athena added. She paused a moment, then looked at me. "So let me turn the question back on you. What would you say?"

"Oh, me?" I put my hand up. "Trust me, I'm not a writer."

"You don't have to be to answer this question. What would you say, Cassia?"

I closed my eyes and gave a moment's thought before speaking. "I would say that life is like a rose. Some seasons are closed tight. We can't see what's inside. Can't see all the way to the center, to the real beauty. But then God sends the wind and water and sun along and they pry it open." I smiled, thinking of how the Lord had done that very thing in my life over the past several weeks, not just in my relationship with Alex, but with my new friendships too. "That's what he's been doing in my life," I said. "He's taken this little bud of a girl, tightly closed, and opened her up one petal at a time."

"Sounds like God has really been working on you since you moved here." Athena reached over to grab my hand. "I'm so glad."

"Me too." My heart swelled with a mixture of joy and pain as I thought about the truth of her words. I'd grown so much over the past few weeks. Coming here to Texas had matured me in a thousand ways.

"One more thing," I added. "I think, hard as it is to admit, that the real beauty comes after adversity. After the rain. After the sun. After the wind. It comes when you're finally opened up. If you think about it, the scent of the flower is sweetest at that point, even though the journey was a tough one."

Whoa. Where had all of that come from?

Stephen looked up from his computer to give me an admiring look. He offered a nod, then went back to typing.

"You should be a writer, Cassia." Athena gave me a comforting smile. "I love the way you word things."

"No thanks. I'll stick to flowers. They're my gift."

"Sure, but be careful not to limit yourself." Athena took a sip of her diet soda. "You are obviously a girl of many talents."

Generous words, coming from someone with so many gifts and abilities. I smiled and whispered, "Thank you." Oh, but how I wished one of my talents included being in two places at once. Then I could stay here with Alex and go to California with my family all at the same time.

After Athena and Stephen left to go to their hotel, she and I continued our conversation by text message. I half expected her to celebrate our family's return to the Golden State, but I could tell from her texts that she felt we belonged here on Galveston Island, and not just because of the show.

We do belong here! I don't want to go anywhere.

Those words kept skittering through my brain as I waited on our larger-than-usual afternoon crowd. But what choice did I have in the matter? If the whole family left, I'd have to go with them. As much as I hated being tied to Babbas's apron strings, I'd hate even more to live without my family.

But I'd also hate living without Alex.

Every time I thought about leaving him behind, a swarm of angry bees took to buzzing around in my belly. Felt like it, anyway. Nothing seemed to lift my spirits, not even humming ten Judy Garland songs in a row. No, the day was shot, and I couldn't get it back again.

Or maybe I could.

At a quarter after five the trio of women from Splendora converged on Super-Gyros, dressed in the brightest neon colors I'd ever seen. Florals, no less. Now, I liked flowers, but this was a little too much for me, and definitely hard on the eyes, especially when you factored in Twila's garish hat, complete with a large silk carnation in a blinding shade of fuchsia. The fact that the back of her skirt appeared to be twisted up in her undergarments didn't help either.

I gestured to her backside, and she wriggled the fabric back down into place, muttering, "Merciful heavens! Why didn't someone tell me?"

"We were down on the island to sing at a women's event," Bonnie Sue said. She pointed at her outfit. "The island beautification society. They had a gardening theme. Very colorful."

"I see."

"They served us a teensy-tiny lunch," Twila said and then rubbed her stomach. "Really, not enough to feed a baby bird."

"So it only made sense to stop by and have dinner at one of our favorite restaurants!" Jolene grabbed a menu and perused it as she continued to talk. "We simply couldn't wait until we got back to Splendora. It's quite a drive, you know, especially at this time of day."

"Oh yes." Bonnie Sue shifted her ginormous lime-green handbag from one shoulder to the other. "It just made sense to stay on the island until evening traffic time was behind us."

Looked like they'd be with us a couple of hours then.

"We bickered over what to have—pizza or gyros." Twila giggled as she clapped her hands together. "I won. I voted for Super-Gyros. We can have pizza anytime, but I don't know any other place to get a great gyro than right here!" She began to sing the praises of our family's shop, and before long the other ladies were shopping our store shelves for a variety of items. Mama joined them and soon they were chatting comfortably as if they were old friends. Then again, the Splendora trio seemed to have that effect on people.

After they'd placed their orders, Mama seated the vivacious gals at a table nearest the counter. She delivered their food a short time later, and Twila asked for extra tzatziki sauce. Bonnie Sue took a bite of her gyro, and her eyes rolled back in what appeared to be delirium.

"Dee-lish-ous!" she proclaimed.

"I know what would be perfect with this. Have you tried our kalamatas?" Mama went behind the counter and came out with a little dish of them.

"Ours are imported, of course. You'll never taste anything like them. I always say they're as ripe as if we plucked them off the tree ourselves."

Bonnie Sue balked when Mama offered her the first one. "I'm not an olive fan, sorry."

"You will be after you taste these." Mama stood firm, bowl of olives in hand.

Though she appeared hesitant, Bonnie Sue took the olive and popped it in her mouth. Her grimace eased into a smile—a broad smile. "Oh. My. Goodness!"

"I know, right?" Mama giggled.

"I can't believe I lived this long without eating kalamata olives. And what a beautiful color they are too!" Bonnie Sue laughed, stuck her plump hand back into the dish, and came out with a second. Then a third.

"Save some for me, for pity's sake." Twila stepped in between Bonnie Sue and the olive bowl. "You're not the only hungry one in this crowd."

Sure enough, we did have a crowd. Our three favorite nuns arrived to purchase enough sandwiches for all of their fellow sisters back at the convent. They greeted Twila, Jolene, and Bonnie Sue with hugs all around, then grabbed their food and headed off.

Looked like Babbas's advertising was really paying off. Dozens of people came in with coupons in hand. Others carried the flyers Babbas had peppered around the island. A couple mentioned seeing Babbas's advertisement in the local paper. Still others shared with gusto about how their friends had sung the praises of Super-Gyros, so they had to try it out for themselves.

Sad that all of this had to happen now, just as we prepared to shut down the place.

Of course, no one but the family knew, and I certainly wasn't going to spoil everyone's good time today. The Splendora ladies were all giggles and smiles as they ate . . . and ate . . . and ate their dinner. When the crowd thinned, they were still with us, now setting up camp in our kitchen, where Mama shared story after story from our years in the restaurant business.

"Sounds like you're just where the Lord planted you, honey." Twila reached to give Mama a hug, and I watched as my mother melted into her new friend's embrace.

"Praise God for his direction in your lives," Bonnie Sue added. "He led you here to Galveston, and he led your sweet Cassia all the way to Splendora to meet us."

"And to meet that handsome nephew of mine." Twila gave me a motherly wink. "He's quite a catch, but then you've already figured that out, haven't you."

I nodded, unable to respond over the lump in my throat. Alex was quite a catch, all right. Only, I was about to let him slip off my hook, wasn't I?

Bonnie Sue reached over to the counter and snagged the last remaining piece of baklava from a sticky tray. This sent Twila into a panic. She began to fan herself, her cheeks blazing as red as the maraschino cherries in the jar nearby.

"Bonnie Sue! You didn't pay for that." Twila slapped her friend's hand and the baklava shot in the air.

Bonnie Sue caught it with her other hand with the skill of a pro baseball player. Before popping it in her mouth, she looked at Mama and said, "Do you mind? I'm happy to pay for it. After I eat it, I mean." She shoveled it in, chewed and swallowed it, then sighed in pure delight. She licked each sticky finger, a look of delirium on her face.

"Pay for it, my eye." Mama pulled out a fresh tray of the sweet stuff and put it in a large to-go container. "You'll do no such thing. You've been such a blessing. Why, you'll never know how amazing your timing is. I needed a bit of social-izing today."

"Oh, well, you're in luck! We specialize in socializing." Jolene eased open the to-go container and weaseled out a piece of baklava, then popped it in her mouth.

"Well, if you can't beat 'em . . ." Twila pulled the top off the container and helped herself to a piece double the size.

This got Mama so tickled that she couldn't

stop laughing. Babbas came into the kitchen at this point, likely wondering what the howling was about. He took one look at all of the estrogen in the room and quickly backed out. I didn't blame him.

When the ladies finally left, I pondered the events of the day. While I secretly thanked the Lord for Mama's blossoming friendships, I had to wonder about God's timing. Why bring so many friends her way just before we left the island? Seemed . . . cruel. And why bless our shop with so many new customers today just as Babbas made up his mind to leave? We would have some unhappy people when the Closed sign went up in a few weeks.

Mentally exhausted, I climbed the stairs to our little apartment. Today I saw the tiny space through different eyes—the brick walls, the beautiful view of the Strand, the solid architecture. How had I overlooked its old-world charm before? I would miss it once we left.

I didn't appear to be the only one. When I climbed into bed that night, all of my siblings gathered around me as if leaning on me for comfort.

"So we're going back to Santa Cruz?" Darian crossed his arms at his chest and rested against the footboard.

"I don't want to go back." Gina pulled the covers over her head. I could hear her whimpering underneath. "I have new friends here. I'm going to miss them."

"You had great friends back in California too." I did my best to sound encouraging, but I felt my little sister's pain. As much as I'd wanted to go back at first, leaving the island seemed impossible now.

Filip nudged the covers with his arm. "Why didn't you just tell Babbas that earlier when he brought it up, goober? He listens to you."

Gina stuck her head back out and wiped her eyes. "I was scared. Sometimes he yells."

"That's the part that stinks most." Eva rose and walked to the window. "I hate that we're all too scared to tell our own father what we think."

"I don't think we have to be anymore," Darian said. "He's . . . changed. A lot. I can see it all over his face."

"Yeah, he does seem nicer now." Filip looked from sibling to sibling. "Haven't you noticed?"

I had noticed, actually. In fact, Babbas hadn't yelled once today. Talk about progress.

"It's just so confusing. I'm not sure what to think anymore." Eva sat in the windowsill and gazed outside. "Even if I could talk to Babbas about what I'm feeling, I don't know what I would say." A little sigh escaped her. She turned to face us, her eyes shimmering with moisture. "I really hated it here at first. You all know that. But now

I'm all mixed up inside. The timing is just . . . weird."

It was weird, all right.

"If we leave now, how will I ever get to build that giant sand castle with you, Cassia?" Gina wriggled her way into my lap. "Remember? You promised to take me to Stewart Beach to build sand castles."

"We can still do that . . . before we go."

"Yes, but who's going to look after it when we're gone?" She sniffled and I knew that tears weren't far behind.

"Sand castles don't last forever." Filip rolled his eyes. "The wind will blow it over or the tide will wash it out to sea, so what does it matter if we're in Galveston or Santa Cruz? Won't make any difference to the sand castle."

"But it will to me!" Gina dissolved into tears at this proclamation.

I held her close. "The point is, you can build sand castles no matter where you go, and we can help you because we'll all be together."

"And you can make lovely flower arrangements wherever you go." Yia Yia's gentle voice interrupted our conversation. I turned to see her standing in the open doorway. With one hand on her arthritic hip, she made her way toward the bed and took a seat on the edge. "Are you talking about the move?"

"Yes." Gina sighed. "I don't want to go."

"Me either," Darian added.

"What about you, Yia Yia?" I asked. "Do you want to go back to Santa Cruz?"

"Where I want to be"—her eyes grew misty—"is with my family. Doesn't matter where, as long as we're together."

I understood. Sort of. I wanted to keep the family together, of course. Staying behind would leave a hole in my heart the size of the state of Texas. But giving up my relationship with Alex—the day in, day out one—would be the hardest choice of my life. Harder by far than leaving my friends in Santa Cruz to come here.

Still, when I looked around the room, when I saw the precious faces of those I loved more than life itself, I knew in my heart that I could never let them go without me, no matter how much it hurt.

Darian suggested we pray together, so we did. That prayer acted as a salve to calm us down, especially when Yia Yia joined us in lyrical Greek, her words laced with emotion and tears. Afterward we all hugged and said our good nights. I wiped away Gina's tears and gave her a kiss on the cheek.

"It will end well," I whispered.

"Promise?" Her pain-filled eyes met mine, and I forced myself to nod.

After turning out the light, I settled into bed, my thoughts reeling. In spite of the prayer, I had a hard time sleeping that night. Who could sleep, when wrestling with the sheets was so much more fun?

Between the hours of midnight and one, I convinced myself that I should stay in Galveston. Pursue my relationship with Alex apart from my family.

Between the hours of one and two, I found my heart nearly as twisted as the sheets every time I thought about Gina growing up without me. And Darian. And Eva. And Filip. We would eventually grow apart if I stayed behind.

Between the hours of two and three, I thought about the flower shop. Marcella wanted to sell it to me. She'd even hinted at giving it to me for a great price, no less. How could I turn down such a generous—and easy—offer? Working with flowers was my dream job, after all. And on my new salary, I could certainly afford an apartment of my own, right?

Between the hours of three and four, I reminded myself that California—vast, beautiful, tropical California—had hundreds, if not thousands, of flower shops. Surely I could find a job in one of them. Babbas would likely champion the idea now that he was taking a softer, kinder approach to life.

Sometime around sunrise, I started thinking about Bella, about her offer to join the other vendors at Club Wed. What a privilege to work with the crème de la crème. My résumé would shine like a new penny. Yia Yia would be so proud.

Yia Yia. My heart felt heavy as I factored my grandmother into this equation for the first time. I couldn't let her go to California without me. At nearly ninety years old, she might not be with us much longer. The very idea caused me to cry. When Gina stirred in the bed next to mine, I pulled the pillow over my head to muffle the sound. That, coupled with the inability to breathe properly, finally caused the tears to stop. Why fight it? I had no choice but to stick with my family, no matter how far it took me away from Galveston.

Galveston . . . Made me think of the beach.

The beach . . . Made me think of bikes.

Biking . . . Made me think of Alex.

Alex . . . Made me think I might just have a meltdown if I left without him.

Just about the time I'd settled on the "I must go to California with my family" decision, I realized how strong my feelings for Alex really were. I remembered the three little words he'd used in his text.

Now if only he'd use the next three words: *I. Love. You.*

They would make my decision a whole lot easier.

27
Just You, Just Me

You might be Greek if you think dish-washers are people.

The next couple of days we all tiptoed around Mama and Babbas. On Saturday morning, just before opening the shop to customers, our father gathered us together. I could tell his smile was painted on as he spoke.

"I talked to the landlord. He doesn't think he will have any trouble leasing out the property. There's a local artist who's been hoping for a spot on the Strand." Babbas didn't look excited by this possibility, but he gave us all a thumbs-up.

"I see." Only two words from Mama. I couldn't tell much from her tone either.

"He's thinking that we might be able to get out of the lease by the end of the month." Babbas reached for a broom. "I'm thinking another week or two and then we'll start the process of shutting things down so that we can get packed up. Cleared out."

"Cleared out." Two more words from Mama. Zero emotion.

Really, Mama? Can't you give us more than that?

On the other hand, I had enough emotion for all of us. Leaving would be bad enough, but closing up shop? Packing up the very things we'd just unboxed weeks ago? Loading and lifting, lugging and hauling? The exhaustion hit me all over again. No thanks. I'd had enough of that already.

Mama simply nodded and walked into the other room.

Babbas looked my way and sighed as he tossed the dish towel over his shoulder. "She hates me."

"She doesn't hate you," I said. "She's just got a lot on her mind."

"No, she hates me." He walked into the kitchen, muttering in Greek.

Gina tagged along behind him, tugging on his apron. "Babbas? Babbas?"

He turned and knelt down in front of her, sweeping her into his arms. "What is it, little monkey?"

She threw her arms around his neck. "I don't hate you. I love you."

"Well, I love you too, Gina." He gave her a kiss on the cheek.

"The yelling kind of love?" she asked. "Or the hugging kind of love?"

The innocence of her question made me gasp out loud. Yikes. Our father's eyes misted over as he pulled her into a warm embrace. "The hugging kind of love."

"Good." She pulled away and put her hands on his shoulders. "Because I have something to tell you and I don't want you to yell."

"I won't." He spoke in a voice filled with genuine sweetness. "What is it?"

"Babbas, I don't want to go back to California. I like it here." She spun in a circle, nearly knocking several pans off the counter in the process.

Babbas stood and straightened up her mess but never fussed at her. "Well now, sweet girl, that is a dilemma. But we have to do what makes sense for the whole family."

"The whole family wants to stay here." She crossed her arms. "All of us!"

Babbas looked at me. "Is this so?"

I released a slow breath and nodded. "I can't speak for Mama, but the rest of us are torn. It's a . . . well, a hard decision."

"One I've made for the benefit of the whole family." Babbas wiped his brow, then reached down to pick up Gina. "I want my little monkey to be happy, but the monkey's mommy must be happy too. You see?"

"But if we leave, nothing will be the same!" Gina's little voice quivered, and soon gut-wrenching sobs followed. Babbas held her close.

My other siblings, likely frightened by the crying, came tearing into the kitchen one after another. Mama followed on their heels. Athena came in behind her, the crinkles deepening around her eyes as she watched Gina weep and wail.

"What's happened?" Mama wrung her hands together. "Are you injured, Gina?"

"She's fine." Babbas put Gina down and smoothed her mussed hair. "We were just having a father-daughter talk. But she knows that all will be well, right, little monkey?"

Gina sniffled and shrugged. "I guess." The sobs started again. "But I really, really, really, really don't want to move, Babbas." She flung her arms around him. "Why do we have to go? I'll never get to build my sand castle. Never, never, never."

"There now . . ." He knelt once more and his arms encircled her.

I felt tears spring to my eyes. Apparently my brothers and sisters were having a tough time with this too. And Mama? She brushed the tears from her eyes and joined Babbas and Gina, kneeling down to join their little circle.

Athena looked my way as if to ask, "What have I missed?" and I just shook my head. There would be plenty of time to fill her in later.

When Gina's cries ended, Mama dabbed her tears away. "We love you, baby girl."

"I know." She looked at our father, whose face was awash with tears. "I was scared to tell you, Babbas. I thought you would yell at me."

"I'm working hard on that, pumpkin. My yelling days are over." He looked at Mama as if to reassure her.

Gina sniffled. "O-okay."

Filip lifted his palms, an odd expression on his face. "Am I the only one who's going to miss the yelling?"

Our father's brows met in the middle as he took in this information. "You . . . what?"

Darian laughed. "I think he's used to a certain decibel level. Maybe you need to keep being . . . well, nice . . . but louder."

For a minute I thought this might upset him, but Babbas started chuckling. "A louder version of nice?"

"Yeah, you could yell nice things at us," Filip said. "Like, 'Hey, you're a great kid! I really love you!' Stuff like that."

Babbas tousled my brother's hair.

"Or what about, 'Hey, you're great at washing dishes!' " Darian added. " 'Why don't you get in there and show me how good you are?' "

Eva groaned, but I couldn't help but laugh. As much as things changed, they stayed the same.

"When we get back home to Santa Cruz, our lives will be different." Babbas now addressed all of us. "I promise. We will have more time together as a family. We will go on vacations."

"Do you mean that, Niko?" Mama crossed her arms. "Or will you go back on this promise like before?"

He looked wounded by her words. "I-I will need to make sure the business is stable, but I promise to go on a vacation." His expression clouded with anger, but I had a feeling he would carry through for Mama's sake.

"Very well. I will put together a plan." Mama's lips turned up in a smile.

"A . . . plan?" Babbas released a slow breath.

"Yes, Niko. That's what people do when they go on a vacation. They make a plan." She waved her hands in the air. "But don't worry about any of that. Just leave it all to me. I know someone."

"You know someone?" Babbas looked concerned.

"In the travel business. One of our customers. I will work out the details."

Now he really looked worried. "But travel agents cost money, no?"

"Don't worry about that part, Niko." She shot him a frustrated look.

The bell on the front door jangled, and Babbas and the boys went out into the shop to tend to the incoming customers. I wrestled with my emotions as I tagged along behind them, my thoughts in a whirl. When we got back to Santa Cruz, life might be different from before, or it might be the same. With Babbas, who could ever tell?

Stephen arrived at lunchtime, and he and Athena took their usual spots in the front booth to hash out ideas for the sitcom. Their conversation of the day focused on Brock, who was set to arrive on the island next Saturday, along with other cast members from *Stars Collide*. My stomach churned as I thought about it.

Then again, my stomach churned for a variety of reasons. I missed Alex. Missed him terribly. And if I missed him this badly now, what would I feel like later, after moving a couple thousand miles away?

I snuck into the kitchen around noontime to call him. He picked up on the second ring. "Cassia!"

"Alex, I just needed to hear your voice." I shifted the phone to my other ear and reached for a rag to wipe the tzatziki sauce off my hands.

"Same here." He sighed so loudly that I felt it down to my core. "That's why I called earlier."

"You called me? I must've missed it."

"Yeah." The tone of his voice changed. "You, um, didn't listen to the message then?"

"Message?" Ugh. I'd missed that somehow too.

"Yeah, I left you a pretty detailed one. That's why I thought you were calling, actually. You, um, might want to listen to it."

At this point Babbas called my name, asking for a tray of baklava to be brought to the front, and I knew my phone call must come to an end. "I hate to do this, Alex, but—"

"Right. You have to go. I hear your dad."

"Yeah. Sorry."

"No problem. Just listen to the message, okay?"

"Will do."

After ending the call, I slipped the phone into my pocket and carried the tray of baklava to the front of the store. The next hour was spent taking care of the crowd. Man, did we have customers or what? I didn't even have time to grab a bite to eat.

Finally, around three o'clock, things slowed down and I remembered Alex's comment about leaving a message. I walked outside with a rag in my hand to clean the outside tables, then reached for my phone and pushed the button to retrieve the message from Alex.

His soothing voice calmed my nerves at once, and the Texas twang seemed richer than before as the message began. Not that the method of delivery mattered. No, all that mattered was the impassioned speech—his words of affection for me, his pleas for me to stay in Galveston so that we could grow our relationship into something that would last a lifetime.

My heart thump-thumped as I listened. Just to be sure I'd heard it right, I played the message again. Yep. Same passion. Same delicious phrases.

Oh. My. Goodness.

Through the glass, Babbas gestured for me to come inside. He obviously needed me for something.

But I couldn't go in just yet. Not now. Not when Alex's emotionally charged "I love you, Cassia" tickled my ear and set my heart ablaze with emotion.

I know it was silly of me, but I couldn't help it. I whispered the words "I love you too" to my now-silent phone, then pulled it to my chest and burst into tears, my heart torn into pieces.

Seconds later I felt someone standing behind me. I turned to discover Mama and Athena had joined me.

"Cassia?" Mama's eyes filled with concern. "Are you all right?"

"Y-yes. N-no!"

"What's happened?" Athena asked.

"I-I just had a message from Alex. He—" I dissolved into tears but then managed to spit out, "He doesn't want me to leave. And I don't want to go either." I glanced at Mama, filled with shame. "I mean, I want to be with the family, but the idea of leaving him is . . . is . . ."

"Is killing you." Mama nodded and put her hand on my arm. "I know that feeling well, sweet girl." She gestured to a nearby table. "Can we sit a minute and talk?"

"Of course."

I tried to get my emotions under control, then the three of us settled into chairs and waited for a group of tourists to pass by before speaking. From across the street, the smell of pizza filled the air as the door to Parma John's opened and several customers walked out. Bella stepped out onto the sidewalk and glanced our way. She gave me a curious look as I dabbed at my eyes with a napkin.

"I'm coming over there," she called out. "I don't care what anyone says." She bravely marched into the street and straight toward us. Well, after dodging the silver SUV with the irate driver.

I could only imagine what Babbas must be thinking. Surely he was watching all of this through the window. But he didn't come outside, thank goodness.

Bella settled into the only remaining empty chair at our table and gazed at me with growing intensity. "What have I missed?"

"Cassia doesn't want to go back to California," Mama said.

"Well, that's good." Bella slapped the table with her hands. "Because I don't want you to go."

"And I don't want you to either." These words came from Mama, who stood and paced the sidewalk. "In fact, I don't want any of us to go."

"W-what?" I shook my head. "Babbas is doing all of this because he thinks you want to go back."

"Ugh! This is all my fault." Athena leaned her head on the table. "I should never have told him that we wanted his input on the show. That's what gave him the idea in the first place. But he certainly doesn't need to be in California for that to happen."

378

"No, Cassia is right. I'm sure this decision of his isn't so much about the show as it is about me." Mama stopped and fussed with a stack of napkins on the table. "He's making a noble gesture because he thinks it's right for me. But now I've painted myself into a corner. I don't want to go, but neither do I want to stay if he's still intent on making a fool of himself to grow this business. I can't bear the idea of arguing with the neighbors all the time. I've lived too long like that."

"He seems to be getting nicer," I said. "Maybe it will stick."

Mama laughed. "I love you for thinking that, Cassia. Your father is a good man, and I do believe the Lord can bring about changes, but Babbas is also a good marketer. He wants to make Super-Gyros the best it can be. Every man wants that for his family—a stable life, I mean."

"So you don't want to go but you don't want to stay?" I shook my head. "I'm confused."

"I want to give the man a wake-up call," she said. "This situation between our two families has to be resolved once and for all."

"I agree," Bella said. "But Uncle Laz is a stubborn old coot. He still wants his business to be number one on the island. He handed over the reins to my oldest brother years ago but then took them back. That's how insecure he is."

"Niko is the same way." Mama sighed. "But I don't care about any of that. I'm done with feuding." She turned to Athena. "I'm sorry if that ruins your sitcom idea, Athena. It's all fun and games for TV, but in the real world we just can't live like this. We are called to love our neighbors, to live together in harmony."

"Right, right." Athena looked a bit dejected. "Should we . . . I mean, should I call my producer and tell him we're not moving forward with the idea?"

Mama shook her head. "No, I'm not saying that either. It would destroy Niko's ego to have that show stolen away from him. He thinks he's going to be famous."

"Uncle Laz would be devastated too," Bella said. "He loved the idea. And I think the people at the Food Network are pleased too. This will draw even more people to *The Italian Kitchen.*"

"So what's the answer, Mama?" I asked. I could tell from the look on her face that she had some sort of a plan brewing.

"I've been giving this a lot of thought," she said. "I believe Niko and Laz need to meet in the middle."

"Meet in the middle?" Bella, Athena, and I spoke the words in unison.

"Yep. Meet in the middle." Mama's eyes gleamed as she looked at the cobblestone street. "And I've come up with just the right way to make that happen."

"Oh?" This certainly captured my interest.

"Yes." She continued to stare at the middle of the street, a devilish gleam in her eyes. "But I can't do it alone." She homed in on the three of us, her voice lowering to a hoarse whisper. "To bring these two men together . . . well, it's going to take a village."

28

Meet Me in St. Louis

You might be Greek if you are summoned
to meals by the sound of a shofar.

A week after my world-rocking conversation with
Mama, we braced ourselves for the implementa-
tion of her big plan.

Okay, so it wasn't just Mama's plan. By the time
it all came together, it pretty much involved every
woman in the Pappas family and the Rossi family.
And heavens, there were a lot of women in the
Rossi family! They all chimed in with their
thoughts, and before long our "wow, I hope this
works!" plan was set.

Midmorning Saturday, we all gathered at the
shop. Athena, Stephen, Alex, his sisters, the
Splendora ladies . . . everyone. Well, everyone on
the Pappas side. Keeping things a secret from
Babbas proved slightly problematic with Alex's
aunt Twila in the mix, but we managed to contain
her before the cat slipped out of the bag.

Mama kicked off the action at 11:45 with a
proclamation: "Niko, I want you to put the Closed
sign on the door."

"The Closed sign?" He looked perplexed. "But we're not officially closing for another week and a half."

"That's not what I mean. I want you to close up shop today. Right now." She pointed to a couple of tables where guests sat eating. "As soon as these last customers leave. You must trust me. No arguments."

"But why? Saturday is our busiest day!" He started to rant in Greek but then stopped himself, a sheepish look on his face. "I will do it, Helena. For you. Anything."

Wow. He really had changed.

At noon, just as Mama rushed the last customer out the door, she hung the Closed sign and gestured for the rest of us—minus Babbas, who still worked in the kitchen—to join her on the sidewalk. We met up with Officer O'Reilly, who gave Mama a thumbs-up. Perfect. Good to go.

I glanced to the middle of the street to make sure everything was in place, then giggled as I reached for Alex's hand. "You ready for this?" I whispered.

He gave me a sound kiss and then responded with a boisterous, "Yep! Can't wait! It's gonna be quite a day."

We exchanged a subtle look of amusement, followed by a high five.

Mama called out for Babbas to join us, and he stepped out onto the sidewalk just as the entire

Rossi family flooded out of Parma John's across the street.

For a moment no one moved—not the Greeks, not the Italians. A lot of staring took place, but no forward motion. Kind of felt like a scene from one of those old Westerns, where the good guy and the bad guy face each other down at the O.K. Corral. Except there weren't any bad guys in our story. Well, not of the shoot-'em-up variety.

"What in the world?" Babbas remained in his Greek statuesque pose, gazing at Parma John's and then at the obvious setup in the center of the street. "What is this?"

"This, my dear, is where we're having lunch." Mama gestured to the long line of picnic tables running down the center of the Strand.

"Lunch? In the middle of the street?"

"Yes, but before we eat, I have something I need to say." She put her hands on her hips and faced him dead-on. "You can go back to California if you like, Niko Pappas, but you will go without me."

"Without you?" He stared at her and then shook his head. "But I'm going *because* of you."

"No. I will not be the reason you flip this family upside down. We love it here in Galveston."

Babbas began to rant in Greek about women and their inability to make up their minds, at which point Yia Yia took hold of his arm and pinched it.

"Already you slip back to your old ways, boy? I raised you better than this!" She wiggled a bony finger in his face. "If you know what's good for you, you will speak to others with kindness, especially the wife God has blessed you with."

"I am kind!" Babbas grunted and muttered in Greek once again. "Did Gina not say just the other day that I'm *too* nice?"

Mama rolled her eyes. "Impossible." She placed her hand on my father's arm. "Now, Niko, we don't want you to lose your personality—heaven forbid—but there's no such thing as being too kind. Remember what the Bible says about loving your neighbor."

"Loving my neighbor?" He grunted again as he looked across the street at the Rossis, who stood on their sidewalk arguing with Laz. He looked about as happy as Babbas did.

"We will meet in the middle," Mama said.

Babbas looked confused. "Meet in the middle?"

"Yes. You will meet me halfway. I will stay, and you will lay down your battle with the Rossis . . . forever."

"But—"

"No buts. And just to reiterate, I'm not going anywhere. You can leave if you want, but I'm staying put, even if you decide not to share a meal with our new friends."

"Helena, surely you don't think that we should—"

"We're having a picnic with the neighbors." She pointed to the beautifully decorated tables, then took a step into the street. "Join us if you like. Or don't. It's your choice."

He looked at the line of picnic tables running down the middle of the Strand. "Are you crazy? Cars have to get through here. And the trolley."

Officer O'Reilly approached and handed Babbas an official-looking piece of paper. "Your wife applied for a permit, Niko. I've coned off the area, as you can see. Plenty of room on either side for cars to get by. And before you start fretting over the trolley, let me put your mind at ease. It's shut down for servicing for the next two hours. Won't reopen until two o'clock, so this little get-together will have to end before then."

"See there?" Mama gave Babbas a knowing look. "So just you hush, old man, and join us for a picnic with friends."

My father continued to grumble, and Yia Yia reached out to pinch him again. Before he could holler "Ouch!" my brothers emerged from Super-Gyros carrying large platters of Greek food to the tables in the center of the street.

Babbas looked mortified. "Where are you going with that?" he hollered.

"We're meeting in the middle," Darian said as he set a tray of gyros down and then headed back inside to fetch more food.

"In the *very* middle," Bella said, joining us with

a large pizza in hand. She called out to Scarlet and Gabi to help her bring out more food from Parma John's—pasta, garlic twists, tiramisu, and more.

Alex grabbed a slice of pizza and slathered it with tzatziki sauce, then took a big bite. "Mmm."

"Meeting . . . in the middle?" Babbas kept his position on the Greek side of the street. He cast a furtive glance at Laz, whose feet remained firmly fixed to the sidewalk on the Italian side. The two men stared at one another, each refusing to budge.

"Stay there if you like," Mama said. "But the rest of us are going to share a meal together as one big happy family. I understand the pizza at Parma John's is quite tasty."

"You wouldn't dare." Babbas turned to her, clearly mortified.

"Try me." She walked over to the table to grab a slice of the Mambo Italiano, then scarfed it down in a hurry. "Yum!"

I couldn't resist, so I grabbed a slice too. So did Darian. Then Filip, then Eva. Gina was the last to succumb, but when she did, her darling face lit up. "The pizza is delicious, Babbas!"

Our father waved his hands in the air as he took a tentative step toward the edge of the sidewalk. "You are all crazy."

"Yes, they are!" Laz called out. "The police will shut this down in a New York minute and have all of you sent to the loony bin!"

"On the contrary." Mama gestured to Officer O'Reilly. "As we've already told Niko, I applied for a permit to meet here for two hours. I have the paper to prove it. And we've asked one of Galveston's finest to join us. This is a family meal, and Officer O'Reilly is family now." She gestured for the officer to sit and he did.

Laz shook his head. "Have you all lost your minds?"

"No, dear." Rosa gave him a firm look as she took a seat and reached for a gyro. "I believe we've found them. Now, are you going to join us, or are we going to have to say grace without you?"

Laz grunted something in Italian. Babbas countered with something equally as irritating in Greek. But Mama and Rosa held their ground as the rest of us—nearly forty, if you counted Greeks, Italians, Splendora folks, and O'Reilly—took our seats.

"Rosa, would you like some tzatziki sauce?" Mama passed the bowl. "My Cassia makes it, and it's the best on the island."

"Sounds divine. I haven't had good tzatziki sauce since . . . well, since you stayed at our house last week, actually. But I can't wait to have more." Rosa turned her attention to my father. "Niko—do you mind if I call you Niko?—your family recipe is the best I've ever tasted."

He grunted a thank-you.

"Almost as good as that Greek pizza recipe

Cassia shared with us," Rosa added. "I still don't care for the name, though."

"Yes," Twila chimed in. "The Venus Flytrap just sounds so . . . hokey."

Babbas crossed his arms and glared at me.

"Of course, we are equally as thrilled that you have shared your secrets with us," Mama said to Rosa. "How can I ever thank you for that recipe for your garlic twists?" She reached for one and gave it a taste. "Mmm."

"You gave away our family recipe for the garlic twists?" Laz's face reddened. "Really?"

"Well, yes," Rosa said. "That's what friends do."

Mama took another nibble. "I've never tasted anything as good. And your homemade sauce— divine!"

"Gravy," Rosa corrected. "We call it gravy."

"Gravy." Mama nodded. "Well, I'll make it every day."

"Over my dead body!" Laz stormed toward the center of the street and pointed his finger at Rosa. "Woman, why have you given away our secrets to the enemy?"

"Enemy?" Rosa reached out and took Mama's hand. Mama grabbed hold of Bella's hand and she took Darian's. He grabbed Marcella's. Marcella took mine. I took Alex's. Alex took Twila's . . . and so on.

Seconds later, we formed a large circle in the center of the street, all hands firmly clasped together.

Well, not all hands. Babbas stood, feet firmly planted, on the Greek side of the street. Laz stood, arms crossed, on the Italian side.

Only when a car came barreling down the Italian side did my father rush toward the circle.

"Whatever it takes to get you here, dear," Mama said, extending her hand.

"But . . ." He couldn't seem to finish his thought.

"Laz, darling, please come and say grace." Rosa's voice rang out above the crowd. "And don't give me any of that 'I don't like to pray out loud' stuff. You do it all the time at home. Might as well pray here too."

I couldn't think of a better place to pray, actually, nor could I think of people I'd rather pray with. Laz muttered a few unintelligible words, then walked toward us. He somehow managed a prayer—most of it in Italian—and then took a seat next to Rosa.

Just as my father succumbed to the temptation to join us—and really, who wouldn't, with all of the tasty dishes on the table?—a limousine pulled up to the curb on the Italian side of the street. My heart rate skipped to double time. I'd waited for this moment for days, after all. The driver got out and opened the back door. With the sun in my eyes, I barely made him out.

Ah yes! There he was!

Brock Benson—Hollywood megastar—emerged,

along with a few other people I recognized as regulars on my favorite sitcom of all time, *Stars Collide*.

Now, I'd dreamed of meeting these superstars all my life, but to find them here, in the middle of the Strand, seemed otherworldly. I could hardly catch my breath. Apparently all of the other ladies in attendance seemed to be struggling with their breathing too, especially Alex's twin sisters, who looked on wide-eyed.

Brock headed straight to the Italian side of the table, talking a mile a minute as Aunt Rosa swept him into her arms and covered his face with kisses. Then the whole crowd came alive. Laz gave Brock a slap on the back, Bella ran to embrace Brock's wife, and Lily and Jasmine both rose with stunned looks on their faces. Oops! We'd obviously forgotten to clue those two in.

Lily couldn't seem to manage a word when Brock walked over to the Greek side of the table. Jasmine, on the other hand, bubbled with nervous energy and couldn't shut up. Brock introduced the twins to his beautiful wife, and before long the ladies were seated and talking like old friends.

Athena tapped her spoon against her water glass and hollered to get the crowd under control. "A huge Texas welcome to our guests!"

The Greeks and Italians clapped in unison. Well, all but Babbas, who looked thoroughly confused.

"You probably recognize Kat and Scott Murphy

from their hit show, *Stars Collide*," Athena continued. "And Brock's wife Erin. I'd also like you to meet Tia, our director, and her husband Jason. He's worked on the show from the beginning. Oh, and Lenora. Surely you all recognize Lenora. She's been on the show from the very beginning."

Athena gestured to an elderly woman about Yia Yia's age and size, wearing, of all things, a ball gown. When Mama complimented her on it, Lenora responded, "Judy Garland, *A Star Is Born*, 1954."

Of course. No wonder it looked familiar. Still, it seemed like an odd clothing choice in the middle of a summer day.

Finally Athena introduced an unfamiliar guest— an older fellow named Rex whose arm was looped through Lenora's. "Rex is our producer, folks. He's the one who took the idea for the new sitcom to studio executives. He and Lenora are married."

"Nice to meet you all. Can't wait to get to know you." Rex glanced at my father and extended his hand. "You must be Niko Pappas."

"Why, yes." Babbas rose and shook the stranger's hand. "How did you—"

"I'd recognize you anywhere from Athena's description." Lenora giggled. "Oh, this new show is going to be *fab*-u-lous!" She grabbed a slice of pizza. "Ooh, speaking of fabulous! This is the yummiest thing I've ever eaten. We just can't get real Italian food in Beverly Hills."

I looked around as everyone began to talk at once. What bliss! I reached to give Alex's hand a squeeze. He squeezed back, then kissed me on the cheek. "I think it's going better than expected. Don't you?"

"Definitely." I couldn't get over the fact that the sitcom producer had so easily swept Babbas and Laz into a common conversation about the show. And Brock! He engaged my father multiple times, puffing up his ego with flattering remarks about all of the fun stories he'd heard.

"Seems like you've made quite an impression on Galveston, Mr. Pappas," Brock said. "People here seem to really love your family and your shop."

"Well, to be honest, we were toying with the idea of moving back to California." Babbas leaned back in his chair, his gaze shifting to Laz and then back to Brock. "But I think we will be staying on the island after all." He glanced at Mama. "It's growing on me." He took a sip of his tea, his eyes widening in delight. "And starting Monday morning, I'm adding sweet tea to the menu! This is amazing."

"Wonderful news, all of it!" Brock took a bite of pizza, then swiped the sauce from his lips. "And just for the record, this show will be comedic—deliberately funny. But we don't expect the two of you"—he pointed at Laz and Babbas—"to really go on feuding just to keep the ratings up."

"Not that it *ever* hurts to keep the ratings up!" Lenora giggled and grabbed a piece of baklava.

Laz gave my father a sheepish look as he reached for a gyro. "I can't really blame Niko here for wanting his business to succeed." Everyone on both sides of the tables grew silent at this proclamation. "That's what we all want, especially those of us with families to support."

Mama lifted her glass of sweet tea and hollered, "Opa!" The Rossis lifted their glasses and responded in kind.

"Must be a guy thing, right, Niko?" Laz looked my father in the eye for the first time all day.

Babbas took a swig of his sweet tea and nodded. "We compete because we care about those we love and want to do our best by them."

"Wait . . . a guy thing?" Bella crossed her arms at her chest and stared at her uncle. "What are we?" She pointed to all of the female business owners in attendance. "Chopped liver?"

"What do you mean, Bella?" Laz gave her a curious look.

"I run my own business, Uncle Laz. And so does Hannah." She gestured to Hannah, who had risen to take photos of our group. "And Sophia. And Marcella. And Scarlet. And Gabi." She pointed at me. "And Cassia too."

"We're all working to keep our businesses going, just like the men," Marcella said. "And it's just as hard for us."

"Maybe harder," Bella said. "Have you ever tried to coordinate a wedding and battle morning sickness at the same time?"

"Can't say that I have," Laz said. "But that doesn't mean you've got it harder because you're female."

Oh. Ouch. The temperature on the Strand shot up by a good ten degrees at that statement.

To his credit, Laz probably hadn't meant to turn this into a battle of the sexes, but that's just what it became. Heated conversations filled the air, most of them between Laz and Rosa, who claimed that she played a larger role in their Food Network show than he did. Laz didn't take that news very well. And by the time Bella's parents joined in with their two cents' worth, I felt like scooting back inside Super-Gyros for some peace and quiet.

Peace and quiet at Super-Gyros? Ha! For the first time ever it occurred to me that my family, loud and crazy as they might be, didn't hold a candle to the Rossi family. They gave new meaning to chaos and confusion.

Before I could give it any more thought, Mama stood and waved her arms to bring the argument to an end. "I need your attention, everyone!" she called out. "Attention, please!"

When the noise level fell, she turned to Babbas and offered a mischievous grin. "I have an announcement to make, Niko, and it concerns you."

"O-oh?" Babbas's unibrow slipped back into place as his forehead wrinkled in concern. I didn't blame him, after the day he'd had.

Her face lit into the prettiest smile I'd seen in ages. As it did, I homed in on the toned-down makeup job. She looked absolutely lovely today. I hadn't even noticed until now.

"Have you ever heard the song 'Mambo Italiano'?" she asked.

" 'Mambo Italiano'?" He let out a noise that sounded a bit like a growl. "Like the pizza?" He pointed to Parma John's.

"The Mambo Italiano special is named after a real song by Dean Martin," Laz said.

"Actually, Rosemary Clooney sang it first, I think." Aunt Rosa dabbed her lips.

Mama sighed. "Point is, I heard it playing at the Rossis' house and fell in love with it. But I don't believe I'd ever paid attention to the words until then."

Babbas grunted. "What about it?"

"It's about a fella who goes back to his home-town in Italy because he misses the scenery—the old dances and songs, that sort of thing." Mama's expression grew more animated. "And that got me thinking." She clasped her hands together, eyes dancing with delight. "Now, brace yourself, Niko. What I'm about to say may come as a bit of a shock."

29

I Could Go On Singing

You might be Greek if your family has a wedding at least twice a year.

Mama practically squealed as she made her announcement: "Pack your bags, Niko! We're going on the trip of a lifetime!"

"The trip of a lifetime?" He shook his head. "You mean to California? Have you changed your mind again, woman?"

"No. To Greece." She gestured to Gabi and smiled. "This precious girl's mother works as a travel agent and has been helping me all week long, ever since you said we could take a vacation."

"Well, yes, but I didn't mean . . ." Babbas put his head in his hands.

"Doesn't matter. We've already come up with a plan."

"A plan?" Babbas wiped the sweat from his brow and gazed at her.

"Now, don't argue, Niko. I've been putting away a little money—"

"You've been putting away money?" My father rose. He did not look pleased by this

397

news. "And where has this money come from?"

"My portion of the tip jar," Mama said. "Why do you think I do my own nails? Cut my own hair? Never ask for a night out on the town?"

"Because we're too busy?"

"Because I'm careful with money—our family budget and my own money besides. Anyway, I've saved enough to pay for our flights to Athens."

"A-Athens?"

"Yes. We're going to enjoy the rich culture and history of Greece, mainland and islands. We'll experience the exotic beauty and romance of Athens and then witness exquisite beaches and breathtaking panoramic views on the islands of Santorini and Mykonos."

"What?" Babbas still looked perplexed. "Have you memorized the travel brochure or something?"

"Yes, I have." Mama nodded. "But before long it will be more than a pipe dream. I'm done with talking about all the things we're going to do someday. We're doing them now."

"N-now?" He looked around, as if expecting suitcases to materialize.

"Well, next month—the fifteenth, to be precise. And that reminds me, we're not going alone. Your brother and his wife are going too."

"My brother?" Babbas crossed his arms, then relaxed them when he realized Athena was looking at him. "I see."

Mama nodded. "This is going to be a family trip."

My siblings had just started to celebrate that news when Mama put her hand up. "Older family members only." She turned to my grandmother and extended a hand. "That includes you, Yia Yia. We're taking you back home to Santorini. You can show us all the places you lived as a little girl, and your favorite vacation spots too."

Yia Yia began to wail about how she wanted us to lay her bones to rest in Greece.

"Well, I hope you're not asking us to do that on this trip." Mama gave her a kiss on the forehead. "We need you to stay alive to show us around." She turned to Babbas. "So what do you say? Are you ready to do what Cassia's always singing about—forget your troubles, c'mon get happy—and take your wife and mother on a trip to a place you've been claiming as your homeland?"

"I . . . I . . ." He raked his fingers through his hair. "When you put it like that, how can I not?" He looked at me. "But with Cassia so busy at the flower shop, who will take care of Super-Gyros?"

"I've got that covered too." Mama pointed to our new friends. "Rosa had the perfect solution."

My father looked panicked at the mention of Rosa's name. "What about her?"

"She and Laz have been in the restaurant business for years and know what it takes to keep a place going. They will check in on the kids every day and make sure things are going smoothly."

"We . . . we will?" Laz glanced over at Rosa, who nodded.

"Over my dead bod—" Babbas clamped his lips shut. Well, actually, Mama planted a big kiss on his lips with everyone looking on. When he came up for air, his cheeks blazed a reddish bronze. I couldn't help but laugh, and all the more when he swept Mama into his arms, tilted her back for a Hollywood-esque smooch, then lifted her back up again. The crowd roared with delight.

When things settled down, I approached my father to put his mind at ease about the shop. "Don't worry, Babbas," I said. "I'll be in and out of the store every day. I'm sure Marcella and I can work out some arrangement." I glanced at my boss and she nodded and smiled.

"I'll help too," Alex said. "I don't know the first thing about running a cash register, but I've watched you whip up the tzatziki sauce so many times I could do it in my sleep. And I'm pretty sure I could make a mean gyro too."

He'd never make a mean hero. A terrific one, maybe, but never mean.

My parents settled back down into their seats, and Bella rose. "Since we're making announcements, I have one too." She looked at D.J. and her eyes misted over. "We, um, well, we haven't really said anything about this publicly yet, but . . ."

"What is it, Bella?" Rosa asked.

"D.J. and I wanted to wait until we were far enough along to make any announcements."

"Far enough along?" Rosa let out a squeal. So did Imelda Rossi.

"Wait . . ." I stared at Bella. "You're . . . you're having a baby?"

She nodded and a little tear rolled out of the corner of her eye. "I am. I mean, we are. I'm eight weeks as of today, and things appear to be going great."

"Oh, Bella!" Hannah squealed and grabbed her hand. "I'm going to take your pregnancy pictures!"

Scarlet ran to her side and gave her a hug. "I'm going to bake the baby shower cake."

"I'm going to make the cutest baby dress," Gabi chimed in. "Well, if it's a girl. If it's a boy, I'll make a little suit."

What could I contribute to this but the obvious? "And I'm going to do the prettiest centerpiece at your shower. Ooh, maybe even a corsage for you. And, of course, a fabulous arrangement in pink or blue once the baby arrives."

A baby! The idea got me tickled.

The Splendora ladies all ran toward Bella at once and wrapped her in their bosomy embraces. This led to a conversation about the baby's birth, and before long they were all talking about the Duchess's delivery. I had to laugh when Twila waved her hand and said, "I still can't believe she deliberately chose a C-section. She's too posh to push!"

This got a laugh from everyone. Babbas lifted his glass of sweet tea and gave a little toast in Greek, welcoming the new little one, to which Laz responded with a hearty "Opa!"

With all of the attention now firmly fixed on Bella, I found myself free to pay attention to the one person who'd been overlooked in so much of the recent chaos. I turned to Alex, my gorgeous Greek Southern gentleman, and whispered, "I love you."

His face lit brighter than the midday sun as he leaned my way. "I love you too." He gave my hand a squeeze and looked around the table at all of the others. "I don't know how I landed an invitation to this memorable soiree, to be honest. I'm not exactly a Rossi, now am I? And I'm not a Pappas. I'm just happy to be included." He kissed me on the cheek. "It's always fun to be part of the family."

Indeed. As I looked around the table, as I listened in on the various conversations, I had to conclude that my family had just doubled in size . . . and I'd never been happier.

The fun continued until one thirty, when O'Reilly reminded us that the trolley would be back up and running soon. The women all stood and started clearing the tables, but Babbas and Laz remained behind, chatting like old friends with Brock and the *Stars Collide* producer, as well as the other members of the cast. I grabbed several dirty plates and stacked them in my arms, then headed into Super-Gyros.

Alex followed behind me, carrying a couple of empty gyro plates. When we reached the kitchen, he looked my way. "I need you to do something for me."

"Oh?"

"Yes." He set the trays down on the counter. "Come with me for a little ride."

"On our bikes?" I couldn't imagine it in this heat. And after such a busy day? "I don't know, Alex."

"Not on our bikes." He took the stack of dirty plates out of my hands and set them in the sink. "The trolley. It's been down for repairs, but they're opening at two o'clock. Remember?"

"But why?" None of this made sense. "You want to show it to Athena's friends?"

"Yes. I think they would like it, don't you?"

I shrugged. "I guess."

"Okay, well, do me a favor. Go upstairs and get changed."

"Huh?"

"Just go upstairs to your parents' room. Athena's there waiting on you."

"No she's not. She's still outside." I walked out into the restaurant and looked through the glass to the street. "Hmm."

"Told you." Alex took my hands. "Now, please don't ask any questions. Just go see her."

"Okay." I practically ran up the steps to our apartment and then bounded into my parents' bedroom. Athena stood in the middle of the room, a bright smile on her face.

"Well, hello there. Thought you'd never get here."

"What in the world are we doing?"

Her eyes widened in false innocence. "*We* are doing nothing. *You* are changing into a lovely new dress that has been supplied for you just for this moment." She opened the closet door. "You wouldn't believe what I had to go through to get this." She giggled as she pulled an amazing Victorian gown out of the closet. "Thank God Rex and Lenora were willing to bring it with them."

I gasped as I laid eyes on the gorgeous red gown with its sweetheart neckline and puffed short sleeves.

"Look familiar?" Athena's eyes twinkled.

I gave it a closer look. "It does seem like I've seen it before . . . but where?"

"What's your favorite movie of all time?"

"*Meet Me in St. Louis.*" I'd no sooner spoken the words than it hit me. Judy Garland had worn this same gown—well, maybe not this exact same one, but close—in the party scene.

"Oh, Athena. How in the world . . . ?"

"Lenora has the most amazing collection of

costumes from old Hollywood days. I asked Rex if he would do a bit of digging to come up with this particular gown, and he did. Long story short, this dress—and yes, it's a copycat—was hanging on the costume rack at the studio. It's not a hundred percent like Judy's version, but it's close. Notice the pinched waistline."

"Well, yes. But why . . . ?" I couldn't formulate words. They'd brought this dress all the way from California?

"Because Alex asked for it."

"He did?"

"Yep. The same day your father gave you the news that you would be moving back to Santa Cruz. So . . ." She grinned. "You gonna stand there all day, or are you going to let us fix your hair so you can get into this knock-'em-dead dress?"

"You're going to fix my hair?"

"Actually, Bella's sister Sophia is helping me. She'll be up in a second. She's going to fix it just like Judy wore it when she danced across the floor in this dress. Sophia printed up a picture from the internet, so don't fret. It'll be perfect."

Fret? Who could fret at a time like this? No, my heart felt like singing!

Sophia showed up with a bagful of hair doo-dads and got to work. I hummed the whole time she and Athena worked on my hair and makeup, then I eased my way into the magnificent gown with its tiny waist and deep red color.

Athena walked back to the closet and came out with a hatbox. She removed the most glorious Victorian hat I'd ever seen.

"Are . . . are you serious?"

She nodded and handed it to Sophia, who pinned it in place over my Gibson girl hairdo.

I stood in front of Mama's full-length mirror and stared at my reflection in awe. With the dress, the hair, the hat, I looked so much like Judy I could hardly believe it.

A knock sounded at the door, and seconds later, after I gave the okay, my father peeked inside.

"Cassia? Alex is wondering if you're ever going to—" Babbas stopped midsentence as he clapped eyes on me. "Oh my." The next few words came out in Greek. I didn't really understand them—well, not all of them—but managed to get the gist of it. He thought I looked lovely.

I threw my arms around my father's neck and gave him a huge hug. "Thank you, Babbas. Now, if you don't mind, I have a trolley ride to take."

"Yes, I believe someone is waiting for you downstairs. A very dapper fellow in an interesting-looking suit. He's been asking for you."

I slipped on the heels Athena passed to me, then gave myself one last glimpse in the mirror. My heart was beating so fast I could barely catch my breath. Oh, but who needed to breathe?

I bounded out of my parents' room and to the

top of the stairs, then slowed my pace to make a graceful entrance.

The shop below was filled with friends and loved ones—Greek, Italian, Californian, and Splendoran. A collective gasp went up as I eased my way from the bottom step into the shop. Twila rushed to me, followed by all of the other ladies, who gushed over my getup. I smiled and did my best to make conversation, but wanted to see— needed to see—Alex.

He was dressed in a formal turn-of-the-century suit that took my breath away. "Oh, wow." We made our way through the crowd, finally reaching each other. His eyes danced with delight as he took in my appearance.

"Just as I imagined you would look." He extended his hand. "Would you take a little ride with me, Miss Pappas?"

"I-I would love to." He slipped my arm through his and led the way out of the shop to the sidewalk. The street had been cleared of all tables. The cones were gone. And the trolley was parked at the corner.

"Oh, Alex!" I almost lost my breath at the sight of the trolley car covered in multiple garlands of roses. Yellows, pinks, whites, and hundreds of reds. "How in the world did you . . . ?"

"I have my ways." He smiled, then ushered me on board.

The whole place smelled heavenly. I closed my eyes and breathed in the scent, then opened them again, noticing our friends and family in the distance.

"Are they coming with?" I asked.

"Not just yet." Alex reached down to the front seat of the trolley and picked up the most beautiful bouquet of Cassia roses in a bright shade of yellow, then handed them to me. "We'll come back for them in a few minutes. I need a little time with you . . . alone." He waggled his brows in playful fashion and gave me a little kiss on the forehead.

My heart went crazy at this point. Alex led the way down the platform to the back. The trolley took off, and everyone on the street followed along behind us, waving. We waved back, but I was shaking so hard I lost my grip and almost went tumbling off the back of the car, nearly losing the bouquet in the process. Alex wrapped me in his arms and held me close. The trolley rounded the corner and we headed off on our way.

"Where are we going?" I asked, struggling to hold on to the bouquet.

"Where would you like to go?" He gazed at me with such tenderness that I felt my heart melt.

If he had asked me this question a month ago, I would've said, "Home to Santa Cruz." Never in a million years would I have said the words now tripping to the end of my tongue. "It doesn't matter, as long as we're together."

He planted several kisses along my hairline, sending tingles down my spine, then our lips met for a kiss so sweet even Mama's baklava couldn't compete.

Oh, how my heart wanted to sing! My toes wanted to tap! I could dance from the back of this trolley car to the front and then back again, if it meant doing so with this amazing man in my arms.

After a couple of dreamy moments, Alex looked at me and grinned. "Um, Cassia?"

"Yes?" I gazed into those gorgeous brown eyes, the same ones I'd taken note of that first day I saw him on the trolley.

"You're doing it again." His whispered words tickled my ear.

"Hmm? Doing what?"

"Humming."

I was indeed. The words to "The Trolley Song" danced their way from my heart to my lips. I simply couldn't help myself.

Then, as the man of my dreams slipped down to one knee, as he pulled out a tiny box and opened it to reveal a diamond ring that even Judy Garland would've swooned over, I realized that my heart would probably go on singing . . . for the rest of my life.

"WELCOME TO PARADISE"

WRITTEN BY
Athena Pappas Cosse, Stephen Cosse,
Niko Pappas, Cassia Pappas

"WELCOME TO PARADISE" JINGLE BY
Cassia Pappas and the
Splendora Sisters

"WELCOME TO PARADISE" JINGLE plays over WIDE SHOT of GALVESTON STRAND midday. Shops open for business on both sides of street, filled with happy customers spilling over onto sidewalks. WIDE SHOT of TROLLEY clang-clang-clanging by. TOURISTS seated on every row of TROLLEY snap photographs of sights as they whiz by. Close-up of PASSENGER near front of TROLLEY. ZOOM IN on BROCK'S face. JINGLE (INSTRUMENTAL ONLY) continues in background.

BROCK
(shakes hands with man on TROLLEY,
looks into camera)

411

Looking for the perfect place to vacation this summer? Why not take a little ride to sunny Galveston Island? The scenery will take your breath away.

Shot WIDENS and camera flies over GALVESTON ISLAND, taking in breathtaking SCENERY along the COAST, where we see suspiciously WHITE SAND and CARIBBEAN-BLUE WATER. WAVES wash in and out. TIGHT SHOT on NIKO and HELENA riding bikes along SEAWALL. CUT TO WIDE SHOT of MOODY GARDENS, flowers in abundance. CASSIA and ALEX are having their pictures taken in FLOWERS by HANNAH.

BROCK
(back platform of TROLLEY,
looking at SCENERY)

Whether you're looking to rest, work, or play, Galveston's got it all. Great beaches, five-star hotels, amazing entertainment, and the best food on the planet.

WIDE SHOT of STRAND, minus TROLLEY. CUSTOMERS flood into various RESTAURANTS. TIGHT SHOT of SCARLET walking out of LET THEM EAT CAKE BAKERY, holding a WEDDING CAKE. She nearly drops it as she attempts to wave at OFFICER O'REILLY, who catches it and smiles.

BROCK
(voice-over)

Looking for a cultural experience? Whether your heart dreams of going back to Italy, Greece, or a thousand other places around the globe, you will feel right at home here.

WIDE SHOT of RESTAURANTS. ZOOM IN on PARMA JOHN'S. LAZ stands outside, welcoming tourists, holding a PIZZA. Camera swings across street. TIGHT SHOT of NIKO dressed in SUPER-GYROS costume, positioned to fly off into skies above. YIA YIA and OTHER PAPPAS FAMILY MEMBERS hand out SANDWICHES and BAKLAVA to TOURISTS walking down sidewalk. THREE NUNS grab SANDWICHES, converse with SPLENDORA TRIO, and they all walk into SUPER-GYROS together.

BROCK
(voice-over)

Good food, awesome surroundings, amazing friendships. You'll find all of these and more on Galveston Island.

LONG SHOT of picnic tables set up down the center of STRAND. PARTY GUESTS (ENTIRE CAST AND CREW) share a meal together.

ALL PARTY GUESTS
(raise glasses of sweet tea)

Opa!

BROCK
(voice-over)

Whether you're ready to shop till you drop or start your own business, there's no friendlier place on the planet.

WIDE SHOT of FLORIST SHOP. Camera ZOOMS in on SIGN with SHOP'S name: A ROSE IS A ROSE. CASSIA and ALEX stand outside, passing off a BRIDAL BOUQUET OF COLORFUL ROSES to GABI.

BROCK
(voice-over)

Preparing for a big event? You'll find some great places to get you geared up for the big day.

TIGHT SHOT of GABI in SEWING ROOM, stitching VICTORIAN WEDDING GOWN. CUT TO WIDE SHOT of SASSY SHEARS HAIR SALON. TIGHT SHOT of NIKO having his unibrow waxed in the middle by SOPHIA. He overexaggerates, crying out in pain. YIA YIA and HELENA look on, cheering at his clean-cut results.

BROCK
(voice-over)

And speaking of the big day, when you're looking to tie the knot, you won't find a more luxurious place to say "I do" than here on sunny Galveston Island.

CUT TO WIDE SHOT of Broadway Street. ZOOM IN on CLUB WED. GUESTS (ALL CAST MEMBERS) are gathered on VERANDA, throwing birdseed as GROOM JORDAN and BRIDE GABI (wearing VICTORIAN GOWN and carrying BOUQUET OF ROSES) run out front door and toward lawn. TIGHT SHOT of HANNAH taking photos. GABI pauses at edge of VERANDA and throws her wedding bouquet of YELLOW ROSES to crowd of ladies standing on STRAND. LILY and JASMINE both catch it and fight over it.

BROCK
(voice-over)

Yes, there's no finer place to ride off into the sunset with the one you love than right here. So why not experience your happily ever after in paradise?

CUT TO TIGHT SHOT of TROLLEY (BACK PLATFORM), where ALEX and CASSIA stand, kissing. TROLLEY begins to move and they grab railing. ZOOM out to reveal TROLLEY (INSIDE) filled with ROSSI CLAN and PAPPAS CLAN, all toasting with sweet tea. CUT TO TIGHT SHOT of NIKO (with a Band-Aid between his brows) laughing and talking with LAZ. ZOOM to back of TROLLEY, where CASSIA and ALEX kiss once more. TROLLEY fades from view in the SUNSET.

BROCK
So what's keeping you? The experience of a lifetime awaits you on Galveston Island!

FULL CAST SINGS
"WELCOME TO PARADISE" JINGLE

FADE TO BLACK

Small circle in center of black screen WIDENS to reveal NIKO flying across the sky in his SUPER-GYROS costume, GYRO SANDWICH in hand. From below, SPLENDORA TRIO tries to snatch SANDWICH out of his hand, but he's too fast for them. They FADE FROM VIEW. NIKO flies over GALVESTON BEACH with WHITE SAND and CARIBBEAN-BLUE WATER, JINGLE playing merrily in background.

FADE TO BLACK

Author's Note

Writing a book is tough work ordinarily. Factor in several health issues and two personal crises (the death of a best friend and the early delivery of a granddaughter), and writing a book becomes more than tough; it can seem impossible. This was the scenario I faced when I sat down to write Cassia's story.

On Valentine's Day 2013, my best friend, Kay Malone, was diagnosed with pancreatic cancer. Her journey over the next couple of months was grueling and painful to watch. I spent countless hours at her bedside, both in the hospital and in her home. She passed away the day after Mother's Day, just two months before this book was due to the publisher.

At this very same time my daughter was expecting her third baby, little Jenna Reese. Complications set in, and we wondered if the baby would make it. On the day after Kay passed away, we received news about the baby that terrified us. We wondered if Jenna would survive. Thankfully, she arrived with few issues and is thriving today. Praise God!

In the midst of all this, I was dealing with perplexing health issues of my own. The exhaustion didn't help. In the back of my mind (as I drove from hospital to hospital, funeral to NICU), I kept thinking, *I have a book due in a few weeks.* But how in the world could I possibly write a romantic comedy? It seemed impossible!

Then something remarkable happened: this story unfolded like a gift from the Lord. I found my spirits lifted, my hope restored, and my joy reignited, all because of a wacky story about a nutty Greek family. By the time it was completed, I felt sure I'd penned one of my all-time-favorite books. I couldn't help but think of Kay as the story came together. I know she would've loved this one. And I know she would have whispered, "Keep going, girl! You can do this!" as I wrote, wrote, wrote.

I miss my sweet friend. But as I gaze into the eyes of sweet baby Jenna, I'm reminded of the circle of life. Somehow in the midst of the battles, we can still experience joy, even in the mourning. Perhaps as you read Cassia's story, you experienced some of that joy yourself. That is my prayer.

Acknowledgments

To my sweet friends Karen and Matt Bailey and Radonna Gideon, who walked with me through the valley of the shadow in the weeks before this book was written. I couldn't have made it through without your prayers.

To my precious daughters. You got me through so much in the weeks leading up to this book. Bless you.

To Jenna. You are the light of Nina's life and bring joy to us all.

To my editor, Jennifer Leep. You are a precious friend and strong advocate.

To my copy editor, Jessica English. What a hard worker you are! I depend on you so much and you never let me down.

To my agent, Chip MacGregor. You are my literary hero.

To my Lord and Savior, Jesus Christ. Take care of my BFF until I get there.

About the Author

Award-winning author **Janice Thompson** enjoys tickling the funny bone. She got her start in the industry writing screenplays and musical comedies for the stage, and she has published over ninety books for the Christian market. She has played the role of mother of the bride four times now and particularly enjoys writing lighthearted, comedic, wedding-themed tales. Why? Because making readers laugh gives her great joy!

Janice formerly served as vice president of Christian Authors Network (CAN) and was named the 2008 Mentor of the Year for American Christian Fiction Writers (ACFW). She is active in her local writing group, where she regularly teaches on the craft of writing. In addition, she enjoys public speaking and mentoring young writers.

Janice is passionate about her faith and does all she can to share the joy of the Lord with others, which is why she particularly enjoys writing. Her tagline, "Love, Laughter, and Happily Ever Afters!" sums up her take on life.

She lives in Spring, Texas, where she leads a rich life with her family, a host of writing friends, and two mischievous dachshunds. She does her best to keep the Lord at the center of it all. You can find out more about Janice at:

www.janiceathompson.com
or
www.freelancewritingcourses.com.

Center Point Large Print
600 Brooks Road / PO Box 1
Thorndike, ME 04986-0001 USA

(207) 568-3717

US & Canada:
1 800 929-9108
www.centerpointlargeprint.com

Spunks